PRAISE FOI.

HISTORY IS DEAD

A ZOMBIE ANTHOLOGY EDITED BY
KIM PAFFENROTH

"*History Is Dead* is a violent and bloody tour through the ages. Paffenroth has assembled a vicious timeline chronicling the rise of the undead that is simultaneously mind-numbingly savage and thought provoking."
—Michael McBride, author of the *God's End* trilogy

"Dr. Paffenroth is a shining literary light who has stitched together an anthology of the undead that will live far beyond anything that has come before. Each entry is a marvel to behold." —Weston Ochse, author of *Scarecrow Gods*

"A prodigious and exciting new approach to the whole genre! This is a must read for any zombie fan." —Devin Trotter, QuietEarth.us

"Tales of the zombie menace from the intimate to the apocalyptic are transformed by transporting the world's favorite monsters into exotic locations in the past. *History Is Dead* is World History 101—zombie style!"
—Lynne Hansen, author of the *Heritage of Horror* series

"For a book about zombies shambling throughout the days of old, *History Is Dead* is filled from cover to cover with fresh and lively tales of the walking dead... this anthology is more fun than a barrel of rotting flesh-eaters in powdered wigs. And it smells a lot better, too."
—Cullen Bunn, Writer, *The Damned*

HISTORY IS DEAD

A ZOMBIE ANTHOLOGY EDITED BY KIM PAFFENROTH

Permuted Press
The formula has been changed...
Shifted... Altered... *Twisted*.
www.permutedpress.com

A Permuted Press book
published by arrangement with the authors

ISBN-10: 0-9789707-9-9
ISBN-13: 978-0-9789707-9-6
Library of Congress Control Number: 2007931789

Table of Contents

THIS RELUCTANT PROMETHEUS by David Dunwoody............1

THE GINGERBREAD MAN by Paula R. Stiles......................11

THE BARROW MAID by Christine Morgan........................19

HARIMOTO by Scott A. Johnson 37

THE MORIBUND ROOM by Carole Lanham 45

THEATRE IS DEAD by Raoul Wainscoting.......................61

THE ANATOMY LESSON by Jenny Ashford 77

A TOUCH OF THE DIVINE by Patrick Rutigliano 97

A CURE FOR ALL ILLS by Linda L. Donahue..................107

SOCIETY AND SICKNESS by Leila Eadie..........................127

SUMMER OF 1816 by James Roy Daley...........................145

THE HELL SOLDIERS by Juleigh Howard-Hobson 163

JUNEBUG by Rebecca Brock..177

STARVATION ARMY by Joe McKinney 193

PEGLEG AND PADDY SAVE THE WORLD
                              by Johnathan Maberry.........209

THE THIRD OPTION by Derek Gunn 227

THE LOANED RANGER by John Peel...............................237

AWAKE IN THE ABYSS by Rick Moore 247

THE TRAVELLIN' SHOW by Douglas Hutcheson 257

EDISON'S DEAD MEN by Ed Turner 271

ABOUT THE AUTHORS 285

This Reluctant Prometheus

DAVID DUNWOODY

"Here you can see some clearly-defined teeth marks. Here, in the bone itself. This is a femur. That's your upper leg bone dear. Over here, this is a shoulder blade."

"That's remarkable—and you say it's all human on human?"

"Yes it is. And over here, this is the fossilized skull of a *homo ergaster*, a subspecies of *erectus* that existed some one-point-nine to one-point-four million years ago in the south and east regions of the African continent, remarkable for their height averaging six feet. We have this exhibit today because an anthropologist named James Milner discovered what appeared to be a burial site at the northern base of Mount Kenya. At the time of *homo ergaster*, in the lower Pleistocene—son, please don't touch that—the dozen glaciers among Mount Kenya's peaks were enormous. I say peaks, plural, because it's actually a dead volcano. Now, *ergaster* is Greek for 'workman', and there is much evidence that these primitive peoples used axes and knives fashioned from rock, as well as fire, as tools in their daily life."

"So back to the teeth marks. The cavemen ate each other? Was that common?"

"Well, it's a bit of conjecture, to say that they actually fed upon one another. Although, in those conditions…"

* * *

Great Man huddled in the lower branches of a fir tree and watched the mammoth cross the plain. It was an adult, alone—uncharacteristic of the animal, but not unprecedented. The sky above was a dreary gray that promised no rain or snow, just bleakness. Great Man tucked his long legs beneath the tatters of his coat and continued to study the mammoth's progress.

It seemed to be gravely wounded, at least from its appearance. Patches of fur and flesh were gone, revealing the red-brown meat beneath, but there was nothing about the creature's slow gait to indicate that it was in fear or pain. Great Man scooted closer, parting the branches to get a better look. Part of the mammoth's face was gone. A gaping eye socket looked out on the cold world as the animal trudged along, and its great teeth, exposed for a lack of lips, gnashed behind a sloping tusk.

Great Man saw the thing's dirt-encrusted guts dragging over the ground and froze.

How does the animal move as if nothing has happened? It has been hunted, attacked and fed upon. It should be dead.

Mouth announced his presence as he clambered down the slope toward Great Man, slipping on grass. His smile—both vertical and horizontal, as his split upper lip yawned—put Great Man at ease. Mouth was two heads shorter than his brother and often stayed in his shadow during a hunt. But this, it seemed, wasn't to be a hunt. Great Man shook his head and pointed through the branches at the mammoth. He gestured at its mutilated face, prodding Mouth's own eye. The boy understood that the animal was no good. But why? What had happened? That question still tickled his imagination. He crouched and peered at the mammoth. It looked like a dead, half-eaten thing. Yet it walked with ease. Toward them. Fear snarled the muscles in Mouth's gut, and he scrambled back.

Great Man pointed up the slope to where the others were, cloistered behind a jutting crag. Mouth left him, and he returned his attention to the animal. He stepped out from the tree's cover and approached it.

The mammoth didn't regard him as a threat; it didn't regard him as anything at all. It simply kept lumbering along. As it passed, he reared back and plunged his hand-axe into its exposed meat.

The mammoth didn't react. Great Man wrenched a handful of stringy muscle out of the creature's side and retreated to the trees. The animal simply continued on its way.

He sniffed the meat. The blood was lukewarm, but seemed fresh, and as he pushed it into his mouth the familiar tang of the mammoth's flavor brought a smile to his face.

We eat.

He let out a roar, and the other males spilled out from behind the crag, running down the slope toward the mammoth with mudstone cleavers in their hands. They leapt onto its sides and back, climbing through stringy hair and burying their blades in its flesh. The mammoth slowed, turned, grunted, but didn't fight; they brought it down with no resistance and opened its belly with a cry of celebration.

His lips brimming with blood, Great Man waved at Black Shoulder as the group feasted on their kill. Grunts could still be heard within the massive body of the thing, but it seemed to be the settling of its guts, not expressions of pain.

Black Shoulder's hard, cracked flesh was spread like a web over his neck and arm. He had been struck by a dagger of light from the sky during a rainstorm. Great Man still didn't understand how the light had thrown Black Shoulder out of his coat and transformed his skin, but it was seen as an affirmation of the man's virility that he survived the experience.

He was reluctant to taste of the mammoth. Mouth grabbed handfuls of bloody meat and thrust them forth, but Black Shoulder shook his head. He was troubled by the look of the thing, how it had shown its skull and innards as it marched across the plain. It was a sign of some sort.

Great Man's mate, Sky, named for the way in which the sheen of her hair captured the light of every new and dying day, fed voraciously. Her belly had grown heavy, and was taking on the firm swell that Great Man recognized as a promise of new life. His first. He watched closely over her as he ate.

They were comfortable here, at the base of this great frozen mountain, where the fir trees rose stubbornly above the rest of the cold world and provided shelter. The loose mudstone could be formed into new tools, bi-faced cutting weapons that would make short work of a mammoth's belly or shatter the skull of a predator. They had not seen many mammoths in recent days, but Great Man didn't know what promise tomorrow could hold. He was glad to sleep here tonight.

Besides Black Shoulder, only one other member of the group didn't feed—Rock Biter, a child so named because he'd used to chew stones with his gums before his teeth came in. He was sick, and sat with his mother beneath the crag, his body trembling as his empty stomach fought the urge to retch again. Black Shoulder hiked a short distance, past the tree line to the glacier's edge, and cut away a handful of ice with his cleaver. He gave it to the child, pressing it into his mouth. Rock Biter leaned against his mother and sucked on the ice with eyes closed. She gave Black Shoulder a grateful look, though it was one tinged with grief, as she didn't expect her son to live much longer.

When the new dawn broke, Black Shoulder shook a fresh snowfall from his hide blanket and surveyed the camp. The others all appeared to be asleep. Stretching his tired limbs as he walked down the slope, he felt hunger gnawing at his belly and looked toward the mammoth's carcass. There was still ample meat clinging to its massive ribcage. Reluctantly, he pulled his cleaver from the waist of his coat and approached the fallen beast.

He heard a low grunting from the thing's open cavity. He froze in place and studied it. Was there a smaller animal inside, feeding? He couldn't see anything, nor was there any movement visible. Black Shoulder crept forward, weapon raised. He realized the sound was coming from behind the corpse's bulk and slowly rounded its foul-smelling haunches.

It was Great Man. He was knelt over his mate, Sky, and Black Shoulder stepped back, thinking they were in an embrace; but then he saw the blood on her swollen belly, and in Great Man's palms, and around his mouth. Sky was dead.

Perhaps she had died during the night, from the cold, or in child-birth, though Black Shoulder was sure the sounds of her pain would have awakened him. And Great Man... was he eating her? Here, in the shadow of their fresh kill? Why? Black Shoulder stood still and watched as his elder dug his hands into Sky's torn stomach, fishing out sheets of red tissue, and a small, soft form with tiny limbs.

Black Shoulder cried out. Great Man turned, and in his eyes there was death and an animal hunger. He lunged forth with a fierce growl.

Black Shoulder spun away, avoiding the gnashing teeth of his at-tacker, and backpedaled from the gruesome scene. The others in the camp were beginning to stir and, as Black Shoulder looked toward them, his heart screamed inside his chest as he saw them assuming strange animal positions, their eyes bleary, limbs trembling with a sort of anxious craving.

Little Rock Biter was hobbling down the slope, sobbing. Behind him his mother let out a baleful moan, blood running down her lips and over the bite marks in her dark breast. Following her were several bloodied men, hobbling forward with dead eyes.

Black Shoulder ran to the child and scooped him up, tossing the thin little body over his scarred frame and running away from the group. Mouth rose and his face opened in three places, ichor spilling over his jowls as he gestured at the pair. He let out a hunter's cry.

We eat.

They were all different, were all animal. Those with whom Black Shoulder had hunted and eaten were gone. In their place were these charging predators. Those who had stood over him in the rain, after the sky swept him across the plain with a hand of light and set him in a mud hole—they were gone, dead inside, and now the dead came at him and Rock Biter.

He ran as fast as he could, heart thudding against his thin ribs, long feet churning the soil and cutting a trail away from the slope camp toward a thick clutch of fir trees. The two dozen at his back made low sounds and pounded the earth as they hastened after their meat.

Rock Biter clung to Black Shoulder's neck, uneven nails digging into his bark-like scar tissue. The fir needles whipped at their eyes and skin like tiny knives as they raced through the trees. Snowflakes, disturbed from their resting places, drifted down and met the cold unblinking eye of the pursuer—Great Man, dead yet alive, all seven feet of him relentlessly tearing through the brittle limbs of trees and scattering small mammals beneath his wide stamping feet. Rocks and seeds dug into those feet, tore viciously at the flesh, and Great Man paid them no mind, pushing his body harder than ever before, like a storm ripping through the forest in pursuit of the soft young one.

Clouds rolling overhead went from gray to black; a growl issued from the heavens met the runners' ears, shaking the trees and saying *the earth feels your hunger; the earth pushes you onward; the earth turns and boils and gnashes its teeth at its dead core. Take them down! Eat! Eat!*

Black Shoulder grabbed the thick arm of an old tree and brought himself up in one sweeping motion, splintering the layers of fir overhead, heaving himself and Rock Biter onto a higher branch. Then another. He slung the boy over his other shoulder, one hand clamped around his tiny arm, and leapt again. Then he clapped his hand over Rock Biter's mouth. Black Shoulder embraced the tree trunk and stared into the child's eyes. *Silence. They hunt us.*

This tree was unusually massive, and Black Shoulder had brought himself and his charge up past the canopy of the forested area. The sky was dark , and the air grew cold and damp; howls sounded throughout the forest. Black Shoulder straddled the branch and held Rock Biter like he would his own son and listened.

They were milling about down below, on the ground. They were grunting nonsense, slapping against each other in passing. They were searching the forest, again and again, for their young meat. Maybe they didn't want Black Shoulder so much, with his tough, wounded skin and sinewy muscles, but the tender meat of Rock Biter's body would be a treat.

The rain came down, and after ensuring the child was calm, Black Shoulder opened his and Rock Biter's mouths to receive it; below there was no change, no reaction. They wanted only the meat. That mammoth… it had looked dead, yet walked. The others ate of it and became dead men walking. In his mind's eye, Black Shoulder saw the passage of a dark, formless thing from one animal to another. He understood. He looked at the dark, blistered star on his shoulder, which erupted into a web of scars running down his arm, and understood that he'd been touched by the hand of the sky to be made aware of this dark thing so that he would not take it into his body.

So he could save Rock Biter, who was a strong boy.

A dagger of light came down across the plain. The dead below screamed and milled about more quickly, looking to-and-fro but never up. Black Shoulder cradled the trembling Rock Biter and watched his former companions. They began to claw at the skin of the trees and rage about, crashing senselessly into one another. Another dagger of light!

Rock Biter looked up at Black Shoulder and let out a bitter cry.

It was answered, below.

Mother.

But not Mother—her breasts were spent of milk, and she clambered for his flesh. She pointed up the tree at her child and howled.

Black Shoulder wrapped Rock Biter in his coat and pushed him against the trunk. He hugged the boy to the tree, and spoke. *Stay.* Then, cleaver in hand, the man fell away.

He splashed down in the mud and spun to bury the rock-blade in Mother's ankle. She tumbled with a cry, and he opened her throat to stop her from calling to her son.

Mouth grabbed Black Shoulder, and the latter delivered a fierce backhand, throwing Mouth into a tree with a crash that was met by a thunderclap. The group surged forth from all directions, pouring through the trees.

Black Shoulder took up a round stone and opened his younger brother's head with it, turning to dash his brother's mate's skull. Light spidered angrily across the sky.

Great Man hefted a massive tree-limb and slung it into Black Shoulder's chest. Black Shoulder flew out of the trees into the open plain, sliding naked through mud. The others swept after him.

Suddenly, a light-dagger tore *up* out of the earth and ripped the great tree apart, spitting Rock Biter out into the night and bringing down a hundred fiery limbs. Bits of light flying through the air were caught by raindrops and married into nothing. Debris showered over Black Shoulder's prone body as the dead ran at him. Flaming branches crashed on either side of him. He seized them, feeling his own chest cry out in agony, and stood to face the dead.

Black Shoulder roared.

They came down on him, and he met Great Man with a pair of torches that had been fashioned by the heavens into white-hot spears. Brittle, they exploded against the leader's skull and sent him flying backwards, heels over head, smoke engulfing his face. Black Shoulder turned to cover Mouth's entire head with embers, knocking him back through the air, flames issuing from his face as if he were a flying star.

Black Shoulder swept another hunter's legs out from under him and crushed his skull with a rock. Heat and light were rising from a depression in the earth where debris had come down; Black Shoulder stoked one of his spears in it and held the fire up to the others. They snarled their intent. Somewhere, away from the flames, through torrents of rain, Rock Biter cried.

Black Shoulder desperately needed the fire, but the rain was still coming down and eating it.

Why? Black Shoulder looked to the sky as if it had betrayed him.

The undead Mouth rose up, a flowering mountain of fire, his face splitting, hands clawing madly at the air, a sight that made all the others fall back, as if in the presence of some new animal, some *GOD*. And he tore through the underbrush in search of Rock Biter, even as the flames ate at his back. Heat and pain filled his vision but he could still hear the meat, mewling somewhere among the trees, fresh meat that would restore Mouth's own aching skin if he took it into himself. He understood through a cold instinct that if he fed on man-meat, his own youth and virility would return... and return... and return. *It is not to make more of us, it is to keep myself... I feed and I keep myself, only myself.*

I eat.

Black Shoulder leapt over Mouth's burning back and sheared his head off with his hand-axe. It was a clean kill, a proud kill, man killing animal. The body of the fiery beast staggered off into the rain, sputtering red, then lay still.

Black Shoulder grabbed Rock Biter and ran for both their lives. He beat the earth into submission with his pounding feet, creating a fearsome percussion that drowned out the howls of the dead at their heels. With leaps and bounds Black Shoulder crossed the plain and left his haggard pursuers behind, water spraying up from between his toes into his unblinking eyes. He pushed the child into his neck and whispered comfort, safety. Now and then, the little one tried to raise his head and look back, perhaps in search of his mother, but Black Shoulder forced Rock Biter down and told him with a grim look that what was behind them was never to be missed.

Safe on a rock ledge, Black Shoulder and his new son watched the others as they teemed below, refusing to eat one another, all reaching their thin rotting arms up for the fresh meat.

There was Great Man, reaching higher than anyone else, his face a shattered and blackened skull with one pitted eye that could barely see. His long arms scraped the rock and ice as layers of flesh sloughed away. They no longer wore their coats of the mammoth's fur, and their hair was falling out in clumps, and in time they wasted away completely. By then, Black Shoulder had taken his boy over the mountain, where they ate only the small animals that scurried along the ground, and always made the meat dark by the warmth of a fire.

* * *

"What do you think led to the end of these people? Is it right to call them people?"

"Why, of course. In the case of this particular find, Dr. Milner's find, it's speculated that in a short period, weather conditions contributed to poor health and disease—and it's believed that food was scarce, food in this case being other animals. This of course raises that question of cannibalism, and all I can tell you is to observe the teeth marks on those bones. Oh! And here, look at this fossilized skull, which splits oddly due to a severe cleft palate—it's known that the inside and outside of this skull was subjected to fire—darn, nicked myself on that tooth."

The Gingerbread Man

PAULA R. STILES

His body arched as life rushed back into it. He sucked in air and water. Blind, deaf, paralyzed. Sharp, pungent decay filled his mouth and nose, making him sneeze. He struggled to get away from the smell, choking on acid water, rolling onto his side, but his hands were caught behind him and his feet stuck together. Something sharp flicked down between his ankles, and freed his feet. He was grabbed under his arms, hauled up, and dragged away from the smell of bog.

No, please. Not again, not again.

He still couldn't see. Water trickled down from his soaked blindfold like tears into the corner of his mouth. It tasted bitter. He knew what his captors would do next. Perhaps it was their first time, but it wasn't his.

What will it be this time? Hanging, stabbing, clubbing? My throat cut by the blood-stone or the garrote tied tight and twisted around my neck? When will they finish with me? He had been trapped for years, and more. He should have died the first time and been free. But that wasn't in his nature.

He tripped over a root and slipped from the grasp of his captors, falling face down. A harsh voice spoke overhead and they hauled him back to his feet. They wouldn't let him escape, even if he'd had the strength. He remembered that, too. It was all a ritual; everything must go perfectly or whatever god they wanted to appease would grow angry. He supposed he was too old for them to care about appeasing him.

If he were still in the bog, still dead, he'd know what these new people were saying. He had been a long time dead, long enough to range his spirit to the edges of the land and discover how he was trapped. While his body rested "safe" and intact in the bog, he could not win free of his prison. He had no choice but to guard this land and make it fruitful, with his force bound into it more firmly than his limbs. His jailers had been clever and he'd get them for that. Someday.

But today they'd kill him yet again.

They dragged him through brush and up to higher ground. The man on his right wheezed and the man on his left stank of some herb he didn't recognize, pungent as the bog but in a different way. They were husky, their arms firm and tight on his elbows, as if they were used to hewing the earth. Farmers. Ugh. A pestilence on them all. As they hauled him out into the open, the wind, brisk and fresh, blew their stink away. He smelled flowers. Spring. He remembered when he'd looked forward to it. Back when he'd been free, when he could take on what form he chose and there were no leaders or followers to call him "trickster" or enslave him, staked down in cold water.

They threw him onto the ground. He landed face down in muddy grass. His bonds were cut and the rags from his last trip above ground were ripped off him, rotten from age. A rough tunic was dragged over his head and then his hands were bound behind him. He had no strength to resist. He was dragged up by his hair. Fearing immediate death, he struggled uselessly. But instead, his jaws were forced open and a drink forced down his throat. He choked on the bitter liquid. This was new. Dizziness seeped through him, even though he could only feel the earth under his knees, not see it. A poison or some drug. What would these mortals think of next? *And why does that scare me?*

As his head cleared, the familiar reek of the bog came back to him. Earth crumbled under his knees; he must be right on the edge of it. He gagged in fear as a noose slipped over his head. It tightened around his throat, cutting off the air. Too soon. Why did they have to kill him so soon before he could savor the spring even a little? They must have known he'd get his strength back with a little more time. Nearby, someone was chanting, but he couldn't hear words through the roaring in his ears. Even as he convulsed, choking, a huge blow struck him in the head and a sharp agony sliced across his throat. Then he was falling after his own blood, plunged under the water and pinned beneath the cold, dead surface by wicker and chanted spells.

He didn't recover for a long time. The water had warmed and cooled again with shortening days before he could think beyond the pain and frozen decay of his own body. He sent his spirit out in cautious tendrils, pushing through his prison of wood to the bog outside, then further into the countryside. It still seemed prosperous, though less so than before. Perhaps his pain was leaking out, poisoning the soil. This was not his land; he was an unwilling exile here. They had caught him in one of their sacred groves, on his way home to his wife and children. Should it be his fault that he hadn't realized it was a crime to take wood there? Wood was wood and since the trees had first marched across the land, chasing the eternal snow as it retreated north, there had been too much of it here.

They hadn't wanted to hear about that. They had sacrificed him the first time, to propitiate the angry god of the grove.

If there had ever been such a god, it no longer existed. He was the only palpable sign of deity here now. Little good it did him. They had him trapped between worlds with wicker and water, and if he gave them bad luck, they would put him through it all again.

He missed his wife, though she must have been long dead by now. A wanderer he'd always been, but even a wandering god liked to put down roots every so often. Just not as a sacrifice in a bog to farmers. He'd seen her dressed in skins in a field, stalking a red deer, and had fallen in love. A trickster, he could take whatever form might please her, live out a short, mortal life with her, then return to his eternal, shapeshifting ways. The elder gods shook their heads but didn't interfere. Love came so seldom, even to gods. She reminded him of the first people who'd returned to this isle after the snows retreated and the seas rushed in—archaic, quiet. She'd been shy of the farmers, said they poisoned the land. He avoided them to please her or he might have known better than to wander into one of their groves. He'd grown cocky in his good fortune with her. Ten years they'd had and three children. All gone now.

The snows came and retreated once, twice, ten, a hundred, a thousand times until he no longer cared if they hurt him or not. Sending out his thoughts again, he pushed the bog's acid outward, spreading it into the surrounding land. His dead, useless body had no control over the air, no matter how much he remembered soaring like a gull or even just the feel of wind through his beard and hair, but the land—he could influence the land, if he didn't mind leaving his body. Since it was now the consistency of tanned leather, he saw this as no loss. It trapped him, anchored him like a raft moored in mid-stream. He could free himself if his body either came back to life or was destroyed. Hanging, bludgeoning, cutting—none of them would help him escape, but burning would free him.

The land was already failing. Hate and fear stalked it as men stalked each other. It wasn't hard to poison the mood. Gathering all his strength, he sent himself out as a coherent spirit, inserting himself into the dream of a great chief to the north, as a dread simulacrum. "Burn me," he whispered in the man's ear. "Appease my spirit. Free me. Burn me."

Nothing seemed to happen. He tried again, night after night in the dark of the new moon until one day, a great crowd came to the edge of the bog with prisoners, animals and wickerwork. He waited for them to unstake him and draw him out. They did not. Instead, they set up the wickerwork in the shape of a man and stuffed it full of people and livestock. By the time he realized what they were doing, they had set the shape on fire at sunset under the pale crescent of the new moon. He tried to stop them, but the chief and his people were too excited to listen to one more spirit wailing on the wind and rumbling in the ground. The fire burned all through the night, the people and animals trapped inside screamed for longer than he thought possible. He pitied them while they burned and envied them when their spirits were set free like birds toward dawn.

After that, he stopped trying. Too weak to send himself out again, he no longer feigned any goodwill toward the land. He withdrew into himself, and for a long time he slept.

The land died around him, becoming as barren as the bog. The mortals dropped more victims into the dank water around him, naked and bound, but they never drew him out again. Some of the victims were willing, but not all. Later they dropped proxies instead, baked food shaped like men. If they remembered that they offered food because they had once eaten their human offerings, they showed no signs of it. The mortals had forgotten him, or feared him too much to raise him again, just as they had once feared to consume his flesh and free him, for good or ill. Neither attitude did him any good. Eventually they fled the barren land, leaving him in peace.

Many springs later he sensed movement around the bog, a building on the land. He had slept a long time, but when he sent himself out, he saw strange things—huge beasts made of shining stone cutting through the bog, ridden by people dressed in odd clothing of woven materials like thick netting. When they discovered one of the mortal bodies, they became excited, chattering to themselves. In spite of his anger and distrust from so many bad experiences, he hoped they meant well. Then they dug out the body. He watched in horror when, after a furtive conversation among themselves, they ripped off the body's ornaments then burned it. He couldn't understand them, but when one of them mounted the great beast and drove it further along the earth, he realized that the bodies were a problem for these people, some kind of curse. This was no group of ordinary grave robbers.

His answer came the next day when two more mortals showed up and engaged in a loud, angry confrontation with the first group. They were thrown off, still shouting, and the mood among the defenders was tense. He didn't trust either group. If they burned him, he might be free. But what if they didn't burn him? What if they carried him off intact and kept him dead? What if they tore him to pieces and scattered them over the countryside? He might never get free then, might never rejoin the elder gods or find his wife's spirit.

The next day, someone pulled up the wicker that staked him down. Their excited voices percolated down to him through the peat.

Then they drew him out. It was the first group, the burners. They laid him in between skins that smelled strange and seemed too smooth to come from an animal with hair, but disturbed him no further. Something about the noisy daylight prevented them from desecrating bodies until the deepest dark of night. At sunset they withdrew, as if to prepare.

He knew he had little time, but his body would not reawaken quickly. He was immortal, not all-powerful. As night settled over the bog and clouds smothered the stars, the wound in his throat finally healed. He woke into a fully living body again, coughing, in the middle of a rainstorm. No one came. Still weak, he worked at his bonds until they broke. He ripped off the blindfold with special, vicious satisfaction. Hands shaking, he pushed back the cover of the top skin and opened his eyes for the first time in so, so long. The storm was ending, the clouds scudding away, and the stars were coming out. He had not seen them with living eyes in so long. He wept.

He had no doubt the mortals would return, for the skins were tough and well cured. No one would leave such valuable objects to rot under the sky. He had little time.

He sat up, his strength finally returning. At worst he could provoke them into burning him, but they would get no more sacrifices out of him. His tunic was rotting off his body like his bonds. He had lain in the water a long time. His skin had cured; his clothes had not. The sacrificial knife they had buried him with—that was still in good shape. It wasn't the gleaming blood-stone that eroded and turned green under the rain of years, but treacherous, enduring obsidian. He found it wrapped in another skin in the shadow of a stone that looked like a huge beast from the ice years. The beast crouched over him, menacing him with its enormous lower jaw buried in the disturbed earth. It seemed harmless, petrified, but he wasn't fooled. It glittered all over with blood-stone in the starlight, reflecting its owners' guilt.

He was cold beyond cold, but as the blood pumped through his body again, he felt more attached to this realm. He didn't want free of this body anymore. He wanted revenge. When he heard the voices of the mortals and saw their lights returning, splashing night vision in blinding arcs across the land, he knew what to do. Night trapped him between worlds as surely as the bog, but dawn was coming and the sun would free him. He could live again. He hid in the shadow of the stone beast and when the first man walked past his hiding place, he stepped out behind him and cut his throat.

As he swung around, letting the body drop, two of those coming behind the man cried out—in fear or rage, he didn't know. He didn't care, either. There were six of them left, six mortals between him and freedom. Oh, yes. He still had uses for this body.

The light on the hills around the bog brightened as the others closed in on him. Their anger vibrated between him and them; they never changed, never. For an instant, his spirit slipped through his fingers into the still air. He sensed something world-huge hovering above him, felt it shift, as one of these mortals might put aside one mask to choose another. It rooted itself in his chest like a gargantuan second shadow, stretching out its deadly grasp to the maniac worshippers who had dared to placate the implacable with his blood. The elder gods had sensed him; they were calling him home.

Not yet. Soon. He bore down on the superhuman vision, dwindling back into himself. He became, again, only a half-naked man, with his back against a stone, a knife in his hand, an ache in his bones, and re-kindled fire in his heart. Everything mortal that he had ever loved had long since turned to dust. He was alone.

Beyond the shadowed hill were sunlight and food and freedom. All that stood in his way were six mortals intent on giving him back to the bog.

He bared his teeth at them. "You want blood? I'll give you blood." He leaped forward, knife first.

The sun rose, bloody as a newborn.

The Barrow Maid

CHRISTINE MORGAN

he death-cry of Sveinthor Otkelsson ripped through the din of battle, as harsh and sudden as the blade that had ripped through his mail-coat. Friend and foe, ally and enemy, all who heard it fell silent. The fighting ceased as men looked to one another, astonished. Could such a cry truly have come from the throat of Sveinthor Otkelsson? Sveinthor Wolf-Helmet? Sveinthor, called the Unkillable?

He had led the first assault against the shield-wall in defense of his uncle Kjartan's fortress, plunging deep into the armies of King Hallgeir the Proud. Arrows had rained all around him but never once touched his flesh. He had beheaded Hallgeir's standard-bearer, then cleaved Hallgeir himself in the shoulder so that the king's torso was hewn nearly to the belt.

A death-cry? Sveinthor Otkelsson, voicing a death-cry?

It could not be believed.

No one moved. No living thing made a sound. Even the cawing of ravens was stilled, and it seemed that the wind itself paused in scudding dark clouds across the sky.

Then, as one, those nearest Sveinthor drew back. He stood alone amidst a mound of bodies, most slain by the thirsty work of his own sword, Wolf's Tooth. The blood ran thick from his belly, spreading over the earth in a wide red stain.

He was Sveinthor Otkelsson, whose ship *Wulfdrakkar* had gone a'viking to far lands, bringing back plunder of gold and silver, slaves, amber, ivory and jet. He had rescued the beautiful Hildirid from becoming an unwilling bride, unmanning her captor with a knife-stroke.

Even if not for the *wyrd* that had been prophesied by the sorceress Sigritha when Sveinthor was no more than a boy, this moment could not have been foreseen. But now Wolf's Tooth had dropped from his grasp, and his hands went to his wound, and the blood was a waterfall between his fingers. His wolf-headed helm, its gilded nasal and eye-pieces red-spattered but still glittering gold, turned this way and that as if seeking out his killer.

A single raven screeched. All who heard it knew it to be an omen of the most fearsome sort. The raven was Odin's own bird, and surely Odin had taken notice of the battle. Perhaps Odin was, even now, dispatching the dreaded Valkyries.

As Sveinthor toppled with his belly split open and the tangle of his guts spilling out of him, there came another cry, furious with rage. It was torn from the throat of Ulfgrim the Squint, long a friend, blood-brother and oathsman of Sveinthor.

In his fury, Ulfgrim charged. Rallied by his actions, the others of Sveinthor's men followed, as did Kjartan's own forces. What came next was not so much battle as butchery. Some of the defenders tried to form again their shield-wall, but too many fled in terror and the rest were soon cut down. The victors moved among the fallen, giving aid to their allies and the final mercy to their enemies, and stripping the dead of their valuables.

Kjartan himself, aged and white-bearded, rode from his fort to the place where Sveinthor had stood. He wept openly and without shame. There had been talk in the mead-halls that Kjartan might make Svein-thor his heir. Now that hope was gone, dashed to pieces like a ship storm-hurled against unforgiving stony shores. Sveinthor was dead.

With his last breath, he had closed his blood-soaked fingers around the hilt of Wolf's Tooth and held it now in an unbreakable grip.

They bore him back to Kjartan's hall. The day was won, the enemy scattered and fleeing, but there was precious little joy and celebration. Three others of Sveinthor's men had perished bravely in the battle. Eyjolf Rust-Beard, and Bork Gunnarsson, and Thrain the Merry were to be placed alongside Sveinthor in honor.

Kjartan had for them a great burial-mound built, a chamber filled with goods for the afterlife. There were bundles of firewood, jugs of mead, furs and blankets, tools, weapons, grain, meat and cheese. Into this tomb was placed Sveinthor's wealth, the plunder of villages and forts and monasteries. Silver cups and platters, gold brooches, piles of hacksilver, beads of amber and jet. Kjartan added many more treasures, so that the mound was as rich as any gold-vault of the dwarves below the earth.

Sveinthor was laid upon his barrow at the center of the chamber. His helm was polished and shining, the wolf's tail that hung from its crown brushed smooth. He was covered with the pelts of wolves, and his sword Wolf's Tooth was set across his breast, its hilt still clutched tight in his dead hand and its blade still clotted dark with the blood of his enemies.

As these preparations were being made, Ulfgrim the Squint sought out Hildirid, who had been Sveinthor's woman. "Kjartan has promised to provide a slave-girl to accompany Sveinthor into the mound," he told her. "There is no need for you to die with him."

Hildirid, who was tall and slender but proud-figured, said nothing. She had hair the color of gold seen by torchlight, which fell past her waist in long plaits tucked through the belt of her tunic. Her cloak was seal's skin, pinned at the breast with a brooch of walrus-ivory, and her eyes were sea-blue and steady.

"You can escape this dire fate," Ulfgrim urged her. "Already, Kjartan's wise-woman is preparing the poison. You have but to agree, and the slave-girl will go in your place."

"Does not Unn of the dimpled cheeks go with Eyjolf, her husband?" Hildirid asked. "Is not Ainslinn, Bork's favorite, being readied to follow him? You would have Sveinthor, who loved you like a brother, go to his grave-barrow with a stranger slave-girl?"

"Thrain does," argued Ulfgrim, "for Thrain had no woman of his own and will need one to tend him in the afterlife. You can live, sweet Hildirid. Live and go forth from here, and marry a strong man and have many fine sons and fair daughters."

He touched her hand then, but Hildirid drew away. "I was fated to be his and his alone, forever," she said. "Skarri the Blind prophesied it to us. It is my *wyrd*."

Ulfgrim scoffed. "And we have seen for ourselves how well the *wyrd* prophesied for Sveinthor came to pass. Mad old women and blind old men! Pah!" And he spat on the ground.

"I was fated to be his," Hildirid said again.

"There is no fate but what a man makes his own. Sveinthor went wrapped in the confidence of his *wyrd*, and it did make him bold and daunted his enemies, but in the end, did his *wyrd* prove true? Look there, Hildirid. Sveinthor the Unkillable… covered with gold and glory, but as cold and dead as a haunch of beef." He clutched at her hand again. "Come away with me, instead. I may not be so handsome as Sveinthor, but I swear I can love you as much if not better."

This time she did not merely draw away, but slapped him so that her palm cracked smartly across his cheek. "I will follow Sveinthor," she said, and her voice was like ice.

Ulfgrim flushed dark, angered and embarrassed. His eyes, already narrow, narrowed further. "It was I who learned of your capture," he said in a snarl. "It was my cunning that formed the plan to rescue you. I would have done it myself, but Sveinthor insisted. By rights, Hildirid, you should have been mine."

She walked away from him then without a word, head high and back straight in her dignity.

Later, when the burial mound was all but finished, Kjartan assembled his people to bid farewell to Sveinthor and his men. There were many verses and poems spoken by skalds, recounting the deeds and honor of their lives, mourning their passing and celebrating their entrance into Valhalla.

Then Kjartan's wise-woman brought forth the cups of poison. Unn of the dimpled cheeks drank first, and kissed Eyjolf's lips before lying down beside him. The woman Kjartan had chosen to accompany Thrain smiled at the great honor she had been given as she raised the cup. Thrain's favorite dog, a great shaggy mongrel called Bryn-Loki, was strangled with a rope and set at his master's feet.

The slave-girl Ainslinn wailed and screamed and would not drink. She tried to flee, then tried to fight, and finally had to be strangled as Bryn-Loki had been. A disgrace, but only to be expected from an Irish girl and a Christian.

And then the cup came to Hildirid, who was arrayed like a queen with her long hair loose and shining.

As she took the cup, she saw Ulfgrim with his dark eyes pleading, but she drank deep of the bitter liquid. As she felt its torpor begin to creep through her limbs, she kissed Sveinthor and sank next to his barrow on a blanket of soft wool.

She opened her eyes to the chill, misty dark and felt a pain throughout her body so sharp and crushing that it was as if she was being rent asunder by beasts. It was Niflheim, kingdom of the dead, realm of the goddess Hel. Was it Hel's own hound, Garm, grinding her bones in its fierce mouth? Was it the dragon Nidhug, leaving off its eternal gnawing at the roots of Yggdrasil the World-Tree?

Then the pain ebbed like a tide, receding from her limbs. Hildirid shivered in the blackness. Her mouth felt dry and parched with a terrible thirst, and her innards were a hollow ache. Slowly, stiffly, she moved. The cold wrapped her like a fog, and she pulled her cloak close around her shoulders.

The air was heavy with a reek of corruption so thick it was like a taste. Yet beneath it, she could smell other scents. Strong cheese. Heady mead. Her dark-blinded hands searched the unseen contours and edges. Soft wool. Hard stone. Rushes and pebbles and loose earth. Stacked logs of wood, the bark coarse beneath her fingers. The lushness of fur. Wolf's fur, from the pelts that covered Sveinthor, and that was when she knew where she was. In the barrow. In the burial-mound. Entombed in the black, entombed with the dead.

Was she dead? Was this death? Was this the truth of Niflheim? Alone and sightless and trembling from the chill? Yet she breathed, and when she pressed her hand to her breast she could feel the quick thudding of her heart. With the little knife she kept on her belt, she pricked her thumb and felt warm blood well from it, which she licked away.

Still groping her way, she rose to her knees and found Sveinthor's chest beneath the pelts. She touched the silver Thor's-hammer amulet he wore around his neck, touched his wiry beard, touched his face. His flesh was like a lump of cold tallow, greasy with a residue that smeared off onto her fingertips. His mouth gaped and did not stir with breath.

Hildirid rested her brow on his chest. Then she searched through the goods in the barrow until she had a candle and the means to strike a flame. The flickering light sent shadows dancing over the wealth and the weapons and the bodies. Unn and the slave-girl were peaceful in death. Ainslinn had died with her eyes bulging in horror, the bruises from the knotted strangling-rope livid on her slim neck. Bryn-Loki, Thrain's dog, lay with tongue protruding and death-rigid legs jutting like sticks. The smells of corruption wafted from them. Hildirid saw skin gone waxen and pallid, flesh sunken and slack. They were dead, dead one and all.

Yet she was alive. Somehow, she was alive. She had drunk of the poison. She had drained the cup to its dregs. It had coursed through her veins. She remembered sinking, sinking like a rock into the bottomless depths.

Her gaze fell upon the jugs of mead, the loaves, the wheels of cheese. Hunger led her to pull off a chunk of bread, but Hildirid hesitated with it at her lips. Should she? Was there any use in eating, in drinking? Why prolong a life that was doomed to a miserable end? Better if she ignored the urges of her body and lay back down to wait for death. Better still if she took out her knife again and seated it in her breast or sliced it across her wrists to hurry death along.

Yet the bread was in her hand. It was stale and nearly as hard as stone, but could not have been more appetizing had it just come fresh from the baker's oven. She tore into it with her teeth, and when it soon proved a chore to chew, opened a jug of mead and soaked the bread to soften it in the potent honey-brew.

Sated, she moved the candle so that its light played over the various treasures. Here was a tiny ship, the *Wulfdrakkar* in miniature, with red shields along the sides above the tiny oars, and its growling wolf's head prow. There was a set of *hnefatafl*-men, two armies carved from ivory and soapstone arranged in ranks on their board. A bone flute. A polished-amber figure of a wolf. Chests of silver and gold. Monk's crosses. A heavy silver plate with designs of Christian saints and angels upon it. A fortune, and all of it useless to her now. Likewise were the many weapons useless. What need did she, Hildirid, have for bows and arrows, axes, shields, and spears? What need for swords? She had her knife, the knife of ivory hilt wrapped in gold wire, and it would do as well as any blade for what she might have to do.

How the men had given good-natured jest to Sveinthor when he'd given it to her! "Provide your woman a weapon," they had said, "and you're all but inviting her to use it on you, should you displease her as all men eventually do."

But Sveinthor had never displeased her. They had never quarreled, not once. He had never raised a hand against her. When he had sought counsel, he had listened to hers with as ready an ear as he had that of any of his men. He had been as fervent in love as he'd been in battle. When his death-cry had rung out, it had been her ending in that instant.

Yet here she was, alive among the dead. Sveinthor would be in Valhalla, and she would not be there to serve him. Who would bring him the great drinking-horns and joints of roasted meat dripping with good juices? Who would arm and armor him when the final call came and Odin's forces assembled against the giants?

She retreated to his side and sat there, huddled in her sealskin cloak. The candle burned low and went out. When hunger and thirst again bestirred her, she rose to take a few bites, a few drinks of mead. Sometimes she would bring out her knife again, and set its point to the swell of her breast, but each time—to her shame—her courage would slip from her. Now and then she lit another candle, but the sight of the treasures did not gladden her spirits, and the sight of the dead as their flesh continued to darken and decay only brought her to despair.

Even in the darkness, though, the dead would make sounds. Tendons creaked as rigor stiffened and relaxed their limbs. Gases gurgled within their bloated bellies. Once, a rancid and rattling corpse-belch produced such a stench that, inured though she was to the odors of the mound, Hildirid was made to vomit up her meager meal.

At last she became aware of new noises. She heard a scratching, like that of rats—faint at first, but growing louder. Next came a harsh grating and scraping, as of metal on stony soil.

And Hildirid understood.

Word of the wealth of Sveinthor's death-hoard must have spread far and wide, the value increasing all the more in the telling, until at last it had won the interest and greed of the lowest kind of dishonorable men—grave-robbers, armed with shovels, come to plunder from the dead, to steal away the gold and silver, the amber and ivory, the cups and platters and other treasures. They would strip the corpses bare of their mail-coats and arm-rings. They would have Wolf's Tooth from Sveinthor's cold grasp, if they had to break off the brittle, rotting husks of his fingers to do so.

In silence and utter darkness, for she by now knew her way as well as she'd ever known her own house, Hildirid took up her knife and went to wait by the entrance. She could hear the digging-sounds louder now, and the voices of the men. As they dug, and cleared away more of the earth, their words came to her ears.

Hildirid was left aghast at all she heard.

Kjartan's enemies had returned in greater number than before, aided by treachery as some of the king's own men turned against him. The mighty fort had fallen. Hundreds of men had been slain, their weapons and valuables taken and their bodies left unburied.

Now Kjartan's feasting-hall rang and thundered with the revelry of his foes. They gorged on food from his store-houses and drank his mead by the barrel. They butchered his goats and pigs, forced the surviving men to fight like bears or horses for their amusement, and made slaves of the women and children. Worst of all, Kjartan himself had been seized as a prisoner. Night after night, he was made by his captors to appear in one humiliating costume after another. Fool's garb, a monk's robe, the clothes of a woman—these things they dressed him in, and led him before the men, who laughed and called and hurled refuse at the white-bearded king. Such mistreatment of the man who had been kindly as a father to Sveinthor filled Hildirid with anger and hate.

Then she clearly heard a voice she knew.

"If she is dead, old woman, I'll hang you by your heels from a tree-branch and leave your body to be picked by the ravens."

The voice belonged to Ulfgrim the Squint. It was answered by the cracked and peevish tones of Kjartan's wise-woman who had prepared the poisons.

"I did as you wished, noble lord," she said. "I mixed in her cup a potion of deep-sleeping, but I told you that you would have to be quick in fetching her out of the tomb before its effects wore off and she woke. I told you that! If she has starved or died of the cold, it is no fault of mine!"

"Peace, brother," another voice said, and Hildirid knew this one as well. It was Halfgrim the Thief, bastard half-brother to Ulfgrim. "If she is dead, she is dead. There are other women and fairer we can find for you. Wealthy as you are now, you can have your choice of them, and never mind that you are ugly as the rump-end of a troll."

Rough snorts and laughter greeted this, though not enough to keep her from hearing Ulfgrim's next words. "I will have Hildirid," he said. "Or I will have no other."

The deadly determination in his voice made the laughter stop for all but Halfgrim, who chuckled all the more. "Then I hope for your sake the maid lives, or she'll be a bedmate even stiffer and colder than the ones you're used to. Myself, it's Sveinthor's gold I want."

"And I," said another voice, one that Hildirid did not know, "want only to piss on his rotting bones for what he did to my father."

"As a favor to me, then, Runolf," Halfgrim said, "be patient and save your pissing until I've gotten off his mail-coat. It should fetch a pretty price in silver, for all it has that hole ripped across the guts."

Runolf, she knew, must be Runolf the Younger, whose father's skull Sveinthor had crushed with his shield-boss in the battle. So Ulfgrim had joined with the traitors, and Ulfgrim had seen to it that the poison in her cup had not been poison at all.

"Yes, yes," Ulfgrim said, aggrieved. "And the blame for that hole, we all know, you lay on my head."

"I do, indeed, brother," Halfgrim said. "You were supposed to slash his hamstrings and then skewer him through the neck. What made you stab him in the belly?"

The breath in Hildirid's lungs had turned to frost, and the blood in her veins to water as icy as that of the far northern seas. "I had no choice," came Ulfgrim's reply. "He realized my intent at the moment before I would have struck, and had I not sunk my blade into his guts, he would have had off my head."

There was more talk as the digging continued, but Hildirid paid it barely any mind. At last the shovels met wood and were laid aside. She heard the splintering crash of axes against the planks. They broke inward. Torchlight poured through the gaps, bright as the brightest sun's rays to her, long accustomed as she was to blackness and feeble candle's flame.

The first man to step through was not Ulfgrim but his half-brother, his gaze fixed greedily on the glitter of gold and the sparkle of silver. Halfgrim never once looked her way until her knife-blade plunged down. He wore no mail, and she embedded the steel to the hilt in his chest.

Halfgrim screamed like a woman in childbearing and staggered back, then fell sprawled at Ulfgrim's feet. The knife had been yanked from her grip and now Hildirid faced them weaponless, but the sight of her revealed by the torches held the men shocked and motionless with terror. A hag she must have been, a filthy crone with dirt on her clothes and her hair hanging in strings and clumps, her eyes as wild as those of a raving berserk.

Then some fled, casting aside their torches and tools into the crude trench of earth they had made to reach the barrow-mound.

"You see?" said the wise-woman. "She lives, as I told you."

Ulfgrim stared at Hildirid, and spoke her name in a strengthless voice. He stepped over Halfgrim and offered out his hand. "Traitor," she said to him. "Foul, murdering traitor! You killed Sveinthor!"

"I did it for love of you," Ulfgrim said.

She flung herself at him, though not in the lover's greeting for which he had hoped. Her nails, long and ragged, raked at his face and dug long furrows in his stubble-bearded cheeks. Ulfgrim grappled with her, his strength more than a match for hers, and soon held her with her arms bent painfully behind her back.

Runolf the Younger pushed his way past them as Hildirid struggled in Ulfgrim's grasp. "You men! There is the treasure, the reward you were promised. I will have satisfaction for my father's death."

"What of Halfgrim?" another asked.

"Leave him," Runolf said. "It is a burial-mound, after all." He turned with torch raised high so that its light was shed over the central barrow.

There he stopped, for the corpse of Sveinthor was sitting upright.

The wolf's pelts had fallen away to the earthen floor. His torn mail gaped where the fatal blow had been struck, and through it could be seen the bulging maggot-ridden fester of his entrails. His eyes, no longer clear blue but clouded and murky as if rimed with muddy ice, peered around from within the gilded eyepieces of his helm.

Then Sveinthor rose to his feet.

Some of his guts slipped from him, swinging against his thighs like a grisly apron. His joints groaned and his bones crackled. Bits of his skin had sloughed away, leaving raw muscle glistening. His lips had peeled back from his teeth, giving him a leering death's rictus of a grin. The sword Wolf's Tooth he still held in his hand, and he extended it now in challenge and invitation.

"*Draugr!*" the wise-woman cried, and threw herself to his knees babbling prayers to Thor and Freya and Christ and to other gods of which Hildirid had never heard . It was a word most used when a man was lost at sea and denied decent burial, so that his restless corpse was doomed to wander. Sveinthor had not drowned, but he was *draugr* nonetheless.

A fierce joy sang within Hildirid's breast, and she cried her lover's name. "Sveinthor!"

"Kill him!" shouted Ulfgrim, retreating and pulling Hildirid as he went.

Runolf had dropped his torch and snatched out his own sword. As the other men rushed forth, waving their axes and shovels, shrieking their horror at this unnatural foe, Runolf hacked down at Sveinthor's shieldless left arm and severed it at the wrist.

No blood gushed from the stump. There was a trickle of thick blackish ooze and a fresh whiff of stink. The hand fell to the ground and twitched there, then turned itself over and began finger-clawing toward the oncoming men.

Wolf's Tooth flashed down, and Runolf the Younger spun away with his face sliced open. From cheekbone to chin it hung down in a flap of bleeding meat, exposing his teeth and gums.

The others, urged on by desperation and terror, raced wildly at Sveinthor. One of them trod upon the severed left hand, which skittered up his leg swift as a spider. His charge became a frantic leaping dance as he beat at himself with his shovel, hoping to dislodge the scrambling hand. He was too slow. It vanished beneath the hem of his tunic and crawled to his groin, where it squeezed and mauled and twisted like someone wringing water from a rag. The man squealed.

A hoarse and rumbling howl came from Sveinthor's throat. Though distorted, it was still familiar. It was his battle-cry, his call to arms. At the sound of it, one by one around the burial chamber, his loyal men rose in answer. Eyjolf, with an arrow still jutting from his eye socket. Bork, the knob of his shoulder-bone showing through pulped and mangled flesh where his arm had been cut off. Thrain the Merry sprang up almost eagerly. They seized the weapons with which they had been laid to rest, and took their places at Sveinthor's side.

Their women rose as well. Faithful Unn of the dimpled cheeks—not dimpled now, but sagging, and the foam of the poison dried to a crust on her lips. The slave-girl, a little creature and young, but hissing like a cat. Even Ainslinn, head lolling on her puffed and swollen neck, got slowly to her feet.

The battle was joined in a furious clangor of metal and screams. The close confines of the burial-chamber became a slaughtering-ground. Flesh struck wetly on the floor and blood flew like sea-spray in all directions. The *draugr* women had no swords, not even knives, but they had teeth and fingernails and fists, and a strength that seemed more than the equal of any two mortal men.

Ulfgrim had seen enough and fled, dragging Hildirid with him. In her last glimpse of the scene within the mound, it looked to her as though the risen dead were not merely fighting their foes, but devouring them… tearing off mouthfuls of meat, lapping hungrily at the blood-spatter, even nuzzling their faces into the guts of the fallen to come up with steaming livers and intestines clenched in their jaws.

The night outside was foggy and damp, turning the distant torches on the walls of Kjartan's mighty fortress to golden smears of elf-light. Though she fought him with every step, Hildirid could not win her way free of Ulfgrim's iron grasp. He pulled her into the broad field, the both of them stumbling over broken spear-shafts and split shields and the scavenger-picked remains of the unburied dead.

"Let me go!" demanded Hildirid, trying to bend back his fingers where they held hard around her wrist.

"They're monsters, you foolish sow!" Ulfgrim shouted. "Did you not see? They'll kill you, or eat you alive!"

"I'd rather that death, than life with you!"

But he would not release her, even when she fell full-length and tangled in a pile of corpses. Taking her by a fistful of hair, he made as if to sling her over his shoulder and carry her the rest of the way.

Then a long shaggy shape hurtled out of the swirling fog and slammed into him, ripping his hand loose from Hildirid's hair and leaving long strands caught in it. He was knocked hard to the wet earth, where a shadow-shape loomed over him.

It was Bryn-Loki, Thrain's dog, who had never liked Ulfgrim. Parts of his fur had fallen out in patches, and the rest was slimed green with mold. He smelled dank and horrible. The growl that came from low in his throat was bubbled and strange. His teeth, though, when he skinned his black lips back from his muzzle, looked strong, and sharper than ever.

Ulfgrim rolled into a crouch, drawing his sword. It was, Hildirid suddenly knew, the same one that had struck Sveinthor that treacherous, fatal wound. Now he thrust it into Bryn-Loki's chest as the dog leaped. The blade sheared through ribs and muscle and gristle, loosing a spurt of foul fluid. Bryn-Loki fell shuddering onto his side. Ulfgrim got up, shaking but sneering victoriously, and wiped the reeking blade on the dog's thick fur.

Bryn-Loki raised his head, snarled, and clambered to his feet. He shook, the way a dog will after a hard rain, and more fur dropped in mangy clots from his hide. Stiff-legged, he advanced on Ulfgrim, who turned again and ran for his life as if all the fiends of Niflheim were on his heels.

There were no fiends save Bryn-Loki, but Bryn-Loki was fiend enough. Hildirid, kneeling amid the dead, watched the chase as Ulfgrim made for the safety of the earthen wall around the fort. The churning mist had nearly hidden them when she saw Ulfgrim madly scaling the wall, and Bryn-Loki make a final lunging leap. His jaws snapped, tearing a chunk from Ulfgrim's buttock. Then Ulfgrim was up and over and gone from her sight.

The dog trotted back to her. As Bryn-Loki came, the first stirrings of fear gathered in her belly. She wondered if it would hurt, the rending of his teeth. She wondered if it would be quick.

She closed her eyes as his paws thumped to a halt on the damp earth only a few paces distant. It seemed she could smell Ulfgrim's blood on his snout. A cold nose bumped her, snuffling thickly. Then a colder tongue, wet and reeking with decay, lapped at her face.

Hildirid opened her eyes. Bryn-Loki sat hunkered on his haunches before her. His head was cocked, his tail making jerky, lurching wags as if he could not quite remember how to do it properly. When he saw her looking at him, he uttered a hollow whine, and the wagging became so energetic she worried his tail might fall off.

Other figures appeared through the gloom. They were drenched in blood, and gobbets of flesh clung to their garments and hair. She knew them, and as they neared her, she stood to face them with the dog sitting beside her and her hand resting on top of his head.

Eyjolf's leg had been hacked to the bone, so that he staggered along nearly lame, leaning on Unn, who swung a tattered scalp of long grey hair—the wise-woman's hair—from her hand. Bork, already lacking one arm, now carried his own head tucked into the crook of the other, his eyes blazing fiercely. Ainslinn could no longer walk, but pulled herself over the earth by her arms. The little slave-girl who had been buried with Thrain held a man's forearm, and munched happily at it as she might have gnawed a pork rib. Thrain himself wore looping strings of intestine around his neck, and his grin was wider than ever.

With them came Sveinthor. His mail was shredded and his body scored with countless cuts that seeped and oozed. He still held Wolf's Tooth, a dark red rain falling from the blade. His severed hand rode upon his shoulder like one of Odin's ravens.

Hildirid went to him, and embraced him, but then stepped back for she knew that his work was not yet finished. He surveyed the battlefield, strewn as it was with the unburied dead, and once more raised his hoarse voice so that it rang and rolled like thunder.

In the fortress on the hill, there was much commotion and alarm. Perhaps when Ulfgrim had come in, they had dismissed his claims as drunken ravings or madness, but now, as one by one the corpses of Kjartan's slaughtered army laboriously raised themselves and armed themselves with what makeshift weapons they could find, the living men flocked to the walls with torches and stared out in horror.

Sveinthor strode among them. They formed into ranks and lines below the earthen wall and the approach to the fort. At the front was a shield-wall, many of the overlapping shields splintered and broken. With slow but inexorable, relentless purpose, the walking dead began their advance.

A storm of arrows descended upon them, and though many found their mark and lodged in flesh, they could not do much harm. Some of Sveinthor's *draugr* were so bristling with arrow-shafts by the time they reached the base of the wall that they looked like hedge-hogs, and still they advanced.

Hildirid stood atop the burial mound, her hair and sealskin cloak streaming around her in the dire wind that had sprung up. Bryn-Loki sat at her side, and her hand still stroked his head and scratched his ears, for he was whining in disappointment at having been left behind from the battle to guard her.

Now from the fort came flaming arrows, but many of the *draugr* had lain so long in the rain and mud that they did little more than smolder. One or two, fatter men in life, burned like tallow, and became shuffling candles in the shapes of men. The smoke from their singed hair and charred, rotting bodies blew back over the wall, filling the fort with an abominable stench.

At last a few of the bravest defenders came out to meet their foes, but they soon fell, and the *draugr* swarmed over the wall and into the fortress. Even from where she stood, Hildirid could hear the cries of pain and anguish and terror, and the ghastly sounds of feeding as Sveinthor's followers feasted on quivering, still-warm flesh.

Later, when quiet had descended and the night was almost done, she took Bryn-Loki and ventured into the fort. Everywhere she looked were *draugr*, plundering the newly-dead and adorning themselves with medallions and arm-rings, or taking trophies of scalps and fingers and jawbones and heads. The living—the women and children and slaves taken from among Kjartan's people—cowered unharmed and ignored.

Then she saw Kjartan himself, freed from his prison and seated upon his great wooden chair draped with bearskins. Ulfgrim's body, bound in ropes, lay before him with a pool of blood around the stump of his neck. His head was held aloft on the point of Wolf's Tooth, raised high by Sveinthor.

Kjartan saw her as well. "He will not stay, Hildirid," the king said. "He must return to the burial-mound, before dawn comes. He has fulfilled his *wyrd*."

No amount of imploring by them could sway Sveinthor. As the sky to the east brightened, the *draugr* left off what they were doing. Almost as one, they left the fort and returned to the field, lying down again where they had died and then arisen. Eyjolf, Bork, Thrain and their women entered the tomb, followed by Bryn-Loki.

Only Sveinthor remained. He had Ulfgrim's head knotted by the hair to his belt, and Wolf's Tooth was finally released from his grip to be sheathed again across his back. With his one good hand, he reached out and caressed the curve of Hildirid's cheek. Then he turned from her, and walked toward the mound.

"Farewell, lord," Hildirid said to Kjartan, and kissed him.

"Hildirid!" the king called. "Where do you go? What do you do?"

"As you said, lord, Sveinthor has fulfilled his *wyrd*." She touched the knife at her belt, and smiled. "Now I shall fulfill mine."

So saying, she followed Sveinthor into the darkness. When the sun rose, the entrance to the mound was covered over again with planks and stones and earth. Never again was it disturbed by mortal men.

And so ends the saga of Sveinthor the Unkillable, and the beautiful Hildirid, his beloved barrow-maid.

H arimoto

Scott A. Johnson

arimoto knelt outside the temple walls, his head bowed in prayer. He asked his ancestors, those who had not yet abandoned him, for strength in his task. He pleaded openly, without concern for any honor lost, for just enough power to finish his quest, to allow his father's spirit to rest in peace. With a deep bow, he stood and took up his father's katana and slid it into his sash. Today was a day of reckoning, an end, one way or the other.

The temple appeared, as did many others in the province, surrounded by a wall of stone, its peaked roof pointing to the heavens. Yet this temple was shunned, feared even, by the villages that surrounded it.

Harimoto found his way to this place, guided by rumor and intuition. At every crossroads he was warned of the great evil that came from the temple during the night, desecrating the graves. The villages were dying, stripped of their ancestral protectors by these evil beings.

Harimoto's honor was lost to these creatures. Bereft of his family's name, he wandered, ronin, searching for the source of the jikininki.

Outside the heavy iron gates of the shrine, Harimoto felt his quest coming to an end. The restless spirit of his father begged for release, a thing denied him by the jikininki. Only through burial could a man find peace. Only through the ceremony of mourning and the final blessing could his spirit rest.

Now, outside the gates of the shrine, Harimoto felt the slimmest pangs of doubt. Jikininki were not supposed to exist. He was always told that they were shadowy creatures invented to frighten children. How could they be anything but? He had, for a time, pitied the creatures, cursed with a half-life for their greed, but it was their method of continued existence, the devouring of the dead, that could not be forgiven. Robbing the dead of their rightful places with their ancestors, stripping those who were to watch over the bodies of their honor, was a thing to be reviled. His heart beat hard. His blood burned with hatred and a cry for revenge.

He stood, brushing the cursed soil from his hakama, and, with firm resolve, walked toward the iron gate. He knew the temple was empty. He'd watched the Jikininki leave, demons in human form, the living dead searching for graves to sate their hunger. The fear he felt when he first saw them was gone. He cursed himself for having felt it. Even if he had no honor, he could at least have courage. The Jikininki had weaknesses, as did any creature. They lived only at night, hiding themselves from daylight inside the temple, lest the Gods find them and reduce their bodies to ash. They had to feed. They could bleed. It was by examining their limitations that he formed a plan of attack: use his father's sword, fell as many as he could, and let the sunlight finish the job. He tried not to think of their power, their strength and ripping claws. A brave man thought not of these things.

Paramount to him was destruction of the source, the one, the creator of all jikininki, a being spoken of only in whispers. Though its real name had been lost over the years, the people who lived in its shadow called it Kama. That one, he knew, would be the most powerful of the jikininki. Harimoto would not, could not, die before he faced Kama and freed his soul.

He reached the gate and flung it wide. "Jikininki!" he cried defiantly. "Kama! I, Harimoto, son of Kesugi, have come for you!"

He heard the guard dogs before he saw them, growling deep within their sinewy bodies as they circled behind him and advanced. Had Harimoto been any slower, one of the beasts might have taken him down and left him for its masters. He leaped, spinning into the air as the creature snapped, tearing a piece of his kimono. When he landed, he stood gaping at the size of the animals. Where other temples were guarded by temple lions, small dogs with ferocious natures, these creatures were immense. Easily smaller than they, Harimoto was awed by the four creatures who stood with foaming mouths and glittering eyes in the dark courtyard. Their fur was short and patched with rot, revealing them for the monsters they were. Their teeth snapped violently as they saw no need for stealth anymore. They barked and growled, letting the young ronin know that trespassing here was a mistake.

One of the creatures jumped at him, snapping and clawing in the air. After a quick flash of steel, the creature fell to the ground, its head separated from its body. It still tried to get to him, unaware that it was already dead.

Two that remained attacked in tandem, each taking a side. While the ronin dodged one, the other bit and scratched. They too fell as Harimoto's blade found its mark. As he slashed at the second of the pair, sending its upper and lower halves in different directions, the fourth attacked from behind, knocking his katana from his hand and pinning him to the ground.

The power of the beast was remarkable. It was all the ronin could do to keep it at bay. The beast tore through the flesh on Harimoto's arms as he tried to keep it from biting his throat. He rolled, floating to the beast's back, and wrapped his arms around its massive head, then pulled with all his might. With a sickening crack, the creature jerked and went limp in his hands, its neck broken.

He stood slowly, making certain that the giant dogs were truly dead. His body was wracked with pain as he turned toward the gate, his kimono and flesh torn. He would get no respite, he saw, for even before the dogs' bodies had stopped twitching, he could see the jikininki returning, carrying the corpses of their latest raid. Harimoto reverently took his father's katana up and moved to where he was certain the jikininki could see him. "Eaters of the dead!" he cried. "You defy the Gods with your existence! You rob the people of their honor, their ancestors, and their lives. I, Harimoto, son of Kesugi, will end your reign of terror tonight!"

It was as if he were watching a wave, for at that moment the jikin-inki dropped whatever it was they were carrying and let out a collective battle cry, an unholy sound that seemed as if it would shake the temple to its foundations. At last, he thought, retribution.

He launched himself, blade first, headlong into the greasy sea of rotting teeth and angry faces. As he slashed and cut, separating heads from bodies, there came over him a feeling, an almost euphoric free-dom, at being able to slash indiscriminately, at being able to fight with abandon. For each face that came into his sight, there were two more to take its place. This was what it meant to be alive. This was what it meant to be a warrior.

He swung hard, lopping bodies apart in his wake, until, drunk with the lust of the battle, he was knocked to the ground and held fast. As the grotesquely distorted faces leered closer, he silently called to his fa-ther's spirit to tell him that he would be alone no longer.

"Enough!"

The voice came from deep within the temple, but was loud enough for all to hear. It resonated with power that could be felt as clearly as wind or rain. Harimoto did not have to look or even guess, for he knew to whom the voice belonged: Kama.

"So Harimoto, son of Kesugi, you think to defeat us all?"

The faces moved revealing the creature known as Kama slowly crossing the courtyard. He was not as the ronin expected. Where the other jikininki were horrifying in appearance, with yellowed eyes and sharpened teeth, with skin that could have rotted off their bones, Kama was a tall man, cleanly dressed with sharp features. More disturbing to Harimoto was that Kama was dressed in the robes of a priest.

"What is it you wish of us, young ronin?" Kama asked smiling

"I will rid the land of you and your evil, or I shall die trying."

Kama laughed heartily, turned and gestured for Harimoto to fol-low. The jikininki lifted him from the ground and led him into the tem-ple.

The main chamber was, as the ronin expected, a testament to filth and decay. Bones piled at every corner told of meals past, and most every holy symbol was destroyed or defiled in one manner or another.

"We are monsters to you, yes?" Kama said without looking. "You see what we do and judge our existence. You look around this room and that is all you see. Rot. Decay. Evil."

He stepped to a door and removed a key from his pocket. "Doubtless you have heard that I am the source of all this evil," he said, unlocking the door and gesturing for the ronin to step inside. "I am not what you think."

The chamber beyond the door was unlike those outside. There was no sign that anything evil had ever been in this room. At its center sat a small table surrounded by zafu cushions. The walls were hung with red silk. On the table sat a small altar with burning incense and prayer tallows. Kama sat on one of the cushions and motioned for Harimoto to do the same.

"Give the ronin back his blade," he said. "And leave us."

The jikininki did as they were instructed and closed the door as they left.

"Tell me, ronin," said Kama. "In all your journeys, have you ever heard of a jikininki being saved?"

"Only once," said Harimoto.

"Tell me."

"Legends tell of a great priest, Muso Kokushi, whose prayers freed the soul of one of your kind."

"And do the legends tell what happened to this priest after he saved the demon?"

Harimoto shook his head.

"I know of Muso Kokushi. The creature he released from this half-life of hell was indeed a jikininki. It too had been a priest that was greedy and wanted more life than was his share. You see, although he was a priest, he feared death. When Muso Kokushi came upon him, he had lived so long that he feared living even more. And so, he begged the priest to save his soul and put him to rest."

"Yes, this much I know."

"Tell me, what was your name before you became ronin?"

"Ogun Harimoto," he said, his eyes turned downward for respect for the family he no longer had.

"Ah! Ogun Kesugi was your father! At last, I understand. But I too once had another name. I was once called Muso Kokushi."

"The priest…" whispered Harimoto in disbelief.

"Yes. It was I who saved the soul of the jikininki, but at a terrible price. You see, the Gods that created us decreed that no soul can be put to rest until another takes its place. I thought that because I was a priest, I would be immune to such rulings, but none are immune from the will of the Gods. In freeing him, I cursed myself to a half-life."

He took a deep breath while searching for recognition in the ronin's eyes.

"I came to this temple and gathered all jikininki that I could find, keeping them here to prevent this curse from befalling any other."

"It is not true!" burst out Harimoto. "I killed many today, laid their souls to rest with the blade of my father."

"They will rise again," Kama said, his voice grim. "They cannot die until another takes their place. You've struggled here, I'm afraid, in vain."

"Are you so certain? Have you tried…?"

"Seppuku? Yes. Although I do not live by the bushido code, I have tried every way of honorably ending my life, and nothing has worked. I always awaken back into this nightmare, feeling the pain of being only half alive." He gazed at the burning sticks of incense, his eyes unfocusing as he became lost in thought. "More come each day. Greedy men who want more of life than their share. They hear of this place, this haven for the damned, and they come, searching for an answer to their continued existence. Nothing can save us. Trying to would mean damning yourself."

"I am already damned," Harimoto said, rising to his feet, his hand on his katana. "You and your kind have taken the honor of my family. You have denied my father's spirit rest. You must be punished."

The priest laughed deep in his chest. "How can you hope to punish that which is already in hell? Is not our existence punishment enough? I pray every day for a way to save all our souls, but the Gods do not answer. They have turned their backs on us."

"Then what am I to do?" asked Harimoto, more to his father and himself than Kama.

"You have only two choices. You could leave this place. I grant you safe passage. None shall harm you. You could leave and never return, spending the rest of your life as a ronin, with no family, no honor, no past, but free to make your own future, or you could take your revenge, unsheathe your blade and split this body, knowing that it will come back together. A hollow victory at best."

"Or," Harimoto said, "I could save your soul, end your torment by agreeing to take your place."

"No!" bellowed the priest. "No such thing shall be done! Ever! My curse is to walk the earth. I will not, cannot allow any other man to endure the same fate as I. To speak of such things is blasphemous! Strike at me if you will! Leave if you will! But this curse begins and dies with me!"

Harimoto thought deeply for a few moments.

"Which would you do?" he asked.

"My choice would be freedom," said the priest sadly. "To know once again what it is to be warmed by the sun, to taste fish or pig, to walk a road knowing that each decision is my own. That would be my choice."

The ronin bowed deeply to the priest.

"I shall honor your memory," he said at last. "You will be remembered for your greatness and your sacrifice, but not for what you have become."

"Thank you," said the priest humbly. "It is more than I could ask."

Harimoto turned and opened the door, not at all surprised to see the faces of so many of the dead-eaters who were listening. In their faces he no longer saw evil or hatred, only sorrow. They despised what they were. He passed through the gates and shut them behind him, reveling in the warmth of the sun. He knelt beside the temple and said a prayer for his father, begging forgiveness, and one for the old priest, begging for mercy.

The Moribund Room

CAROLE LANHAM

Ridley had never noticed it, but Corliss had broad shoulders. Sad to say, the gaps between the prison bars were only so big. "Tug, Ridley, tug," Corliss begged, twisting her body in the narrow slot.

Ridley tugged until the girl's face coursed with tears but, alas, shoulders will not bend iron.

"It's no use," Corliss said. "I'll never fit through this window."

When you're a deaf man, it doesn't do to turn your back on a person's lips, but Ridley's knees had begun to buckle. He slumped to the ground on his side of the wall, coming face to face with his reflection in a puddle of horse piss. Corliss was right. They were beating their fists on a prison tower that had known the beating of fists for five hundred years. He wondered that he ever thought he could save her.

Ridley beat anyway.

A handkerchief fluttered from the window. In the piss, the reflection of a man wearing a hanky on his head gazed up at Ridley. He drew the lace down over his eyelids and pressed it to his nose. Lemon balm. Pennyroyal. Lavender.

Ridley stood up.

"There's someone screaming in the surgery," the girl's lips informed him. "You should go back to your uncle."

Ridley's uncle was the barber surgeon and Ridley was his helper. Recently gout had been swelling up ankles from Gloucestershire down to Chelsea.

"He's cut off another," Corliss said. "I suppose my last hours will be spent listening to this?"

Ridley dug a lump of talc from his pocket and scrawled his answer on the ragstone sill: SOMETIMES IT'S THE ONLY WAY TO SAVE THEM. No sooner had he scratched the words than a plan to rescue Corliss sprang to mind.

* * *

Ridley woke in the dark on his back with a pounding head and something resting on his chest. The last thing he remembered was fetching the brand iron from the surgery. After that, the world went black. Scrabbling for answers, he examined the thing on top of him; tracing flaps of skin, the tip of a bone, and a crinkly thatch of hair before getting to the crux of the matter. When his fingers met up with fingers that did not belong to him, he knew he was in the Moribund Room and he knew who'd put him there.

At first light, Corliss Pracy was scheduled to lose her head. While Ridley wondered how much time had passed, the amputated arm sat on his stomach, behaving as though it possessed the muscle to pin him to the floor. He flung it so hard, it bounced back and he had to throw it again. Thanks to the bump on his head, his skull was ringing like high noon.

"Do you know what 'moribund' means?" his uncle had asked when he first showed Ridley the room. Uncle Ambrose was proud of his secret room, naming it as carefully as he would a son. "'On the point of death,' Ridley. That's what it means. Everything in this room is dying or trying its damnedest to cause death and I want to know why. On the king's map, it shows the room as destroyed, but I needed a place to store the half-dead and what's left of the place suits me fine."

Uncle Ambrose kept a lamp in the corner and Ridley had no choice but to squish about on hands and knees if he wanted to find it. Before he stumbled on the lamp, he found the ax. The handle was broken off and the blade was crusted with hair and filth. While he was stuffing it in his pocket, his toe brushed the lamp. Five scratches of flint later, Ridley had the thing lit.

Someone had written something in red ochre on the wall: I WILL LET YOU OUT WHEN THE EXECUTIONER'S WORK IS DONE

Ridley threw his fist at the door and blood from his knuckles dripped through a second set of red words: IT'S FOR YOUR OWN GOOD RIDLEY TOM

* * *

Ridley Tom was the nephew of Ambrose Pratt, barber surgeon to the king of England, and thus his fate had become inexplicitly linked to the moldering of royal appendages.

The year before, when Ridley turned nineteen, there was an outbreak of sweating sickness. Uncle Ambrose needed a man with a strong stomach and tight lips. In a letter to Ridley's home at Honey Acres he wrote, "I require a helper who will not feel inclined to prattle on about my private medical experiments."

Ridley was not a prattler and the Toms were dedicated Congregationalists of the highest accord. There was a sign hanging over their front door that read, "WHO TRAVELS FOR LOVE FINDS A THOUSAND MILES NOT LONGER THAN ONE." The Toms lived by this belief; therefore the letter was folded and put next to his mother's heart and the matter was settled as easy as that. Ridley would leave the sun-bleached brood boxes of his father's apiary to help his uncle in the blood-stained salt house in Brick Tower used as the royal surgery. This was just as well, his father said, blinking back his tears. Bees, unlike barber surgeons, were known to thrive on gossip.

What Uncle Ambrose failed to mention was that a barber surgeon had not survived a winter at the Tower in three years. The same was true for helpers. Uncle Ambrose, it turned out, failed to mention a good many things. Consequently, Ridley was knee-deep in his uncle's secrets when the king came to seek him out.

* * *

Because few people could carry on a conversation with a deaf man in writing, Ridley had learned to draw. Most days, he went about his business in silence, but upon occasion it served his purpose to sketch someone or something. Shortly after Ridley's arrival, the king began to notice a flurry of little drawings tucked into servant's waist bands and propped in the corners of dressing table mirrors.

One day, while searching out the second cook, the king spied Ridley sitting atop a pile of green cup cabbage sketching one of the castle's toilet courtiers on a piece of broken shoe sole. After learning that the barber's helper could not hear or speak, the king had Ridley brought to his mural gallery.

As Hercules suffered to choose between Wisdom and Folly on the ceiling overhead, the king peered at Ridley over the rim of his goblet, gulped loudly, and wiped his lips on the back of his hand. "Thin as a starveling, aren't you, boy? Still, I suppose you'll do."

Ridley read between the smacks as the man dug into lunch. "I am in need of a wedding present for my new wife-to-be and I would like you to draw her picture."

Ridley glanced at the gods charioting up and down the walls in expert strokes of russet, cyan, and parrot green. Even a starveling knows that kings and queens are painted by court painters, not bee-keepers turned barbers. The king's favorite at this time was a square-jawed fat man called Hans Holbein the Younger, who had painted a great many royal heads in his time. In contrast, Ridley was untrained, inexperienced, and still trying to come to grips with the work of a bone saw, but the king didn't appear to care about that.

"The lady has an affinity for the unhearing," he explained. "She's always said as much." With that, he called for his wife-to-be.

Not his first wife, whom he had divorced after she failed to give him an heir. Not his second or third wives either, for each of them had met with a miserable end.

"Ah, here she is," the king said, gesturing with a chicken leg. "Mister Tom, meet my future queen, Corliss of Lenoncourt."

* * *

On the day Ridley left home, his mother solemnly instructed, "Remember son—God loves a cheerful giver."

Ridley was prepared to do whatever he was asked to do but his schedule was busy. Afternoons, he buried the contagious in a dead garden behind the bell tower and covered the barrow tracks with a sweep of his boot on the way back. Come three o'clock, he prepared a second set of coffins to be handed off to the loved ones of the contaminated dead—six stout stones for a tall man, two for a child. Evenings he held down the maimed and fevered beneath his uncle's knife. Outside of a few quick scribbles here and there, there was no time for drawing.

In the middle of it all, there were the experiments.

WHY KEEP A FINGER? Ridley once asked.

"Study, my boy! Cutting away disease can't be the best way to save lives. I want to fix the disease."

Ridley was a busy man. Indeed, he was living in the hub of modern society.

* * *

"Did they slather your ears with fox grease and stuff them with hare gall?" Corliss wanted to know five minutes after making his acquaintance. The girl was only seventeen but she was not without experience when it came to the deaf. "My mother lost her hearing when she was a child and they made her sleep with sea shells under her pillow for a year. Didn't work though."

Seeing how Ridley had popped from the womb in his present state, he'd been put through a great number of "cures" in his time. "What's the worst they did to you?" Corliss of Lenoncourt wanted to know.

Being a noble, it was a good bet Corliss could read in both English *and* French. In order to avoid telling a pretty girl something unpleasant, however, Ridley drew a picture of himself with a stick in his ear. In this way, Ridley Tom was spared the ordeal of writing about the urine mixed with garlic he'd once gulped down while standing on one foot. Better still, the stick made the pretty girl laugh so hard, he could almost hear it.

"I have an affinity for the unhearing, Mister Tom. I've always said as much."

Ridley liked the girl right off but he got down to the job at hand and finished with her in a day.

"No! No!" the king said. "I want detail. I want color. This will take you weeks to complete."

Ridley was not *that* sort of artist but the king was the king after all. Ridley asked for a supply of salmon-pink paper, four bottles of brown ink, and some red and black chalk, and made up his mind to be colorful.

Each day, Corliss was rustled from her bed at cockcrow to perch for long yawning hours on a cushion of pointy seed pearls. In the afternoon, Ridley continued in the surgery. "Bring me that arm from yesterday," Uncle Ambrose would say, or else he might ask for a toe or a thumb.

Picking through parts in the Moribund Room, Ridley would often find himself wishing he was in the bedchamber of the king's soon-to-be-wife, quill bobbing between fingers stained with equal parts old blood and ink as he worked to put the sparkle of a ruby to paper.

"Cut it open along the wrist," his uncle was often inclined to instruct. "Let's see what's going on in there."

It was a strange thing, digging under people's skin.

Then came the day that Uncle Ambrose brought the boy back to life....

It was the celandine tincture that did it and it had worked two other times as well. In the first instance, the woman lived. In the second, the woman lived but died again the next day. This time it was the son of the king's deputy, a ten year old with a sluggish heart by the name of Phinneas Grey. Uncle Ambrose anointed the child's head with the essence, and the boy perked up like a feather plume.

Like most barbers, Uncle Ambrose was not schooled in medicine. Rather, he was a Lullist, a self-proclaimed disciple of the great Doctor Illuminatus, Raimondo Lull. Tucked away in the dead mathematician's teachings, Uncle Ambrose had stumbled upon a recipe. The Fifth Essence, he called it, for it stirred up something well beyond the four elements of fire, water, air, and earth found in all living things. Uncle Ambrose had copied the recipe word for word:

Roots of celandine flowers for man's history
Cumin seeds for his ancestry
Saffron for the inner light found in all humble creatures
Shavings of box for the fragile perimeters of the human existence

Lullists, like Congregationalists it seemed, were constantly called to serve. Uncle Ambrose shook, bruised, and pestled the Fifth Essence as if he were a priest at holy sacraments.

He explained his calling like this: "Sometimes, when a person leaves the world, I see a sort of rope dangling along behind them and I know I must try and grab hold. For those precious few, I rub the Fifth Essence on the skull above the brain and let it abide for twenty-four hours. If nothing becomes of it, I know for certain that the rope was beyond my reach."

Like most men, Uncle Ambrose grew more philosophical the more cider he drank. Uncle Ambrose, Ridley had learned, was philosophical most all the time.

Phinneas Grey had been dead an hour, his father still pacing the outer ward and awaiting news, when Uncle Ambrose decided the boy might yet be within reach. The way the child shot up seemed a promising sign.

WILL HE LIVE, UNCLE?

Uncle Ambrose gulped his tipple. "We best see that he does."

* * *

It was an odd road Ridley traveled. Separated by but a few cobbles, there were the embroidered pillows and velvet counterpanes of Corliss Pracy's bedchamber, immediately followed by the gray flesh, black boils, and purple swellings of the surgery. He might have liked the former better had the king ever seemed the least bit pleased with his efforts. As it happened, the man demanded numerous re-starts and threw regular tantrums. "Try it by the window. She looks too gloomy this way.... Tear it up! I want something more serious."

Ridley ripped and balled-up and burned his work and the weeks turned into a month. As time rolled on, he found himself in the unlikely confidence of England's future queen. Corliss told Ridley how the king had looked at dozens of portraits and bloodlines and political connections before deciding that marriage to the sister of a leader from the Schmalkaldic League offered the best possible chance for securing the neutrality of France. She explained coronations, the Ceremony of the Keys, and other monarch matters to Ridley. She spoke of her endless worries. "He nearly dropped dead on the boat docks when he saw me in person," Corliss said. "He thinks I look too much like his daughter Mary."

Ridley read her lips but did not answer. The day before she had confided that the king was concerned she would give him a deaf heir. Corliss Pracy's greatest fear was that the king was disappointed in her.

"They say Mary and I might well be twins if not for the fact that she's seven years older than me. But then, I suppose you've heard the gossip?"

Ridley replied in sanguine chalk: NOT A WORD

This made Corliss smile. "How is it that you know how to write, Mister Tom?"

Sometimes it was almost impossible to remember the simplicity of life in the valley of Buttermere. In those days, Ridley's hands and thoughts were always clean. Life was golden. MY FATHER TRADED THREE BARRELS OF HEATH HONEY SO WE COULD GO TO PETTY SCHOOL.

"We?"

Ridley nodded. HE SAT IN A LITTLE CHAIR WITH HIS KNEES TO HIS CHIN LEARNING SENECA BESIDE LADS IN SKIRTS.

"Your father did this just for you?"

Ridley scratched his answer in chalk. WHO TRAVELS FOR LOVE FINDS A THOUSAND MILES NOT LONGER THAN ONE.

Her eyes got dark. "My family is not like that. One mile would prove a thousand."

Ridley couldn't imagine coming from such people. His brothers and sisters had eaten once a day for four months so that Ridley could go to school and learn to converse through their father.

"It must be wonderful to be loved like that."

Sometimes Ridley pretended to contemplate Corliss for the purpose of a pen stroke when really he just enjoyed looking at her. Her fingers were constantly playing at threads or gold rings or lose strands of hair. Corliss was like the damselflies that fluttered round the horsemint back home, her hands a delicate whirlwind of wing beats.

"What's your Christian name, Mister Tom?"

RIDLEY.

"R-id-ley." He liked the way she said it—the "R," a kiss; the "id," a pink flicker against the roof of her mouth; the "ley," a slow uncurling of her tongue. He could have watched her say his name all day. "Do you think I look like his daughter, R-id-ley?" she asked, fingers settling on a red-brown curl like a jewelwing on a marigold.

THERE'S ALL THE DIFFERENCE IN YOUR SMILE.

Corliss smiled and, with a kiss, a flick, and a curl of tongue, said his name in a way that made him stare too long, pen and breath suspended until the damselfly fluttered on to other things.

* * *

There didn't seem to be much danger in loving someone who could not love you back. Ridley understood that he was more suited to the rough hands of the skinner's widow whom he sometimes comforted out back against the slaughterhouse wall. That didn't stop him from dreaming of Corliss Pracy's soft hands. He'd felt them once when she slid a loose eye lash off his cheek. Her fingers were as soft as silk, and they didn't smell a bit like rabbit either. "Make a wish," she'd commanded, presenting the lash before his lips on the tip of a silken finger.

Ridley could not have wished for one thing more at that moment so he moved the finger over to her own lips and gave her his wish.

Corliss closed her eyes. "I wish I were not sick with worry all the time."

She blew the wish away.

* * *

One morning, it became clear to him that the subject was studying the artist more closely than the artist was studying the subject and this was no small feat.

"Wash your face," she said at last, her eyebrows scrunched as if he'd done something to make her angry. Why should Corliss be angry, he wondered? "Use the bowl over there."

Ridley scrubbed until his face was cleaner than it had been in months.

"Look at you," Corliss said, her brow scrunched even more than before. "You're perfectly pleasant under all the dirt, aren't you?" With that, Corliss Pracy burst into tears.

Ridley rolled a piece of chalk between his fingers and waited for her to transform again into the damselfly he'd come to know.

"Oh, what's to be done?" her lips said. "I may as well accept it."

She put her arms around his neck and kissed him with all her might.

Ridley wanted Corliss more than he had ever wanted anything, yet he held her from him and scrambled for his quill.

HE'LL HAVE YOUR HEAD ON A PIKE FOR THAT.

"That's rather the point, I'm afraid." Tears trickled from her eyes. "Does all of this feel right to you, Ridley? You're a barber, not a court painter. Don't you see? My picture will never be good enough until he's gotten what he wants—a way out."

Ridley's brother had once tricked him into kissing a girl by leaving gifts that falsely hinted at adoration, but Ridley Tom had never run across a truly devious act in his life. He read Corliss Pracy's lips, but he didn't understand what she was saying.

"The man can scarcely break the arrangement he made with my brother, can he? He wants *us* to break it for him."

Ridley knocked over a candle in his haste to answer. Across splashed wax, he wrote, I WILL REFUSE TO DRAW YOUR PICTURE.

Corliss laid her soft fingers over his, making him drop the pen. "Then we will die innocent *and* stupid."

* * *

"Distressing news, nephew," Uncle Ambrose said when Ridley came to work an hour after. "I've moved the boy to the Moribund Room."

YOU PUT HIM WITH THE FINGERS?

Phinneas Grey had turned out to be a frightful botch. The boy's body had returned to the living but his mind had not. It'd been necessary to report him dead to the family since the truth would mean the chopping block for Ambrose Pratt. A coffin of stones had been tearfully put to rest in the church yard one week before.

"I want you to see this for yourself," Uncle Ambrose said.

Through an archway of red eyes and pink tails they traveled, hopping oily puddles and scrabbling up a crumbling staircase to emerge in a draft with their candles snuffed at a room reserved for hacked limbs. When Uncle Ambrose re-ignited the wicks, their eyes fell on the window in the door. A jagged row of nubs was all that remained of the iron bars that had been there hours before.

Keys were extracted and inserted and turned. The door was opened, just a crack, and they peered in, one face above the other.

Phinneas Grey, if he could still be called by that name, lunged from the darkness; his little fish teeth snapping.

Uncle Ambrose slammed the door, locked the lock, and they both backed away, panting. "Did you see it?" Uncle Ambrose said. "He's eaten the fingers and toes."

All night, they debated it until ink, along with words, ran out. At sunrise, Uncle Ambrose took an ax and returned to the Moribund Room. "From now on the dead stay dead," he said.

* * *

His fingers were trembling too much to draw. "Poor, Ridley," Corliss said. "This has you out of sorts." She took the chalk from his quivering fingers. "I know just what you need."

Down came Ridley's trunk hose.

"You're the only person who's ever listened to me, Ridley," she said, laughing at the irony of it all.

Off came Ridley's nether stocks.

"You're the only person who's ever loved me." She unhooked a strand of glass pearls and let them drop away. "You do you love me, don't you, Mister Tom?"

He rubbed his cheek against hers, up and down, up and down, and they fell on the rushes that carpeted her floor, rolling until wild snippets of cowlslip and daisies poked from their hair.

Most nights Ridley curled up on gummed flagstones in the surgery and made do around the dross. Corliss slept in a room for a queen. She shook a petal from her hair, and Ridley watched it weave through the air like a golden magic carpet.

The portrait sat untouched on the easel for seven days yet Ridley's life had never had more color.

"How far will you go for me?" Corliss asked.

Ridley wrote his answer with his finger tip on the inside of her wrist. AS FAR AS I HAVE TO.

Not long before this, Uncle Ambrose had stitched the finger of a corpse onto a living hand. With shiny eyes, they'd watched the new finger flop against the others as if it had no bone. The next day it turned black and the patient was more ill than before. The day after that, Uncle Ambrose did away with the entire hand. In the end, the patient died.

Kissing Corliss felt a whole lot like putting a dead finger on an otherwise good hand. It was a fix that was bound to kill but Ridley couldn't stop himself. Some things were more important than living.

Eventually they were caught. "Run Ridley! Run!" Corliss cried, as the king's men stormed her room.

Ridley was out the window before they could catch up.

* * *

Corliss was put in the Record Tower and word spread that the king's intended had a secret lover.

Corliss insisted her virtue had been stolen at knifepoint by a stranger at her window but the king didn't believe her. "If it was the deaf boy, he will die soon enough for my surgeons do not live long. But if, as you say, it was a stranger at your window, this is because you are a tart who smiles at every man she sees. Either way, you've made a fool of me."

"Happy to be of service, my dear," she said.

The execution was to take place on the day set aside for Corliss of Lenoncourt's coronation.

* * *

In the Moribund Room, Ridley could feel the ghosts of a dozen abandoned fingers curling up from the carnage in an effort to trip him. He feared to turn his back on the bone piles, lest they might reassemble themselves, and come after him in revenge. *How dare you leave us to be sucked clean by that little monster!*

Even as Ridley steered clear of irate digits, he felt grateful to that little monster. In life and in death, Phinneas Grey had carried the girth of wealth. Ridley was thin as a starveling. Though Phinneas had found the strength to rip iron bars from wood, he didn't have the trim size to make an escape. Ridley *almost* did.

The removal of the bars was the first thing Ridley was grateful for. The second was the ax. Uncle Ambrose must have left it behind as useless. The door planks were thick as a Cromwell Bible but they were also old and rotten. Ridley scraped at the opening, whittle by whittle, and the window grew bigger. When the size was right, he kicked off a dozen phantom fingers, squeezed out of the cell, and went off to rescue Corliss.

"I was worried I'd never see you again," Corliss said when Ridley tossed a pebble at her prayer book. Ridley had already given the guard a good knock in the temple. He held up the saw.

Corliss went back to praying.

To do the job properly, the left arm would have to go and part of the shoulder too. "Better a limb than my head," Corliss said, though it made her turn green saying it. She tied a rope around her waist, handed the tail to Ridley, and drank down the malmsey he'd pinched from his uncle.

Ridley tied his end of the rope around himself so that there was no slack between them. He stuffed a wool stocking in her mouth and had her step on an old leather jerkin. The rope was to hold Corliss upright, the sock to stifle the screams, and the jerkin to soak things up, but Ridley didn't tell her that. He angled her arm on the window sill and put a finger to his lips.

Shhhh.

It took eight minutes to get it off and, if Corliss screamed, Ridley didn't know it. He only knew that, when it was done, the jerkin could have been wrung out three times over. Using the rope, he pulled her up, praying she would fit.

She did.

Then it was into the death cart and off to the surgery where an empty coffin waited. Ridley's intent was to put her in the box and drive her out, using the papers for a woman who had died that morning. It was a late hour for such business but it would work. It had to. By the time the king realized what had happened, they would be half-way to Buttermere.

* * *

Uncle Ambrose was not happy to see that Ridley had escaped, especially after all the trouble he'd gone to keep him safe. "Blast you, boy! Do you want to die? Think of your poor Mum!"

Uncle Ambrose being Uncle Ambrose, he was too deep in his cups by this point to do anything but help with Corliss and mutter like an old hen. "A man who will stick his fingers with equal carelessness into a hive of bees, a chest cavity, or the King of England's bride is a danger to himself and others. If you had any brains at all, you'd have stayed back with the arm." He put his ear to the girl's chest and listened for a long time.

"She isn't breathing, Ridley."

Ridley shook Corliss again and again and again. He listened for breathing. He shook her some more. He scratched on the wall with a stub of chalk: BRING HER BACK

"You know I can't do that."

Ridley thumped on the words he'd written. Thump. Thump. "No."

It took a single punch in the nose to change the man's mind. Uncle Ambrose brought out the bottle of celandine he'd hidden in his good fur hat and he rubbed the tincture on Corliss Pracy's pale forehead.

They watched. They waited.

The girl's eyes shot open.

DOES SHE SEE ME UNCLE?

"Lord God, I hope so."

They were putting the coffin on the wagon when Ridley noticed that every window in the tower was lit. "They're looking for her," Uncle Ambrose said. They hurried the box back inside. "Take her to the Moribund Room, Ridley. No one will look for you there."

She wasn't next to him when he woke up and the lamp was broken on the floor. Ridley felt around, finding a wall, a pebble, a bone. He still had his candle and set about lighting it.

It caught on the first try and, in a flash; he came grimace to grimace with Corliss, a breath away from his nose. He dropped his light. The candle rolled into his knee along with something else. Was that a finger brushing along his forearm? Something wiggled near his ankle. Ridley scraped the lighting stone, fervently wishing he could hear or speak. He was so grateful to see that Corliss still lived, he could scarcely grip the slick candle in his hand. He felt a puff of air near his cheek. A breath. Then another. Scratch. Scratch. Scratch. The stone sparked.

She was against the far wall, her dress soaked through with blood. When he held up the candle, he noticed something stuck to the back of his hand. An old ear. He dropped the candle again and Corliss disappeared just as she began to move toward him. He rubbed the flint faster. He hadn't meant to fall asleep. The last he could recall, he'd been counting her breaths.

At last, the wick caught and Ridley reminded himself to keep the thing lit this time, no matter what. He moved the light from one corner to the next, the flame a circle of gold in the Bubonic black. There! Corliss sat with her knees drawn up to her chest, blocking the glow with splayed fingers.

Ridley smiled.

Corliss leapt.

He reared back so fast, he almost lost his candle again, but she only wanted the arm lying against the far wall. With round eyes, she raised it to her mouth and bit.

It took time to understand what he was seeing and by then, she had picked the bone clean and was coming across the room at him. Ridley pulled the ax blade from his pocket and climbed to his feet.

At that same moment, he caught a familiar gleam in the dark pools of her eyes. *How far will you go for me, R-ID-LEY?*

When she chomped her teeth, he had no choice. Ridley raised the ax as if it weighed more than the sun. Heart thundering in his chest, he sank the blade in flesh and bone, stopping Corliss in her tracks.

For a full minute, she looked at him the way she'd looked at him before her mind went bad. That one minute was enough.

When her eyes clouded again and she barred her teeth, Ridley slumped down in the gristle and tossed his beloved his thumb.

Theatre Is Dead

Raoul Wainscoting

The stage was set. The crowd quieted to a murmur under the mid-afternoon sun as the narrator appeared. Entering from stage right, he glided regally to the edge of the stage. His handsome costume was new and flawless. He took a moment to study the crowd. The better-paying patrons sat comfortably in the shade on the far side of the Globe.

Squinting against the light, the narrator spoke. "Good people, hear thee now our tale of woe. The family royal Puglia, rulers of Brindisi, undone by the politics of man, while amongst them the dead do walk."

The crowd's murmur rose briefly. The rumors were true, the play did concern the postvitals. A few amongst them rose to depart, mortified by the idea of using such tragedy as entertainment. Backstage, while the narrator strolled through the introductory monologue, the cast was rushing to complete its preparations. A debut performance was always challenging, but when breaking in a new theatre, doubly so.

"Come now, into your costume!" William yanked on the cords, tugging the cape snugly about the young man's neck. "Prince Risoni enters the first scene shortly, boy!" William shoved him toward his assigned post near the stage to await his cue.

Henry Darcy, the young man in the costume of the doomed Prince Risoni, cradled his wounded hand, hidden beneath the cape. His brow was damp with pained perspiration, attributed to a mild case of stage fright. He swept the cape aside for a moment, peeking at the hand once more. It had happened in an instant, on the way to the theatre. That foul drunk, staggering along the cobbles, smelled of the sewer. Putrid and stinking, the drunk had crashed into Henry, forcing him to shove him away. As he pushed the stinking body, the old man had bitten him! Now costumed, Henry studied his hand. The arc of small, festering cuts on his palm betrayed the bite mark, but he had to go on. He needed this job, and this troupe was the only one willing to take him. This was his last chance in London.

Nearby, lurking in a shadowy corner, stood the officer. Quietly, Lieutenant Richard Litchfield of Her Majesty's Royal Navy observed. He caught William's eyes and drew him over. William offered his hand, the pair shook, exchanging looks of tired relief. It had been a maddening few months for both of them. William thought back to their first meeting. His carriage, returning him from family business in Stratford, had struck and been overturned by an unexpected mob of postvitals on the road. His first encounter with the walking dead was terrifying. The staggering mass of rotting corpses had seized upon the coachman and his horses, giving William and the other passengers time to escape. They were soon being pursued. A slow, relentless chase drove the passengers of the ruined coach across the field, carrying the others who could not walk. It had seemed like hours. The temptation to drop the injured and save himself had been overwhelming. Just when hope had seemed lost, help had arrived.

Richard recalled their first meeting as well. The outbreak from the small village had gone unchecked for too long. His team, atop armored horse and with their war wagon carriage, had trampled, impaled and slashed the corpses in quick order. He had personally crushed the lifelessness from the last few corpses with his metal gauntlets around their necks.

It was then that William, an enthusiastic survivor of the assault, had seized upon his plan. After hearing Richard's profane complaints of how the citizenry was too stupid to follow a few simple rules for preventing such outbreaks, he had made his offer. "Teach me these rules, as you would have them know, and I shall present them in grand form!" William had said there on the gore-soaked hillside. "Come to London with me, consult on the production of my new play. We shall take the city by storm, entertaining, educating, and making a good name for my troupe; and you, you shall gain allies in your battle."

Richard had scoffed at the idea, having no interest in sitting on the sidelines. A rising star in the Royal Navy, he had proven himself at the postvital outbreak in Portsmouth, leading his men, charging the fallen city from the docks. After that, he found himself seconded to the Royal Army, teaching them to roam the countryside, chasing down reports of the increasingly-frequent outbreaks. He had no idea the power of this maddening playwright, who had Lord Chamberlain reach out to have Richard seconded again to this new branch called "Relations with Her Majesty's Public." He had spent the last few months in frustrated misery, teaching artistic young fools to stagger and lurch in the manner of the dead. That had been easy, compared to the task of arguing with the arrogant, petulant playwright over details he was supposed to be reinforcing in their play—how to prevent the dead from rising, how to deal with those who had risen, or been bitten or befouled by them. Simple rules, needlessly complicated by their inclusion in this miserable, clichéd storyline of a fictional royal family.

William smiled. Ignorant of Richard's true feelings, he was happy to see the loyal officer standing by to the last, ready to assist during the play as needed. "We shall do well, you shall see. Your service here is most appreciated, and I shall make sure your superiors know of it, Lieutenant." William tossed off a flippant salute and returned to shuffling the cast backstage.

Onstage, the first scene had begun. Two Princes of the royal Puglia family had begun their part. Their third, the quietly-suffering Prince Risoni, waited for his cue. He wiped his brow again, his face growing ever-paler as the throbbing in his wounded hand slowly spread up his arm.

"What hear you of Count Gemelli's plans, good brother?" asked Prince Paccheri, eldest son of the King, his majesty Fiori Puglia.

"I trust not that man, but our father's ear he doth have," replied Prince Filini, the second eldest.

"I wager it is war he doth seek, to usurp the crown, aided by our falling in battle, good brother," said Prince Paccheri.

Prince Risoni, the youngest of the three princes, lurched onto stage a few beats after his cue. He appeared somewhat dazed, raising an unexpected titter of laughter from the crowd. "How now, good brothers!" Prince Risoni finally managed to squeak through the growing pain in his arm. Backstage, Lieutenant Richard Litchfield held his ears, hiding in the shadows. He tried to block out the back-and-forth dialogue of the elder Princes, as they explained for the audience the state of the conflict with the Calabria family, sworn enemies of the Puglia royal family, and how the mysterious court advisor, Count Gemelli, seemed to be making things worse.

William, seeing a lull in his backstage work, once more approached the tortured officer. "So, how do you think it is going?"

"Fine! Just stay on script and get the message across." Richard fought his urge to strangle the infuriating playwright.

William nodded. "I've been meaning to ask you, were you really there? Against the Armada? I heard some of the cast talking. They said you were." William pressed himself against the wall to let some bodies pass in the narrow space backstage, readying themselves for the upcoming onstage battle.

Richard perked up. At least this would distract him for a moment. "Yes, I was there. I was serving aboard one of the ships that met them. And, yes, the rumors are true. The dead walking amongst the crew of the Spanish galleons were a factor in their defeat, but only in part."

"And, is it true that…" William began.

Richard cut him off. "The rumors of British intrigue being the cause of the enemy vessels' infection are just that." Richard smiled at William from his shadowy hiding place. "Just rumors."

Onstage, the ambush began. The soldiers of Calabria, sworn enemies of the Puglia, swarmed onstage, all three of them. The three Princes fought valiantly to fend off their attackers. Richard, backstage, shielded his eyes against the sight. No matter how he shouted at them, these actors could not manage to make a sword fight look authentic.

Wild, chopping swings and lengthy pauses for heroic poses made them look like fools, but the audience lapped it up, laughing and "oohing" appropriately in time with the action. Most importantly, they gasped on cue as the brave young Prince Risoni fell, victim of a final stab from the departing, defeated enemy.

"Brother! Thou hast fallen!" shouted the elder Princes, joining the brave Risoni as life failed him. The illness of the actor beneath the costume was acute. The throbbing in the wound upon his hand had spread to the rest of his body. His gasps of pain made his character's death seem all the more real. Henry Darcy joined his character in death, there upon the stage.

Even Richard had to admit, it looked pretty good.

"Now, brother, flee us to seek aid, to move our littlest brother's body," said Prince Paccheri.

"A noble carriage for his noble body," agreed Prince Filini.

The pair moved offstage, leaving the body alone. The audience murmured, some of them aware of the folly of leaving a fallen body alone, unmolested, in these dark days.

William watched as Risoni remained at rest. "Get up now! Your lines!" William hissed at the prone actor. His moving soliloquy on the nature of death and the rest it might bring was going wasted! The audience rustled, curious at the pause in the action and the general state of immobility of the actor at center stage.

Richard nodded approvingly. For weeks he had battled the writer and his cast, insistent that the dead not be portrayed as speaking. As far as he could tell, the good Prince was playing dead to perfection.

"Next scene!" William signaled backstage, and the cast and crew rushed to comply. The narrator rushed onstage to explain to the crowd the terrible mistake the elder Princes had made, leaving a recently-fallen body untended. While the chances were slim, the horrible new condition that afflicted those rare few might lead the body to rise again. A mindless killer, wandering, feeding, spreading the curse to others through their wounds.

The Prince's body was dragged offstage as the intrigue between Count Gemelli and Queen Bavette was established. He had dirt on her, and it would prevent her from disrupting his plans for disposing of King Fiori.

The body of Prince Risoni continued to play its part. That which had killed him, so painfully, was now reanimating him. Slowly, the body of the costumed Henry Darcy twitched upon the wooden floor and began to rise.

"Funeral scene!" William signaled backstage and the cast and crew set to work. The costumer rushed to Prince Risoni, ready to throw a damp gray cloth over the actor's head, the better to appear a lifeless corpse. Upon seeing the actor, he decided the Prince didn't need it. Someone else must have already prepared the actor, he already looked the part. Risoni's body let out a low moan, reaching for the man, the hunger for flesh already consuming what passed for its mind.

"Come on!" Prince Paccheri and King Fiori grabbed Risoni's barely-animated corpse and dragged it onstage, flopping it onto the flimsy bench next to the trapdoor in the stage. The scene was set, the body was atop the Puglia family's royal crypt, and the rest of the royals had assembled for the ceremony.

"Curse be to mine enemies, having our son from us ta'en!" King Fiori bemoaned his loss, shaking his fist skyward. The actors playing Queen Bavette and Princess Barbina wailed in falsetto at their loss. Count Gemelli skulked in the corner, lurking, to remind the audience of his evil, traitorous nature.

"We beseech thee, look with favor upon—" the priest began, as the body of Prince Risoni began to rise from its prone position. "Not yet!" hissed the priest, pushing the corpse back down onto the table.

Backstage, William grimaced at the miscue by the young actor.

The funeral continued, with soliloquies on the nature of life and death bursting forth from the King and Queen. Frequent interruptions by the body at the center disturbed them, the actor apparently wildly confused as to when it was his turn. The trapdoor was slid open and the body was hoisted off the table by the cast for its deposit into the crypt.

The dead Risoni flailed, this time on cue, and gripped a convenient arm, that of the actor wearing the wig and dress of Queen Bavette. The cast gasped and erupted with a horrified "Zounds!" to emphasize their surprise over the rise of the dead. The audience was less impressed, having seen it coming due to the frequent miscues by the dead actor.

Prince Paccheri immediately drew his stage sword and moved to dispose of the animated corpse. Just as quickly, the King, reinforcing the family's tragic misunderstanding, ordered him to hold. "Thine own brother thou wouldst stab in death? What manner of love is this?" questioned King Fiori.

"One speaketh so often of that which is rotten in Denmark, what say you of the rot before thee?" retorted the Prince, gesturing widely at the struggling corpse.

Risoni's body lurched again in their arms, tugging itself toward the Queen. It clamped its jaw around the arm it held, digging its teeth in. The Queen, played by one of the eldest boys in the cast, howled and cursed as the actor tried to tug away, his artificial royal bosom shaking with the effort. "Not so hard you fool!" he hissed at the corpse as he saw blood erupt from his broken skin.

Risoni's body was now poised over the trapdoor, and the rest of the cast, upset with the actor's fumbling of the scene, simply dropped it through the hole. The fierce grip of its hand and jaw drug Queen Bavette along with it, through the trapdoor. The unexpected headfirst dive of the Queen and the howls of painful surprise echoing beneath the stage shocked the audience with its realism.

Backstage, William howled in pain of his own. "She's not supposed to go in there! Just Risoni! He gets buried, then comes back up! What are they doing out there? We need the Queen for act two! And three!" He stomped his feet and flailed his arms for an immediate scene change.

Richard, meanwhile, had grown suspicious. Drawing a hidden dagger from under his uniform, he grabbed a stagehand and dragged him along as he sought access. "If I'm not out before the next scene ends, set fire to the theatre!" Richard hissed at the shaken stagehand.

"I don't think Mister Shak…" the frightened stagehand began.

"I don't care what he thinks. We have a bigger problem than some botched lines!" The officer dove below through another trapdoor, barely touching the ladder during the short drop. He disappeared into the dark space beneath, seeking his prey.

The next scene began quietly. The priest and the nefarious Count Gemelli were discussing the latest developments, explaining to the audience the reasons for the rise of the dead Prince. They carefully recited the checklist of the ways one might ensure that the recently-deceased would not rise again, as well as delivering a tedious lecture on the nature of the bites they leave. The more astute audience members wondered why they seemed to be avoiding any mention of the departed Queen. The occasional muffled thumping and moaning noises coming from beneath the stage only added to their confusion. William was incensed by the noises and sought out someone to explain the activity. The stagehands claimed ignorance of anyone doing work below.

Richard reappeared with a streak of blood across the breast of his uniform and some sticky mess upon his fearsome dagger, but it was the angry look upon his face that scattered the cast and crew as he stalked through the backstage spaces.

"What have you been doing down there?" William demanded, furious over the awful noises he had heard.

"The Queen is dead," Richard stated flatly.

"Yes, I know, those damned fools. What were they thinking? We'll need Princess Barbina to step up for some additional lines." William snapped his fingers, then jabbed them at King Fiori, who nodded and went to find the boy wearing her dress.

"We require Prince Risoni for the next scene, did you manage to retrieve him?"

"No. But I shall. You need to stop the show. There is a..." Richard spoke through tightly-gritted teeth.

"Stop the show? On opening day? I think not!" William laughed, pointing to usher the next group onto stage. "You just sit back here, keep out of the way. And find Prince Risoni for me!" William scampered off to correct the order of the Calabrian soldiers, lining up for their next entrance.

"I intend to." Richard stalked off to explore another corner of the backstage maze, hopeful that the mindless corpse had not discovered an exit.

Minutes later, the officer had cornered his prey. The walking dead weren't terribly clever, but they had their moments. Having found its way out from the depths beneath the stage, the lifeless Prince Risoni was now hopelessly tangled in the costumer's line of over-sized dresses. Richard aimed his dagger, intending to stab the lengthy blade through one hazy white eye and into its brain, ending the poor actor's new existence. His thrust was interrupted by William and one of his crew swooping in and whisking the lifeless creature away. He was required on stage.

"William!" Thundered Richard, catching up and spinning the playwright around to face him. "That is a postvital. It must be ended!"

"Oh, please, you do carry on. He's just acting the part, staying in character!" William dismissed the officer with a deferential wave.

But Prince Risoni was not interested in his entrance. It had taken the opportunity to attack the stagehand escorting it. The youngest Prince's teeth ripped at the neck of the poor man, as it dragged him down to the floor. William leaped in to cover the victim's mouth, muffling the scream, lest it erupt from backstage and ruin the performance.

"Move!" Richard demanded, shoving William aside with a swift boot. "I must do this!" He stared into the stagehand's eyes, hoping he understood and would forgive him. The stagehand fought to escape, kicking and clawing at the Prince tearing at his throat. The lifeless corpse's grip was broken and the stagehand rolled away, clutching at the wound on his neck. Richard could see it was not immediately fatal, a shallower cut than he had expected.

"Don't! I'm fine!" The stagehand protested through pain-clenched teeth. On his knees, he backed away from Richard.

"You know I have to, you're going to be one of them soon. You know this is the right thing for everyone." The officer moved closer, preparing to stab at the stagehand, to end his suffering and prevent the foulness from spreading.

Behind him, William saw his opportunity. He scooped up the momentarily-sated Prince Risoni's body and aimed it toward the stage. The Prince's lifeless face appeared strangely pleased with itself. Its grey tongue probed at a trickle of blood running down its jaw.

"William! No!" Richard objected, caught in a rare moment of indecision between the two who must be put down. The stagehand took the opportunity to flee. Awkwardly, he rose and staggered painfully away from Richard, seeking refuge. In the other direction, William and the Prince reached the stage, only a few beats after the corpse's cue. With a forceful shove in the back, the lifeless Prince Risoni was propelled, staggering awkwardly onto stage. William wrung his hands nervously. Something was terribly wrong here.

Onstage, the trio of lusty harlots had been awaiting the entrance of the undead Prince. They were played by the same trio of boys who served as the soldiers of the Calabria family, well-practiced for their rapid costume change. The lifeless one's escape from the crypt was to be observed in the village below the Castle Puglia, thus fueling rumors to the other royals that their dead Prince still walked, and the play needed some saucy language to keep the audience interested during the second act.

"How stiffly thou movest," observed the first of the town harlots, in his best falsetto.

"'Tis good, for the stiffer thou art, the greater thy use shall be," suggested the second, earning a rowdy chuckle from the crowd.

"Stiff he does move, but perchance to remain so as I should require?" agreed the third, causing the trio to laugh and point at the Prince. The dead one took no offense, but staggered forward, its arms raised in anticipation. It began to moan, its breathless voice rising as it called out, eager to feed.

The trio of harlots used wild gestures to feign offense at the smell of the walking dead.

"Thy breath stinketh of the dirt, good sir!" The first fanned her hand before her nose.

"A horse, a horse," the second harlot began, "thou stinketh as doth a horse!" The trio broke down laughing at this.

Backstage, Richard finished chasing the bitten stagehand and gave him a thorough skull-stabbing. Disposing of the body through a trapdoor, he turned again to the primary problem, the wandering Prince Risoni. Rushing toward the stage, he was stopped by the other two Princes.

"You can't go out there! You'll ruin the scene!" Prince Paccheri objected, as they struggled to keep the officer from his duty.

"I must! It will kill them!"

"He's just acting. You should be proud. He's doing that walk you taught us better than anyone," Prince Filini noted with admiration.

On stage, the harlots began to taunt the poor Prince, running to and fro, their dresses lifted immodestly for better mobility.

"Staggerth thou as if from a tankard house fled!" the first one cried.

"Thy odor precedes you and doth linger well after!" the second one offered.

"Hence, rotten thing—" the third one's line was cut off by Prince Risoni grabbing the harlot as she passed. "Hey, wait, that isn't in the…" the harlot said as the dead one struggled to bite at the tempting neck flesh. The pair stumbled, tripping and staggering backwards, locked in a struggle. The other two actors chased after, leading the entire ensemble on stage to crash out of sight and back into the wings. Horrible screams were heard from the now-hidden party.

The audience, confused, began to grumble louder. Some howling and hissing of disapproval erupted. William struggled to keep the play moving. He shooed the next scene onto stage early, with whispered instructions to stretch their part out, as the Calabrian soldiers might not be immediately available for their entrance.

William was right about that. The three young men set to play those soldiers, and more recently the town harlots, were being efficiently dispatched by Richard. When William found him, the officer's blood-soaked uniform sleeve rose and fell again, putting to rest the last of the three new postvitals, before they could rise and kill.

"You must end this, sir!" Richard demanded as he rose to meet William with a glare. "It is over! We must clear out the theatre, save the patrons."

William, shaking with panic, lashed out at him. "No! We have to go on. Our generous benefactor, the Lord Chamberlain, the other investors, they need this to work. I need this to work. I am gambling my reputation, my fortune on this."

"You won't have enough actors to go on, they are already infecting each other!" Richard gestured at the new corpses at his feet. "Listen to the crowd!"

71

Indeed, the crowd was turning. The raucous noise of hissing and hooting was growing as the dwindling cast made the best of the scene. Backstage, the shadowy forms of Prince Risoni and its newly-deceased companions staggered haltingly in the shadows, eager to feed on their former colleagues.

William sagged. It was true. His mind reeled as his carefully-crafted denial collapsed on him. The terror of his first encounter, that day with the carriage, came back to him, the horrible noises they made, the sight of them tearing apart the coachman. He shivered at the memory. They were here.

Onstage, the remaining members of the royal family delayed, improvising lines as they awaited the surprise arrival of the traitorous Count Gemelli and his allies, the now-missing soldiers of Calabria. They turned as one when they caught sight of an entrance. King Fiori began to stride onto stage to demand answers from his formerly-loyal court advisor. Only a few of the audience members, seated at just the right angle, witnessed the King's just-as-sudden exit, clawing at the wood of the stage as unseen forces dragged him away by his ankles. His screams were short-lived.

The actors stood silent, waiting for direction. The audience responded, renewing their howling and shouting, many moving to depart. A few token rotten vegetables were launched toward the stage, as if testing their range before a full volley.

Richard shook the playwright by the shoulders with gore-soaked hands. "End this!"

"I have an idea," William rasped, his throat dried by fear. He gulped loudly as the sounds of violence grew around them.

A bold voice shouted over the chaos in the theatre. A resplendently gaudy royal costume strode onto stage. It was Richard, officer of the Royal Navy, dressed as the King. The new King Fiori, with loud and efficient shouting, belted out the lines that William had pressed upon him. His words were orders, jarring the other actors and silencing, for the moment, the audience.

"My family, my kingdom, it is undone!" shouted Richard. "Undone by our lack of wit. Ignorant we were of this vile scourge, this walking of the damned dead!"

Stumbling, William entered, clad in the trademark green suit of Count Gemelli. The stains of blood from the recently-slain actor hardly showed at all through the dark color. "I beseech you sire. Forgive me now ere this wretched scum taketh me!"

It was a significant leap forward in the script, but the remaining cast, two Princes and the Princess, stood their ground, waiting to see what would happen next.

"Another day shall I deal with thy traitorous nature, Count. For now, we must fight to live!" The new King Fiori began to whisper quick commands at the cast. The Princes drew their stage swords. They turned as one, backs to the audience, and waited. The silence in the theatre was such that everyone could hear them—the postvitals. Former cast and stagehands, moaning and thumping about backstage. They were coming.

"This royal throne we defend to the last!" King Fiori waved his own sword, one not fashioned for the stage, but for real combat. He handed his dagger to Princess Barbina, a slender actor, who held it nervously with both hands.

A shadow broke the entrance to stage right. "But soft! What corpse through yonder window breaks?" William, as Count Gemelli, stammered.

"The first thing we do, let's kill all the postvitals!" Richard, the new King Fiori, waved his sword and attacked the shambling forms emerging from backstage. The audience shouted with enthusiasm, hoping for a blood-soaked finale to save the day. They were quieted with shock at how real the blood looked, spurting from the newly-decapitated body of the first one to emerge from backstage. Richard's sword was a blur as the crowd screamed for more of the amazing tricks of costume and makeup that made such a graphic death possible on stage.

The battle was upon them. The actors stabbed and clubbed their weapons against the lumbering wall of corpses taking the stage, while Richard's sword carved great gashes in their necks and gouged deeply into their eye sockets. As the horrible, gruesome battle played out on the stage, the audience that had remained was enthralled. Prince Paccheri was the first to fall, taken down by teeth clamped upon his jugular.

Prince Filini joined him soon after, the pair set upon by the grotesque creatures. Richard moved quickly to disown the lot of them of the contents of their skulls.

William himself managed to club and push back one of his stagehand's corpses, nearly tossing himself from the stage in the effort. The corpse he clubbed spun about, halting itself as it faced the unguarded back of Princess Barbina. The actor in the dress was distracted, attempting to dislodge his dagger from the neck of a fallen corpse, and was set upon without warning.

The carnage ran its course. It came down to William and Richard, as Count Gemelli and King Fiori, backed up against the edge of the stage. The last of the postvitals moved forward. It was the former Henry Darcy. The tattered, blood-soaked remains of Prince Risoni's costume hung about him like wet feathers. The body shuffled toward the pair of survivors. Richard reached into his costume and pulled out his last surprise, a small pistol, which he moved to charge with powder and ball. The hungry moaning of the corpse grew louder, deeper, as the corpse neared, arms outstretched.

"We're supposed to die now," William admonished in a quiet whisper to his officer. "The script says everyone dies, the lesson of not heeding the rules about these creatures."

Richard paused and stared at the playwright incredulously.

"This is a tragedy, it has to end this way," William explained.

Richard nodded and smiled. "Fine. Follow my lead."

As the arms of the corpse reached for the pair, they fell down, shouting with feigned pain. The surprised corpse halted, seemingly wondering where its prey had gone. Then it noticed the audience. It moaned loudly, hungrily.

Richard lifted his body up, on one arm, as if to gasp out a final, breathless proclamation. Instead, the silence of the theatre was broken by the sudden explosion of Richard's pistol. The crowd screamed in shock and awe as the corpse's skull volcanically erupted blood and brain and bone. The wrecked body of Prince Risoni fell to the stage for the last time.

The bodies, the living, the dead, and the dead-again, lay still on the stage as the audience went mad. The screams and cheers put to shame their earlier protests.

Lying prone on the stage, the playwright and the officer spoke to each other with short shouts over the noise.

"I think I'm starting to like the theatre, William." Richard said, a gruesome smile spreading on his gore-spattered face.

"Yes, but I don't know how we're going to manage to top this one, or even put it on again. We deviated from the script rather sharply." William sighed heavily and then laughed.

"And you seem to be short a few actors." The pair laughed uncomfortably before rising to take their bows. The audience, too stunned to wonder why the other actors remained motionless, showered them with thunderous applause.

The next day, the word was out. It was said that the play was an unconventional, uncompromising, revolutionary look at the future of theatre. The signs went up around the Globe, announcing a temporary hiatus for some necessary upgrades. This move only stoked the rumors.

The next week, the advertisements went out. New actors were required for an expanded version of the hit new play. Other ads sought out new stagehands, with preference given to those with experience in animal handling. The theatre was besieged. Quietly, elsewhere in London, a new program for dealing with outbreaks was established. The disposal of postvitals went on as it had previously, but stories were told of some Royal Army squads conducting careful round-ups of the walking dead. Hushed voices explained it to be part of an experimental, more humane, less traumatic program for disposing of the problem.

The next month, the theatre reopened with a new cast and expanded costuming and makeup magic. It was said that the actors playing the postvitals in the cast were masterful in their impersonation, and the way they died on stage was simply the most realistic depiction of graphic, bloody violence the stage had ever seen.

The Anatomy Lesson

Jenny Ashford

"I'm cutting the rope now, Hendrik. Get under his legs."

Johannes, the Preparator, teetered on the wooden ladder, the knife clutched in his right hand. He heard Hendrik moving into position, the man's bulky frame making the boards of the gallows creak. "Are you ready?"

Hendrik grunted an affirmative. Johannes began to cut.

It was only an hour past sunset, but already the streets around them were deserted. It was mid-January, and bitterly cold; Johannes expected the canal to freeze sometime in the night. For now, though, he still heard its waters lapping gently at the boat hulls. That and the huffing breath of the horse standing nearby were the only sounds in the settling darkness.

Johannes finally managed to saw through the fibers, and all at once the corpse dropped into Hendrik's waiting arms, almost knocking him off his feet. Johannes hurried down the ladder to help, tucking the small blade into his coat. "Steady, there. I've got his arms. Lift his legs and we'll get him down the steps. Careful how you go."

Between the two of them, they maneuvered the body of Aris Kindt down from the gallows and onto the waiting cart. Pieter, the driver, turned to look. "Poor bastard," he said in his gruff, low Dutch.

"Yes. Well, justice is swift." Johannes pulled a handkerchief from an upper pocket and wiped at his fingers. Hendrik patted the horse on the flank; the animal nickered, and breathed icy crystals from its nostrils.

Johannes had just begun to climb onto the cart for the ride back to the anatomy theatre when he saw a light several hundred yards away, swinging slightly and coming closer. It appeared to be a lantern. This was confirmed when Johannes heard footsteps on the cobblestones a moment later. He stepped back off the cart and motioned for Pieter to wait.

"Ho there!" A cloaked man approached, his arm raised in greeting. His shuffling footsteps and pained movement suggested an old man, but Johannes could not yet see his face. His dark figure made an eerie apparition in its flickering pool of lantern light.

Johannes raised a hand in return. "Is there something you need, good sir?"

The man limped toward them, pushing back the hood of his cloak. His head was massive and misshapen, and nearly bald aside from a few gray wisps. His face was a rough mass of wrinkles, as though it had been hewn out of soft wood. "Forgive me for interrupting your work, gentlemen," he said, nodding to each of them in turn. "If I am correct, you are taking Master Kindt to the surgeon's guild for dissection?"

"You are correct," Johannes replied. The horse whinnied and clopped its hooves behind him, eager to be on its way.

"And may I ask what you will do with Master Kindt after the dissection is completed?" The man held the lantern closer to his face. His eyes had once been blue but were now filmed over with cataracts.

Johannes frowned. "Why do you ask this?"

"A favor, sir, if I may ask!" The man cackled, his mouth splitting like a rotted fruit, his teeth like blackened stalactites. "If your good self has no more use for Master Kindt, sir, then might I be allowed to take possession of him? Afterward, I mean?" His expression was odd, sycophantic and sly all at once. His milky eyes twinkled.

Johannes crossed his arms. "Certainly not. Whatever makes you request such a thing?" He could hear Hendrik and Pieter muttering darkly behind him.

"I can pay!" From among the folds of his cloak the man produced a small cloth bag that jingled pitifully. "Not much, sir, as I am not a rich man, but a few gulden, for something you'll have no further need of!"

Johannes sighed. The cold was beginning to get to him; his coat was not as heavy as it could have been, and his uncovered fingers were beginning to go numb. "Did you know Aris Kindt? Was he a relative of yours?"

"My son! Yes!" The man still held the bag of money out in front of him. "Surely you can't refuse a father taking the last remains of his son when you are finished with them. Surely not, sir!" He shook the bag, making its contents clink. The sound suddenly seemed loud, as did the slow lapping of the nearby canal.

Johannes glanced back at his helpers. Their brows were knitted suspiciously. Hendrik pulled at the canvas that covered the body, then thrust his chin out. Johannes turned back to Kindt's alleged father. "Keep your money, old man," he spat. "If you're so keen on having him, then I suppose it can't do any harm. Although I'd prefer if you kept the transaction to yourself."

"Of course, sir! I understand!" The glee on the man's face was horrible to see, distorting his features into something resembling a gargoyle's. He tucked the money back into his cloak. "And when may I...?"

"Come to the anatomy theatre at just past sundown tomorrow," Johannes said. "Do you know the alley that runs parallel with Nieuwmarkt?"

"Yes, sir."

"Come that way to the back of Da Waag. There is a large gray door. Bring your cart there and wait until I come for you. And try not to be seen."

The old man pulled his hood back over his face and gave a little bow. "Thank you, sir," he said, his eyes nearly white in the glow from the flame. "I will be waiting." He turned slowly on his heel and shuffled off into the night, the yellow light from his lantern throwing his hunched shadow across the cobblestones.

His jaw set, Johannes checked the body again, securing the canvas with rope. Without a word, he climbed onto the cart and motioned for Pieter to drive.

* * *

"Ordinarily," began Dr. Tulp, gripping the forceps in his right hand, "we would begin with a study of the viscera, but today I wanted to point out an item of particular interest to me. You will notice I have made the incision here." He indicated the arm of the pale corpse of Aris Kindt. "And this," he said, lifting a muscle carefully from the arm with the forceps, "is the flexor digitorum superficialis." He pulled at the muscle with the forceps, causing the corpse's fingers to flex. Then he demonstrated the motion with his own hand.

At that point, the observers crowded more closely around, and Johannes could no longer see what was happening. This did not bother him; he had witnessed many of Dr. Tulp's lessons. Instead he stood back and surveyed the crowd in the anatomy theatre. It was the usual collection of wealthy merchants and the cream of Amsterdam society, all dressed in solemn black for the occasion, their white ruffs crisp in the dimness.

Near the front, though, Johannes spotted a lone figure, clad in scruffy brown robes many years out of fashion, with a broad, workingman's face and reddish hair curling around his ears. The man held a sketchbook, and was taking in the scene with great intensity. Johannes thought this must be that artist from Leiden that he'd heard so much about. Dr. Tulp had mentioned commissioning a group portrait, though Johannes wasn't certain what kind of a portrait this young scalawag would be able to produce. Still, Master van Rijn did have a sterling reputation, despite his tender age, and had come at the recommendation of Constantijn Huygens himself, so Johannes supposed his doubts were likely groundless. The artist's rough appearance vexed him, though; the man stood out like an elephant in a field of tulips.

Dr. Tulp continued his dissection, his voice becoming a singsong of meaningless sounds to Johannes's ears. The Preparator divided his attention between the crowd surrounding the corpse and the earnest face of the artist, who was sketching madly when he wasn't engrossed in the spectacle.

As the day wore on, Johannes began to feel warm and uncomfortable, despite the deep chill that pervaded the theatre. He never should have promised the cadaver to that old man. What if someone saw him? He could lose his position, even be charged with grave robbing. The subjects of the annual dissections were supposed to be handed over to the secular authorities for disposal; no executed criminal could be interred in hallowed ground. He wondered if that was what Kindt's father proposed to do—weasel his son into an undeserved Christian burial. Johannes squared his shoulders. He wasn't going to allow it. When the old man came for the body, he would tell him to go away. Better still, he would tell him that the authorities had already come to claim the body. The Preparator smiled to himself, his discomfort easing. Yes, everything would be all right.

When Dr. Tulp had finished his dissection and the crowd had begun to disperse, Johannes stepped forward to remove the body from the operating area. The incisions on the corpse had been stitched closed to keep the organs from spilling out during transport, but the cut in the arm was still open and flapped redly. Johannes curled his lip and placed the arm across the man's sunken chest, hiding the worst of the wound. He glanced up and noticed that Dr. Tulp had crossed the theatre and was now deep in conversation with the scruffy-looking artist, peering at the sketches and nodding approvingly. Grunting with the effort, Johannes pushed the body on its wheeled wooden cart to the preparation room behind the main chamber.

The Preparator could still hear buzzing voices from without, but thankfully this back room was empty. He pushed the cart up against the wall, averting his gaze from Aris Kindt's naked, bluish carcass. It had started to rot, despite the freezing weather, and Johannes could just catch a whiff of decay when he turned his head.

Through the high, narrow windows the sun was blazing orange; it was nearly sunset. He looked around the room critically. He would have to hide the corpse if he didn't want to give it to the old man, but where? The preparation room was small and cramped, with sturdy wooden tables lining the stone walls. There was a tall cabinet in the corner that offered possibilities, but when Johannes opened it he found that it was already packed tight with instruments and supplies. He muttered under his breath, wishing he'd done a better job of keeping the area free of clutter. Well, it was too late to bemoan his poor housekeeping. The old man would be arriving soon, and the body had to be gone.

Moving as swiftly as his gangly frame would allow, Johannes pulled a length of canvas from under one of the tables and threw it over Kindt's body, tucking the loose ends underneath his slack limbs. Then he wrapped the grisly package with four lengths of rope, keeping the knots fairly loose so they didn't sink into the flesh.

That done, he lifted the body from the cart, holding it against him as though he was waltzing with it. The smell this close was nauseating, even though he was used to dealing with corpses. He dragged Kindt across the room, heading for the back door. He wished he had thought to bring his own cart around, but someone might have seen him and wondered what he was up to. In any case, he could hide the body in the rubbish piles behind Da Waag, and then bring his cart around after darkness fell. From there he could take it to the authorities, dropping it anonymously in front of the building if need be.

His back aching with the strain, Johannes undid the latch on the back door and prepared to push it open.

It was at that moment that someone knocked, softly but definitively.

* * *

Before the door had even opened, Willem Kindt knew something was amiss.

He could hear a distinct grunt, and then the sound of rapid footsteps, and large furniture being shifted around. He smiled, his milk-white eyes gleaming. So, the Preparator was planning to go back on their agreement. No matter; he had suspected as much. The old man reached into his cloak and fingered the silver dagger he kept there. Then he reached up and knocked again.

At last the gray door swung open and the Preparator stood there, looking flustered and sweaty in a dour black waistcoat with one button missing. The old man bowed. "I have come as you asked, sir," he said in his most deferential tone. "And I have kept myself unseen."

"Ah. So here you are." The Preparator's foot tapped on the stone, and he stared down at the old man as if he didn't really see him. "Yes. Well, I'm afraid there's been a… bit of confusion."

"Confusion, sir?" Willem had taken the knife from its leather pouch. He held it in one hand, concealed by a long sleeve.

"Yes. The authorities, you see, the ones who normally take possession of the bodies, well, they have…." The Preparator glanced over his shoulder. "They have already come. It's most unusual, and I am sorry that I cannot honor our agreement."

The old man smiled and bowed his head. "It certainly isn't any fault of yours, sir," he said. Then he arranged his face to suggest sorrow. "I would have liked to see my boy at least once more, though, sir. Even though he was a thief and a brute, he was still my son."

"Well, I do apologize." The Preparator's fingers twitched on the door latch.

"You did what you could, sir, and I do thank you." Willem held out his hand, the one that didn't contain the dagger. "I'll not trouble you again."

The relief was visible on the Preparator's face. He reached out to grasp the old man's hand.

With speed and agility shocking in a man so ancient, Willem clasped the Preparator's hand and pulled the younger man down toward him, simultaneously slicing upward with the dagger and connecting with the flesh of the Preparator's chest. The flow of blood was immediate and hot. While the younger man was still reeling from the attack, Willem threw him to the ground and stepped over his writhing body into the preparation room. The area was small, and Willem could see immediately where the corpse lay, crammed haphazardly beneath one of the big wooden tables. His sandals slapping on the stones, he crossed the room and knelt to drag the body free. He had been outside Da Waag for a while, watching the comings and goings; he knew most of the observers had gone, but a few still lingered, so he would have to work quickly.

The Preparator moaned, but not loudly. Willem ignored him. Aris Kindt had been a thin man in life, but in death he seemed to have gained several pounds. The old man struggled mightily, pulling his canvas-wrapped burden across the floor. His cart was just outside in the alley; he didn't have far to go.

As he stepped past the Preparator, the younger man reached out and grabbed his ankle, but the grip was weak. The man was dying. Willem shook his hand off and bent down to lift the corpse. At last, after much effort, the old man had succeeded in getting Aris onto his cart. It was now full dark outside, and the road around Da Waag was deserted.

Before he mounted behind the horse, Willem used his foot to push the Preparator's limp body back into the building, closing the door on it with a massive heave. There was a thick pool of blood cooling on the stones, but the old man didn't think anyone would notice it until morning. His clothes were another matter, but he couldn't worry about that just now.

Nodding to himself, he climbed onto his cart and urged his horse forward.

* * *

When he finally slowed, he had come nearly two miles from the center of Amsterdam and was in one of the worst sections of the city. The houses were caked with filth. Half-naked ragamuffins ran the streets at all hours of the night. The only buildings with lanterns burning were the pubs, which spilled noise and drunken revelers into the crooked, narrow alleys. Willem had not lit his lantern on the journey here, in order to keep a lower profile. Now he was glad he had not. He traveled in darkness, keeping to the shadows, avoiding the few shady figures he spotted walking along the open and refuse-clotted sewers.

He finally arrived at a gray boarding house , which had a torch burning above the door. He drew his cart even with the door, and climbed down from his perch. He thought he could smell the fetid odor coming off Aris's corpse, but it might have been sewage or any number of other horrible things that Willem didn't care to imagine.

There was a long silence after he'd knocked at the door. For a moment his heart dropped, thinking the woman was not here or had forgotten their agreement. Then he heard the clank of a metal key in the lock, and the door opened a crack. A yellowed eye peered at him. "Brought it, have you?" a voice croaked.

Willem gestured to the cart in lieu of answering.

The door opened wider, revealing a small, hunched woman dressed in several layers of ragged wool shawls. Her long white hair was gnarled and tangled, emerging wildly from beneath a faded red cloth wrapped around her head. She raised a wizened hand and beckoned with one skeletal finger.

Willem lifted the corpse from the cart, still wrapped in its canvas shroud. The woman stepped back and let him carry it into the front room of the boarding house, which was lit by a single lantern and appeared to contain no furniture except a single wooden chair and a battered cooking pot sitting on a hearth that looked as though it hadn't been lit in quite some time. As there was nowhere to put the body down, the old man simply laid it gently on the floor. The stones were as cold as ice; he could feel them through his thin shoes.

"You pay?" The woman was standing directly behind him, her breath rattling and stinking of old meat. Her hand was extended like the claw of a bird of prey.

Willem dug in his cloak and produced his cloth bag. It only held a few gulden, all that he possessed in the world. He shook the coins into the woman's hand. She stared at them as though they represented the riches of a sultan. A moment later, she had secreted them somewhere amid her shawls. "You will wait upstairs," she commanded, pointing to a rickety ladder in the corner that Willem had not noticed.

"Am I not to witness it, then?" he asked, drawing himself up to full height.

"No! I must do alone. You may come down afterwards." She chewed at her lips with her blackened gums. "Go now. I call for you when it is finished."

Defeated, Willem glanced once more at the body of his son, nearly shapeless under the canvas, and made his way toward the ladder.

* * *

Dr. Nicolaes Tulp ascended the stairs at Da Waag, up to the living quarters above the anatomy theatre. Master van Rijn, the painter, had been staying there for the past few days while he worked on the commission, but this was the first time that Dr. Tulp had gone up to check on his progress. He had heard that Rembrandt worked quickly, so he hoped there was some substantial progress to see.

He knocked discreetly and at Rembrandt's call he entered. The room was small but pleasant, with a large window looking out at the Nieuwmarkt, which was bustling at this time of day. Rembrandt himself stood before his canvas, a brush in his mouth, his diminutive frame draped in his trademark brown robes. He looked, Dr. Tulp thought with some amusement, like a particularly unkempt monk. As he watched, the painter leaned forward and scraped at the canvas with the end of his brush handle.

"Good day, Master van Rijn," Dr. Tulp hailed, removing his round-crowned hat, an emblem of his status. "I hope I'm not interrupting anything, but I was curious to see how you were coming along."

"I'd be honored, sir," Rembrandt said with a little bow, backing away from the painting so that Dr. Tulp could have a closer look at it.

"Why, this is extraordinary!" Dr. Tulp leaned close, his nose almost touching the canvas. "The composition is most wonderful. I've never seen another like it."

"Thank you for saying so, sir. I did wish to capture a certain… movement. In addition to focusing attention on your good self, sir."

"Well, you've certainly done that," Dr. Tulp said, obviously pleased. "You have worked on this a great deal, I see. It looks almost finished."

"Yes. It does need more work in some areas, such as here on the arm of the corpse. My sketches of it were not as detailed as they could have been, I fear. Perhaps distance was a factor there, sir." Rembrandt had picked up another brush and was drawing the stiff bristles between his fingers.

"Well, I have plenty of anatomical texts, if you need a reference. They are in my study, just down the hall here. You may borrow them any time you like; the door is never locked."

"Thank you sir. That would be most helpful."

"Indeed." Dr. Tulp took one last appraising glance at the painting and then turned to leave, placing his hat back upon his head. "I must say I'm happy that Master Huygens recommended you for this position. I think this work will be a credit to you, as well as to me and my profession."

"I hope so, sir." Rembrandt bowed again, his brush still in his hand, his robes spattered with paint.

"Good day, then." Dr. Tulp stepped over the threshold, then remembered something and turned back. "I say, Master van Rijn, did you hear of that awful business last night in the Leidsestraat? The murder?"

Rembrandt looked up, startled. "No. Who was murdered?"

"Damned if I can remember his name. Main executioner, he was. Ironic that, isn't it?" He chuckled a little then coughed. "Well. Not safe to walk the streets at night, sad to say. In any case, I'm sure the person responsible will be brought to justice. In the meantime..." He tipped his hat with his hand. "Again, good day, Master van Rijn."

"Good day, sir."

Dr. Tulp left the studio and closed the door quietly behind him.

* * *

Willem Kindt sat in the room's only chair and stared at his son in the flickering lamplight.

He could hardly believe what the woman had done, even now, even twenty-four hours later. Aris was slumped against the far wall, his eyes glazed but open and presumably seeing, his white fingers beating a nervous rhythm on the knees of his tattered trousers. He didn't appear to be breathing, but he lived, by Hell. The old man crossed himself, knowing that this small piety could not atone for the abomination he had wrought.

"Tonight, again?" said the woman, who was bent over the hearth, stirring an evil-smelling broth in her cooking pot.

"Yes," Willem said. "The executioner is dead. Tonight he will revenge himself upon the sheriff who convicted him, and perhaps upon the man who fingered him for the crime, if he can find him."

The woman cackled. "Your son will live until his revenge is complete. No matter how long it may take."

"Yes. I understand that," Willem said. Aris was looking dumbly back and forth between his father and the old woman, understanding little or nothing. Willem's heart broke, seeing his emotionless face hanging there in the dimness. This was not his son resurrected, as much as he would have liked to think so; it was merely a body animated by bloodlust, by a rough kind of justice. He peered through the window and saw the moon, full and orange, floating above the horizon. *Soon*, he thought to himself.

The woman poured her reeking concoction into two bowls and handed one to Willem. He held his breath and sipped, trying not to gag. It didn't taste as bad as it smelled, but that wasn't saying a great deal. He considered taking the bowl to Aris to feed him, but he already knew it would be pointless. The thing that Aris had become was no longer human and no longer needed human nourishment.

When the soup was gone and the lantern had burned down a little further, Aris began to stir, getting clumsily to his feet as though he was a marionette on a string. Willem stood also, keeping well back; the woman had said that these specimens were sometimes erratic, and might turn on those who were helping them. Aris, though, seemed not to notice his father at all, and instead turned his head toward the door, making his way toward it with deliberate, shuffling steps. The woman nodded, and Willem began to follow, keeping a safe distance.

Once they were away from the house, Willem stepped up his pace, trailing Aris at the distance of about a yard. The streets were dark, but the moon provided ample light, and Willem had no trouble keeping his ghostly son in sight.

The night before, Aris had headed west, toward Leidsestraat, but tonight he turned east, trudging along with his single-minded purpose.

The city seemed silent around them. The sound of the corpse's footsteps on the stones was blasphemous.

The old man struggled to keep up over the long trek; Aris was tireless, and kept a constant pace. The moon had risen farther in the sky by the time they turned into a wide avenue lined with respectable houses. Lamps blazed on every corner, but the street was eerily devoid of life.

Aris mounted the steps of a particularly fine house with whitewashed shutters and stone lions flanking the entrance. The door was dark green and had a gold knocker. Aris, however, did not knock, but simply opened the door and stepped inside. Willem, as he had done on the previous night, waited outside on the street, pulling his cloak around him to fend off the cold.

He heard the sounds. As much as he wanted to stop his ears, he would not, because he knew he must participate in some small way. He must accept a modicum of responsibility. He told himself that the sheriff was getting what he deserved; he had executed an innocent man, after all. As true as this was, it did not make hearing the sounds of his death any easier.

It seemed both an eternity and a matter of seconds before Aris emerged from the house, his hastily assembled clothes (since he'd come from the anatomy theatre naked) soaked with red. His face was as slack and emotionless as ever, his eyes like two silver coins glinting in the night. The noises the sheriff had made in dying had apparently awakened others; Willem could see candles being lit in windows around the street. His heart hammering in his chest, he gestured for Aris to hurry, not having any idea if his son could understand him.

As they made their way up the avenue and back into the darkness, he thought he could hear shouting and barking dogs. He quickened his pace to a trot, which was as fast as his bones would move these days. Aris was still a few steps behind, but he caught up easily and passed his father, loping along as though he hadn't a care in the world.

Willem hoped that the one murder would be enough for one evening, but this hope was dashed when Aris turned, not toward the boarding house, but south toward the Mauritskade. His legs aching, Willem followed.

The second man was drinking in a pub nearly half a mile from the sheriff's house. Aris stood outside and stared in with his strange, stupid gaze, his black hair falling limply across his forehead. Willem stood in the shadows a few yards away, shivering in his thin cloak. He didn't know how long they would have to wait, but the old man hoped it wasn't long enough for him to freeze to death.

Fortunately, it was no more than half an hour before the man staggered out, alone, into the darkened alley beside the pub. He burped then laughed to himself before bracing himself against the wall with one hand. His piss steamed as it spattered onto the stones. He sang a snatch of song, nearly fell, pissing on his shoes in the process, then righted himself. Willem was almost glad to see the man in this state; at least he wouldn't comprehend what was happening to him.

Aris approached from behind, and he was nearly upon his victim before the drunken man turned. He didn't seem surprised in the least, but muttered something that sounded vaguely companionable. Aris reached for him and closed a long, thin hand around the man's neck. The drunk's eyes got bigger, and he opened his mouth to protest, but all that came out was a beer-smelling belch. Aris squeezed, and Willem heard something pop. The man fell to the ground, groaning. Aris bent over him like a vulture, his clawlike hands tearing at his clothes and skin. The man's cries grew weaker and weaker as Aris leaned closer and closer, going at the man with fingers and teeth. At some point Aris must have severed an artery, because blood sprayed against the alley wall, mingling with the cooling urine and producing a noxious aroma of copper and ammonia. Willem turned away, but he could still hear the wet sounds of flesh being torn from bone, the sounds of bone being crushed by teeth. The sounds from the pub seemed far away, part of another world.

When Aris had finished, there was little left of the man but blood and a pile of shredded rags, smeared here and there with gobbets of skin and fat. Willem fought the urge to vomit, stepping out of the alley and breathing deeply of the frigid night air. Somehow his killing of that officious Preparator had not bothered the old man nearly as much as seeing the same crime perpetrated by his only son. He wasn't sure why this should be, but he couldn't deny it.

Aris appeared a moment later, looking like a parody of a painted devil, crimson from head to toe. Sighing, Willem removed his topmost cloak and threw it over his son's shoulders. The boy's face was still a fright, but perhaps no one would notice in the dark.

His teeth chattering, the old man followed as the corpse shambled in a northerly direction, back toward the boarding house. The three murders had been carried out; justice had been served. Willem was saddened by the fact that his son would now be well and truly lost to him ; while it was true that this mute monstrosity before him was no replacement for the real, living Aris, the corpse still bore his son's outer trappings, and this, Willem reasoned, was enough to stir sentimental feelings within him. When morning came, he thought, he would lay Aris Kindt to rest with the knowledge that he had avenged his wrongful execution, and may God forgive him for that.

The moon had passed the halfway point in the sky, meaning dawn was but a few hours away. The cold was like many tiny knives biting into his flesh, and the walk had all but exhausted every ounce of energy he possessed. He would be glad to get back to the boarding house, even glad to sip at a bowl of the woman's foul stew. The house was surely not far now.

But it seemed that Aris was not walking toward the boarding house. He had turned again, this time to the northwest, toward the center of Amsterdam.

As soon as the old man realized this, his heart began thumping again. There was no one else responsible for the execution; he was certain of it. And the woman had promised that Aris would only live as long as it took to take revenge on those responsible for his death. So what was happening now?

Willem went after him, mystified, forgetting about his tired legs and his frozen fingers. Aris seemed as unconcerned as ever, moving deliberately along the streets, not feeling the cold at all. Before long, the old man thought he could hear the lap of the canal in the distance.

Moments later, a large stone building that looked like a fortress loomed before them. Without pausing to look or consider, Aris made his meandering way toward it, and Willem hurried to follow.

* * *

Rembrandt had been sleeping, but woke when he thought he heard a noise on the stairs outside his room. He lay on his cot, straining to hear. No one else was supposed to be in the building at this time of night; normally he didn't mind the solitude, but the stories about the murder had stoked his already active imagination.

He had almost decided that the sound had been a mouse, and that he should try to go back to sleep, when it came again—a dragging, furtive sound, definitely made by something much larger than a mouse. He sat up and felt for his cloak. The moonlight was streaming in the window, providing just enough light to make his easel look like a hulking beast with spindly legs. He pulled his cloak around himself and lit the lantern on the table near the cot. The room appeared as ordinary as it had when he'd retired to bed, but now the sound was louder, a scraping right outside his door. Frightened, he lifted the lantern high and crept toward the door. "Who's there?" he called.

There was no answer, but then he thought he heard a knock, albeit one that sounded somehow meaty and damp. He shuddered. "Who is it?"

There came another sound, labored breathing and a quick patter of footsteps.

"I am sorry to disturb you, sir. I'm not sure why we've come."

Relieved to hear a human voice at last, Rembrandt crossed the room, lantern in hand, and opened the door. For a moment he didn't understand what he was seeing, and when he did he nearly dropped the lantern. "What the devil…"

"Sorry again, sir." An old man in woefully inadequate clothing appeared behind the horror that stood swaying upon the doorstep. "This is my son. I suppose he wishes to see you."

Rembrandt stepped back into the room, glad to move away from the thin, pale monster who appeared to be covered in blood and who smelled like a slaughterhouse. The old man came into the room first, worming his way around the younger man, who didn't move from the threshold. The son's eyes were metallic and empty. After a long moment, he staggered into the room. The old man closed the door behind him.

Rembrandt had nothing in the way of refreshment to offer the pair, so simply motioned for them to sit on the cot he had recently vacated. The old man sat wearily, but the son just stood, his shoulders slumped. His gaze seemed to be fixed upon the painting that Rembrandt had nearly completed, the one that he hoped would make his fortune in Amsterdam. As the artist watched, the savage-looking man hobbled over to the canvas and stopped a few feet in front of it, tilting his head to one side. "He won't damage it, will he?" Rembrandt whispered, but the old man just shrugged and shook his head.

The silence of the room was broken only by the harsh rasp of the old man's breathing. At last, the younger man stirred and turned away from the painting. For a brief second, understanding seemed to flicker in his silver-coin eyes, and he stared at Rembrandt, as though trying to remember where he might have seen him before. The artist felt his blood run cold at the scrutiny. When the man moved, Rembrandt stepped back, his arms half raised to ward off an attack, but the monster simply shuffled forward and sat at the table that served as Rembrandt's dining area.

He flopped his pale arm onto the wooden tabletop, letting the incision made by Dr. Nicolaes Tulp flap open, exposing the muscles and nerves beneath.

The artist gasped, recognizing the wound immediately. Surely this could not be the same man he had witnessed on the dissection table just a few short days before? As he studied the features—the low, heavy brow, the slightly upturned nose, the scruff of beard at the chin—he knew for certain that this man had been the unwitting model at the center of his painting, *The Anatomy Lesson of Dr. Nicolaes Tulp.*

The man was sitting still, as though waiting for something. The wound on his arm still looked fresh, and Rembrandt remembered how Dr. Tulp had pulled at the flexor digitorum superficialis with his forceps, causing the corpse's fingers to flex. Rembrandt had made several sketches of the action, but he hadn't been able to get it exactly right. It was this that was holding up the satisfactory completion of the painting.

Then, understanding dawned.

Moving as quickly as he could, he lit the remaining three lanterns in the room; the light was far from adequate, but it would have to do. He pulled his easel closer to the table and added linseed oil to the pigments he'd ground before going to bed. "Is this right?" he wanted to ask the dead man, but he knew it was, so he didn't ask.

Loading his brush with red lake, he began laying in the detail on the corpse's arm, sketching in the muscles with long thick strokes, then going back over them with more refined movements. As he worked, he heard the old man come up behind him, his breath warm on the artist's neck. He pointed at the canvas. "That's my boy there," the old man said. It was almost a sigh.

"Yes." It was all Rembrandt could say. There were so many questions he wanted to ask the old man, about what had happened, but he dared not speak them out loud. One did not question a miracle.

Just before the moon set behind the horizon, Rembrandt stood back and surveyed his painting, a smile creeping across his ample face. The muscles of Aris Kindt's arm now lay exposed and glimmering and perfect, laid open forever for the entire world to see. The old man leaned in and reached toward the image, his fingers trembling just inches away from its surface, and then he brought his fingers to his lips and held them there. Rembrandt thought he saw tears sparkling in the old man's eyes.

"It is finished." The artist directed this statement to Aris Kindt, who still sat at the table as though he would never move, his face as blank as the face of a Greek statue. He did not look at the painting, but simply lifted his arm from the tabletop then rose from his chair. It was time for him to go.

The old man clasped Rembrandt's arm. "Somehow he remembered." It was all he could manage, but it was all that was necessary. Rembrandt nodded his head, not speaking but saying volumes with his silence.

The dead man and his devoted father made a bedraggled parade toward the door of Rembrandt's temporary studio. The old man opened the door and let his son walk out before him. Then he turned. "Thank you, sir," he said. He seemed to remember something then, for his face went distant and melancholy, but the emotion was gone in an instant.

He bowed his bald head, and then disappeared into the shadows of the outer hall.

Rembrandt stood and watched the door for a long time after they had gone. He glanced at his painting again. Aris Kindt's body seemed to glow with a kind of inner light, a humanity that emanated from him, making him more than just a corpse being dissected upon a slab. Rembrandt laughed, a little sadly. Dr. Tulp would likely view himself as the star attraction of this portrait, but the artist would always know where its true heart lay.

A Touch of the Divine

Patrick Rutigliano

Even through the elongated nozzle of the leather mask and the aromatic combination of healing herbs within, Stephen's lungs burned with the thick smoke permeating the city. The fires had been lit with the intention of purifying the pestilence from the air, but as it combined with the overpowering scent of human rot and decay, the scent was no more wholesome than the charnel scent of the Pit itself. The once thriving streets were all but abandoned, the residents too terrified of contracting the disease to leave their homes or doomed to remain indoors due to the rules of quarantine while their relations beside them died one by one. All that remained outside were the corpses.

Bodies in every stage of decomposition crowded the doorways, their grossly contorted features and death throes frozen in time as they awaited their entry into consecrated ground. Stephen could not repress a shudder for he knew it was a wish that was destined to end in disappointment. He had seen the immense trenches even before entering London, the emaciated victims of the cruel affliction laid side by side like freshly threshed wheat before the earth was grimly piled upon them without any semblance of ceremony or mourning.

Stephen had already been witness to innumerable blasphemies and horrors since leaving the monastery. Faith gave way to debauchery as the weak raced to experience every vice imaginable before judgment was passed upon them, while others scourged themselves en masse in a vain attempt to assuage the wrath of Heaven with the flaying of their own corrupt flesh. Stephen's travels had long ago confirmed that both were useless endeavors.

For two years, he had tended those struck by the plague, their curses and prayers assaulting his ears time and time again from deathbeds as both the wicked and pious fell to the scourge in droves. His treatments seemed to do little good aside from providing some temporary false hope, but aside from the last rites' bleak assurances, it was all he had to offer.

Stephen's survival was as much a mystery to himself as to his few remaining peers. He had tended to countless victims in the worst stages of the disease, breathing the same miasmic air that had circulated through their ravaged bodies and feeling the grip of their seizing hands upon his own, yet no harm had befallen him despite these typically fatal experiences. A higher power had chosen him to alleviate the peoples' suffering, of that Stephen was sure, and he would do all he could to live up to those weighty expectations. In the heart of London, during the country's greatest catastrophe, was the best opportunity to carry out that wish.

Even in York, word of the newest and most astonishing variation of the pox had reached him by way of the affected area's nobles, their ranks desperate to attract any clergymen or doctors who might offer some insight into the hideous new form of the disease that they struggled to contain. The case descriptions that had been entrusted to Stephen in an invitation from the lords had been completely outlandish, unbelievable in their depictions of the new danger that had manifested itself in the city. Still, he had decided to take the men at their word, eager to find any trace of a legitimate explanation for the wholesale suffering that had swept through the continent with such virulent and tempestuous force. The answer was hidden somewhere in the smoke-choked maze of alleyways, obscured behind worm-eaten timber and beneath thatched roofs, but he would find it. Grateful to find no bodies piled in front of the threshold as of yet, Stephen rapped on the flimsy door of the ramshackle home that was his destination, its position clear on the map of the small but crowded section of the city upon which the investigated cases had been marked.

Through the mask's clouded lenses, dark eyes warily peered at Stephen as the portal cracked open, the cold reservation in their pupils soon eased by a knowing glance at the instrument bag clutched in his hand. The cold, embittered voice of a woman issued with the wanton clarity of a winter chill.

"I was there when it happened. There's nothing you can do for him now. You do realize that don't you?"

After a moment of shock at the realization that the deceased man had not yet been interred in one of the sprawling mass graves, a forced nod proved response enough for entry, the barricaded door to the house gradually giving way with an exasperated sigh echoing that of its occupant.

* * *

Scores of candles accented the hearth's illumination. The flickering lights cast sinister shadows across the walls and floor. Their combined vapor was incapable of masking the putrescent and unmistakable odor emanating from the home's only other room. Beneath the layer of leather, Stephen wrinkled his nose at the scent's proximity and strength, wondering how the woman could continue to lead him toward the source with such stoicism. It had been her husband after all.

"He's in there. Do what you will with him just so long as you keep him bound, otherwise he'll end up wandering around the streets deaf and dumb like all the others." A frightened, desperate look stole across her rigid features as she looked back at the stupefied monk.

"I'll have to ask you to end things when you've finished. I don't have the heart for it, but it needs to be done. Just as his soul's left him, his body's got to go too. I can't do it myself."

Stephen's hand tightened on the bag, the large dagger resting amongst his other instruments reminding him of the duty he might soon have to perform if the unthinkable were true. The woman left the doorway in favor of a roughly crafted chair in the main room, her back facing the monk as the candlelight danced on her unmoving form. Bracing himself for any combination of the abominable possibilities he had faced in the past, Stephen looked aghast at the creature fastened to the bed.

The man bore every sign of the plague. Egg-sized growths bulged from under his arms and around his neck beneath the layer of cloth covering his body, the deep purple patches of internally clotted blood visible beneath the sheer material and taut, sallow flesh. A string of saliva hung from the slightly protruding tongue, its transparent fluid marred by flecks of blood and phlegm. Never before had Stephen seen all the signs of the plague's various incarnations at work in one person, nor had he ever seen an individual in such a state of decomposition still indoors, for surely one look beneath the cloth was enough to confirm that the man should already be at rest within the ground.

The blistered light blue flesh of the corpse had already begun to creep up to the chest from the abdomen, its vile appearance accentuated by a wholesale swelling of the front half of the body. Fingernails had become claws and hair long and unkempt while the flesh had continued to recede, the ashen skin already ruptured at various points where the corrosion of tissue had been worst. Indeed the woman had been right, there was nothing he could do, but neither did he see any sign of anything but madness at any allegation that life still crept somewhere within the ruined human frame. Chancing a glance back at the woman's haggard form, Stephen could not help but be moved to pity by the insanity that had surely taken hold of her at the passing of her husband, and reaching for the long knife within his bag, moved to put her unstable mind at ease the only way he could.

The blade was half-way through the tough sinews in the neck when the man's lids began to flutter. White and soulless orbs stared blankly at Stephen, his digits frozen on the dagger's handle while the putrefied, viscous blood continued to run like some polluted river from the gaping wound. There was no indication of pain or any other expression on the creature's face, but the decrepit limbs began to push against the ropes that held them, comprehending them, *testing* them, as would an animal caught in a trap. The dead eyes traveled from Stephen's mask to the hunched figure in the chair, the formerly resolute position of her head and shoulders now lowered in a convulsive cringe.

"Weren't you told that it always starts at night!? Remember what I told you man! Finish it! Finish it!"

Bile rose in Stephen's throat as his trembling hands sawed through bone and muscle, all the while the dead eyes staring at the woman now weeping in her chair with what almost seemed an air of repressed apology. The task at last complete, the stricken monk covered the remains with the shroud as best he could and stumbled back into the main room, bloodied dagger still in hand.

A look of overwhelming pity flashed over the woman's face as she watched him struggle to collect himself, the routes the tears had taken still wet upon her cheeks.

"I'm sorry Brother, I truly am, but there wasn't another living soul willing to get near him after the last time, and I couldn't do it myself, not to him."

The unsteady light of the dying candles gave way to moonlight as she continued. "If they actually tried to hurt you it would be easier, but all they do is wander around as if they were alive, trying to return to their homes after they claw their way out of those shallow graves, or knocking on their doors after they've been left outside to be taken away. There aren't too many yet, a few dozen maybe, but there'll be more. Everyone in the area would have left already if the damned lords would let anyone go across the border, but they're just interested in having someone around to work the land and keep the shops running, whether they're suffering or not doesn't mean a thing to people like them."

Beneath the glass frames, Stephen's eyes widened as if he had been struck, the blade falling to the floor and sending its metallic cries echoing through the house. The woman gaped at him for a moment in stunned amazement.

"Nobody's been allowed to leave the area in months. Didn't you know?"

* * *

The truth of the woman's words had been confirmed that same night. Stephen had disposed of the husband's body as discreetly as possible, leaving thereafter to ascertain the true nature of his situation. The guards who had been eager to allow him entry earlier denied him exit, citing the orders of the local authority, a decree which they had been happy to omit from their earlier greetings, and threatened the monk with arrest should he attempt to leave. Normally, Stephen would have sought refuge from the nearby church, but experience told him all too well of the glut of corpses that would welcome him from within its once holy walls, the blessed structure now little more than an oversized crypt for those who had been fortunate enough not to be left on the streets. Besides, after the evening's earlier proceedings, sleep was impossible. There was much to see.

The list of patients afflicted with the strange disease had supposedly been a half-dozen cases, but the filthy labyrinth of vermin-infested avenues told a different story. Not one of the typical heathen revelers walked bleary-eyed from the taverns, nor did the shifty eyes of any thief or prostitute surreptitiously follow him as he traveled the roads. These were the nocturnal life-blood of any city, the vagabonds and criminals who favored the shadows and preyed upon the unsuspecting who would dare invade their moonlit territory, but here they did not exist. It was the sounds of shuffling feet and the scraping of elongated fingernails against familiar doors that had replaced the raucous laughter of the drunkards and the crescendos of the normal fighting in the alleyways, their pitiful resonance all that remained to cleave the nocturnal silence of the tomb.

The woman had been right, their numbers were not overwhelming, but there seemed to be at least one or two on every street, their pitiful imitations of life dominating the forlorn region of the city as they drove all others behind the safety of barricaded doors. To dispatch the creatures would be all but impossible, a drop of their infected blood would surely kill any who dared venture close enough to strike, and an accidental touch of their bodies while transporting their remains would be all that was required to birth a new walking corpse to stalk the night. Eventually, the creatures would congest all of London if they escaped the fortified border, their ranks destined to devour and dwarf the vulnerable population to which they had once belonged; and all the while, the people had no chance to flee.

Stephen's teeth gnashed at his betrayal and the state of fear and anguish that those in power had only compounded with their avarice. He had primarily done his work in the smaller villages, traveling only once or twice to the larger cities under the protection of his holy brethren, but he had heard stories of such devious invitations as the one he had received. Farmers were normally the victims of such deceptions, the promise of high wages coaxing them to accept employment only to be held captive on the land, a substitute for a worker who had already fallen victim to the plague's accursed touch. Still, Stephen's reputation for immunity had apparently been more widely known than he realized, and the possibility of one who would comfort and tend to the increasingly dissatisfied masses without need of replacement was no doubt a prospect that had been too attractive to refuse. Stephen doubted that any courier would be willing to travel the disease-ridden streets or risk the guards to convey a message of the treachery outside the city, but as the rising sun drove the creatures back to the shadowed haunts from which they had earlier emerged, the answer came to him at last.

* * *

Stephen had little trouble finding the lords' estate the following day, its fortifications and imposing stature a far cry from the humble lodgings that orbited its impressive bulk, the cold veneer of stone hiding the repugnant indifference that festered like a cancer within its confines. There would be no dealing with such men. Either the plague would pass or Stephen would before he would be allowed to leave, his every step falling on a spot where another body had fallen and another abomination would stand. He now understood that the disease he had become so familiar with had nothing to do with the monstrous human parodies that strode restlessly through the sunless streets they had walked in life. He knew what had to be done to lift the curse that had been placed upon them. Even with the revenue at their disposal, the lords had barely been able to entice enough soldiers to guard the boundaries of the diseased area, let alone their residence. Only a handful defended the massive door that sealed it. The creatures' affinity for familiar surroundings and the proximity of their homes to the hastily dug graves had kept them from venturing near the manor, but that might be changed.

The moon rose wan and spectral that night to find Stephen again walking the abandoned streets. One by one, he sought them, their blank eyes drawn from the doors to the symbol that Stephen anxiously carried, their disconnected memories recalling something of importance in the emaciated figure that adorned the cross. Whether it was a recollection of hope or betrayal that drove them to seek the image, the monk did not know, but before long, a small army trailed behind him as he held the crucifix, their ungainly march ending a short distance from the front of the doors leading to the ones who had damned them all. Their bulk blocked the only entrance and exit from the grounds. The terrified guards looked on in horror at the undead ranks that silently poured in. Stephen pulled at the straps of his mask, the unfiltered scent of decay circulating through his nostrils for the first time since he had arrived.

"Our business is inside! Order the doors to be opened and you will be spared!"

Indecision tore at the guards as they stared at the wall of rotting flesh that barred their exit. A note of cold resolve worked its way into Stephen's voice as he called to them again. "Lads, surely you know that they're responsible for them. Are they really worth dying for? Are they really worth becoming one of *them*?" Stephen took a step forward, his motion echoed by dozens of exposed and scraping joints.

No more negotiation was required. The door swung open to allow the guards and the servants who had overheard the conversation from within to stream out like ants from a ruined hill. Their quaking forms lined the outer walls of the estate as they allowed Stephen and his weird congregation entry. The diseased bodies cut a swath of festering affliction through the opulent surroundings as they sought its master, the bulk of their numbers filling room after room in their search. Not a single sword or pike opposed them as they made their way through the cavernous hallways to the upper reaches of the small fortress. A single portal barred their way, a sturdy two-paneled door of construction similar to the one that had blocked the entrance to the building; its hinges were denied movement by an obstruction on the other side.

It was while pondering how to move past this obstacle that Stephen noticed a marked difference in those following him, spreading with all the violent ferocity of the plague itself. No longer did the clouded eyes fix themselves on the gaunt form of the forgiving savior; only the door's obstinate frame was reflected in the moist surfaces of the pale orbs. The ruined bodies threw themselves at the door even after their bones had cracked, some clawing and even gnawing at the stubborn oak where even the smallest splinter had appeared in an attempt to rend it apart. Slowly, minute fissures began to appear in the heavy panels, the fractures gradually widening with the unrelenting assault until the heavy bar beyond became barely visible through the cracks.

Dim candlelight bled through the gaps, the flames growing brighter as more of the door split beneath the tireless blows until horrified shrieks reverberated through the castle's yawning halls. Stephen never saw any of the conceited men, the mass of silent assassins converging over their cowering forms before he could catch a glimpse of the luxuriant clothing or a flash of the clumsily flailed weapons before all were torn to pieces. The overturned candelabras and the spreading flames found easy prey in the expensive tapestries and rugs, their growing volume soon leaving only a wall of fire beyond the doorway.

Stephen watched the manor burn after making his way outside, his fingers clenched around the crucifix as he watched the new scourge cleansed from the world until only ash remained inside the eviscerated husk of stone, a fittingly grand monument to those who had finally found their peace. After reciting the last rites one final time, he raised the cross reverently to his lips.

"Thy will be done."

A Cure For All Ills

LINDA L. DONAHUE

London, England
September 1665
From the personal journal of Dr. Henry Mortimer:

More than seventeen thousand people died in July; more than thirty thousand died in August. September looks to be worse. More houses than not are seen with a red cross painted on the door in St. Giles-in-the-Fields and the districts of White-chapel, Westminster and Southwark. I travel these areas frequently.

Many of my colleagues, cowardly physicians undeserving of the honor of being doctors, have already fled, some of them having turned their backs on London's citizens at the onset of plague. Now that plague has progressed, the city's remaining doctors, save myself, have moved to the countryside. To my way of thinking, refusing to treat patients in need breaks the Hippocratic oath.

I shan't run from this plague, no matter how black or dark the times become.

* * *

Patrolling London's streets, I was easily recognized by my "uniform." Leather breeches worn beneath a full-length robe of thick, wax-coated material kept out the poisonous air. Along with leather boots, leather gloves, a hat and mask, the uniform left nothing exposed to the miasma choking London. Glass lenses in the mask protected my eyes. To purify the air I breathed, a mix of herbs and spices filled my mask's beak-like attachment.

Dawn's light barely cracked the sky when the bells resumed tolling. The tower bells rang continuously, announcing deaths instead of time. 'Twas the start of another day in which I couldn't possibly see everyone who required medical attention.

My heart cheerless, I trudged through Whitehall's empty cobbled streets carrying a satchel and the yellow staff the Lord Mayor had decreed plague doctors must carry so they might be visible from a distance.

Nowadays, London's nicer districts were as deserted as the poor ones were becoming. Street stalls and markets had closed. Corners were vacant of beggars and girls selling posies.

A bedraggled boy tacked the weekly *Bill of Mortality* on a post. Seeing my approach, the boy fled, leaving one corner flapping.

In bold print, the death toll announced that 8,297 people had died this past week. My shoulders sagged from having borne this dire duty alone. I clutched my satchel, full of useless treatments. I fought a war I couldn't win, yet I refused to be among the deserters. I'd rather die fighting.

Across Old London Bridge, feeble moans rode the wind. With so much death about, all beauty in the world seemed lost. Even the sunrise was naught but a blood-colored sky. The growing piles outside the city walls made it seem that death was England's newest crop, blooming heavily with corpses.

A hunched woman knelt at my feet, her arms held protectively over her head. "You're a doctor, isn't that right, sir?"

"Dr. Henry Mortimer at your service." Noting she still cowered, I lowered the yellow staff, promising, "I won't strike you." That was another of its purposes—to drive away desperate, panicked mobs.

"Please, good doctor," she begged, tears filling her rheumy eyes. "It's my boy. Only nine he is."

Too young to die and likely too young to survive, I thought. A stout teen stood the best odds of recovering. Nevertheless, I nodded, hoping to instill some hope where there could surely be none. "Lead on, poor mother."

Gingerly she laid a hand on my sleeve. "Kind, sir, you won't report him, will you? I'll keep him in, I will."

It was a doctor's duty to report all cases. Nonetheless I smiled reassuringly, even though I knew my full-head mask hid my expression. "Dear woman, you appear in good health. Perhaps your son suffers some small case of ague and not the plague." I knew the lie, even as I spoke it; yet for the brief glimmer it brought to her eye, the sin was worth the price.

"May God bless you, sir."

On the street where the woman lived, three houses in a row were nailed shut, crosses painted on the door along with the words "Lord have mercy on us." Guards stood outside those homes, ensuring that those families remained sealed in, even if only one family member suffered from plague.

The woman crossed herself on passing each such house.

Her home stood at the end of the cul-de-sac. Like all the houses in this impoverished area, it was of timber and pitch with a thatched roof.

The herbs stuffing my beak counteracted the stink inside. Animal droppings speckled the urine-stained straw covering the floor. A thin hog lay on its side against one wall and a mangy dog curled beside it.

A boy shivered on a rag pallet beneath the sagging ceiling. Blackish mold streaked the wall beside him.

I knelt beside the lad. "What's your name, son?"

"Thomas, sir." He coughed.

"A good, strong name." I patted the boy's head then took a firm hold. "Relax. I must examine you."

Black pustules spread behind his ear, at his temple and the base of his throat. "Have you many more of these?" I asked.

"Yes, sir. A couple more." He wheezed and coughed harder.

"Just point them out. Don't try to talk." It seemed to weaken the lad.

Thomas pointed to a spot below one shoulder and another midway up his rib cage. Between his thumb and finger, blood had caked over an angry welt.

Taking his hand, I asked, "What's this, Thomas?"

Thomas wheezed, then said, "Rat bite."

"He got it two days ago," the boy's mother said, "right before the black swelling started."

Rat bites weren't usually deadly. Yet the timing of the bite fit with the plague's incubation period. With only five visible spots, and none ruptured, Thomas was likely in the early stages.

"Open your mouth." I studied his tongue. "No signs of bloating." I asked his mother, "Has he been vomiting? Complaining of headaches or any other pains?"

"His joints are sore, sir," she answered. "Can barely hold his cup without wincing. And he barely keeps his broth down."

It was plague.

On the inside, I ached from anger and frustration. Yet a doctor must maintain a calm, detached and clinical demeanor. What helped maintain that facade most was my fervent belief that perhaps the boy's mother had sought help in time, that perhaps young Thomas could be saved. Too often, a family tried to hide sickness, even knowing the consequences. That had led the Lord Mayor to hire Examiners to find and report cases of plague.

I searched my satchel, digging through bundled posies, a jar of leeches, a pouch of tobacco, philters of laxatives and a bottle of mercury; all of it useless.

"I've fed him broth as hot as he'll take it, and shoved posies in his pallet and hung a charm over his head," the boy's mother said, wringing her hands.

She'd tied willow sticks with ribbons and tacked them to the wall. Her folk cures were neither more nor less effective than those devised by learned physicians. I could bleed Thomas to anemia and still he might die. Laxatives could empty the boy's bowels, yet the disease would persist. It always did. Nothing came from coating a patient with mercury besides increasing his suffering and nausea.

"Good woman, I should like to take your son with me. He requires constant care if he's to have any chance of outlasting the plague."

"Take him?"

"To the hospital." Even in the continental countries, boorish rulers had enough compassion to designate pest houses for victims. However, in England, the seat of the world's greatest power, plague victims were sealed in their houses to die. "You have my word, good mother. I shall personally see to his care."

"We can't afford no hospital, Dr. Mortimer."

"Then it's fortunate I have no intention of charging you."

Her knotty hands trembling, she wrapped a moth-eaten blanket around Thomas's thin shoulders. "Take good care of him, kind sir. He means the world to me."

Thomas wobbled, barely able to stand.

Handing the boy my yellow staff, I said, "Lean on this. There's a good lad."

* * *

With Thomas to care for, I moved into the vacant hospital. More than ever, London needed the collective minds of its doctors to discover a reliable cure for the Black Plague. Yet the College of Surgeons was as empty as at Christmas holiday.

Therefore I alone tended the sick while making a study of the disease. For the purposes of the latter, I slipped out that evening while Thomas slept fitfully. At least the boy was resting.

The tolling tower bells echoed through the streets. Soon only the dead would inhabit London. *The dead.* The study of corpses had furthered mankind's knowledge of human physiology. Perhaps the final ravages of illness might provide some clue to its cause and cure.

I prowled the poorer districts in search of Reapers—those who carted the dead to plague pits. For my purposes, I required someone freshly dead, before decomposition set in. For two shiny shillings, I purchased a body, along with the Reaper's services and his silence.

* * *

In less than a week young Thomas had wasted away to half his size. Though I labored late into the night dismembering plague-ridden corpses, I was no closer to a cure. The boy was dying. I needed another approach.

Before fleeing, my colleagues had postulated that blood was the key—hence the use of leeches. Perhaps their thought was right, but their method wrong. It wasn't a matter of removing sick blood, but of infusing the patient with healthy blood—such as the blood of someone who wasn't sick. Or better, someone who was immune. For all my dealings with plague patients, I remained plague-free. Ergo, whatever coursed through my blood making me immune would surely do the same for the boy.

I rolled up my sleeve and drew a vial of blood. Carefully, I injected my healthier, stronger blood into Thomas's vein. "My blood will make you well," I explained.

For a week, I repeated the treatment morning, noon and night. That Thomas survived more than two weeks with plague was a miracle. Clearly the treatment was doing some good, yet Thomas remained tired and weak, barely able to stomach food. He wasn't progressing as I had hoped.

Still, he hadn't died either.

* * *

A voice echoed through the hospital's stone corridors calling out, "Dr. Mortimer? Henry? Are you here?"

I stumbled toward the door, scratching my arm. "In here," I called. A light cough rattled in my heavy chest.

Lord Mayor Blutworth approached, a nosegay covering his mouth. Though London's betters had fled, Charles II had commanded some city officials stay behind to carry out plague orders. "I'd thought you'd finally come to your senses and left for the countryside, doctor," Blutworth said. "Then I heard mad rumors you were treating patients in hospital. Whatever were you thinking?"

"Not patients, but patient. Young Thomas. And I suppose I was thinking," I defended, "that it's my duty."

"Duty be damned, sir. They'll die with or without your ministrations. 'Tis God's wrath, I say."

"Which explains why His clergy fled, no doubt," I said humorlessly.

"My God, man, you look as filthy and unfit as the peasantry you've been treating."

I raised a brow. "Is this visit meant to rally my spirits?"

Blutworth scowled. "Besides taking in the sick, I hear you're buying corpses." The Lord Mayor wandered toward the laboratory door, flicked a glance inside then blanched. "Really Henry, for what purpose can you want those bloated atrocities?"

"For study."

"Then I suggest you clean up after you're through. When the clergy return, there'll be literal Hell to pay. You know the Church's stand."

"Apparently it's on its feet and running."

Blutworth chuckled despite his troubled expression. "Thankfully the number of deaths is beginning to drop. Before year's end, I expect Londoners will have returned. It wouldn't do for anyone to discover those dissected corpses. You'll be drummed out of surgery. Worse, you'll be named a heretic."

"I'll send for a Reaper when I'm through."

"Pay him off properly and, though it goes against your nature, Henry, you would do the fellow a favor by stressing the importance of keeping his tongue in his mouth in regard to this matter."

I nodded to whatever the Lord Mayor said; anything to hurry him along. I was tired and had much work ahead of me. Before disposing of the cadavers, I wanted to finish cataloguing every detail of the disease in its final stage.

Once alone, I peeled back my sleeve. A black spot had appeared inside my elbow where I'd been drawing blood for Thomas. The sore did explain the incessant itch.

I set a candle beside Thomas's bed. Grabbing the needle I said, "Time for another injection."

The boy didn't stir. Feeling a cold dread gnaw at my innards, I checked the boy for a pulse, for breath, for any sign of life. Nothing. Poor, thin Thomas was dead, starvation as likely a cause as plague. If only he had managed food, perhaps he might have survived. Or he might have lived had I tried my own blood as a cure sooner.

I slumped against the wall. Tears streamed down my face. I'd come so close to success. Aching sorrow welled inside my chest, pressing against my ribs and heart. I wheezed, trying to draw air. Spots danced before my eyes and, for a split second I swore I saw a shade hovering over Thomas's pallet. When I blinked, the apparition, along with the spots, had disappeared.

Never had I felt London's emptiness as much as I did then. I desperately desired company, but not that of the dying. Leaving my uniform behind, I took to the streets, hiding budding signs of plague beneath my clothing.

The inns and boarding houses were closed, yet a few taverns did business behind heavy curtains, with lookouts keeping their eyes peeled for Watchers, Searchers, and Examiners—street guards, nurses paid to search out the dead, and people hired to report outbreaks, respectively.

By the time I'd meandered to the far end of town, the sun hung half-way to the horizon. I paused before an empty church. Vinegar filled the basin beneath a stone cross. A few sixpence and half-penny coins rested in the vinegar, the liquid believed to kill plague germs.

Kneeling, I dug out a coin, offered a prayer for Thomas's soul and for forgiveness for having failed the boy. It was but a gesture, for I still felt every ounce of guilt burdening my soul. Nonetheless, I tossed the coin into the vinegar, praying for salvation.

From within the shimmering pool, a shadowy reflection gazed up. A dark hood surrounded a skeletal face. Two coins in the basin appeared to rest in the skull's eye sockets. Startled, I looked over my shoulder for whatever had cast the image but saw nothing.

Wanting only a single night of peaceful sleep, I staggered toward home, and not the again vacant hospital. Around every street corner, I glimpsed a dark, tattered robe, or saw a bony hand reach out to touch an oblivious passerby.

Wearily, I waited for night, sitting beside my window, listening for the cry of, "Bring out your dead," followed by the ringing of a hand bell. After meeting with the Reaper with whom I'd done much business of late I paid him, then sent him to the hospital to cart off Thomas and the tightly wrapped, dissected corpses.

* * *

For days the fleeting image of Death stalking London's denizens haunted me like waking nightmares. I saw Death everywhere, a shrouded army of spectral skeletons invading the city. Unable to bear the apparitions, I chased the phantoms until overtaking one. Then I stared face to bony face with the nightmarish creature.

Death seemed as tall as the Tower looming above London's rooftops. His rictus grin added to his perverse, grotesque horror. His tattered shroud smelled of earth and peat, the flesh having long rotted from his bones. When he opened his jaw, a stench rancid with decay rolled forth.

"What fool seeks death?" the skeletal apparition asked .

I pushed back my sleeve. Three more spots had joined the first. A dozen more, as of this morning, covered my body. "I recognize the signs. I know you'll soon come for me."

"And you wish to end your suffering early?"

"Quite the opposite actually. I won't go willingly. I'll fight you every step. You'll have to drag me from this world."

"I am not the enemy. Most welcome my appearance, for I deliver man from mortal suffering."

"What you call 'mortal suffering,' Spectre of Death, we call life," I said. "Touch me with your claws of putrescence if you will. Yet long after you give up trying to claim my soul, I'll still be here, fighting for my life."

"Are you challenging me, Henry Mortimer?" Death cocked his head, the gesture generating the sound of neck vertebra rubbing together.

"Consider it fair warning." I puffed my chest, wishing I could quell the shaking in my bones, but fear, hunger and plague wore at my tiring body. "I've devoted my life to defeating you and see no reason to cease the battle now."

Death laughed and a mist-like snake escaped his toothy jaw. "Then you have wasted your life, for all life ends in death."

"Eventually. But every year, we learn new ways to hold you at bay. There is a cure for this plague and I won't rest until I've found it."

Death's skeletal hand raked the air before my face. "Brave words for a man I touched days ago." As the shrouded figure receded into the shadows, his voice whispered ominously, "Stay on this world, Henry Mortimer, and you shall know of things worse than plague, worse than death. Stay, and you shall beg for my return." Death momentarily vanished, only to reappear in an alley where it touched a passing man.

The man staggered and coughed. I watched him walk onward, never suspecting that Death had marked him with plague.

You haven't won, Spectre.

* * *

I spent the better part of three days bedridden. When I felt strong enough to spoon cold soup into a bowl, I couldn't keep it down. Plague sores covered me. Swollen glands burst, oozing yellow pus streaked with blood. Fever wracked me with shivers. Spots danced before my eyes and spasms kept my muscles twitching.

My throbbing head felt like an overripe melon, ready to burst with the least pressure. I curled on my side and closed my eyes, almost—but not quite—ready to surrender to Death.

For a blissful moment, I felt nothing but the sweet peace of deep, unfeeling sleep, free of all sensations, free of dreams, as though my soul no longer inhabited my poor, diseased body, but rather the soothing darkness of infinite space.

Then I opened my eyes, dispelling the void of darkness.

My fever had broken. The pounding headache receded. My joints, though stiff, loosened as I moved about. Although plague sores remained, they appeared dead on my flesh. I scratched one and bits of it flaked off.

I survived. I should be dead. I raised my fists skywards. "You hear that, foul Spectre? I've defeated you! I, Dr. Henry Mortimer, have defeated Death himself!"

I threw open the shutters, wanting to shout my victory to the world, but settled on inhaling deeply. Across the street, a boy posted the weekly *Bill of Mortality*. I cocked my head. That shouldn't go up for another two days.

How long had I slept? No matter. I was awake now and cured.

***

October gave way to November. Rains swept in on colder air. The change of season heralded the first trickle of returning Londoners, mostly clergymen and a few lower ranking court officials.

With winter's approach, the number of plague cases dwindled. Yet it was just as deadly to any who caught it.

I mewed myself in the still-vacant College of Surgeons to study while I recovered. My skin still bore faint bluish swellings, the last remnants of plague pustules. Otherwise I felt fine. Actually, I felt nothing.

Having almost cured Thomas then having survived plague myself convinced me a cure was within my grasp. Because the Black Plague had troubled England since the fourteenth century, I renewed my research with older tomes, which chronicled the disease's history.

Medieval doctors wrote of the four humours: (Choleric, melancholic, phlegmatic and sanguine. *Yellow bile, black bile, phlegm and blood.* Their names alone evoked an image of a plague victim. I already knew the importance of blood in developing a cure. Surely, I was at last on the right trail.

I drew samples of all my bodily fluids. With them I concocted a medicinal tonic infused with a tincture of woodworm. I held the vial to the light. Sunlight streamed through the liquid, casting a halo. Deep in my bones I knew I'd discovered the cure.

If only I could have used it to save Thomas.

My first test case, a woman of twenty, survived.

The miracle drug cured men and women. It cured the old and young. It cured everyone. By the time winter fully arrived, London was free of plague.

***

I slept much during winter. As I had no patients, I had time to rest at last. No need to wake. Besides, I had little appetite. No doubt as an effect of having starved much during the past year, my body had become accustomed to eating less.

* * *

April, 1666

Spring thaw revived me, yet the hard winter of fighting plague had worn me out. I felt older and stiffer. Bone weary, I shuffled to the mirror to shave.

Oddly, no beard had grown. Dark rings sagged under my listless eyes. My sallow cheeks were sunken. My lips appeared bloodless. Dry skin cracked across my knuckles. Elsewhere, scaly black patches flaked worse than ever. Yet surely new skin was growing just beneath, waiting to push through.

I stared out the window.

Fresh rain had renewed London. Flowers bloomed. Color returned to the sky. People crowded the streets. Noise filled the air. London again smelled of life, of wood smoke and roasting meat, of sweat and grime, of living flesh.

Hunger awoke within me. My stomach knotted, yet I couldn't go out, not like this. I looked like death, almost. Perhaps if I covered up….

A hard, rapid knock intruded. A youth's voice shouted, "Doctor Mortimer? Me pap needs you bad. It's done come back. Everyone says ain't no one but you can save him!"

Spring had revived the plague, too, it seemed.

It gave me a reason to cover. I donned the uniform then followed a red-haired boy to the so-familiar, poorer districts.

The smell of fresh herbs stuffing the beak made me ill, but I had to wear the mask. People couldn't see me like this. They wouldn't understand.

A street vendor sold meat pies. Cloying, fried, fatty odors turned my stomach. I should have forced myself to eat more during winter. Yet nothing had appealed to my sense of taste.

Finally, we reached the boy's hovel. A man huddled over a table. The signs were clear. Plague.

But I possessed a cure. The only cure.

When I left, I felt confident the man would recover.

A chicken screeched, drawing me to a halt. A new scent wormed past the herb-stuffed beak. A salty, tangy, delicious smell. Blood. Fresh blood.

I licked my cracked lips. My dry, sticky tongue flayed off a thin layer of dead, peeling skin. Ignoring that, I followed the rich, tangy, tantalizing smell. It came from around back of the thatched farmhouse. A milkmaid squatted, feathers scattered about her. She held the dead chicken to her lips. Blood rimmed her mouth as she chewed on raw flesh.

Her hollow gaze lifted. She cocked her head and smiled.

"I know you," I said.

"Doc-tor," she said, struggling to speak.

I'd cured her last year. She'd been one of my first successes.

"Raw meat is not…" I licked my lips, shredding a bit more dried skin. The torn, raw, bloodied meat looked delicious. So tempting. But medicine taught differently. "You should not…" I quivered, wanting a taste of raw meat.

Fighting every urge to stay, I fled the scene. Yet my desires would not be squelched. The body craved foods for a reason. Perhaps it knew what it needed to heal. To grow new skin.

I stopped at the butcher shop and bought a pound of raw pork and a plucked chicken. That night, my stomach finally quit growling.

* * *

Every day, I treated new plague cases. I visited old patients. Validating a miraculous cure required a follow-up study. All my cured patients had slept much of winter. All craved raw meat, so I prescribed an all-meat diet. When the stomach was ready, it would accept cooked foods and vegetables.

As time passed, however, raw pork and chicken left my hunger more and more dissatisfied. I tried freshly killed game. Fresher was better. The blood still ran. For a time, that quelled the gnawing in my gut.

Every week, another letter arrived from the College of Surgeons, requesting I share my cure, but the study was incomplete. I still hadn't completely recovered myself.

My skin was still blackened, still flaking. Moreover, I found myself staring, standing listlessly, my mind blank. Every day, it seemed my thoughts became harder to focus. Words, too, harder to form.

A deep wanting drove me to the streets. The coarse fabric of my uniform used to feel itchy. Now it didn't bother me. My legs trembled. My hands shook. I staggered aimlessly for hours, staring at my fellow Londoners.

I'd emptied the mask's beak of cloying herbs so I smelled everything…everyone. People smelled good. Fresh. Clean. Delicious. Human flesh would surely be the sweetest meat. Everyone I passed smelled ripe for eating.

The thought repulsed me. Yet the craving was overpowering. Horrid, insistent whispers nagged my thoughts, making inhuman suggestions, creating horrific images I could not purge.

Fighting the unacceptable craving, I veered into Whitechapel's darker streets, then turned down an alley.

A miasma of foul odors choked me. Sweat. Blood. Urine. Cheap wine and ale. Beneath it all, flesh. Meat. Food. *Nourishment.*

A drunk slept against a wall.

I ripped off my mask. I knelt beside the slumped man, reeking of beer. He'd been stabbed. Robbed. Left for dead. But not dead.

His pulse was weak. Too much blood lost. His head lolled back. An eye opened. Both eyes opened wide. He shuddered. Tried to scream. Then fell slack. Now dead.

Hunger overcame me. *Waste not.*

I tore a mouthful of flesh from his neck. I chewed heavenly, bloody meat. A delicious shiver filled me. Every bite renewed me. My dizziness abated. The gnawing ache in my belly was at last sated.

I ripped away the man's shirt and feasted on his shoulder. I tore into his chest. Organs were the answer. Heart. Kidney. Liver. Brains. I should've realized that. Organ meat was always prized over muscle, and it provided more in the way of vitamins.

Soon I felt my old self. Even my concentration improved. My joints ached less and I stood without shaking.

A shriek erupted from the alley's entrance.

I looked up, wiping blood from my mouth against my sleeve. A prostitute screamed again, then grabbed her skirts and ran.

I picked up the mask and chased after her. "It's not as you think! I did the man no harm!"

People scattered. They pointed and screamed. In the ensuing panic, I ducked into a shadowed doorway and donned the mask. There, I waited until those who had seen my ghastly face had gone. Staying to darker streets, I made my way home.

* * *

Headlines in *The London Gazette* read: ZOMBIE SEEN IN WHITE-CHAPEL. In the article, the writer hypothesized that a zombie, a creature of African slave voodoo magic, must have stolen aboard a ship importing molasses and rum from the French plantations in the West Indies. The paper called me, though not by name, the "Monster of London."

"Nonsense," I muttered. Nevertheless I thought it wise to stay indoors awhile.

Each edition of the *Gazette* reported new sightings, mostly in the once plague-ridden districts. Soon, theories of a French conspiracy arose. This, the article claimed, was the start of a new war with France.

Yet I hadn't gone out.

Perhaps it was time I did. The hunger was growing. I couldn't concentrate. The stiffness had returned. Along with dizziness. Fatigue. Weakness.

I needed to feed on human flesh. Morally it was wrong, yet my body demanded it. Needed it. Without it, I'd die.

I refuse to die.

First, I planned to seek out zombies. If I found none, then hysteria had spawned rumors. One person reported a monstrous sight and achieved fame, so others copied. Surely that was all.

I walked stiff-legged but brisk. I stared at the ground, knowing the way. Once across Old London Bridge, I slowed and searched the crowd. Looked down every street.

In the poorest pocket of town, I found them. Two men, a woman and a boy huddled over another body. They tore off limbs. They ate flesh and sucked on bones.

Horrified, I watched. That I wanted to join them disgusted me. Time seemed to cease.

The boy looked up and tugged on the woman's tattered, bloodied skirt. All four looked at me and waved.

The woman, her face decomposing, said, "Doc-tor. My my frrr-end."

The milkmaid I'd seen eating a raw chicken. I knew the boy, too. I'd treated them all.

Fighting my desires, I dragged myself away.

Behind a haystack, two youths feasted on an old woman. In a dilapidated barn, a married couple, their flesh withered and gray, were eating their children, two already dead, one dying, and another tied to a stall. Inside a thatch hovel, a woman scooped out her husband's brains. In another, a man devoured his wife's bowels.

Every "zombie" had been a patient, one I'd thought cured.

I trembled and collapsed to my knees. Hunger clawed at my gut. I wanted to feed but not to murder. My patients had killed. Were killing.

Murder was wrong. Even to survive.

I didn't kill that man. He was already dead.

I groaned. Loathing myself, I admitted the truth. *I would have killed him.* I wanted to kill now. I wanted to eat. To feel alive again.

Alive? I peeled off my gloves. Stared at grey-fleshed hands. I had no pulse. Reaching inside my robes, I found no heartbeat.

My patients hadn't survived. The philter was no miracle. Rather than cure the Black Plague, I'd created something worse. I'd created zombies. Living dead to feast on the living.

I am the Monster of London.

I crawled to my apartment and barricaded the door. I prayed that as I grew weaker, it would trap me.

* * *

Late August, 1666

Weeks pass. Henry live. He no die. Life be his punishment. His Hell.

I realize I think of self in third person. It seem I no longer me. Henry seem someone… something else… some creature else. Henry the body and I disembodied thoughts. The ability to think come and go. My mind deteriorate like my body. Decompose. But not die.

Time have no real meaning.

Henry bash into wall. Rotted flesh tear. Streak old paint. Still he—I—no die. Knife in heart not kill. Something must kill. *Please, God.* If not die, Henry eat. He so hungry. But hunger wrong. I not let Henry eat.

That thought drive Henry mad. "No eat," I scream. My words garbled. Hard to force out. "No feed. No kill. No murder."

But others kill. I hear his voice, my voice, in head. Patients kill. They feed. They hunt streets. No one safe. Zombie plague worse. Black Plague better.

"Better to die," I sob.

Must die. Even Henry, my body, agree. But how?

Need help. Henry fumble but find parchment. Find ink. Find quill. Take long time… but I write thoughts. Henry drop message out window. Drop coin to boy. Lord Mayor Blutworth's name on front. Boy know where to go. Boy will help. Boy like doctor.

Henry and I sag into chair. My body long ago stop pretending. Henry no more breathe. He barely speak. All we want is peace. And forgiveness.

I try pray. Words hard. Maybe God see heart. Maybe see heart that not beat. No harm meant. Intentions good. But actions do wrong. Cause harm. Cause hurt.

I ache deep. Want to cry. But no tears. No more fluids. Henry no bleed. Humours all gone.

Hours pass. Lord Mayor where? He note get now? He come must. Must help us.

Henry stagger. Pull at barricade. Piece fall. Some move. Door now exposed.

Then knock.

I call out. "Cccc-ome… in."

Slow door open. Push stuff aside. Lord Mayor head poke in.

"My God, Henry. Is that really you?" Lord Mayor lurch back. Horror in face hard for me. Make me sad. "When I received your missive, I thought it a joke. The writing was so bad. Never mind. What can I do to help?"

"Burn. Must burn." Thought of death soothing. Give strength.

"Burn what?" Blutworth asked.

"Burn all. All like me." Henry lean on heavy desk. Open drawer. Ledger. Names of patients. Henry shuffle to door. I sputter words, "In here. Names. Sick. Burn."

"Burn your book?"

"No. Burn names. Burn me. All like me. Burn. Must die." My body sag. "No cure. Burn. Fire clean."

"Henry, you're asking me to kill…"

"No!" For me, Henry shake head. "Not killing dead. All dead now. Undead. Please. Help." He grab knife. Plunge it chest deep. Lord Mayor gasp. No blood issue. Henry pull out. Show knife. He stab deeper. "No live. Burn. Must destroy. Bad plague."

His face like ghost, Lord Mayor nod. "I'll make the arrangements." He reach out. Almost pat Henry shoulder. Almost. But not touch it… me… monster I become.

*　*　*

September 2, 1666

Midnight tower bong. All old patients gather. Lord Mayor bring them. Shop belong to king's baker. Maid here one of patients. I know her.

Henry, me, last enter shop. Lord Mayor stand outside. He no move long time.

I want ask, *Why here?* But no words. Tongue useless. Henry only cock head.

"Yes, old friend. It's goodbye," Lord Mayor say. "At least here it'll seem like an accident."

Bakeries often catch. Ovens dangerous.

"It's on the edge of town, so the fire should be easily contained," Blutworth continued. "Besides, I know the baker. The king made Farynor a handsome offer. He'll rebuild his shop on the other end of town and never speak a word of how the fire really started or why. The maid attacked his son yester eve, so he understands the importance."

I groan. Still no word. No way ask about son.

"The lad's fine, doctor. She bit him, but a few stitches fixed him up. In a day or two, he'll be right as rain."

That some relief. I struggle to draw last breath. Still can't say, *Get all?*

"Don't worry, Henry. I've gathered every name on the list. Farynor left the oven fire burning and a stack of firewood. I'm trusting you, old friend. I can't bring myself to do it."

Lord Mayor close door. Clock bong one o'clock.

Henry weave through crowd. They pat him, me. Gurgled moans greet us. They look up to us. Trust us. Hope they understand. Hope they forgive.

Henry knock embers out of oven. Wood pile catch.

As flames grow, zombie patients shrink back. They hold hands before face. Lifeless expressions still show terror. Fear. Much pain.

Fire engulf walls. Ceiling burn. Glowing timbers fall. Fire burn brighter. Engulf screaming undead. First ones die. Through window, I see fire spread to neighbor's building.

But shadow catch gaze. Shrouded figure step forth. Hold out skeletal arms for embrace.

I welcome Death. Peace at last.

Society and Sickness

Leila Eadie

"It is a truth universally acknowledged, that a woman of a certain age must find a husband or be the bane of her father's life thereafter."

Miss Katherine Alders and her family had, through entirely no fault of their own—except perhaps Mr. Alders' sense of honour—been forced to leave their fondly loved Kellsby Hall to find more modest accommodations. Yet Mr. Adlers would speak no wrong of his brother, even though that gentleman's accumulation of debts and subsequent death had left his only brother the bearer of that heavy weight. So it was that Mr. Edward Alders and family came to live in the North Downs, to Hartford Cottage, part of the Hartford estate that belonged to a good-hearted second cousin twice removed.

The cottage was not altogether unpleasant, being a sprawling building, which although certainly smaller than Kellsby Hall, had enough room for the Alders family. Mr. Alders had been blessed with one son, Henry, and three daughters, from the eldest Katherine, to Millie, to the youngest, Elaine. Unfortunately, Henry had died of a terrible fever while serving as an officer abroad, and this remained a constant source of sorrow for those he left behind.

Within a month, the family was settled in the area, having been introduced to the local nobility, eligible bachelors, and other young ladies. There had even been talk of Katherine attracting the attention of Colonel Foster. Foster was not overly handsome, but he possessed a large estate adjoining theirs, a house in town and the happy sum of six thousand pounds a year.

Mr. Alders had been starting to suspect that Katherine, at two-and-twenty, would be with him forever, plaguing him with her ideas about constructing pipes leading from the cottage's well direct to the house, and the creation of automated lawn shears. The girl was handsome enough, with a fine figure, but her accomplishments left a lot to be desired. She could sing and play the piano, but she was more interested in drawing. And did she draw genteel things such as birds, flowers and landscapes? No, not Katherine. She drew abominable engines, mechanical nightmares, and the like. Mr. Alders sighed. What brave man would take her off his hands? So he hid the drawings, burned them when he could, and instructed the servants to do the same.

Millie was little better, though she was different from her sister. A sillier girl could not be found in the whole south of England. Happiest covered in bows and flounces, all Millie wanted was romance. Her belief was that love would overcome all, and she actively looked in the most unlikely places for her heart's desire. Mrs. Alders had found her talking to the cowherd, batting her eyelashes like the boy's animals, and had forced her to return to the cottage. Could the girl not see his poverty? The terrible skin and wracking cough that resulted? Mr. Alders supposed he had this all to come with Elaine, once she reached her teens in a few years.

Mr. Alders' reverie was disturbed by the cottage door being thrown open then slammed.

"My dear! Do consider the furnishings," he heard his wife admonish, and then the sobbing started. Mr. Alders considered barring the door of his study, but he was not quick enough to turn thought into action. Mrs. Alders burst in with Katherine and Millie in tow.

"Mr. Alders," she said, pushing Katy into the seat across the desk from her father, "you must hear what has happened."

"By all means. I was only contemplating how we are to afford food for the winter ahead. Nothing that cannot be interrupted, obviously."

Ignoring her husband's mutterings, Mrs. Alders drove a hard finger into Katy's upper arm. "Tell him."

Katy looked up. It was not she who had been crying, Mr. Alders saw, but Millie, still sniffing in the doorway.

"It is Colonel Foster," Katy started reluctantly. "I fear he has changed in his affections toward me."

"Oh, yes? How so?" Mr. Alders asked, endeavouring to ignore Millie's renewed weeping.

"It is just terrible!" Mrs. Alders added.

Katy frowned at her mother and continued. "I met him in the lane as I was returning from the village. He was most disarrayed. His coat was torn and he was not wearing a hat. Even so, I bade him a 'Good morning,' and did not receive a reply. Indeed, he looked at me and grunted."

"This is most unexpected. I considered the Colonel a perfect gentleman, of good breeding."

"Indeed. But not this morning. Upon consideration, I wonder if he was not ill."

"Ill, you say?"

"It must be so. He was uncommonly pale. His eyes were not their usual bright selves. I am not sure he recognised me, even though he stared directly at me."

"There is talk of an illness in the ports on the coast. Something new spread from over there." The family knew *over there* was the source of most evil. They nodded gravely.

"There you have it. The Colonel has been at Dover seeing to business. He was to return yesterday and visit with us today," Katy said.

"So, ripped attire, no hat, pale complexion, rudeness. I believe I will investigate. Was he on his way to Yarwell Manor?"

"No, he was moving toward the village. He was moving slowly, on foot, not a-horse. That too was strange. I rushed back here straight away, so we may still catch him before he reaches the village."

"Very well." Mr. Alders stood and walked past his women to the cottage's hallway. Katy followed him, and he stopped her at the door. "I will go alone. There may be things said unsuitable for a female's ears."

"Nonsense. I will come with you Father. I wish to know what ails the Colonel."

"She does have an interest in the matter," Mrs. Alders said from the study doorway where she still stood, comforting Millie. "Why, any day now we expect Colonel Foster to ask your permission to…" She trailed off, seeing her husband's expression darken.

"You will remain here Katherine. I will return to tell you what I have learnt." With that he opened the front door, stepped out and pulled it firmly closed.

He knew that Katy would follow him despite his instructions to the contrary. She was a willful girl. It would be her downfall, he knew it. He strode on, swinging his cane, ignoring the flash of colour that was his daughter following behind.

Mr. Alders caught up with Colonel Foster as he approached the outskirts of the village. The man was in a bad way; that much was obvious. His shooting coat was missing an arm, ripped off along with the shirt sleeve underneath by the look of it. He was limping; his right ankle looked most unsteady each time it was called upon to bear his weight. Indeed, as Mr. Alders watched, the whole foot slid sideways in a manner that suggested the joint was broken. The man must be in considerable pain! Yet he continued on, making no sound other than the heavy breathing Mr. Alders clearly heard.

"Colonel Foster!" he called as he drew nearer. "Are you hurt? May I assist in any way?"

There was no response from the man, who trudged on as if he had not heard the greeting. Mr. Alders caught up with him and caught his shoulder turning him around. He immediately loosened his grip on the man. The Colonel did look ill. His face was deathly pale, his eyes clouded and apparently unseeing. His coat was unbuttoned, as was his shirt, and on the pale skin of his belly was what looked like a bayonet wound, fresh with clotted blood.

"Colonel, it is I, Alders. Do you not recognise me?"

The man had stopped his painful walk toward the village and turned his blank gaze onto Mr. Alders.

"Uhhg," he said. A grunt, as Katy had said. The Colonel reached up his unclothed arm and gripped Mr. Alders' coat sleeve.

"You appear unwell," Mr. Alders said, trying to pull himself free of this grip. "Shall I fetch Dr. Norris?"

The Colonel, his normally fine blond hair matted with something that could have been mud—but could have been dried blood—pulled Mr. Alders closer to him and bared his teeth.

"What is it, man? What are you doing?"

Somewhere close by, a gun fired. Mr. Alders, staring into the Colonel's cloudy eyes, was splattered with a viscous liquid and released from the grip a moment later. He fell to the compacted earth of the road and wiped the stinging fluid from his eyes. The Colonel was the recipient of the shot. It hit him in the side of the head. As the disarrayed figure crumpled to the ground, Mr. Alders saw that it had done the man considerable damage. Blood and pink jelly oozed from between sections of exposed, shattered bone. Mr. Alders turned away, clapping a hand across his mouth. In his distress, he heard footsteps approaching. It must be Katy.

"No, my dear, do not look!" he said, his own eyes firmly closed, but the footsteps came on until they stopped by his side. He looked up and saw Katy holding his hunting rifle trained on the twitching remains of the Colonel.

"You! You did not—"

"Get up father," she said, satisfied that Colonel Foster would not be rising again. "If he has a sickness, we must wash his blood off you. Let us return to the cottage quickly." She offered him a hand and helped to pull him back to his feet. She kept hold of his hand and tugged him away from the pooling blood.

"You are not to touch my gun, you know that."

Katy ignored him and continued her brisk pace back along the lane.

"Someone will find him."

"They will. I must return immediately with some oil and set fire to the Colonel."

"Why? What good will that do? His relations will no doubt wish to bury him in the family vaults. They will not be pleased."

"I do not care."

"You *should* care! It is just this sort of impropriety that will see you a spinster, living with me until I am hounded into my grave!"

"I fervently wish for us both to live that long." Beyond this comment they remained silent until they reached the cottage. Mrs. Alders was waiting in the parlour with Millie and Elaine. They rushed to greet the returning pair.

"How is the Colonel? Edward, what is that on your face and hands? Is it blood? Has there been an accident?"

"Not now. Fetch some water."

"No, father, we will go to the stream."

"I will not wash in the stream like a commoner for everyone to see."

"I will not have the cottage tainted by that infected blood," Katy said, tugging him through the cottage and out to the back yard, beyond which lay the stream.

"Infected? What is going on?" Mrs. Alders said. She received no answer, so told her younger daughters to stay in the parlour and hurried out into the yard after her husband. Katy had succeeded in getting him to the stream where he knelt and splashed himself with water.

Picking her way carefully through the pasture, Mrs. Alders approached the bank and asked again, "What has happened?"

"The Colonel was indeed most unwell," Katy said. "He died."

"She shot him!" Mr. Alders said.

"Katherine, you did not! Tell your poor afflicted mother that you did not shoot the man you are going to marry?"

"I am not going to marry Colonel Foster. Not now, at any rate."

Mrs. Alders covered her face with her hands. When she lowered them again, her eyes were hard. "You wish us to live out our dotage penniless, do you? You can not behave like this!"

"There's no telling the girl," Mr. Alders put in.

"He would have hurt father. I could not let that happen."

"I was only talking to the man," Mr. Alders said, and at this, Katy turned and walked back to the cottage with her lips pursed tightly together.

"We will never find her a husband now," Mrs. Alders said to her shivering husband and let out a wail.

* * *

"It seems you were correct." Mr. Alders called to his daughter as she passed the open door of his study.

She backtracked and entered the room. "What's that, father?"

"There is a sickness in the village. I heard today from Lord Fothergill's man, who was here to drop off an invitation."

Katy raised her eyebrows. "Oh yes?"

"We are invited to Verity House for an end of season ball."

"What of the sickness?"

"A nasty business. I should not have mentioned it."

"I too have heard a little. They say it leads to loss of interest in everything except raw meat. And biting."

"Enough! Where have you heard such lurid details?"

Katy shrugged. Her father tutted at the unladylike behaviour. "You should stop up your ears in preference to letting such thoughts enter your head."

"I think the Colonel would have bitten you, Father."

"Nonsense! Do you not have anything to do? Go assist your mother."

"Yes, father," Katy said and left, pulling the door closed behind her.

* * *

The End of Season Ball was a smaller affair than originally intended. The sickness had affected many in the area, spreading with a speed that scared people, who left rather than risk its depredations. The attendees were fewer, but determined to make just as merry as if Verity Hall were full to bursting.

Katy was distressed at how few people were there. The sickness had taken a larger toll than she had anticipated. She had heard the maids whisper about news from the village and beyond, but had not suspected it was so virulent.

As she passed through the diminished crowd, she heard more talk of violent deaths and cannibalism. It was no ordinary sickness, but Katy had realised that when she saw the Colonel. That sense of unease had prompted her to fetch her father's gun, and she was glad enough she had. With her inborn sense of caution allied with her imagination for design, Katy had also made some preparations to keep the cottage and its inhabitants safe. It was a terrible thought, but this sickness had provided her with the best opportunities to pursue her particular interests. Katy thought she might not get another chance, if her parents had their way, and she was determined to make the most of it.

She heard the announcement of Mr. and Mrs. Warburg's arrival and shook her head. She knew the couple liked to arrive late to make a grand entrance when everyone was present to watch them, and a grand entrance they made: Mrs. Warburg in all her finery dragged an obviously ill Mr. Warburg. Watching them, Katy thought Mr. Warburg hadn't quite reached the stage of mindless hunger, but he did not look far off. If the sickness spread as she surmised, through an infected bite, then she had better round up her family and depart, even though the dancing had barely begun. Millie was not going to like it. As Mr. Warburg was dragged into the crowds near the hall's entrance, Millie was dancing with a soldier in dress uniform, a bright smile on her eager face. Katy decided to tackle her parents first.

"Mother, father," she said as she approached them. They were talking to Mr. Alders' second cousin twice removed, and they did not look happy to see her.

"Ah, Katherine. I was just telling Mr. Worthington about your skill at the piano."

"Mr. Worthington," Katy said, dropping a curtsey to the round, bald man. "Please forgive me, I beg you. I am afraid I must speak with my parents for a moment."

"Of course, of course, my dear. Please do, and remember that you have an open invitation to use the piano at Hartford Hall any time you please."

"Thank you, sir," Katy said with a smile, and waited until Mr. Worthington saw someone else he should talk to before turning to her waiting parents.

"Well?" Mr. Alders said.

"We must leave. Mr. Warburg has arrived and he has the sickness."

"I don't think we should go now. Lord and Lady Fothergill might take offence if we left so early." Mrs. Alders waved to an acquaintance before turning back to her daughter. "You really should make an effort. There are many gentlemen here who have looked upon you favourably on previous occasions. Now that Colonel Foster is no longer of interest, you must find a replacement."

"Mother!" Katy said, barely succeeding in her effort to keep her voice low. "This is important. The sickness is here, in this room. You could fall ill if you stay. Do you understand?"

"I'm sure you are mistaken," Mr. Alders said, looking around the room. "Everyone seems in good spirits. Perhaps you should be more like your sister. See, she is enjoying herself. Is that a lieutenant, my dear?"

"I believe so. And so handsome. He looks at Millie with a certain light in his rather fine eyes, I think." Mrs. Alders clasped her hands together at her breast. "We may yet have a wedding this year."

"Please," Katy insisted, "let us leave. I will say I am unwell, if it pleases you, but we must not stay here."

They both returned to staring at their eldest daughter, not happily. "Please," she said again. "The sickness spreads quickly."

Mrs. Alders shook her head and opened her mouth to say something but never got the chance. A scream rang out through the high-ceilinged hall, cutting through the conversation and the music equally. Shocked silence followed as the music died away. Then a muttering began rippling around the room as people asked each other whatever could be the matter.

"Have them bring the carriage around. I will find Millie and we will join you there," Katy told her father and then pushed her way through those who had been watching the dancing. All faces now stared at a point to the left of the platform where the musicians were arranged. Katy followed their stares and saw Mrs. Warburg desperately trying to pull Mr. Warburg to his feet. The gentleman writhed on the polished marble floor, groaning. He looked even more ill than when he had arrived, if such a thing were possible.

Suddenly he was still, having fallen back limp, giving up his struggle. Mrs. Warburg dropped his hand and peered down at him, her mouth a perfect O of shock. Just as suddenly, Mr. Warburg lurched forward onto his stomach and attacked the stockinged leg of a gentleman who was attempting to assist Mrs. Warburg. The man leaped backward, but Mr. Warburg's teeth were affixed to his leg, and he pulled Warburg with him for a pace before toppling to the ground himself. A bloom of red stained the white stocking. Mrs. Warburg joined in with a lusty scream as the newly fallen man yelled. The panic spread among the meager crowd. It jumped from one bystander to another, and all rushed for the hall's big double doors.

Katy was roughly shoved from one side to another as people rushed away from the scene. She could not see anything to do that might help, so instead she sought out Millie. Her sister's sweet face was not among those distraught people running toward and past her. Nor was she among the group trying to exit via the veranda.

Mrs. Warburg continued screaming, and Katy looked again at the tussle on the floor. Mrs. Warburg's helper now lay still as Mr. Warburg chewed on his throat. The slurping sound, barely audible over the sound of those fleeing, was particularly unpleasant. Katy skirted the fallen men and took Mrs. Warburg's arm. "Will you join me, Mrs. Warburg," she inquired, as if nothing was amiss, "for a stroll on the veranda, for you are quite pale and I think some air would aid you greatly."

Mrs. Warburg was unresponsive, but moved when Katy pulled her arm. They were among the last of those using the tall veranda windows as an exit. Katy helped the blank-faced woman into the cool night air. They followed the group hurrying away from Verity Hall. Those who had managed to find their carriages were jamming the driveway; one coach had overturned in its haste to reach the gate. Men were arguing about whether the horses could be persuaded to go around, and who was going to move it, and because it was not their fault they did not see why it was their job to solve the problem.

Now that she had brought Mrs. Warburg safely out of the hall, Katy did not know what she should do with the woman. In the light shining from the hall, Mrs. Warburg looked pale and unwell, which was not at all surprising, considering what she had witnessed. It was a miracle that the woman was still on her feet.

"Perhaps you had better return home with us tonight," Katy said, and because she did not expect any response, she led Mrs. Warburg along the edge of the grand lawn toward the gates. Katy looked around for her family, but did not see them. She hoped that they had made a good start away from Verity Hall.

There came a crash as a figure burst through one of the windows by the veranda. Katy looked back, and guessed that Mr. Warburg had finished with his entrée and was ready for more sustenance.

"Come along, Mrs. Warburg," she said and increased her pace. Her companion was having trouble keeping up; no doubt shock was setting in. Katy heard the woman's harsh breathing and slowed slightly. "We cannot stop, I am afraid. We need to reach a place of safety."

Men must have moved the fallen carriage clear, as wheels were rolling again. A cry startled Katy. She stopped, unsure whether to run or attempt to hide. The carriage that was passing stopped. Millie's head poked through the curtains. She called, "Climb in, Katy!"

Whispering thanks under her breath, Katy did just that, first passing Mrs. Warburg up. Katy pulled the door shut behind her and looked around. Her family was all there, plus the soldier who had been Millie's dancing partner, and Mrs. Warburg, who looked as if she were going to be ill . There was little room left in the full carriage, but Katy perched on the edge of the bench next to her father. He would not look at her. His thin-lipped mouth was tightly shut, his eyes wide. Mrs. Alders sat beyond her husband, clutching his arm. Millie sat across the carriage, between the soldier and Mrs. Warburg, whom she was watching with curious eyes.

Mrs. Warburg began to sob, taking deep shuddering breaths. Millie looked unsure whether to join in or not, and looked to her soldier for reassurance. He stared out of the window at the people they passed as they endeavoured to escape.

Katy was not quick enough to react when Mrs. Warburg fell forward, almost landing in Mr. Alders' lap. There was little light present, but by whatever illumination did make its way into the carriage, Katy saw it shine off Mrs. Warburg's bared teeth.

Millie shrieked, as did Mrs. Alders. Mr. Alders did not understand what was happening, and tried to help Mrs. Warburg back to her seat. He yelped as her teeth clicked together just a hair's breadth away from his wrist. The soldier sprang into action and, grabbing Mrs. Warburg's legs, pushed her up and out of the carriage's window.

The driver must have heard that all was not well. He slowed, so Katy shouted, "Keep going! We must reach Hartford Cottage at all costs!"

The carriage regained speed.

"May God bless you for your quick thinking," Katy said to the soldier.

"Lieutenant Johnson," he said, bowing his head in her direction, "at your service, Miss." He paused, then said, "I do not know quite what happened. I am pleased you think it was the correct course of action, but—should we go back for the lady?"

Katy smiled briefly. "No, assuredly not. It is the sickness. Her husband must have infected her. I did not know, or I would not have..." Much vexed, Katy broke off and turned to her father. "Are you unharmed?"

"I think so," he said. He stared at the window, where Mrs. Warburg had vanished. "Why would she do that?"

"It is the sickness. We must get away. More will be suffering its effects tomorrow."

The carriage made a left hand turn, swinging everyone within. "We're almost home," Millie said, clutching Lt. Johnson's arm in imitation of her mother. The carriage stopped before the cottage's gate a short while later.

"Lt. Johnson, you will accompany us, will you not?" Katy said, with a glance to her father, who nodded approval.

"If it pleases you," he said, looking warily around.

"We should be safe here for a while at least," Katy said, following his glances. "Stick to the path."

"Upstairs," Mr. Alders said. "It would be best if we gathered upstairs. We can keep a watch, and fend off anything that tries to mount the staircase."

"A good plan, sir," Johnson said as they made their way to the house as quickly as possible without breaking into a run.

Once inside, with the door barred and both men armed with guns, Mr. Alders seemed considerably less concerned.

"They will not come this far," he stated.

"We cannot know *what* they will do," Katy said.

"Do not frown, dear," Mrs. Alders advised her. "It will line your face." She looked from Katy to the Lieutenant. Millie saw this and folded her arms beneath unhappily pursed lips. She took several steps nearer to the soldier until she was almost leaning on him.

"You women should try to get some sleep." Mr. Alders waved them toward the door. "We will watch out for trouble."

"I will stay and watch too," Katy said, and would not leave. Millie was unwilling to leave the Lieutenant alone with her sister, and declared that she could not possibly sleep. Mrs. Alders said that she certainly was not going to be on her own, and so they all remained where they were.

As time passed without event, Mrs. Alders fell asleep. Millie soon followed, curled up on the chair behind Lt. Johnson, and even Katy felt her eyelids slipping closed more and more frequently.

All at once there were bells clanging in the stillness of the night.

Katy snapped awake and rushed to the window. "They are out there."

"What?" Her father joined her at the window, rubbing his eyes.

"I set the cowbells to warn us if anything approached the house. Lt. Johnson, be ready."

"Yes, Miss." He stood to attention, as if she were his commanding officer. Katy could not enjoy the feeling, because the bells continued and were only silenced by a crashing noise.

"The pit! They have reached the pit."

"What pit?" Mr. Alders asked.

"We dug it earlier today," came a small voice from behind them. Elaine stood in the doorway with the maid, both yawning. "Have they come then, Katy?"

"Yes, dearest," Katy said to her sister. "But they will not get any closer. You remember what else we did?"

Elaine nodded. "Can I come and watch?"

"There is nothing to see; it is too dark. Why don't you sit with Millie, and then we will all be together?"

Elaine hopped up on the chaise-langue next to her sister and watched those clustered around the window with bright eyes.

Mrs. Alders took Katy by the arm and pulled her away from the window. "What have you been doing with Elaine? You have not been involving her in your unnatural ideas and plans, I hope?"

"I would not dream of doing such a thing, Mother," Katy lied.

In the silence that followed that statement, Millie spoke up. "Why are they coming here?"

"They have probably eaten everyone else," Elaine said with all the innocence of childhood. For a moment she had everyone's attention, and then a new noise began.

They were thumping on the door. Heavy blows rained down upon the sturdy wooden front door then stopped. After a pause they started again, accompanied with guttural grunts.

"Lt. Johnson, may I ask : do you possess a tinderbox?"

The soldier nodded and pulled the item from his pocket. Katy smiled and took it from him. She struck the flint against the steel and the tinder caught after a few tries. When she was sure it was alight, she stepped up to the open window and threw the whole box out. Johnson bit back his protest as, within moments, a roar arose. He stepped forward to look outside.

"Oil?" he asked.

"Yes," Katy said, "and a little brandy."

Mr. Alders yelped and barged past them to see what had happened to his special reserve liquor. Flames sprung up from the grass in front of the house.

"I have placed bundles of firewood there too. We should have a fire until dawn now."

The banging on the door stopped and an inhuman wail arose; the watchers saw a figure afire stumble away from the house. It got as far as the gate before falling and lying perfectly still as it continued to burn. A second figure tottered away on unsteady legs then vanished from view.

"He has fallen into the pit," Katy said, and indeed the flames and screaming began again, rising from the ground as if hell itself had opened a gateway through the earth.

"The fire," Mr. Alders said. "It is awfully close to the cottage. I fear for our safety. The whole place could take light."

Katy frowned. "I don't *think* so."

"But you did not cut a barrier between the oil and the house?" Johnson asked.

"No."

The Lieutenant and Katy raced downstairs, closely followed by Mr. and Mrs. Alders. The fire looked considerably closer from the downstairs windows.

"The fire will keep the sick ones away," Katy began.

"But it may burn us to cinders!" her mother interrupted.

"We must create a space next to the house where it cannot burn." Johnson explained that he had some experience of such things from his time in India, where fires were common. He set the family to fetching water and shovels and a boundary was established with hard work, but no trouble from the infected.

The sun was climbing above the horizon as they gathered inside, back upstairs where Elaine now slept again.

The view from the window was not heartening. In the lane beyond the blackened, burning grass, stood many of the sick. They were still, merely watching the house. Waiting.

The grass was burning low now, the fuel almost used up. The pit also still burned, but was useless as a deterrent, being now full to overflowing with inert bodies.

The sky grew lighter.

One by one the afflicted filed into the garden. Dresses and trousers caught light, but now others reached the door unscathed and began their ceaseless pounding.

Johnson and Mr. Alders checked their guns and took their places at the head of the stairs. The women watched from the bedroom where they had passed the night.

They waited.

The first board splintered. This was soon widened to a hole through which dead eyes and hungry mouths could be seen.

The sisters and their mother huddled together, sure that despite all their efforts, the end was near.

"What's that?" Elaine asked.

"What, dearest?" Mrs. Alders said.

Elaine pulled free of her mother's embrace and stood at the window. "Horses."

Katy joined her. "I cannot hear… Wait! She is right, it sounds like a whole troupe of horses."

All four women gathered before the window. Katy began to wave and shout as the first of the riders came into view. The others soon joined in and were not slowed by the sound of the first gunshot behind them.

The riders, soldiers by their uniforms, stopped in the lane, shooting any of the sick who stood before them. The commander waved the majority of the troupe on, and they continued toward Hartford Hall and the village. Six men remained after the commander followed the main group, but they had guns and put them to good use. The afflicted fell, being fired upon from within and without. Some struggled to rise up again, and they received more shot for their trouble until finally, all lay still.

"Hallo in there!" a soldier called. "Are you hurt?"

The Alders, servants, and Lt. Johnson cautiously made their way out into the garden. Johnson approached the soldiers with recognition, and a friendly reunion was observed by the family. He returned to the Alders, grouped by the smashed front door. "This is the remainder of my regiment. We were sent here to look into the reports filed by Colonel Foster's man, and now that we know what we are up against, we will quarantine the area. You should be safe now; we will cleanse the area of these creatures, but you may be restricted to the cottage for a week or two while we ensure the sickness is fully spent." He bowed to Mr. Alders first, then to Katy. "I must thank you for your kindness in offering me escape and shelter last night."

"Thank you, sir," Katy said, and Mr. Alders nodded.

"I will rejoin my men. We go to the village and the surrounding estates."

"Good luck to you."

"Come back and visit us," said Mrs. Alders, looking from the Lieutenant to Katy, then to Millie.

Johnson smiled and saluted. "Ma'am." He turned and ran to the waiting soldiers. Jumping up behind one of them, he saluted again, and with a flurry of hooves, they were gone.

Mr. Alders raised his gun and shot a twitching body, startling the Alders women. "Look at this mess," he said, using the gun barrel to indicate the burned lawn, the bodies, the mud, and finally, the ruined door.

"I think we should thank Katy for saving us," Elaine said, gazing up at her sister and tucking her small hand within Katy's.

"Hah!" said Mr. Alder. It was expressive enough, but he added, "Thank her, eh? For creating all this chaos? For nearly burning the cottage down to the ground with us all still inside? *With my brandy!* Hah!" He turned and stepped on the broken-in door. It slumped to the ground as the last hinge collapsed. Pausing, he looked over his shoulder at Katy and said, "And where is the money coming from to fix this, I ask you?" He continued on into the cottage, still muttering. Mrs. Alders watched as his back vanished into his study, then she surveyed the lawn.

"So many dead." She came to a decision. "We will have to move. We cannot stay here."

"The soldiers will take care of the sickness, mother," Katy said.

"Oh, it's not that. With so many dead, there will be no chance at all of finding suitable husbands for you here." With that, she followed her husband into the house. Millie, starting to weep at the prospect, ran after her, leaving Katy and Elaine standing hand in hand in the garden. The sisters looked at each other, sharing many unspoken thoughts, then turned their backs on the devastation and joined their family inside the scorched cottage.

Summer of 1816

JAMES ROY DALEY

She was a writer who couldn't focus, couldn't think. The words on the page came slowly, painfully—if they came at all. After an hour and ten minutes, Mary Shelley, frustrated, lowered her head and dropped the pen from her hand, allowing the ink to drip. She slid her high-back chair away from the lavish table an inch, maybe two. She had no concept, no story. Inspiration was thin at best.

It was time to quit with the scribbles, call it a night.

The downpour of rain, the violent lightning, the excessive thunder—these things brought darkness and gloom, painting an image of misery while casting an enormous eclipse over the city. Tonight, like every other night this month, the storm was dominant, making it virtually impossible for Mary to maintain a level of attentiveness or concentration.

Would this storm never end?

Mary knew *why* the weather had become hostile. The Tambora volcano erupted in Indonesia three weeks earlier, spewing 1500 cubic kilometers of ash into the atmosphere. The explosion killed 10,000 people instantly, while another 92,000 were killed by the eruption, and

82,000 died of starvation. In total, 184,000 people were dead. It was the largest eruption in historic time.

Mary knew these facts, most of them anyway. She put two and two together: Big, bad volcano went with big, bad weather. Simple as that.

Some thought the horrific weather conditions marked the beginning of the end, the apocalypse.

Somehow Mary doubted it.

Tapping her fingers on the table, an image floated within the constructs of her mind. It was the face of a friend, Lord Byron.

She closed her eyes, sighed.

Byron was losing his faith in her, and Mary didn't want that. Didn't want the man to mislay his confidence, his belief. The writing circle was all she had, or so it seemed more nights than not. Lord Byron was the biggest part of the writing circle. If he lost faith, cast her aside—what then?

Expelling a deep and shaky breath, Mary visualized a smug look on Byron's face. She imagined him grinning and laughing. Then without realizing it, her hands became fists and her knuckles turned white.

A horror story, Bryon had challenged.

Damn.

Shuffling her thoughts, she considered another friend, another circle member—John Keats. Keats was no smarter than Byron. He was no better. Of course, he did have some good qualities. He was handsome, well dressed, well spoken. He had strong hands, wide shoulders, and a kind face. She thought about Keats from time to time, when she was alone, away from her husband. When she felt needy, adventurous. Mischievous. But she didn't *like* him.

Or did she?

Mary wasn't sure.

John Keats didn't understand Mary Shelly's complexities. He never thought about her, never looked at her the way she looked at him, with ravenous eyes and fervent desire. No. John was too absorbed, and something of a character. He was slain by his own ego, his own designs—filled to the brim with self-esteem, pride and arrogance. To make matters worse, John Keats *loved* Byron's idea of writing a horror story. He adored it.

Mary opened her eyes and unraveled her fists. She looked at the design of the stones beneath her feet and the mug of tea sitting next to her pen. She looked at the unfocused scribbles on the page. The word *disappointing* came to mind; her writing had become sloppy in more ways then one.

I want to stab myself in the heart, she thought uncharacteristically, while fighting the urge to scream out in frustration.

Then, without hesitation, Mary thought of Keats. Again.

* * *

"You solicit the darkness," Keats had said on the heels of Byron making his horror story suggestion. The words rolled off his tongue as if he were an actor in a play. His back straightened. His smile engulfed his face. "And I am but the spark to light that darkness, that malignant imp. A fine and justly wicked proposal. Excellent my dear man, austerely excellent."

Laughter from another room seeped through the doorway.

"Keats," Mary whispered, thinking the laughter to be his.

She felt a knot in her stomach and hated emotions that messed with her thoughts. She had become as confused as a schoolgirl. Sometimes she wanted to embrace Keats. Sometime she wanted to strangle him. Sometimes she wanted to strangle Keats and Byron both.

Her eyes became thin, frightful slits.

They wanted horror.

It occurred to Mary, as she sat away from the desk, that her husband, Percy Shelley, had agreed with the horror story idea as well. He smiled with delight upon hearing it.

What was he thinking?

Was it not bad enough that Mary had fallen in love with Percy, a well-known, married man? Not bad enough that she was guilty of destroying his marriage, and was held responsible for his wife's suicide? Could Percy not see her misfortune, her heartbreak, her turmoil?

Did he not care?

Mary had *too much* horror in her real life. They all knew it. Why in God's name create more?

Her father had disowned her; her sister committed suicide mere weeks ago—two closely related suicides in one year no less. Her marriage was surrounded by fierce public hostility. She was driven out of town. Now, Byron challenges the writing group to create horror?

Horror?

Is he a fool, she wondered. *Or does he secretly hate me?*

With the question came fury, merciless and swift.

Sweeping the pages from the table, Mary leapt up and circled the room. Thoughts and words were complicated inside her mind no more. Her thoughts were flowing, burning. If she had an ax, she would split the table in two. No—in four! She would drop the blade as many times as she could, until blisters in her fingers were created and blood dripped from her hands.

Her muscles tightened; her teeth clenched.

Needing a drink more than she ever had in her nineteen years, Mary checked the cabinet on the far side of the room. Sometimes a bottle of wine would be there, sometimes two or three.

Today there were none.

Didn't matter. She didn't want wine. Not really. She wanted something harder, something cutting. She needed time alone, time away from the group and the castle they were residing in. Time to think, time away from this hell she now called home.

The thought of sneaking off to the Orchid Street Pub had barely crossed Mary's mind when a snap of lightning lit the sky, illuminating the castle's giant wall of windows. She glanced through the glass and peeked outside.

Streets had become rivers. Valleys had turned to ponds. It was another intense August evening, muggy and humid, rainy and gusty.

Was a drink really worth the trek?

Mary crossed the room, approaching the hallway door with slow, cautious steps. She placed her ear against the thick of the door. Listened. Heard nothing, then voices. She heard Byron laugh, Keats laugh. She heard Percy speak.

Her small hands became white-knuckled fists.

It was decided. She would go.

Tonight Mary would leave the writing group in search of inspiration and walk the dark, watery streets alone.

* * *

He was a huge man, who looked like a warrior, but served as a grave keeper. His name was Frank, and he sat alone in the Orchid Street Pub. His arms were pythons; his legs were tree trunks. He had an eye with no sight, and a scar the length of a long blade around his neck. With four of his front teeth missing, he appeared to be the largest, meanest man in Europe.

Some thought him to be the largest man in the world.

The cemetery, which sat less than one hundred-twenty yards from the small, empty pub, had the bodies of two men, a woman, and a child rotting inside posh wooden coffins, deep in the basement of the yard's pantheon-style mausoleum. With each passing day, the stench of the dead grew more fetid, more rotted and foul. Rats, disfigured and diseased, would gather around the caskets in distressful numbers. This was no good. Graves needed to be dug.

Frank understood this, but was getting nothing accomplished. He couldn't work in this weather. The storm had lasted three weeks. It was growing stronger, getting worse, and stopping his workday before it began.

He swayed and turned his head.

William the barkeep was sitting on a stool in the corner of the pub cleaning glasses. He looked up, smiling. Then, keeping his hands busy, he eyed Frank, wishing that he would leave.

William didn't want to sit inside a near-empty bar. He wanted to be home, in the company of family. Of course, he would never say anything, not to a man of *Frank's* size. He valued his neck and guarded it watchfully.

Mary opened the door and stepped inside. She was soaked. Her clothing hung from her body like an oversized wet glove. Hair dangled in long, thin strands. Water ran from her chin.

She looks like a drowned cat, William thought, placing a glass on a table. He stepped behind the bar. *And she appears to be alone—how unfortunately odd.*

"My lady," Will said. "What brings you out on a night as dreary and as dreadful as this? Surely you can't be alone."

Mary shook off the rain the best she could. She pulled her hat from her head, slapped it against her leg and made her way across the room. Sitting on a stool not far from Frank, she glanced his way but did not see him.

"My only desire is to be out," Mary said to the barkeep, shifting her meager weight inside her sopping attire, "to be away from those who have cluttered my thoughts and dampened my heart. I am alone— here for the same reason that anyone would come to an establishment such as this, on a night so sodden. To wash the pain and grief from my tired mind, and drink my sorrows away."

"Aye," the barkeep said. "But to be a woman, young and alone? It is not common, nor considered wise. The necropolis sitting but a stone's throw away, is teeming to the gates with brave young women, fearless women, women who died by the cursed ways of the streets."

"I would think it less wise to travel alone on a handsome night," Mary quickly responded, "a night in which the streets were thick with men, intoxicated men. Obtuse men. Tonight there is none of that. There *are* no men. The streets are wet, I question that not, but the streets are safe enough for the likes of me. The pathway is innocent, innocent as it is apt to be. This I reckon to be true."

"Aye," the barkeep said again, seeing the wisdom of Mary's thinking. "Then, my lady of the storm, what shall it be? Perhaps an Irish tea to warm the blood?"

Mary smiled, ran her fingers through her dripping hair. "Perhaps a dry cloth?"

William smirked. "Of course. Let me check the back room. I'll find something for you."

"Thank you."

"Not at all."

As William walked away, Mary's eyes fell upon Frank. For the first time, she *looked* at him, really *looked* at him. His stature sent a shock of anxiety through her body; he seemed more monster than man.

"My name is Mary Shelly. I live down the way."

The words fell from Mary's mouth before she knew she would say them. It was an act of nervousness, not bravery or desire for companionship.

Frank turned toward Mary. He rubbed his giant hand against his chin and grinned. "Are you not fearful of me, woman?"

Mary sat straight, wondering if she had initiated an unwise conversation. A moment passed. "Should I be?"

"Most are."

William re-entered the room and handed Mary a towel.

She thanked him, crushing the fabric against her body, hair, and face. She ordered a glass of scotch. William fetched the drink and Mary paid for it. A moment later, William returned to his stool and lost himself in his work.

"You failed to answer the question." Mary said after taking a pair of sips from her glass. The alcohol burned and soothed as she spoke.

"Aye."

"Well? Will you answer it?"

Keeping his eyes on his drink the grave keeper said, "A woman should be afraid of what gives her fear, be it wise or be it not."

"Yes, of course. But should I fear you?"

Frank's eyes rolled in their hollows, like pool balls into a pocket. "Not of me. I know what I am and what I'm not. I am a man of peace, not anger and violence. Fear me none."

"Oh?"

"Aye."

Mary took another drink. This time the alcohol burned less.

"Then why, might I ask, do you have the look of a man who has seen a great deal of violence? Perhaps you were born with that scar around your neck. Is that so?"

"I was born with no scar," Frank said, his voice becoming quiet. He was not amused.

"So you *do* know violence."

Mary didn't know why she challenged the giant. It seemed unwise, yet for some reason she enjoyed playing with danger.

Frank could see what Mary was doing, the way she was manipulating the conversation. He didn't like it, and he began to ignore her.

He drank from his cup. In time, they drank together in silence.

Frank ordered another drink, as did Mary. William filled both glasses and returned to his work. Then Mary eyed Frank one last time, baiting him with her stare.

Still, Frank didn't budge.

Mary thought her little game with the giant was over. After she had given up all hope of conversation, Frank surprised her, saying, "I have something that would fill your heart black with dread, woman. You need not fear me, foolish girl who walks the streets of a thousand murders—*alone*. But I do hold a key, be it physical, *and* metaphorical. It is the key to the greatest fear I have ever known. It is the face of the serpent, the true hand of shadow."

In mid sip, Mary froze. She lowered her glass, turned her head and swallowed. Her eyes were round and wide. Her lips briefly quivered. "What did you say?"

"You know what I said, woman. You heard my words, and know their meaning."

"The hand of shadow?"

"Aye."

"The face of the serpent?"

Frank nodded, grinned. "Aye."

Mary expelled a great breath. Putting an arm on the bar rail, she whispered, "Lucifer? Lucifer of the fallen angels?"

Frank pulled himself away from his drink, seeing Mary with the only eye with which he could see.

He shrugged.

"Where?" Mary snapped.

If Frank had consumed less alcohol, he would have said nothing. Instead he spoke without considering the consequence. "Not here, woman. In the mausoleum."

"You lie." Mary quickly spat with anger growing inside.

"I do not lie."

"You do! You wish to lure me there—to bury me after having raped and killed me! I am a scholar, and not easily fooled. I know the likes of you and your kind. You are not a man. You are a beast!"

Frank had had enough of Mary's insults. He slammed his hand on the bar, spilling his drink. "You've asked me if I'd seen battle, and I did not answer. But I shall answer you now. Yes! I *have* seen battle. I see battle every week of my life. A man my size can know not peace. I am a target, a marked man. I am the man others wish to knock down, to prove themselves men. They come at me often, drunk and brainless—like *you* woman, like you. They come alone at first, then in packs. The violence—it's always the same. I find bloodshed and carnage waiting at every corner around which I turn. I long for peace. I swear it, I do. But I shall never find peace. Not with the likes of you, and not until someone strikes me down. I shall not find harmony and serenity until I am dead, though my heart longs for its calm and tranquil shores. I pray for a life of peace, though I shall never get it."

Seething with anger, Frank turned away, wanting to smash something.

Mary gasped. She was speechless; she was touched. The giant man was no ogre. He was intelligent, educated and passionate. He spoke like a scholar, a teacher, a poet. Seconds passed, and Mary felt the overwhelmingly bitter sense of shame. "A book should not be judged by its cover," she said. "Nor should man. I am sorry and ashamed. You have done nothing to make me believe that you are a creature of violence, yet it was the conclusion to which I arrived. I feel a fool."

Frank groaned like an animal. He said, "Don't bother. This cross is mine to bear, not yours. Just leave me be."

"But a man does not choose the size to which he grows. He grows until the Lord commands it not."

"I suppose."

"It is true. I've known it, yet I was blind. Blind like a bat in the night. Again, I am sorry, truly sorry."

"Forget it, woman. It's nothing."

Mary finished her drink, and William poured them another. Time passed. Then changing her tone, she said, "The face of the serpent?"

"Aye."

"Will you show me?"

Frank closed his eyes. If Mary had been nicer to him, he would have said *no*. Instead, spite encouraged a nod of his head. "Aye."

Mary shifted her weight, moved closer. "How can I be sure that your intentions are pure? I am a young woman, of nineteen years. I have been called beautiful. Most men considered noble would find themselves swimming with impure thoughts."

"I am not most men."

"Yes, yes, of course. But how do I know?"

Frank swallowed half his ale. "William!" he said. "Come."

William slipped off his stool, and approached the couple. "Another ale to warm the gullet?"

"No."

"No?" Will seemed puzzled. "Then what is it?"

"You know me?"

"Aye, that I do."

"Be truthful now. Do men, women, and children fear me?"

William leaned back; stroked his chin lightly. "You are a man of great stature, of great physical strength. I believe they fear you."

"You've seen me fight?"

William nodded. "Aye."

"Have I ever picked a fight, picked one with a man who did not ask?"

"No. Not one. Men seem drawn."

Frank glanced at Mary. "Have you seen me harm a woman or a child?"

"I have not."

"Am I known to *be* a man that harms women, children?"

"No." William said. "You are not."

"Thank you William."

"Not at all, Mr. Stein. Would you like another ale?"

"No thank you. I believe we are finished here. Isn't that right, *woman*?"

Mary bobbed her head. "Aye."

As William returned to his stool, Frank said with a doubtful tone, "I am to show you then?"

"The hand of shadow?"

Frank tapped a dirty finger against his dead eye. "The face of the serpent."

* * *

They walked through the burial ground as rain bounced off the tombstones, created lakes, drowned the grass and drilled holes in the mud. Frank led the way, finding the highest ground, where the ponds were shallow beneath his feet. They approached the mausoleum, which sat near the center of the cemetery. Made of sandstone, the building was of considerable size, larger than most houses. Trees and shrubbery were plentiful around both sides of the structure. Headstones were abundant, separated only by Christian statues and stone pathways. Smooth, slippery steps led to a six-pillar entry, centered by a tall black door with a long brass handle. Some thought the handle looked like gold.

Frank approached the door and produced a ring of keys, also made of brass. As he shuffled through them, Mary waited patiently. Frank found the appropriate key, slid it into the keyhole.

They stepped inside.

The crypt was a great hall with several rooms on each side. The air was musty, stale, and polluted with the stench of death. On the floor, mice scattered. Against the wall, unlit torches sat bundled together on a shelf, next to a dozen long, hand carved matchsticks.

Frank lifted a match from the shelf. He dipped it into a small asbestos bottle, which had been filled with sulfuric acid. The match ignited. Using the tiny flame, he lit a torch, and handed it to Mary. Then he lit another torch, which he kept for himself. The burning torches revealed an elaborate portrait on the ceiling. The stones became an everchanging flicker of cherry red faces and beautiful landscapes, the toils of an unknown artist.

Frank walked past the empty rooms, and approached a staircase. Mary followed.

"To the basement," Frank said, running fingers through his sopping wet hair. He briefly pulled his shirt away from his body, hating the way it felt.

"Is it here?" Mary asked with a growing sense of fear.

"Aye, that it is. The face of the serpent is in the cellar, near the base of the stairs. As you may or may not know, this crypt was a jail in secret for many years. Or so it has been said."

"Not a secret. I've heard those rumors since I was small. This is true of a great many mausoleums."

"But things are different now. I've worked the grave a long while, and known not a single man kept in the dungeons of this place. That time has come and gone, it seems. Until…"

"Until now."

"Aye."

Mary coughed twice and stroked her fingers along her dress. "The hand of shadow—this is a man in a cage?"

Frank grinned. "It is no man. But there is something locked in that cage. In fact, there are four of them."

"Four?"

"Aye. Four demons. Spawned from hell, the dark abyss, with skin rotting and eyes washed in the depths of fire. They don't breathe. They don't eat. They don't talk. They just wait, observing the living as the skin rots from their bones. And how they moan. It sounds appalling, abysmal."

Mary looked shocked. Her mouth hung wide, like her jaw had been broken. Finally she snapped her lips shut and said, "How did they come to be here, these creatures of anguish?"

"They came on the day the storm began, all of them. Loved ones brought three. The other came from the hospital. They were just people then, dead people—nothing new for a place like this. I put each body in a coffin when it arrived, as I always do. A service was given in the rooms upstairs. We do that sometimes, if the weather is bad, or if it is requested. We charge more for an indoor service so it is not called for often, and when the storm breaks—which usually takes no more than a day or two—we bury the deceased in the yard with the others. But in that time between the service and the burial, we keep the bodies downstairs, locked in a cell."

"Locked? Why locked? They're dead, are they not?"

"Yes, of course. But from time-to-time there have been thieves. They break the door, come for jewelry, or the gold in their teeth. At some point I stopped leaving the corpses upstairs. I bring them to the cellar now and lock them away." Frank giggled without happiness. "This time, something peculiar happened. Perhaps the storm brought it on. I do not know. Strange time this is. No dead since the storm arrived. None that I know of, anyway."

An odd droning hum came from the basement.

"What is that?" Mary asked.

"It is the dead. They have opened their eyes, woman. They have risen." Frank sighed. "I know not why you've come this far. You must be mad. But it is not too late to turn away. Satan has not seen your face yet."

Mary huffed. She wanted to leave but needed to see. "Can I leave whenever I decide to?"

"You can leave now. I shall not stop you."

"No. Not yet. I long to see. I need to know."

"I know why *I* come here," Frank said. "I come to see that all remains well, but you? Why? Why place yourself within the grasp of a demon? Do you not fear your soul to blacken, your heart to wither?"

"You would not understand."

"But I would."

"No!" Mary said, louder than intended. Immediately she wished she had remained silent.

"Have I instilled no trust in that mind of yours? Am I so obtuse?"

"No."

"Then why would I not understand? Is it because I am a man?"

Mary wondered what to say, what to do. And she was afraid. If Frank wanted to hurt her, it would be easy now. No one would see or hear. Help would not come. She was alone with the giant, and at his mercy. He could tear her head from her neck with his bare hands. He could snap her arm like a dry stick.

Mary shuffled her conflicting thoughts.

Frank seemed trustworthy. She sensed no hostility from him. He was another tortured soul, like she was. He was an innocent and locked inside the prison of his own body. She hoped.

"If you must know," Mary whispered, as if the demons in the basement were listening, "I am a writer on a quest, in pursuit of inspiration. I've been asked to write a horror story, but find I am without insight. My mind works in tragedy, for mine is a life of misfortune. My sister died three weeks ago, and still I cannot summon a tale of horror. If you were to show me the face of the serpent, the hand of shadow..."

"You will write it."

Mary winced. "Perhaps, perhaps not. Seeing the hand of shadow is not a tale in itself. There is no love interest, no conflict. I need inspiration, not obscure news banter."

Frank nodded, turned, and walked down the stairs. "Then my dear, you shall see the true face of horror."

* * *

Mary followed along, entering the basement upon heavy legs. She heard growling and moaning. A putrid smell made her stomach turn. Reaching the bottom step she realized that the rainwater had made its way inside somehow. The floor was littered with puddles.

Frank lifted his torch. He nodded and turned away.

"Are you to leave me?" Mary asked.

With the sound of her voice, the moaning and growling stopped dead.

"Yes. The demons are here. They remain secure. That is all I need to know. Do not stand close to the cell and you shall remain unharmed."

Frank disappeared up the stairs.

Mary took a step. Then another. The cell was within an arm's length now, but she could see nothing unusual.

"Hello?"

No answer. Silence.

Mary moved closer than Frank had suggested. She held the torch against the bars and felt a chill. The cell seemed full of ice.

Then a boy appeared. He moved without speaking, without breathing. His fingers were long and thin. His stomach was bloated. Recessed eye sockets were drawn and dark. Ten years old and soulless, with skin that had turned from light and fair to black and purple. The eyes were red, shocking red, like glistening orbs of blood.

Looking into those eyes, Mary could see that the boy was not human, not now. He had the pupils of a demon, a serpent. Nothing from this earth could lurk behind those chilling red orbs, those deep haunting spheres.

Looking closer, Mary realized that she was not looking into the eyes of a single demon. She was looking at hundreds of demons—perhaps thousands, millions—all living inside the corpse-child together.

And *he* was the cold one. The chill was coming from inside *him*.

Mary stepped away.

A man and a woman crept forward. Both were stinking, rotting. It was obvious that the man had been killed in some type of accident. His head was split open. The gray matter from his brain had leaked down his neck. The woman was tall with long dark hair. Her dress was torn open; her wilting breasts were exposed. Rope marks circled her neck.

The corpse woman grinned. Pointed. She began to laugh with a multitude of voices. Her voice was a carnival of living death—an eerie rattling grind, a handful of sticks pressed against the slow moving spokes of a coach wheel.

Mary's eyes widened. Her legs felt weak.

"No," she said, her tone overflowing with pain. "Dear God, no! This cannot be!"

A forth corpse approached, limping on a broken leg. It lifted a gnarled hand as murky dribble flowed from its tattered mouth.

A moment later, Mary ran for the staircase screaming.

* * *

Frank waited by the front door for his guest to return. It didn't take long. Within two minutes she came to him. Her face was shocked; her skin looked bleached.

Frank said, "So, Mary the brave, the fool, did you find what you were looking for? Did you find inspiration deep inside the tomb of the living dead?"

"That I did," Mary replied, with a trembling voice. A shaky hand wiped tears from her checks.

"Will you write the first great novel of horror, or was this blackening of your soul for nothing?"

"I do not know, nor do I care. I found more than I had bargained for, inside that cursed cellar of yours. I care not if I write another word. This event has shaken me to my core, my foundation."

"I warned you."

"No, Mr. Stein, you don't understand. The woman in the basement, the one that had been hanged; her name is Fanny Imlay. She is my sister."

* * *

In time Mary thanked Frank, left the mausoleum and walked home alone. She was already wet, so the rain didn't bother her; however, the dark roads and alleyways did. She kept thinking that *something* was watching her.

Something dead.

It was a little after one in the morning when Mary arrived home. She entered through the castle's back door, the servant's entrance. She had left it unlocked.

A fresh change of clothing and a dry pair of shoes later she was in her room, safe and sound. No one realized she had left. The event took less than three hours.

After tidying her desk and lifting the scattered paper from the floor, Mary placed a fresh sheet of paper in front of herself and surrounded herself with candles. She dipped her pen into her inkbottle, smiled nervously, and began to write:

It was on a dreary night of November that I beheld the accomplishment of my toils. With an anxiety that almost amounted to agony, I collected the instruments of life around me, that I might infuse a spark of being into the lifeless thing that lay at my feet. It was already one in the morning; the rain pattered dismally against the panes, and my candle was nearly burnt out, when, by the glimmer of the half-extinguished light, I saw the dull yellow eye of the creature open.

She wrote those few words, no longer caring about Keats, Byron and Percy—what they were thinking, what they were saying. Her inspiration had been found. The first paragraph had been written.

A year later, in May of 1817, *Frankenstein* was completed. It was published January 1, 1818, and although she didn't know it then, her words would outlive them all.

The Hell Soldiers

Juleigh Howard-Hobson

The bend in the river was leafy and green with old trees that hung their thick branches out and over. The shadows were almost black at some points along the bank, spreading gradually to grey green, then dappling away into nothing by the middle of the water. The sunlight sparkled gold and white on the dark waters. The bank was deep. It consisted of sand and mud and rock, climbing up to a granite wall topped with an earthy ledge where the trees began their crowded presence.

It was a good place to hide. It was a good place to find myself hidden. If any place was good anymore.

The battle had been raging for three days just a few miles down river. The stink of sulphur and gunpowder reached the small bank and hung in its tree-walled air. The smell of death hung there too. Other smells, that I didn't notice at first, came to me as I got used to the overarching stench of burning weaponry and rotting meat—smells of blood, of charred flesh, of fear—they came too.

Came and settled in the bend.

Still, though, smells aren't the same as the things that make the smells. A man can live with stink, with stench, with ripe odors that tug the gut until his ability to ignore them is made so strong that the stink can't reach deep inside anymore. Just like a door getting closed. A window shut.

Daniel Stampley knew if he waited long enough he would cease to smell the slow, filthy decay of his brothers in arms. Stampley also hoped if he stayed where he was, in this hidden bend on this backwater river, deep in these wooded hills that no man so far had bothered to turn into farmland or chop down for wood, he could wait out everything.

The Ninth Virginia Infantry, his unit, was all gone or as good as gone. That last battle was the end of them. There hadn't been many to start with. Not in this battle. Not now.

Most of them were picked off back when they crossed with Union snipers a month ago toward the end of winter. Hemmed in by Yankee sharpshooters, flanked by Yankee artillery. For two weeks while snow came down and rain washed blood into the narrow creeks that surrounded the area, the Virginia farm boys fell, one by one or in messy bloody knots of frightened men, to the snapping report of rifles or to the gut thundering roar and thud of cannon fire.

No matter what they were doing—getting water, using the outhouse, burying another soldier—they did it with the knowledge that death could fall any second, any minute, from anywhere. Sometimes one of them would be outside, ordered to stand guard or hunt whatever small prey still lived in the closest lot of blasted trees, and he would disappear. Nothing left of him. Hunted down and gone. Silently. Completely.

There was no fighting back. The enemy was invisible, all knowing, all seeing, unkillable. At least they seemed like that.

Then they went away. The men who were left in the Ninth woke up one morning to pale sunshine and asparagus shoots pushing up from the ground.

But no death.

No death by the well when water was being drawn out by a man who waited for it with gut wrung and shoulders hunched. No death by the woodpile for the men who lifted each piece waiting for the sharp crackle and final burst of lung. No death by the outhouse. No death by the close edge of trees where squirrels chattered and looked down from thickly scarred branches while ragged men too thin for their uniforms took unsteady aim with slingshot and pistol at the small animals that stood between them and starvation.

No cannon balls came. No bullets came. Nothing came to take the men away to death. Spring flowers showed their pink and yellow faces to the sun. Weeds and grasses waved bright green leaves in breezes that hinted of warm days and the sun reached higher into the sky, lightening the dark forest, changing it more each day from a black expanse to a brown copse.

The Yankees had disappeared, leaving all that was left of the Ninth behind. Not many of the surviving men stopped to wonder why. Why'd do such a thing? Especially now, now that the air and the earth were warm and it would be comfortable and easy to sit in the forest and kill every man . It would be a pleasant task, a barrel shoot, an easy victory. But the enemy didn't take it. They simply went away.

So the Ninth pressed on.

Westward, across and down to the places where the farms no longer stood. Down to the places where the woods were shattered, and the creeks were filmed with slimy muck, choked and clogged with swollen bodies in winter uniforms, hair swaying in the small ripples that pushed through past the dead flesh and rusting weapons. Down to where the banks were clawed and churned by hands long since drowned and fallen back into the stink of the creek, and the shadows fell jagged and stark and there was nowhere to look that had not been turned into a staging area of death, of battle, of war.

Before this war these places would have been different. Their smell would have been of earth freshly turned for planting, of newly born colts and calves that cropped sweet grasses with their mothers in fields sunny and warm, dotted with wild flower and alive with the assorted sounds of bees and crickets and small birds. The creeks would have been sparkling fresh with a small urgent rushing sound to them as the spring thaw brought new waters down from the snow-melt in the hills to fill them gently to the tops of their low banks.

There would have been the noise of peace time—men yelling "Hey!" to plow beasts, laundry flapping, cart wheels creaking, perhaps children and women coming out to make their mark on their world. Laughter. Gentle voices. Contented animals.

But this was not before the war anymore. These places were only for the dead now. Cold. Still. No sounds except the sounds of the men who passed through these places, their marching no longer regular, their steps no longer proud. The slow-paced plod of men who have no wish to go any further, but must. The slow death march of men who know they have survived too much but have not survived enough. A column of men not yet battle dead, but close.

Hungry. Tired. There was no food to be found. There was no place to rest here. They must just get through it. They must get past this barren, blasted spot, to a place not yet barren, not yet blasted. They must march.

They were ordered to continue until they came to a big river.

The river—least wise the section they would come upon—was wide and deep and hemmed in on both banks by woods and un-pathed wildness. It was a part of the river that had no bridge yet, and that must not have a bridge built upon it. The Yankees would love to cross the river there, to ford it, and then to bridge it, so they could roll their cannon across, march their troops over.

Fresh troops. New men coming everyday from ships that brought strong men from Ireland, from Europe, from across the ocean, to the northern ports where they became Union soldiers before they touched the streets of the new country they swore to defend. Men who were not yet tired out from this war.

So they must not have a bridge they could cross.

When the Ninth arrived at the big river, it was afternoon. The sun was high, the air carried no chill, the ground no damp. The river they could see was not a river of death. There were no battle signs. There were no upturned carts. No horses, gut torn and kicking. No scattered bloodied traces of men and boys. The Ninth had seen many—too many—soldiers blown to nothing more than parts that weren't good enough to be called meat.

If Stampley closed his eyes, he could see things he didn't want to see. Unbidden, the images presented themselves to him in the darkness of his shut lids. A hank of bloody blond hair hanging from the side of a flesh peeled and shattered head. A bloodless white hand with the thumb torn off, ending in a grizzled red knot of wrist joint. A leg still bleeding in its grey woolen uniform, dangling from a shattered tree trunk, carried up into the tall pines by a cannon ball and left where it had been caught.

And other things.

Things no living man should see.

An old churchyard, riddled with cannon balls. The old stones blown apart and the gutted ground forced to shake loose what it had long held in a deep embrace. Unearthed coffins and desiccated corpses splayed on the rutted surface of the little grounds where horses and men had thundered over and across, splintering and pulverizing whatever fell between them and the earth. The Ninth coming upon this cemetery two days after the melee and seeing wounded men, dying men and newly slain men left mixing with the cloying dust of the long ago dead.

All that bodily remained of a red haired union soldier lying in a small hollow on the edge of a field that the Ninth plodded through, his skull caved in, his flesh chewed and torn from the bones by whatever animal had dragged him in there.

A pile of gnawed human shanks lying in a nest of last autumn's leaves and the rotten shards of homespun grey linen.

Teeth marks on the ends of arms and legs of the dead who lay bloated and blue and rotting damply in the creeks.

Stampley shook his head, trying to clear the visions from his mind. For the time being at least. But the image of the bear bites wouldn't budge. They stayed stuck in his head, vivid and bright. And wrong. But how wrong? They were bear marks. They had to be bear marks; the pattern was like no panther bite Stampley had ever seen.

Stampley shook his head again and this time drove the image out as he thought about bears and where they would hide when a battle raged and razed the woods and blasted caves and underhangs. Perhaps in the new holes made by the blasts.

It made little difference in the end. Bear or not bear. Dead men were dead men, and Stampley had had his fill of them.

The section of the river where the bridge had not been built had not stayed serene for long. The Yankees arrived, more Yankees than the Ninth ever thought were possible. They arrived in long lines of blue that stretched out past the trees, across the dusty fields and down past the curves of the far off hills. Who knew how many were back there, behind those far off hills?

The Yankee soldiers arrived without cessation for the whole day. They assembled themselves across the river and set up stout tents and hot fires. Soup pots and spits strung with rabbit, squirrel and other game soon sputtered in front of the tents.

The tired and worn Ninth watched fitfully, from where they were camped without fire, without food, hidden in the thick brush that grew beneath the trees. Some were driven half crazy by the smells of the Yankee cook fires, the aromas of real coffee mingling with vapors of roast meat, breeze-borne across that river and right into the cold food-less encampment of the ragged Confederates. If it was an encampment at all. More like just a place where men no longer marched, but dropped on their blanket rolls and stayed, unseen but not unseeing.

A lean man with dark unkempt hair that clung damply to his pale brow was the first man to die on that side of the river. He died quietly and without dramatics, his throat slit by their captain.

Stampley knew the dead man, Harlon McBride, from before the war; he was a good man, had a wife, three young ones, but still, Stampley knew it had to be done. McBride had begun licking his lips and quivering his nostrils early on, and by midday he had a small cluster of fellows ready to swim against the odds and the current and grab whatever it was over there the Yankees were cooking.

Stampley would have let him go, let them all go, let them go get their asses shot off halfway across the river, except he wasn't the captain and except that their asses weren't the only ones going to get shot. The Yankees had no inkling the Ninth was there, and Stampley sensed the captain aimed to keep it that way as long as he could. No one said the words, but the idea of *maybe them Yankees would just move on in the morning, maybe they weren't here to build no bridge*, hung like a fitful hope in the air around them.

Maybe the Ninth would wake up to nothing more than birdsong and damp fog on the other side. After all, this had happened before, them Yankees just up and going away, so the idea of *"maybe"* had to be worth something.

Worth more than a skinny assed dirt farmer with no more sense in him than a panther in season anyways.

So Stampley had no bones with what had to be done. As McBride dropped dead, and was quietly dumped into the edges of the under-brush, the rest of the men who reckoned they'd make some of that Yankee food their own, melted back into the hungry shadows.

"Wait," was all that the captain said to them.

Wait. And they waited. While the daylight bled away into grey chilly damp mists. While the mists slowly became black night. While the cold of the river ran across the tree line and settled down to cloak the Ninth.

The smells of those Yankee cook fires were a constant torment. And the noises. The assorted noises—horses nickering, men smoking, men talking, men playing, while the Ninth leaned fitfully on muscle-sprung haunches and were made aware of all they did not have. Would probably never have again, seeing as most of them would die here, fighting, if not well fed, at least somewhat fed Yankee soldiers. So they spent that night, their first night there—for many, their last night any-where—by that river with no bridge.

When the morning light came beaming down weakly from in be-tween the high branches, it showed the dead man still laying there, half-hidden in the edge of the underbrush, the damp soil beneath him sticky with blood. His limbs tilted at angles not made by any man but a dead one.

One big tall fellow walked toward the body. Weller, the man's name was. He walked slowly, pulling his belt in, sucking his teeth, saying if he weren't going to get no food, at least he weren't going to be made sick at the sight of McBride lying there all day—ain't no decent man could do that, no matter how the bastard died.

"Better git something to use for a shovel then, Weller, if you think-ing of burying him. Collins, Rice—you two, up and help him find him-self a shovel," the captain said distractedly.

The three men shuffled off, toward where the trees ended and the bank began, looking for a suitable branch or root.

"Take care to keep hidden now."

Stampley watched, too tired and too hungry to care much beyond realizing he wasn't a decent man anymore because he didn't care if McBride laid there until hell froze, he wasn't going to waste any energy to dig a hole for him.

The first tendrils of coffee-scented air were starting to reach the Ninth's side of the river. Stampley wondered idly if bacon was something the Yankees had with them. Bacon, maybe ham, maybe some johnnycakes. Hot biscuits too, with butter and honey.

His mind wandered back to breakfasts he had had before the war took men like him away from things like breakfast. He tried to remember whether his wife had ever made cornpone or if it was his mother who used to serve it, cut up and fried in drippings. He thought of how his wife would cook up fried eggs, cooked till they were crispy on their white edges, and how their yolk would stay golden and creamy, until it broke and spread across...

There was yelling. Too much yelling. It cut through Stampley's famished daydreams and he reached for his rifle.

The men had returned from the tree edge, having found a root with a scoop-like end to it that would shift damp earth easily enough. But the root was lying on the ground, they weren't digging with it. They were yelling. One of them was shrieking and pointing at McBride.

Stampley could hear the noise carry over the water. The captain reached the man before he did, and punched him in the face. The shrieks stopped abruptly; the man crumpled over and began rocking silently, holding his hands to his face. But the yelling continued with the two others, and the rest of the Ninth were coming over, pulling their tired bodies up out of the bushes where they had set up hastily rigged shelters, and coming over.

Stampley looked down at where they were all staring.

There was the body of McBride alright, at least wise, most of McBride. But where the top of him should have been, there was none. The fingers were gone too—chewed off, it looked like. Bits of hair, skin, blood, meat, bone were all over the bottom of the bushes where McBride's head and neck and some of his shoulders should have been. There was spoor.

Looked like man spoor.

Had to be panther shit.

Maybe.

A younger soldier began puking, just hawing and heaving. He had nothing in his gut to puke up.

The soldier who had been punched in the face began laughing—a shrill, high laugh. As Stampley stared at him, the man fell over on his side, his laughter coming to an end as he began rambling, talking fast and loud, like a man with a demon inside of him, "Them things got him. Them things got him. I tol' them they was things in there. They done and got him. They been eating all along. But not this close... now they gonna get us... now they gonna get us all... yes they will, all of us now..." He began to keen and shriek. "All! All!"

A rumble, like thunder clapping on a close-by mountain, and then the swift, roaring, hot *thud-thud-thud* of cannon balls ripped into the Ninth's makeshift bivouac.

The men scattered. McBride's body disintegrated under a direct hit. The shrieking man went with him, forever gone with a split second's roar and blast.

Stampley threw himself to the ground, rolling out of the way into the shelter of the bigger trees, back beyond the encampment. Cannon balls hit the river bank, the bushes, and the provisional sleeping areas that the Ninth had occupied. The sounds of tearing and crushing, men screaming and dying, began to fill the morning air.

Hidden by a tangle of bush vines and a thick wall of overhanging willow branches, Stampley readied himself to fight. He loaded his rifle. He gritted his teeth. Keeping down low and making no sound, Stampley dug in and waited for whatever it was that was going to come to get at him first—the man-eating panther, or the Yankee army.

It was the armies that came.

The Yankees first. How they got there so fast, Stampley couldn't rightly tell. There was still no bridge, but there they were. He could see them coming in from beyond the fringe of the trees, dripping wet, bayonets gleaming. The Yankees, masses of them, faces expressionless, had gotten to the encampment.

Already. Right there.

And, coming in from behind the trees, from somewhere on the other side of the encampment, from out of the thick growth there, there came men clad in the same uniform that Stampley wore. More Rebel soldiers than Stampley thought were in those parts, more than Stampley had seen, moving, in a long time.

His first impulse was a glad jubilation at the sight, but something about them made him still, made him feel guarded and watchful at the sight of the Confederate soldiers coming in from the darkness of the forest. They, like the Yankees, were expressionless.

Union and Confederate—they were both there, faces pale and blank, the men moving with strange jerks and twitches. They swallowed up the tiny ragged fragment that was the Ninth as they fell to their fighting. Sudden, fierce, terrible fighting.

It was not fighting like Stampley had ever seen fighting. Leastwise between men.

Cannon and the few frightened shots his fellow Ninth were able to squeeze off were the only things that made Stampley know for sure that this thing he was seeing was not some delirium caused by a damp cold night on a stomach filled with nothing more than jerky and a few huckleberries.

Because this fighting was not soldiering-fighting. Not man-fighting. This fighting was tearing. This fighting was pulling. This fighting was soldier falling upon soldier and biting, clawing, tearing, rending and shrieking. Like dogs but not like any dogs Stampley had known. These were like hell dogs.

He could see that there was red flesh flying, chunks of it being torn and chewed out of each other, but there was no blood coming out of the wounds or the meat. There were hands and ears and innards being torn away from bodies, but it didn't stop them. They went at each other. Earless or with rib cage torn right open so the guts of them was hanging out, they kept on chawing and clawing at each other.

Bloodlessly.

Like nothing Stampley had ever seen.

Didn't seem to matter how much of them was hurt, the soldiers clad in blue or gray grasped and grappled their opposites and pulled and bit and chewed upon each other, and they both set upon any of the Ninth they happened upon.

Yankee or Johnny Rebel, Stampley couldn't see any difference in who would set upon the men of the Ninth and rip them apart. The hell soldiers went for the limbs of his fellow soldiers first, and then they'd split the heads open like they were no more than oyster shells, and with both their hands inside the men they would pull the brains right out and start chawing on them.

The dual metallic tangs—fear and blood—released by the dying Ninth seemed to Stampley to drive the hell soldiers into pitched frenzies. They tore and dove at each other to get at pieces of the freshly killed men. The brains of them, especially. Grey or blue, whole or hacked away, it didn't matter; the hell men pushed each other away to get some of the Ninth in their mouths.

Were they just crazy from being starved? If they were, Stampley never saw crazy like that before, so crazy they kept fighting each other with no legs left, snapping and biting in the dust, dribbling blood of the Ninth infantry out of their mouths.

Stampley made no sound. Stampley slowly backed away. Every moment that he backed he wondered what he would be backing into.

This was no cowardice impelling him; this was no act of self-survival perpetrated at the cost of his fellow men. There were no fellows left back in the encampment—least ways none that would get out of there. He saw about half a dozen pulled to pieces right there in the first few minutes. How long could the others last, if they were still alive now at all?

From across the river, the cannon balls kept arriving, heaving their chaos into the fray. The heavy artillery drowned the shrieking with its thunderous roaring, and it sent pieces of charred flesh—blood, bone and brain—high in the air.

The hell soldiers, some of them, raised their battered faces in the din and, sniffing the air, chased after the large bits of blown men as the cannon explosions ended.

They came close—too close—to Stampley.

He froze.

But the smell of the cooked flesh, the sulphur and the burning camp was stronger than the scent of one man. They didn't find him. This time.

They would though, if he stayed. It was only a question of when. There were so many of them, and they were fighting and fanning out as he watched. Already spreading their territory of gore into the first undergrowth around where the Ninth had spent the night.

Stampley stopped backing up slowly. Stampley got down on all fours and he skittered forward like a rat as fast as he could go. He skittered and he slid and he forced himself across that forest floor, hitting face first into thorny berry vines, stumbling with his bare hands across fetid patches of what were probably other confederate soldiers once, catching his knees and palms on roots and jutting rocks, but he kept going.

He didn't stop.

He didn't look back. He didn't quit until he couldn't feel the ground shake with cannon balls. Until he couldn't smell burned human meat and bone and hair anymore. Until the shrieks and screams had faded then receded into nothing and didn't come back. Until he had found a place where the river doubled back on itself and he had to scrabble down its banks by way of a sheer granite rock face it had carved itself into.

Then he stopped.

The bend in the river was leafy and green with old trees that hung their thick branches out and over. The shadows were almost black at some parts on the banks, spreading gradually to grey green, then dappling away into nothing by the middle of the water. The sunlight sparkled gold and white on the dark waters. He'd been there, in the secluded river bend, for three days now. Eating green huckleberries, and raw crawfish he caught as they came to inspect the bits of scabs he dropped in the water from his knees.

Every so often, along with the rank sourness of death, the wind brought the shrieks of the hell soldiers. Sometimes it seemed to him like the shrieks were louder, closer, than they were the time before. Once he thought he could hear the captain's voice, calling him by name.

Stampley knew that a man's mind could play tricks in a place like this, but he knew that if he could stay hidden, he would be all right. Just so long as they didn't know he was there.

So long as the wind didn't change and bring his scent back where they were.

Stampley shivered despite the fact that it was mid afternoon, shivered and wondered how long he had, waiting there....

Junebug

REBECCA BROCK

I t's almost soothing, waking up in the warm dark. I can hear Momma singing "Amazing Grace" somewhere far away from me. I listen for a while, waiting for Daddy to join in on the second verse, the way he always did in church. I always loved his deep voice, even when he couldn't hit the right note or carry the tune. He sang for God's glory, he always used to say, so it didn't matter how good it sounded. I always thought it sounded pretty.

I don't know where I am. I'm not in my bed. It's hard beneath my back, like lying on the floor. When I raise my hand I feel rough wood right on top of me. Like a coffin.

But that's not right. Can't be right. I'm not dead.

The day we heard the news, almost a month after Mr. Lincoln's War ended, Momma dropped to her knees and started praying and thanking God for bringing on the Last Days during her lifetime. She made all the kids get down with her, even Ethan, who didn't want to thank God for anything after all he'd seen in the war. Ethan had always been trouble for Momma and Daddy. Before he went off to fight, he always used to argue with them and say they should think for themselves instead of listening to Preacher Hollis down at the End Times Church. Daddy used to take the switch to him for that and whip him 'til the welts on his back started bleeding. He was only nineteen now, but Ethan had always seemed like an old man. He was smarter than everybody in the family, especially me. That's probably why I loved him most of all. And that's exactly why Daddy hated him so.

The singing's coming from above me, Momma's voice leading what's left of the church choir. Now they're singing my favorite hymn, "Just a Closer Walk with Thee." Such a pretty song. I used to like to imagine walking in a garden with Jesus, holding his hand and asking him all kinds of questions about why He did the things He did. Next to Daddy I thought Jesus was the most handsome man I'd ever seen— but I never told nobody that, just in case it was sinful to think of Jesus that way.

I thought about the portrait of Jesus that hung in the hallway of our house. His eyes used to follow me around, like He was watching me special, and I used to curl up underneath it to go to sleep whenever I woke up from a bad dream. I always felt like Jesus loved me more than anybody else in the whole world. Even when the bad things started happening and people started saying mean, sinful things about God and Jesus, I knew He still loved me and my family. And I knew, no matter what anyone said, that it wasn't His fault.

It was mankind that brought on the End Times. Not Jesus.

After the Dead started coming back to life, touched by the glory of God in all His wisdom, everything changed. We lived way back in a hollow, in a part of Tennessee that everybody but the Lord had forgotten about, but we still heard news coming in from people traveling out of the cities. They came to church and testified on Sunday mornings, then they told us what they were seeing out there in the world.

The sickness came out of the North, they said. Out of the cities. Some people said it was God's punishment for winning the war, but I didn't believe that. They said that the bodies of soldiers started getting up on the battlefields and wandering into the towns nearby, hurting anybody who got too close to them. Ethan told me about the things that happened during battle, and I couldn't imagine acres of dead men rising up to walk again. He told me about walking in mud that was made of dirt and blood, trying not to step on the bodies of the men who'd fought beside him just a few minutes before, hearing nothing but screams and explosions and prayers that God wouldn't hear. Ethan always said that God had turned His eyes away from Shiloh that day.

The last news we heard was from Captain Robert Hayes, who was on his way home to Mississippi to find his wife and sons. He'd said that New Orleans was burning, and that no living person remained north of Virginia. He'd seen the Dead massing along the roadways, and it was a sight he wished he would have never witnessed. He said it didn't matter what color a man's skin was, because after he came back from the dead, it all turned the same shade of gray.

Everybody in the church wanted to be baptized again that day after Captain Hayes spoke. After the service, Preacher Hollis walked us all down to the creek and dunked us one more time, just to make sure our souls were saved. Ethan refused to do it, even after Daddy tried to make him. Later that night, after everybody else had gone to sleep, Ethan sat on the porch with me in the dark and said that he didn't think he believed in God no more. He said that he stopped believing as soon as he stepped foot onto the battlefield and realized he was actually going to have to kill somebody. He didn't think that any God he wanted to believe in would make him do that.

After Captain Hayes's news, Daddy knew what to do. He always knew what was best for his family. He told Momma to start gathering up all the food she could and to go ahead and start canning the summer vegetables we grew in the garden. She had me and Suzie and Maryanne to help her out, so it didn't take no time for us to put up a whole bunch of pickles and beets and apples. We kept the potatoes and onions down in the cellar. Daddy and Ethan went out hunting and brought back a couple of bucks and a wild pig that'd been running around the hills. We spent one whole Saturday skinning and cleaning the carcasses so the meat could be smoked and laid up for lean times later.

No matter what happened, Daddy always said, his family was gonna be ready. God provided all.

Something thumps on top of the lid. Daddy. He must have realized that his Junebug was awake and was coming to get me. But then I feel grit sifting down into my eyes, onto my cheeks.

Dirt.

I try to yell but something's not working right in my throat. I move my hand up to my mouth and feel around in the dark. I try to scream again and can't make a sound.

But I don't think it'd matter anyway. I think I'm already under the ground.

We'd always gone to church every Sunday, but after the first few weeks of the End Times, we started going every day. Preacher Hollis wanted his flock close at hand, so we would be together just in case that was the day that God decided that the final trump would blow and Jesus would come back to gather us home. We spent most of the day at the church at the bottom of the hill, just praying and singing hymns and waiting to hear that trumpet.

I didn't mind it too much. I liked Preacher Hollis because he reminded me of Jesus. He had a beard, too, but he cut his hair short because it said in the Bible that only women should have flowing hair. That's what he told us, anyway. I always wondered why Jesus had long hair in all the pictures if it was wrong, but I never asked that. Preacher Hollis didn't like to have people asking too many questions.

We'd walk down to the church every morning after the sun had been up a couple hours. That gave us time to do chores and eat something and read our Bible lessons. Then Daddy would get his rifle and he'd have Ethan follow us down with the shotgun. They were both good shots. I was never afraid to go outside when they were around.

We were lucky where I lived, because we were so far out from town that we didn't see too many of the Dead. We heard stories though. One family passing through said that they saw so many of the Dead walking into the Mississippi River that by sundown that night there was nothing but bodies floating shoulder to shoulder from one bank of the river to the other. Every once in a while, one of 'em would slog out of the water and keep walking.

Preacher Hollis told us a lot of these stories in the lunch break between morning and afternoon prayers. The little kids were taken down in the church basement with Mrs. Hollis so she could read Bible stories to them, but the grown-ups talked about what was going on out there. I got to sit with the grown ups and hear about it. Sometimes I wished I could go down and be with the babies.

I never thought that it was unfair that the world was ending and I was just fifteen years old. I knew that God had a plan. That's what everybody kept telling me. God had a plan and His plan would be for the salvation and glory of all the true believers. I didn't think about how unfair it was that I'd never had a boyfriend or even been kissed. Those things were sinful anyway. I wanted to be pure for Jesus.

Sometimes Preacher Hollis would talk to the young people separately while Daddy or one of the other deacons preached the day's lesson. I liked it when Preacher Hollis talked, because he had such a pretty voice and pretty eyes. One day, he talked to us about being pure vessels for God's word. He told all the girls that they had to be virgins so they could enter the gates of Heaven and told the boys that they had to keep their thoughts and hearts pure of temptation. It was embarrassing, and I didn't understand why he kept looking at me when he talked. I remember staring at my lap, at the violets and baby's breath flowers in the pattern of my dress, but knowing that he was staring right at me.

I never told anybody about it. I wanted to be special, and I didn't want to make Daddy mad. Daddy always said that I was *his* little Junebug and no one else's. I was the eldest of the girls, so I was first in his heart the way Ethan was first in Momma's. He used to come see me special at night, when everybody else was sleeping, and tell me how much he loved me.

I didn't tell him about Preacher Hollis smiling at me. and I didn't tell him about the time Preacher Hollis told me he needed to check to make sure I was still a virgin. He didn't do anything but poke at me with his fingers, but it hurt, so that meant I was still a virgin and still pure in God's eyes. I remember the way Preacher Hollis looked at me while he did the test. He breathed hard, panting like one of our old hound dogs, and got all funny looking around his eyes. I didn't much like it, but I didn't tell him to stop. Preacher Hollis knew what was right for me, for all of us.

I let him do what he wanted. I just didn't tell Daddy.

Now they're singing "Rock of Ages" and I can just barely hear it. Maybe I'm not buried all the way yet. Maybe somebody can hear me if I pound on the lid, kick my feet, do anything I can do to make noise.

I wonder how much air I have left in here. I wonder why they thought I was dead. I wonder why nobody's realized what they've done and dug me up already. Momma knows I have fainting spells… why didn't she just tell everybody to wait it out until I woke up?

My fist goes through the thin wood of the lid. I feel dirt, wet and heavy. The smell reminds me of when me and Ethan used to dig up nightcrawlers for fishing.

I guess I'm going to have to dig my own self out of here.

Preacher Hollis asked Daddy if I could stay with him and Mrs. Hollis and help them watch their kids. They had three little boys, and they all liked me well enough. Daddy said it was fine with him. He didn't want me to be away from home, but Preacher Hollis reminded him that God wanted his flock to share the bounty of His goodness. Daddy couldn't argue with that.

Mrs. Hollis had come down sick not long after the dead people started rising. It was her nerves, Preacher Hollis told me one night as we drank warm well water and listened to the crickets. She couldn't take what was happening out in the world and was shutting down. That's what he called it. Shutting down. The only thing she was good for, he said, was reading Bible stories to the little kids. He couldn't talk to her anymore.

I felt real bad for Preacher Hollis, and Mrs. Hollis too. She was a good Christian woman. I thought it was terrible that she couldn't act the way she used to act.

But then Preacher Hollis told me Mrs. Hollis hadn't been acting like a wife to him, either, and he hated to make her do wifely things when she was so sick.

Now he had me, and in the eyes of God and Jesus and all the angels, I would be his new wife.

I've never been in such darkness before. I close my eyes to get away from it. Somehow it's better to be in my own darkness. I feel the wood splintering and can hear it cracking under my hands, but it seems like I'll never get the hole big enough to crawl out of. Dirt is falling on top of me, heavy on my chest. I don't care. I just want out.

I wonder how deep they put me. Probably not very, since there're not many of us left now. I bet Daddy dug the grave himself. He got good at digging them over the last couple of months.

I feel around the edges of the hole, wondering if it's big enough for me now. I can't do anymore right now. I hurt all over. Every joint feels like it's on fire. My bones feel hollow and heavy all at the same time. And my stomach... I've never been so hungry. I want...

I don't know what I want...

I stayed with Preacher Hollis for four months straight. Daddy and Momma never knew our secret, because God didn't want them to know it. They'd ruin everything, Preacher Hollis told me. They'd want me to leave him and come home.

So I stayed with Preacher Hollis. He kept telling me to call him Joseph, like Mrs. Hollis did, but I couldn't ever feel right calling him that. Even though he made me wear Mrs. Hollis's nightgowns to bed, even though he did things to me that hurt and didn't feel like anything God would have wanted for me, I always thought of him as Preacher Hollis.

Then I started getting sick in the mornings. Real sick. Mrs. Hollis caught me throwing up in the outhouse one morning and went and told the Preacher.

Then Preacher Hollis didn't want to be married to me no more and sent me home to Daddy.

I stood at the door and heard him tell Daddy that our family wasn't welcome in the church anymore because we was all a bunch of dirty sinners. Especially me. He told Daddy that I crawled into his bed at night and made him commit all manner of sin against his wife and God and that I was a Jezebel and a whore.

Then he told Daddy about the baby.

It was the first time I ever seen him cry.

It's bad. I'm so afraid and it's so bad it almost makes me scream. But it's not as fierce as the ache in my stomach. I'm so hungry...

I press my hands against the edges of the hole I made. The wood's rough, like Daddy didn't take the time to sand it down or polish my coffin before nailing me up inside it. Splinters sink into my skin but I don't feel them. I don't feel anything anymore.

I push into the dirt. I can feel it giving way. It's not packed in tight. God must be watching over me.

Daddy hit me as soon as Preacher Hollis left the house. It was a slap across the face, but it hurt deeper than anything I'd ever felt before. He'd never hit me, not ever. Momma didn't say anything. She just cried into her handkerchief and looked at me like she believed what Preacher Hollis had said.

Daddy said the baby would be born a bastard and that I had sinned so bad in the eyes of God that both me and the baby would go straight to Hell, no matter how much we went to church or prayed. Jesus would not forgive such treachery, he said. Then he hit me again. He hit me until he busted my lip and saw the blood. He never looked me in the eye again.

But he kept hitting me every chance he got.

I remember the story of Lazarus that Mrs. Hollis taught us in Sunday school when I was just a kid. It always scared me. Except for Jesus, dead people were supposed to stay dead.

I am Lazarus now.

The baby took root in me real good. That's what Daddy always said about Momma when she was pregnant with baby Jaynie. By the time the fourth month passed, I was getting big. I couldn't stand up without help, but by that time, Daddy wasn't letting nobody do anything for me. He didn't turn me out, but he didn't want me in his home, neither. He never talked to me. Never even looked at me. It was like I was dead.

It hurt. I wasn't Daddy's Junebug no more. Now, if he had to say something to me, he just called me plain old June, and he said it like he was saying the foulest cuss word he could spit out.

The first time my baby kicked, nobody knew it but me. That was the same day Mrs. Hollis killed herself with the Preacher's razor.

I can't dig no more. My hands feel numb, like I've slept on them too long, and fat and heavy and useless. I try to make a fist but the muscles won't do what I want them to do. I can't see them, but I know my hands are just curled into claws.

I want to scream. I want to scream and kick and pound and get out of the dark and get rid of the hunger in my belly and make them see that I'm not gone, that they don't need to be crying and mourning over me yet. I can't even move and that makes me want to scream even more. I open my mouth and try to make a sound but I can't.

Preacher Hollis was out visiting with Mrs. Johnson down the road when Mrs. Hollis did it. She knew what the Preacher was doing, and it wasn't giving comfort and support to the recently widowed Mrs. Johnson. I guess she just couldn't take no more.

Daddy heard that Mrs. Hollis turned into one of those things. He called it God's punishment for committing suicide, but I don't think it mattered how she died. She'd already killed two of her boys and had just started on the third, little John, when the Preacher finally got back home. Then she got him and ate what she wanted before wandering off into the woods. There wasn't enough left of the boys to come back, and that was a good thing, I think.

Daddy was out chopping firewood when Preacher Hollis came up the road, just like he used to do when he fetched me for babysitting. I heard him tell Momma that he could smell the Preacher from twenty feet away. Mrs. Hollis had gone for the soft parts of his belly and all his intestines were dragging in the dirt behind him. Daddy said he smelled like a dead rat in an outhouse hole. He let him get almost up to the house before he pulled out the shotgun and put him out of his misery.

I stood in the shadows of the open door and watched every bit of it. When I remembered how much it hurt when he put his thing inside me, I wished I was the one pulling the trigger.

The baby kicked at the exact second Preacher Hollis hit the ground, like she knew her daddy was gone, but I was glad of it.

Daddy turned around and caught me watching him. I could tell by looking at him that he wished I was just as dead as the Preacher.

I think it's raining up there. The dirt's turning into mud. The more I dig, the closer I get to the surface, the thicker and heavier it gets.

I remember rain. I remember playing in the puddles and the way the drops felt tickling through my hair and the way the water always tasted so clean on my tongue.

I'm not dead. They made a mistake. I can't be dead if I remember.

Can I?

I was sitting on the couch sewing on a baby blanket when Daddy decided he couldn't bear the sight of me no more.

He walked into the room, saw me sitting there, and the next thing I knew he had his belt out of his pants loops and bunched up in his hands. He caught me across the chest with the first swing and called me a whore.

I tucked into a ball and tried to cover my belly. Sometimes he liked to kick me, too.

I lost count of how many times the belt came down. He called me every bad name he could think of while he hit me. I peeked up once and saw his face and he looked like he was possessed by the Devil. I closed my eyes after that.

I heard Momma crying in the other room and figured she was keeping the little ones out of Daddy's sight. She never did much when Daddy took to whaling on me. She never tried to help me. I think she liked that he was punishing me. I'd fallen in her eyes, too.

I took my beating in silence, like usual, while Daddy cursed and swore at me and Momma cried.

Then, all of a sudden, it stopped.

When I looked up and saw Ethan grabbing Daddy's arm and yanking the belt away from him, I realized that I couldn't feel my baby moving. I couldn't feel her tossing and turning and kicking anymore. I'd gotten so used to feeling her inside me that when it stopped, it felt like I'd gone all hollow.

Ethan crouched down beside me and helped me sit up. He saw the blood puddling between my legs before I did.

Then Daddy hit him.

I never saw Daddy hit another man before, but he busted Ethan's nose so hard blood spurted out of it.

Ethan got up and faced Daddy and it was like he was possessed, too. They fought all the way out to the porch, then Daddy threw Ethan down the steps and told him to get gone, that he wasn't his son no more. I don't think Ethan minded much, 'cause he never really liked the idea of being Daddy's son no way. Daddy didn't even let him pack a bag or take a gun. He just sent Ethan walking down the dirt road from our house. I watched from the front porch, with my arms wrapped around my big belly, my back stinging from the belt. Ethan never looked back. I know he wanted to, though. I know he wanted to wave goodbye to me, at least.

But he kept walking, and I watched him all the way down to the bend in the road, just like the day he went off to war. Then Momma hollered for me and I had to go inside the house. The last memory I have of Ethan is him going down the road, with his head down and his hands in his pockets.

My belly felt like it was on fire, and I could feel the blood running down my legs. Momma threw an old towel my way and told me to go clean myself up. She didn't ask if the baby was okay. Daddy looked at me like he wanted to pick up the belt and start in on me again. He didn't. He just stared at the blood on the floor and the blood on his hands and went out to the tool shed. Never said a word.

I locked myself in the outhouse for a long time. I could feel the blood running out of me, like it used to do when my time of the month came. I could taste the blood in my mouth, like I'd been sucking on old pennies.

I didn't want to think about my baby not moving around. I couldn't.

God's will. It would prevail.

It had to.

I remember the baby.
My stomach's flat now. No baby in there. Not anymore.
My baby's gone.

Daddy was madder than fire, and he didn't calm down for a long time. The night Ethan left, he made all of us get down on our knees with him and Momma and pray that Ethan would see that the Devil had gotten into him, making him dare to raise a hand against his father. I didn't do it. I didn't want Ethan to come back and be beat down by Daddy again, so I prayed that Ethan would find some people who would help him out and that he'd go off with them.

I prayed that my baby would kick me again, even the kicks that really hurt or the ones that made me pee on myself a little.

I'd even picked out a name for her. Jenny. I knew it would be a little girl, just deep in my bones knew it. Her name would be Jenny and she'd have blue eyes like me and a dimple in her chin like Preacher Hollis and she'd be the prettiest baby ever born.

That night, while I was lying in bed, I felt her move again.

I praised the Lord. It was a miracle.

I don't want to remember anymore. I don't want to think about it.
I just want to get out. I want to go home. I want…
I want my baby.

Two weeks later, Ethan came home.

I don't know how he managed to make his way back. Maybe he hadn't gotten far before those things got ahold of him. Maybe he remembered all the shortcuts we used to take when we'd walk to town. Maybe something just steered him.

But he came home. Just like I'd prayed for him to do.

I don't feel the hunger anymore. I don't feel the pain or the cold or the rain or the mud falling into my eyes and mouth. I want out. I dig until I can finally sit up, half of me in the coffin and half of me buried in the mud. I don't care. I dig harder. Faster.

But the memories are coming back. Even though I don't want them.
I don't want to remember…

Daddy was on the porch shucking corn when Ethan came stumbling up the road. I was sitting in the living room reading the Bible, petting my belly every time Jenny decided to do another somersault.

Momma and the girls were down in the basement, putting up another summer's worth of vegetables.

I heard Daddy shout something. Then he came running into the house to grab his shotgun. His face was whiter than the sheets Momma had hung in the backyard that morning. I looked out the window and saw Ethan coming closer.

Half his face was gone. I only recognized him by the calico patch on his overalls. I'd sewed it on there myself a long time ago, back when he could talk me into doing his chores by promising me piggy-back rides on his shoulders.

Daddy stopped when he saw me, and I think that was the moment he got the idea. I saw his eyes change, going mean.

He got his shotgun then grabbed me by the arm.

I can feel cool air on my hands. My arms are over my head. One good push and I'll be outside again.

It's like being born again. Only I don't think Jesus ever thought it would be like this.

By the time Daddy pulled me out onto the porch, Ethan was in the front yard. He had one eye left, but he saw us just fine. His arms reached out straight ahead of him and he changed direction, following us on the ground while Daddy dragged me along the porch.

I couldn't stop crying. I fought Daddy as best as I could, but he was too strong. He didn't say anything at all.

He pushed me down the steps, into the backyard with Momma's fluttering sheets, and stayed up on the porch with his shotgun in his arms. I could see Ethan's feet beneath the hems of the sheets, could hear him moaning over the flapping and snapping of the sheets in the wind. He grabbed one of the blankets in his hand and left a bloody print and all I could think about was how mad Momma was going to be when she found that mess.

I wasn't afraid of Ethan. Not even then. He was my brother and I loved him.

When he came at me, I didn't move.

And Daddy watched it all. He watched with his gun in his hand when Ethan fell on top of me. He watched and didn't move when Ethan bit into my throat. He watched my blood exploding into the air and all over Momma's sheets.

Because Ethan was doing Daddy a favor. Ethan was doing God's work that Daddy was too cowardly to do himself. Even as the Lord leveled His mighty punishment on him, Ethan was an avenging angel, punishing the sinner.

I remember...

I remember Ethan's teeth in my neck, ripping at the muscle, tearing at the skin.

I remember Jenny kicking in my belly, like she was trying to fight for me, trying to save me.

I remember Daddy smiling as he finally... finally... leveled the shotgun.

I remember Ethan's head exploding in a mist of red, tasting his blood in my mouth when he fell on top of me.

I remember all of it now.

I didn't know I was dying. I didn't hurt. Not even in my throat. I felt a gush of wetness between my legs again and knew that Jenny was coming out. I felt her slide out of me just as easy and gentle as can be... just a little bit of a cramp and then she was gone.

I missed her.

Somewhere behind me I heard Momma and the girls running out of the house. I heard Jenny crying. I wanted to pick her up, to at least hold her, but I couldn't move. I laid on my back and watched clouds drifting over a blue, blue sky. Such a pretty day for my baby's birthday.

"She come out here to take down the sheets," I heard Daddy say. "Ethan must have surprised her. I couldn't save her."

Then Daddy was standing over me, reaching down between my legs, lifting Jenny by one of her feet and holding her upside down as she squalled.

"There's something wrong with it," he said, even though I know he knew better. He just didn't want the reminder of my sin. "It's one of them things."

Just like that, he threw my baby away. Whipped it out of his hand like he was bouncing stones on the creek. Jenny hit the side of the house and went quiet.

Momma cried. The girls cried. They sounded further and further away from me, like I had cotton stuffed in my ears.

I cried as I watched the clouds float by. Felt the warmth of the sun on my face and the breeze on my skin and…

… and then I woke up in my grave.

There's candlelight flickering in the living room window. I hear Daddy's voice all the way out here. Reading Revelations again. He loves his end of the world stories, even though they scare the little ones. That's probably what he likes best about them.

The rain has stopped. That's good. I can walk better now. I can point myself toward that light in the window and walk home by myself.

For my baby. My Jenny.

And for Daddy.

God's will would prevail.

Starvation Army

Joe McKinney

From the window of his abominably small second story room, Jonathan Nettle could see the alleyway where he'd found the body earlier that morning. He'd stumbled on the corpse quite by accident, while he was wandering the huge, unending slum of London's East End, looking for the homeless shelter on the Mile End Road where he was to take up his new post as assistant minister. He'd smelled the stench moments before he came across the blackened, mangled body of the homeless man. He'd spun on his heel and vomited all over the sidewalk when he saw the black, iridescent flies swarming around the mouth and eyes. After that, he'd stumbled out of the alleyway and grabbed the first policeman he saw. He babbled and pointed and grunted until at last he made himself understood enough for the policeman to follow him.

The policeman looked at the body, at the bruise-like splotches on the skin that weren't bruising but lividity, at the emaciated, rail-skinny arms and legs, and nodded.

"Yer an American, ain't ye, sir?"

"Huh?" Nettle said, the back of his hand against his lips. "Uh, yes."

"What are ye doin' here in the East End?"

Nettle told him he was looking for the homeless shelter. The policeman nodded. "The peg house yer lookin' for is over there," he said and pointed over Nettle's shoulder.

Nettle could barely take his eyes off the body, but he did so long enough to see the tumbledown, soot-stained building the policeman pointed out for him. He looked back at the policeman—at the bobby, he reminded himself—and said, "What... happened to him?"

"This bloke? Prob'ly starved to death'd be my guess, sir."

"Starved?"

"Aye," the bobby said.

Nettle had said nothing to that, only nodded as he tried to take in the wonder that a grown man could starve to death in the middle of the largest city on Earth, in the heart of the most powerful empire the world had ever known. He tried, but couldn't wrap his mind around it.

His stay was to be brief, long enough for him to get some experience with the great things William Booth and his "salvation army" were doing for the poor here in London. The church elders hoped he might learn enough to put those same practices in effect in the Methodist ministries in New York and Boston. But a few hours here were enough to tell him that the "problem of the poor" that such great orators as the Reverend Merle Cary of New York had spoken of so eloquently to audiences along the New England seaboard all that preceding summer of 1875 was far greater than anyone had imagined.

Just then several men began lugging bags of garbage out of the hospital across the street and dumping them on the sidewalk below Nettle's window. The bags split open on the ground and soon there was an almost liquid pile of corruption festering in the open air. Nettle watched the pile grow into a shapeless mass of rotten vegetables, scraps of meat, orange peels, and bloody surgical rags and blankets. The street was a miasma of squabbling and obscene yelling and fighting, yet no one said a word about the garbage. Indeed, after it had been sitting there for a few minutes, children converged on it, burying their arms in it up to their shoulders, digging for any kind of food they could find and devouring it on the spot.

One boy, a runt of perhaps six years, came up with something black that might have once been a potato and tried to steal away with it.

Several older boys surrounded him, punched him till he fell, then kicked him till he gave up the nasty potato-thing he clutched near his groin.

For Nettle, it was too much. His sister Anna had put a dozen oranges into his luggage as a treat for him. Fully aware that indiscriminate charity is cruel, he made up his mind to be cruel. He collected the oranges in a paper sack and went down to the street.

"How old are you, son?" he asked the boy.

"Twelve, sir," the boy said.

Nettle blinked in shock. Twelve! He had imagined the boy a runt of six. *How this place must beat them down*, he thought.

He handed the boy the oranges, and the boy's eyes went wide, like he'd just been given all the jewels in Africa.

"Go on," Nettle said. "Enjoy."

The boy was gone faster than the sun from a November day. Nettle, feeling a little better, went back to his room to write a letter to his sister in New York.

* * *

The porter's name was Bill Lowell. He was a weathered, bent-back old man charged to watch the door to the shelter and tell the poor wretches who came there for shelter when there was no more space available. Most nights, there was room for between twenty and fifty people, depending on the shelter's food stores and what work needed to be done—for the cost of a bed indoors and a hot meal was a day of hard, hard labor.

"We open the doors at six," Bill said to Nettle, who'd been told he'd work at each job in the shelter so he could better learn its overall operational strategy, "but the line'll start formin' 'fore noon. By four the blokes'll be lined up 'round the corner."

"Even when there's only room for a few of them?"

Bill shrugged. "We'll need to search 'em as they come inside. Sometimes, they try an' sneak tobacco inside in their brogues, and they ain't allowed that."

Nettle glanced through a window next to the door, and sure enough, a long line had already formed and was snaking its way down the sidewalk and around the corner. Word had gone out earlier that to-night there was only room for twenty-five, yet no one in the line seemed to want to leave his spot.

The faces he saw all looked hollow, the eyes vacuous. It wasn't un-til several days later that Nettle learned why everyone he saw shared the same corpselike expression. London law didn't allow the homeless to sleep outside at night. The idea was that if the homeless weren't allowed to sleep outside at night, they would find somewhere indoors to sleep. To those who only saw the problem from the stratospheric heights of wealth and power, it was a clear example of *give a man a fish and he eats for a day, teach him to fish and he eats for a lifetime.* The reality, though, was a homeless population constantly driven from one doorway to the next by the police, forced to stay awake by the toe of a boot or the bite of a ba-ton. This resulted in an expression of slack-jawed exhaustion that stared back at Nettle from every pair of eyes he met.

Bill himself had nearly shared that fate, he told Nettle. He had had a family once—a wife, three daughters, and a son—but had outlived them all. His wife and daughters he'd lost to scarlet fever, all within a month of each other, but the son survived, and had helped Bill in his work as a carpenter in days past.

One day, Bill had been carrying a load of nails that was too much for him. "Something in me back just broke," Bill said. His load of nails had spilled, and he'd ended up flat on his back, unable to get up. He was taken to a hospital, but they refused to admit him, telling him, essen-tially, to "walk it off."

This he had tried to do, but two hours later was on his back again. He was taken to a different hospital, and this time spent three weeks in bed. He emerged a broken man, unable to do the hard labor that was the only kind of work that he and most of the men like him were quali-fied to do, only to learn that his son had fallen from a rooftop and died the week before his release. The boy was buried in a pauper's grave along with a dozen others.

Bill lived on the streets after that—carrying the banner, as the ex-pression went—chased from one doorway to the next by the police, until, as luck would have it, he ended up in the Mile End Road shelter on the day they had an opening for a porter who could also do a little light carpentry. His nine pounds a year salary made him a practical Croesus among the East End's poor.

Nettle thought idly that such a man as Bill, who had narrowly escaped a cruel death by exposure and malnutrition, would be more charitable toward his fellow men, but such was not the case.

Bill, much to Nettle's unease, seemed heartily to enjoy his position of relative power over the poor, and stared down his scabbed-over nose at all who entered, demanding from each his name, age, condition of destitution, and what kind of work he was good for, before searching them all with a rough, hard hand.

In one of his searches he found a ragged pouch of tobacco inside a man's sock. Bill proceeded to beat the man with a stick he evidently left by the door for just such a purpose, and probably would have gone on beating him indefinitely, Nettle figured, had he not intervened.

When Nettle tried to berate him for his violence, Bill only scoffed. "Why 'e's nothin' but a worthless beggar, 'e is," he said, and, with all the sour disposition of a man who kicks the cat because he's afraid to kick his wife, went to the door, where a wrecked shell of a man stood on the threshold waiting for admittance, and said, "Be gone, you. Full up!"

"Please, sir," the human wreck said. "Please, I ain't 'ad food in me belly for five days."

"Full up!" Bill said.

Nettle's heart broke to see the pain in the man's eyes. Before Bill could close the door, he was at Bill's shoulder and said, "We can take this man in, I think."

"But, sir," Bill said, "there's only room for twenty-five tonight. We're full up."

"That man," Nettle said, pointing at the bleeding bag of bones Bill had beaten for the insolence to smoke cheap tobacco, "was to be number twenty-five. Now, I believe, this man is twenty-five."

Bill said nothing, but his eyes did.

"Thank 'e, sir," the wreck said and walked inside.

Bill's other job at the shelter, after the doors were locked and the homeless shuffled inside, was to monitor the bathing room.

Making the homeless take a bath seemed like a good idea to Nettle—that is, until he saw the process in motion. The overnighters were lined up and led one by one down into a dark room with a single tub of warm water and a single threadbare towel hanging from a hook on the wall. Each man used the same water and towel as the man before him. By the time the man Nettle had forced Bill to let in got his turn, the water in that tub was a frightful stew.

But the human wreck didn't notice. He stripped off his rags. His appearance made Nettle gasp. His body had no meat on it. He was all ribs and distended belly, his back a mass of dried and fresh new blood where he'd been attacked by vermin.

He cleaned off several layers of dirt and blood and changed into a shirt and pants from the shelter's wardrobe. Then he followed the others to the dining hall for a meal of stale bread and skilly—a sort of oatmeal mixed with tepid water so unclean Nettle doubted a dog would drink it—and he would have received that meal had he not had the misfortune to pass Bill on his way inside.

"You!" Bill said.

Nettle glanced up at the sudden rage in Bill's voice.

The man stopped in his tracks.

"Look who we 'ave 'ere," Bill said loudly, looking around at the crowd.

Slowly, every head in the place turned to look.

The man kept his eyes on the floor.

"I'll be damned if it ain't Barlow the Butcher. Look 'ere. We got us Barlow the Butcher!"

This meant nothing to Nettle, but it clearly did to the peg house crowd, for in short order they became a riotous mob. They fell on Barlow and began to beat him with a savagery that would have made a tribe of cannibals blush.

Nettle waded in and pulled Barlow out of the flurry of fists. Barlow, though, didn't wait around to thank him. As soon as he was clear of the mob, he ran for the door and fled into the night.

Nettle was left with a decision to make. He was ringed by angry faces, some of them bleeding where they'd been hit by others trying to land blows on Barlow, and he had a feeling he knew what would happen if he stayed there, now that they had the taste of blood. He went for the door himself, stepping into the street in time to see Barlow, or, rather, a crowd of homeless at the end of the street separating for Barlow as he rounded the corner onto Stepney Green.

Nettle ran after him, and managed to follow him for a good ways before he lost him in the maze of the East End's soot-stained back alleys. He became lost in short order, every cross street and alley meeting him with endless vistas of tumbledown misery and bricks.

Walking with his head on a swivel, trying to find something familiar, he eventually stumbled onto the Brown Hay Road, where he stopped in front of an abandoned warehouse. It was a blackened, eyeless hulk, not a single window down its entire length. It made him feel strangely uneasy. There were, Nettle had seen already, few empty buildings in London's East End. Real estate, *any* real estate, was at a premium. Landlords could pack as many as eight families into a home no bigger than the small apartment he had shared in New York with his mother and his sister Anna. One was more likely, he'd been told, to see a giraffe swimming down the Thames than to find an unoccupied building in the East End.

The moldy warehouse in front of him was most certainly abandoned. Something about it made the skin crawl down his spine. Then someone was there, staggering toward him from the other side of the street. A patchwork of shadows played across the man's face, but the little Nettle could see was ghastly. The man's joints had swollen. His body had withered away to almost nothing. His skin was black in places, almost mummified, like it had begun to rot, and it wasn't until he got halfway across the street that Nettle could tell part of the man's leg had been torn up as if by some sort of animal.

The man raised his hands and flexed his fingers in a weak grab at Nettle, moaning as he stumbled closer. At first Nettle thought it was a moan, meaning nothing beyond the pain it obviously conveyed. Then he recognized the word inside the pain.

"Fooooood."

Nettle turned on his heel, thinking robbery, and started to walk the other way.

"Foooooood," the man groaned again.

"See here," Nettle said, "I don't have anything for you."

He was close to running then and had already stepped up his pace, when a hansom cab lurched around the corner at a full sprint and mowed the man down. The driver of the hansom never slowed. A moment later, he was gone.

Nettle was frozen with shock. What was left of the man after he'd been trampled by the horses and his body sliced open and dragged by the hansom's wheels was in two gory pieces, connected by a clotted smear of liquefied meat.

The man's legs were still in the street, but his torso was near the curb. Nettle staggered that way, hands over his mouth, and knelt down next to the mess the hansom had made of the man.

He started to pray for the man's soul. Nettle was rocking back and forth, sobbing at the horror of it, when the man opened his eyes.

Nettle fell backward onto the wet cobblestones. The man's eyes were horrible, like staring into the void.

"Foooooood," he groaned, and tried to claw his way toward Nettle, his fingers digging so hard into the edges of the cobblestones that the fingernails ripped and tore loose.

Nettle got up and ran. He ran till he broke down. Then he cried. He was still crying when, by chance, he stumbled back onto Mile End Road.

* * *

The next morning, still badly shaken by his encounter, Nettle packed his bags and knelt by his bed to pray. He fully expected to leave that afternoon, but his prayers took him in another direction. When he rose to his feet he had made the decision to stay. He had also convinced himself that what he had seen the night before couldn't have happened. He was upset, nothing more.

Nettle's faith had never led him astray. The events of the next few days, and a chance encounter with the man the mob had chased out of the peg house on his horrible first night there, reinforced the decision he made during prayer.

Nettle took to wandering up and down Mile End Road, watching people as they struggled for existence. He noticed a curious thing. The homeless always seemed to keep one eye on the spittle-flecked sidewalks. When they'd see a morsel, they'd snatch it up and eat it on the fly. Most, it seemed, could pluck an orange peel or an apple core from the cobblestones without ever losing a step.

Nettle had been watching people go by late one afternoon. Barlow had been coming the other way on the same sidewalk. Barlow had stooped to pick up something. When he rose, his nose collided with Nettle's chest.

"Oh, hello," Nettle said, and had a devil of a time over the next few moments trying to assure the man that he had no intention of braining him.

They talked in the eaves of a pub. Gradually the look of a rabbit trying to find an opening through a pack of hounds faded from Barlow's eyes. Then a strange thing happened. Nettle, whose over stimulated humanitarian urges were in danger of melting down if he didn't find some specific point, some single human face to put on all this misery he had been witnessing, bought a pint of beer for Barlow, who was desperately in need of some kind person to buy him a pint of beer. It was the first pint of beer Nettle had ever bought, and it was the first full pint of beer Barlow had had in a long time. Nettle bought a second round. By that afternoon, as the windows of the pub sizzled with rain, he had come to a conclusion. He was not going to be the salvation for *all* the world's poor—indeed, there was no way he could be, and it was vain to think so—but he could be the door to *this* man's salvation.

Nettle finally had a project, something he could manage.

They sat in the pub, the rich, well-meaning American, and the homeless, nearly starved Londoner, and the American talked about God and goodness and reward, and the Londoner drank his beer and nodded.

* * *

They met in the afternoons at the same pub over the next week. Gradually Nettle began to realize that it wasn't the man's grotesque, almost troglodyte appearance that had sparked his philanthropy, but rather his cynicism. The man cared little for his own life, and not at all for anyone else's. Nettle found it hard to believe that a creature who so hated life could actually go on living.

"Beer," Barlow said. "Beer's what makes a man feel like a man. You can take all the rest of it away, but you take away a man's beer, and there ain't no reason left for 'im to go on bein'."

Nettle squinted at his own almost untouched beer and thought about that as a philosophy of life. It seemed tragic, empty.

"What about a family?" he asked. "A home? A wife and children?"

Barlow snorted. "I saw enough of that growin' up. I saw what me ma did for me old man. That was enough. Made 'im mis'rable, she did, always a-bangin' me brothers and sisters about, makin' 'is 'ome a noisy racket. 'E no sooner walk through the door and she'd be a-yellin' at 'im, barkin' at 'im like a dog. Take me word for it, mate, and don't waste yer time on a wife 'n kids. Do nothin' but take yer 'ard earned money and keep you from drinkin' a beer when it suits you."

Nettle was stunned, bewildered. Such a wasted life! His mind raced for a response, for something worthwhile to say. At last, he found it. "William," he said, "I want you to pray with me. Will you do that?"

"Pray?"

"Yes, William. There's a power in prayer that has sustained me through my hard times. I think it can do the same for you."

A wan smile crossed Barlow's face. "Let's pray for another beer, mate. You want me to pray? I'll pray for that."

* * *

Barlow wasn't Nettle's only project. He was still expected to learn how to run a shelter. He spent time in each of the numerous jobs that were necessary to keep the operation going on a day to day basis. A few nights later he was back with Bill, the porter, passing out blankets in the sleeping quarters. The overnighters would come in, take a blanket from Nettle and head to a long, narrow room with two large oaken beams traversing its length. Rough pieces of canvas were stretched between the beams. The men slept on the canvas. When he first heard about the arrangement, before he had seen it, Nettle thought of seamen in hammocks, rocking to sleep with the rhythms of the sea, but the reality was nothing like that. The actual arrangement lacked any of the adventurous dignity a landsman could envision a sailor's life at sea to be. The men were packed in shoulder to shoulder. The room was dreadfully noisy with snores and coughs and breaking wind. In the right light, the whole room shimmered with a living cloud of fleas.

He was watching this sad display with a heavy heart when Bill appeared at his shoulder.

"What are you about, sir, talkin' with Barlow the Butcher?"

"Excuse me?" he said.

"You become 'is reg'lar drinkin' mate's what I 'ear."

"I have not," Nettle protested. He stammered, trying to rise to his own defense, and finally managed to tell Bill his plan, how his goal was the man's salvation.

Bill just laughed.

"What's wrong with going after a lost sheep?" Nettle said.

"'E ain't no sheep," Bill said. "A devil, aye, but 'e ain't no sheep."

"What do you mean, a devil?"

"There's an em'ty warehouse down on the Brown Hay Road. D'you know it? A big, ugly brute of a buildin'?"

"I've seen it," Nettle said, cringing inwardly at the memory of the beggar and the hansom cab.

"Your mate used to be the union man there, 'bout twenty years ago."

Nettle nodded. He knew that.

"Did 'e tell you 'bout the people 'e killed there?"

"Killed? What are you talking about?"

"Aye, I thought not."

"Tell me what you mean, sir. You cannot accuse a man of such a crime and not state your proof."

Bill only shook his head. "Nothin' was ever proved 'gainst 'im. Didn't 'ave no blood on 'is 'ands. None that the courts could see, anyway. But 'e killed 'em all right. Just as pretty as you please."

Nettle searched the man's face for some indication that this was a joke. It had to be. He searched the creases in the old man's face, the cracked red map of lines that colored the whites of his eyes, but found nothing to indicate that this was a joke.

"When you say killed, do you mean…"

"I mean 'e murdered 'em. Sure as the Pope eats fish on Fridays. Murdered more'n an 'undred people. Men, wimmen, and children, just as pretty as you please."

Nettle felt the muscles in his legs turn to water. He fell against the wall and said, "A hundred people?"

"Aye."

"But how?"

"Why, 'e starved 'em. Locked 'em in that warehouse for full on twelve days. When they finally opened 'er up, every one of 'em—men, wimmen, and children—was dead as dead can be." His smile was ugly. "I 'eard tell some of them bodies was eaten on."

"That's impossible," Nettle countered. "How could he do such a thing?"

"I already tol' you, sir. 'E was the union man, and those people went on strike. The comp'ny tol' 'im to fix the problem, and 'e did."

"A man can't starve to death in twelve days," Nettle said.

"You've seen these men," Bill said. "Not a one's more than a week away from death's door."

"But somebody would have done something to stop him," Nettle said. "You can't just kill a hundred people and expect to get away with it. Somebody would have said something."

Nettle didn't need to see the blank expression on Bill's face to know that wasn't true. Not here in the East End.

Feeling angry, confused and betrayed, Nettle ran from the peg house and set out for the pub where he and Barlow had been meeting in the afternoons. He found Barlow in the alley behind the pub, rifling through a paper bag of trash he'd found on the curb, pulling out little bits of orange peels and tearing what remained of the pulp from the pith with his blackened front teeth.

"Mr. Barlow," Nettle called out from across the street.

Barlow looked up and smiled. Then his smile fell. Perhaps he saw the savage expression in Nettle's eyes, or heard something sinister in his tone. Whatever it was, his expression instantly changed, and he took off running into the night.

Nettle didn't bother to chase him. It was enough, for the moment, to see him run. That was all the proof he needed that Mr. Barlow, also known as Barlow the Butcher, was a devil of the lowest sort.

* * *

Some men snap by degrees. Like green wood, they bend a long way before the tension takes its inevitable course. Other men break like porcelain. They shatter into thousands of pieces, their edges razor sharp.

Nettle was of the later sort. When his mind snapped, it came with the illusion of sudden clarity. It seemed he was thinking clearly now for the first time. The path before him seemed plainer than it ever had before. He suddenly saw in Barlow, not an individual's face to put on all of humanity's troubles, but a cause of its misery. There was only one thing to do with such causes. The fact that he had befriended such a beast, that he had bought such evil a drink, for God's sake, didn't terrify him so much as instill in him a sense of personal responsibility. His proximity had given him ownership over the ending to Barlow's sordid little history, and he set out to bring that history to a close.

He carried the banner that night, walking the streets of the East End without stopping for rest or sleep, ferreting out the places where the homeless hid. He caught up with Barlow in a doorway. The man was sitting on the top step, his knees bunched up to his chest. his head bent down between them, trying to sleep.

Nettle kicked his foot. "Wake up," he said. "I want a word with you."

Barlow thought him a policeman at first and had half pulled himself to his feet when the haze of sleep left him, and he realized who was standing in front of him.

"You owe me an answer, Mr. Barlow."

Barlow didn't stand still to give it. He turned and ran with all the energy a scared, weather-beaten, prematurely old man could muster.

Nettle followed him at a jog yelling "I want an answer!" over and over again at Barlow's back. As they slipped deeper and deeper into the warren of slimy streets that made up the bowels of the East End, a cold, light rain began to fall.

Nettle finally closed on him in a back alley off Brown Hay Road, the streets deserted now and splashy beneath their feet. Barlow had curled up under a flight of stairs and was trying to hide his face with his arms.

"You have some explaining to do," Nettle said. The rain rolled off his face unnoticed.

Barlow stared up at him with abject fear.

"What did you do? Answer me!"

"For the love of all that's 'oly, sir, please don't yell. You'll…"

"I'll what? Wake the dead? Go on, you villain, say it! Say it! Are you afraid they'll hear us?"

Barlow looked seasick. His eyes pleaded for silence but got none.

"Spill it!" Nettle roared. "Tell me what you did."

Nettle waited, and for a moment there was no sound but the pattering of a gentle rain on cobblestones. Then it came, as both Nettle and Barlow knew that it would. The sound of slow, plodding feet dragged on the cobblestones behind them.

Nettle looked over his shoulder and saw a small crowd of shamblers had appeared out of the mist. There were men, women and children in that crowd. Their faces were dark with disease and their cheeks empty from hunger. Their eyes were carrion eyes, and a smell that could only be death preceded them, filling the street with its sad, inexorable power.

A man in the front of the crowd raised his arms as if he would grab them. One hand looked like it had been partially eaten. He groaned, "Fooooood." Barlow jumped to his feet and tried to run.

"Where are you going?" Nettle yelled after him. "Don't you know you can't run from this?"

Barlow didn't make it far, only to the middle of Brown Hay Road. There he stopped, whirling around in panic, surrounded by the dead. They stepped out of every doorway, out of every alley, from behind every staircase, taking shape out of the shadows.

He fell to his knees in front of Nettle and started to cry.

"Please," he begged.

"Tell what you've done," Nettle said.

Barlow looked at the groaning, starving dead, and he shook his head no. NO, NO, NO, NO, NO!

"Say it," Nettle said. "While there's still time."

But there wasn't any more time. Barlow could no more belly up to the magnitude of what he'd done than he could force himself to stop breathing. As the rotting dead shouldered their way past Nettle and closed on Barlow, all that he could do was close his eyes.

The dead tore at Barlow with their hands and their teeth, ripping his flesh like fabric. Nettle stumbled away into the dark. As he walked he heard Barlow's screams echo on and on. They seemed to go on longer than possible for any one man to suffer, but go on they did. They echoed in Nettle's mind even after their shrillness disappeared from his ears.

He had no idea a man could scream like that.

Nettle wandered, his mind unhinged, until he began to see people. These he tried to tell what he had seen, but they flinched away from him, alarmed at the intensity in his eyes and the urgency in his voice and the complete lack of sense in his speech.

Dawn came as a russet stain behind plum colored smoke clouds. Nettle collapsed less than fifty feet from the doors of Stepney Green Hospital. He lay there, lips moving soundlessly, eyes still as glass beads, until an orderly from the hospital knelt beside him and said, "Hey, mate, are you hurt? What is it? Are you 'ungry?"

Though he felt dizzy, one thought was perfectly clear. *Eat*, he thought, and sensed his body in complete revolt at the idea. *God no, I'll never eat again.*

Pegleg and Paddy Save the World

Jonathan Maberry

I know what you've heard but Pat O'Leary's cow didn't have nothing to do with it. Not like they said in the papers. The way them reporters put it you'd thought the damn cow was playing with matches. I mean, sure it started in the cowshed, but that cow was long dead by that point, and really it was Pat himself who lit it. I helped him do it. And that meteor shower some folks talked about—you see, that happened beforehand. It didn't start the fire either, but it sure as hell *caused* it.

You have to understand what the West Side of Chicago was like back then. Pat had a nice little place on DeKoven Street—just enough land to grow some spuds and raise a few chickens. The cow was a skinny old milker. She was of that age where her milk was too sour and her beef would probably be too tough. Pat O'Leary wanted to sell her to some drovers who were looking to lay down some jerky for a drive down to Abilene, but the missus would have none of it.

"Elsie's like one of the family!" Catherine protested. "Aunt Sophie gave her to me when she was just a heifer."

I knew Pat had to bite his tongue not to ask if Catherine meant when the cow was a heifer or when Sophie was. By that point in their marriage Pat's tongue was crisscrossed with healed-over bite marks.

Catherine finished up by saying, "Selling that cow'd be like selling Aunt Sophie herself off by the pound."

Over whiskey that night Pat confided me that if he could find a buyer for Sophie he'd have loved to sell the old bitch. "She eats twice as much as the damn cow and don't smell half as good."

I agreed and we drank on it.

Shame the way she went. The cow, I mean. I wouldn't wish that on a three-legged dog. As for Sophie… well, I guess in a way I feel sorry for her, too. And for the rest of them that died that night, the ones who died in the fire… and the ones who died before.

The fire started Sunday night, but the problem started way sooner, just past midnight on a hot Tuesday morning.

That was a strange autumn. Dryer than it should have been, and with a steady wind that you'd have thought blew straight in off a desert. I never saw anything like it except the Santa Ana's, but this was Illinois not California.

Father Callahan had a grand ol' time with it, saying that it was the hot breath of Hell blowing hard on all us sinners. Yeah, yeah, whatever. We wasn't sinning any worse that year than we had the year before and the year before that. Conner O'Malley was still sneaking in the widow Daley's backdoor every Saturday night, the Kennedy twins were still stealing hogs, and Pat and I were still making cheap whiskey and selling it in premium bottles to the pubs who sold it to travelers heading west. No reason Hell should have breathed any harder that year than any other.

What was different that year was not what we sinners were doing but what those saints were up to, 'cause we had shooting stars every night for a week. The good Father had something to say about that, too. It was the flaming sword of St. Michael and his lot, reminding us why we were tossed out of Eden. That man could make a hellfire and brimstone sermon out of a field full of fuzzy bunnies, I swear to God.

On the first night there was just a handful of little ones, like Chinese fireworks way out over Lake Michigan. The second night there was a big ball of light—Biela's Comet the reporter from the Tribune called it—and it just burst apart up there and balls of fire came araining down everywhere.

Pat and I were up at the still and we were trying to sort out how to make Mean-Dog Mulligan pay the six months worth of whiskey fees he owed us. Mean-Dog was a man who earned his nickname. He was bigger than both of us put together, so when we came asking for our cash and he told us to piss off, we did. We only said anything out loud about it when we were a good six blocks from his place.

"We've got to sort him out," I told Paddy, "or everyone'll take a cue from him and then where will we be?"

Pat was feeling low. Mean-Dog had smacked him around a bit, just for show, and my poor lad was in the doldrums. His wife was pretty but she was a nag; her Aunt Sophie was more terrifying than the red Indians who still haunt some of these woods; and Mean-Dog Mulligan was turning us into laughing stock. Pat wanted to brood, and brooding over a still of fresh whiskey at least takes some of the sting out. It was after our fourth cup that we saw the comet.

Now, I've seen comets before. I seen them out at sea before I lost my leg, and I seen 'em out over the plains when I was running with the Scobie gang. I know what they look like, but this one was just a bit different. It was green for one thing. Comets don't burn green, not any I've seen or heard about. This one was a sickly green, too, the color of bad liver, and it scorched a path through the air. Most of it burned up in the atmosphere, and that's a good thing, but one piece of it came down hard by the edge of the lake, right smack down next to Aunt Sophie's cottage.

Pat and I were sitting out in our lean-to in a stand of pines, drinking toasts in honor of Mean-Dog developing a wasting sickness when the green thing came burning down out of the sky and smacked into the ground not fifty feet from Sophie's place. There was a sound like fifty cannons firing all at once. The shock rolled up the hill to where we sat. Knocked both of us off our stools and tipped over the still.

"Pegleg!" Pat yelled as he landed on his ass, "The brew!"

I lunged for the barrel and caught it before it tilted too far, but a gallon of it splashed me in the face and half-drowned me. That's just a comment not a complaint. I steadied the pot as I stood up. My clothes were soaked with whiskey but I was too shocked to even suck my shirt-tails. I stood staring down the slope. Sophie's cottage still stood, but it was surrounded by towering flames. Green flames, and that wasn't the whiskey talking. There were real green flames licking at the night, catching the grass, burning the trees that edged her property line.

"That's Sophie's place," I said.

He wiped his face and squinted through the smoke. "Yeah, sure is."

"She's about to catch fire."

He belched. "If I'm lucky."

I grinned at him. It was easy to see his point. Except for Catherine there was nobody alive who could stand Aunt Sophie. She was fat and foul, and you couldn't please her if you handed her a deed to a gold mine. Not even Father Callahan liked her, and he was sort of required to by license.

We stood there and watched as the green fire crept along the garden path toward her door. "Suppose we should go down there and kind of rescue her, like," I suggested.

He bent and picked up a tin cup, dipped it in the barrel, drank a slug and handed it to me. "I suppose."

"Catherine will be mighty upset if we let her burn."

"I expect."

We could hear her screaming now as she finally realized that Father Callahan's hellfire had come aknocking. Considering her evil ways, she probably thought that's just what it was, and had it been, not even she could have found fault with the reasoning.

"Come on," Pat finally said, tugging on my sleeve, "I guess we'd better haul her fat ass outta there or I'll never hear the end of it from the wife."

"Be the Christian thing to do," I agreed, though truth to tell we didn't so much as hustle down the slope to her place as sort of saunter.

That's what saved our lives in the end, cause we were still only halfway down when the second piece of the comet hit. This time it hit her cottage fair and square.

It was like the fist of God—if His fist was ever green, mind—punching down from heaven and smashing right through her roof. The whole house just flew apart; the roof blew off; the windows turned to glittery dust and the log walls splintered into matchwood. The force of it was so strong that it just plain sucked the air out of the fire, like blowing out a candle.

Patrick started running about then, and since he has two legs and I got this peg I followed along as best I could. Took us maybe ten minutes to get all the way down there.

By that time Sophie Kilpatrick was deader'n a doornail.

We stopped outside the jagged edge of what had been her north wall and stared at her just lying there amid the wreckage. Her bed was smashed flat, the legs broke; the dresser and rocker were in pieces, all the crockery in fragments. In the midst of it, still wearing her white nightgown and bonnet, was Sophie, her arms and legs spread like a starfish, her mouth open like a bass, her goggle eyes staring straight up at heaven in the most accusing sort of way.

We exchanged a look and crept inside.

"She looks dead," he said.

"Of course she's dead, Pat, a comet done just fell on her."

The fire was out but there was still a bit of green glow coming off her and we crept closer still.

"What in tarnation is that?"

"Dunno," I said. There were bits and pieces of green rock scattered around her, and it glowed like it had a light inside. Kind of pulsed in a way, like a slow heartbeat. Sophie was dusted with glowing green powder. It was on her gown and her hands and her face. A little piece of the rock pulsed inside her mouth, like she'd gasped it in as it all happened.

"What's that green stuff?"

"Must be that comet they been talking about in the papers. Biela's Comet they been calling it."

"Why'd it fall on Sophie?"

"Well, Pat, I don't think it *meant* to."

He grunted as he stared down at her. The green pulsing of the rock made it seem like she was breathing and a couple of times he bent close to make sure.

"Damn," he said after he checked the third time, "I didn't think she'd ever die. Didn't think she could!"

"God kills everything," I said, quoting one of Father Callahan's cheerier observations. "Shame it didn't fall on Mean-Dog Mulligan."

"Yeah, but I thought Sophie was too damn ornery to die. Besides, I always figured the Devil'd do anything he could to keep her alive."

I looked at him. "Why's that?"

"He wouldn't want the competition. You know she ain't going to heaven and down in Hell… well, she'll be bossing around old Scratch and his demons before her body is even cold in the grave. Ain't nobody could be as persistently disagreeable as Aunt Sophie."

"Amen to that," I said and sucked some whiskey out of my sleeve. Pat noticed what I was doing and asked for a taste. I held my arm out to him. "So… what you think we should do?"

Pat looked around. The fire was out, but the house was a ruin. "We can't leave her out here."

"We can call the constable," I suggested. "Except that we both smell like whiskey."

"I think we should take her up to the house, Peg."

I stared at him. "To the house? She weighs nigh on half a ton."

"She can't be more than three hundred-weight. Catherine will kill me if I leave her out here to get gnawed on by every creature in the woods. She always says I was too hard on Sophie, too mean to her. She sees me bringing Sophie's body home, sees how I cared enough to do that for her only living aunt, then she'll think better of me."

"Oh, man…." I complained, but Pat was adamant. Besides, when he was in his cups Pat complained that Catherine was not being "wifely" lately. I think he was hoping that this would somehow charm him back onto Catherine's side of the bed. Mind you, Pat was as drunk as a lord, so this made sense to him, and I was damn near pickled, so it more or less made sense to me, too. Father Callahan could have gotten a month's worth of hellfire sermons on the dangers of hard liquor out of the way Pat and I handled this affair. Of course, Father Callahan's dead now, so there's that.

Anyway, we wound up doing as Pat said and we near busted our guts picking up Sophie and slumping her onto a wheelbarrow. We dusted off the green stuff as best we could, but we forgot about the piece in her mouth and the action of dumping her on the 'barrow must have made that glowing green chunk slide right down her gullet. If we'd been a lot less drunk we'd have wondered about that, because on some level I was pretty sure I heard her swallow that chunk, but since she was dead and we were grunting and cursing trying to lift her, and it couldn't be real *anyway*, I didn't comment on it. All I did once she was loaded was peer at her for a second to see if that great big bosom of hers was rising and falling—which it wasn't—and then I took another suck on my sleeve.

It took near two hours to haul her fat ass up the hill and through the streets and down to Pat's little place on DeKoven Street. All the time I found myself looking queer at Sophie. I hadn't liked that sound, that gulping sound, even if I wasn't sober or ballsy enough to say anything to Pat. It made me wonder, though, about that glowing green piece of comet. What the hell was that stuff, and where'd it come from? It weren't nothing normal, that's for sure.

We stood out in the street for a bit with Pat just staring at his own front door, mopping sweat from his face, careful of the bruises from Mean-Dog. "I can't bring her in like this," he said, "it wouldn't be right."

"Let's put her in the cowshed," I suggested. "Lay her out on the straw and then we can fetch the doctor. Let him pronounce her dead all legal like."

For some reason that sounded sensible to both of us, so that's what we did. Neither of us could bear to try and lift her again so we tipped over the barrow and let her tumble out.

"Ooof!" she said.

"Excuse me," Pat said, then we both froze.

He looked at me, and I looked at him, and we both looked at Aunt Sophie. My throat was suddenly dry as an empty shot glass.

Pat's face looked like he'd seen a ghost, and we were both wondering if that's what we'd just seen in fact. We crouched over her, me still holding the arms of the barrow, him holding one of Sophie's wrists.

"Tell me if you feel a pulse, Paddy my lad," I whispered.

"Not a single thump," he said.

"Then did you hear her say 'ooof' or some suchlike?"

"I'd be lying if I said I didn't."

"Lying's not always a sin," I observed.

He dropped her wrist, then looked at the pale green dust on his hands—the glow had faded—and wiped his palms on his coveralls.

"Is she dead or isn't she?" I asked.

He bent and with great reluctance pressed his ear to her chest. He listened for a long time. "There's no ghost of a heartbeat," he said.

"Be using a different word now, will ya?"

Pat nodded. "There's no heartbeat. No breath. Nothing."

"Then she's dead?"

"Aye."

"But she made a sound."

Pat straightened, then snapped his fingers. "It's the death rattle," he said. "Sure and that's it. The dead exhaling a last breath."

"She's been dead these two hours and more. What's she been waiting for?"

He thought about that. "It was the stone. The green stone—it lodged in her throat and blocked the air. We must have dislodged it when we dumped her out and that last breath came out. Just late is all."

I was beginning to sober up and that didn't have the ring of logic it would have had an hour ago.

We stood over her for another five minutes, but Aunt Sophie just lay there, dead as can be.

"I got to go tell Catherine," Pat said eventually. "She's going to be in a state. You'd better scram. She'll know what we've been about."

"She'll know anyway. You smell as bad as I do."

"But Sophie smells worse," he said, and that was the truth of it.

So I scampered and he went in to break his wife's heart. I wasn't halfway down the street before I heard her scream.

* * *

I didn't come back until Thursday. As I came up the street, smoking my pipe, Pat came rushing around the side of the house. I swear he was wearing the same overalls and looked like he hadn't washed or anything.

The bruises had faded to the color of a rotten eggplant but his lip was less swollen. He grabbed me by the wrist and fair wrenched my arm out dragging me back to the shed; but before he opened the door he stopped and looked me square in the eye.

"You got to promise me to keep a secret, Pegleg."

"I always keep your secrets," I lied, and he knew I was lying.

"No, you have to really keep this one. Swear by the baby Jesus."

Pat was borderline religious, so asking me to swear by anything holy was a big thing for him. The only other time he'd done it was right before he showed me the whiskey still.

"Okay, Paddy, I swear by the baby Jesus and his Holy Mother, too."

He stared at me for a moment before nodding; then he turned and looked up and down the alley as if all the world was leaning out to hear whatever Patrick O'Leary had to say. All I saw was a cat sitting on a stack of building bricks distractedly licking his bollocks. In a big whisper Pat said, "Something's happened to Sophie."

I blinked at him a few times. "Of course something happened to her, you daft bugger. A comet fell on her head and killed her."

He was shaking his head before I was even finished. "No... *since* then."

That's not a great way to ease into a conversation about the dead. "What?"

He fished a key out of his pocket, which is when I noticed the shiny new chain and padlock on the cowshed door. It must have cost Pat a week's worth of whiskey sales to buy that thing.

"Did Mean-Dog pay us now?"

Pat snorted. "He'd as soon kick me as pay us a penny of what he owes."

I nodded at the chain. "You afraid someone's going to steal her body?"

He gave me the funniest look. "I'm not afraid of anybody breaking *in.*"

Which is another of those things that don't sound good when someone says it before entering a room with a dead body in it.

He unlocked the lock then reached down to where his shillelagh leaned against the frame. It was made from a whopping great piece of oak root, all twisted and polished, the handle wrapped with leather.

"What's going on now, Paddy?" I asked, starting to back away, and remembering a dozen other things that needed doing. Like running and hiding and getting drunk.

"I think it was that green stuff from the comet," Paddy whispered as he slowly pushed open the door. "It did something to her. Something *unnatural.*"

"Everything about Sophie was unnatural," I reminded him.

The door swung inward with a creak and the light of day shone into the cowshed. It was ten feet wide by twenty feet deep, with a wooden rail, a manger and stalls for two cows—though Paddy only ever owned just the one. The scrawny milk cow Catherine doted on was lying on her side in the middle of the floor.

I mean to say what was *left* of her was lying on the floor. I tried to scream but all that came out of my whiskey-raw throat was a crooked little screech.

The cow had been torn to pieces. Blood and gobs of meat littered the floor, and there were more splashes of blood on the wall. Right there in the middle of all that muck, sitting like the queen of all Damnation was Aunt Sophie. Her fat face and throat were covered with blood. Her cotton gown was torn and streaked with cow shit and gore. Flies buzzed around her and crawled on her face.

Aunt Sophie was gnawing on what looked like half a cow liver. When the sunlight fell across her from the open door she raised her head and looked right at us. Her skin was as gray-pale as the maggots that wriggled through little rips in her skin; but it was her eyes that took all the starch out of my knees. They were dry and milky but the pupils glowed an unnatural green, just like the piece of comet that had slid down her gullet.

"Oh… lordy-lordy-save a sinner!" I heard someone say in an old woman's voice, and then realized that it was me speaking.

Aunt Sophie lunged at us. All of sudden she went from sitting there like a fat dead slob eating Paddy's cow and then she was coming at us like a charging bull. I shrieked. I'm not proud; I'll admit it.

If it hadn't been for the length of chain Paddy had wound around her waist she'd have had me, too, 'cause I could no more move from where I was frozen than I could make leprechauns fly out of my bottom. Sophie's lunge was jerked to a stop with her yellow teeth not a foot from my throat.

Paddy stepped past me and raised the club. If Sophie saw it, or cared, she didn't show it.

"Get back, you fat sow!" he yelled and took to thumping her about the face and shoulders, which did no noticeable good.

"Paddy, my dear," I croaked, "I think I've soiled myself."

Paddy stepped back, his face running sweat. "No, that's her you smell. It's too hot in this shed. She's coming up ripe." He pulled me further back and we watched as Sophie snapped the air in our direction for a whole minute, then she lost interest and went back to gnawing on the cow.

"What's happened to her?"

"She's dead," he said.

"She can't be. I've seen dead folks before, lad, and she's a bit too spry."

He shook his head. "I checked and I checked. I even stuck her with the pitchfork. Just experimental like, and I got them tines all the way in but she didn't bleed."

"But... but..."

"Catherine came out here, too. Before Sophie woke back up, I mean. She took it hard and didn't want to hear about comets or nothing like that. She thinks we poisoned her with our whiskey."

"It's strong, I'll admit, but it's more likely to kill a person than make the dead wake back up again."

"I told her that and she commenced to hit me, and she hits as hard as Mean-Dog. She had a good handful of my hair and was swatting me a good'un when Sophie just woke up."

"How'd Catherine take that?"

"Well, she took it poorly, the lass. At first she tried to comfort Sophie, but when the old bitch tried to bite her Catherine seemed to cool a bit toward her aunt. It wasn't until after Sophie tore the throat out of the cow that Catherine seemed to question whether Sophie was really her aunt or more of an old acquaintance of the family."

"What'd she say?"

"It's not what she said so much as it was her hitting Sophie in the back of the head with a shovel."

"That'll do 'er."

"It dropped Sophie for a while and I hustled out and bought some chain and locks. By the time I came back Catherine was in a complete state. Sophie kept waking up, you see, and she had to clout her a fair few times to keep her tractable."

"So where's the missus now?"

"Abed. Seems she's discovered the medicinal qualities of our whiskey."

"I've been saying it for years."

He nodded and we stood there, watching Sophie eat the cow.

"So, Paddy me old mate," I said softly, "what do you think we should do?"

"With Sophie?"

"Aye."

Paddy's bruised faced took on the one expression I would have thought impossible under the circumstances. He smiled. A great big smile that was every bit as hungry and nasty as Aunt Sophie.

* * *

It took three days of sweet talk and charm, of sweat-soaked promises and cajoling but we finally got him to come to Paddy's cowshed. Then there he was, the Mean-Dog himself, all six-and-a-half feet of him, flanked by Killer Muldoon and Razor Riley, the three of them standing in Paddy's yard late on Sunday afternoon.

My head was ringing from a courtesy smacking Mean-Dog had given me when I'd come to his office; and Pat's lips were puffed out again—but Pat was still smiling.

"So, lads," Mean-Dog said quietly, "tell me again why I'm here in a yard that smells of pig shit instead of at home drinking a beer."

"Cow shit," Pat corrected him and got a clout for it.

"We have a new business partner, Mr. Mulligan," I said. "And she told us that we can't provide no more whiskey until you and she settle accounts."

"She? You're working with a woman?" His voice was filled with contempt. "Who's this woman, then? Sounds like she has more mouth than she can use."

"You might be saying that," Pat agreed softly. "It's my Aunt Sophie."

I have to admit, that did give even Mean-Dog a moment's pause. There are Cherokee war parties that would go twenty miles out to their way not to cross Sophie, and that was *before* the comet.

"Sophie Kilpatrick, eh?" He looked at his two bruisers. Neither of them knew her and they weren't impressed. "Where is she?"

"In the cowshed," Pat said. "She said she wanted to meet somewhere quiet."

"Shrewd," Mean-Dog agreed, but he was still uncertain. "Lads, go in and ask Miss Sophie to come out."

The two goons shrugged and went into the shed as I inched my way toward the side alley. Pat held his ground and I don't know whether it was all the clouting 'round the head he'd been getting, or the latest batch of whiskey, or maybe he'd just reached the bottom of his own cup and couldn't take no more from anyone, but Pat O'Leary stood there grinning at Mean-Dog as the two big men opened the shed door and went in.

Pat hadn't left a light on in there and it was a cloudy day. The goons had to feel their way in the dark. When they commenced screaming I figured they'd found their way to Sophie. This was Sunday and the cow was long gone. Sophie was feeling a mite peckish.

Mean-Dog jumped back from the doorway and dragged out his pistol with one hand and took a handful of Pat's shirt with the other. "What the hell's happening? Who's in there?"

"Just Aunt Sophie," Pat said and actually held his hand to God as he said it.

Mean-Dog shoved him aside and kicked open the door. That was his first mistake because Razor Riley's head smacked him right in the face. Mean-Dog staggered back and stood there in dumb shock as his leg-breaker's head bounced to the ground right at his feet. Riley's face wore an expression of profound shock.

"What?" Mean-Dog asked, as if anything Pat or I could say would be an adequate answer to that.

The second mistake Mean-Dog made was to get mad and go charging into the shed. We watched him enter and we both jumped as he fired two quick shots, then another, and another.

I don't know, even to this day, whether one of those shots clipped her chain or whether Sophie was even stronger than we thought she was, but a second later Mean-Dog came barreling out of the cowshed, running at full tilt, with Sophie Kilpatrick howling after him trailing six feet of chain. She was covered in blood and the sound she made would have made a banshee take a vow of silence. They were gone down the alley in a heartbeat. Pat and I stood there in shock for a moment. Then we peered around the edge of the door into the shed.

The lower half of Razor Riley lay just about where the cow had been. Killer Muldoon was all in one piece, but there were pieces missing from him, if you follow. Sophie had her way with him and he lay dead as a mullet, his throat torn out and his blood pooled around him.

"Oh, lordy," I said. "This is bad for us, Pat. This is jail and skinny fellows like you and me have to wear petticoats in prison."

But there was a strange light in his eyes. Not a glowing green light, which was a comfort, but not a nice light either. He looked down at the bodies and then over his shoulder in the direction where Sophie and Mean-Dog had vanished. He licked his bruised lips and said, "You know, Pegleg… there are other sonsabitches who owe us money."

"Those are bad thoughts you're having, Paddy my dear."

"I'm not saying we feed them to Sophie, but if we let it get known, so to speak. Maybe show them what's left of these lads…"

"Patrick O'Leary you listen to me—we are not about being criminal masterminds here. I'm not half as smart as a fencepost and you're not half as smart as me, so let's not be planning anything extravagant."

Which is when Mean-Dog Mulligan came screaming *back* into Pat's yard. God only knows what twisted puzzle-path he took through the neighborhood but there he was running back toward us, his arms bleeding from a couple of bites and his big legs pumping to keep him just ahead of Sophie.

"Oh dear," Pat said in a voice that made it clear that his plan still had a few bugs to be sorted out.

"Shovel!" I said and lunged for the one Catherine had used on her aunt. Pat grabbed a pickaxe and we swung at the same time.

I hit Sophie fair and square in the face and the shock of it rang all the way up my arms and shivered the tool right out of my hands; but the force of the blow had its way with her and her green eyes were instantly blank. She stopped dead in her tracks and then pitched backward to measure her length on the ground.

Pat's swing had a different effect. The big spike of the pickaxe caught Mean-Dog square in the center of the chest and though everyone said the man had no heart, Pat and his pickaxe begged to differ. The gangster's last word was "Urk!" and he fell backward, as dead as Riley and Muldoon.

"Quick!" I said and we fetched the broken length of chain from the shed and wound it about Sophie, pinning her arms to her body and then snugging it all with the padlock. While Pat was checking the lock I fetched the wheelbarrow, and we grunted and cursed some more as we got her onto it.

"We have to hide the bodies," I said, and Pat, too stunned to speak, just nodded. He grabbed Mean-Dog's heels and dragged him into the shed while I played a quick game of football with Razor Riley's head. Soon the three toughs were hidden in the shed. Pat closed it and we locked the door.

That left Sophie sprawled on the barrow, and she was already starting to show signs of waking up.

"Sweet suffering Jesus!" I yelled. "Let's get her into the hills. We can chain her to a tree by the still until we figure out what to do."

"What about them?" Pat said, jerking a thumb at the shed.

"They're not going anywhere."

We took the safest route that we could manage quickly and if anyone did see us hauling a fat blood-covered struggling dead woman in chains out of town in a wheelbarrow it never made it into an official report. We chained her to a stout oak and then hurried back. It was already dark and we were scared and exhausted and I wanted a drink so badly I could cry.

"I had a jug in the shed," Pat whispered as we crept back into his yard.

"Then consider me on the wagon, lad."

"Don't be daft. There's nothing in there that can hurt us now. And we have to decide what to do with those lads."

"God… this is the sort of thing that could make the mother of Jesus eat fish on Friday."

He unlocked the door and we went inside, careful not to step in blood, careful not to look at the bodies. I lit his small lantern and we closed the door so we could drink for a bit and sort things out.

After we'd both had a few pulls on the bottle I said, "Pat, now be honest, my lad… you didn't think this through now did you?"

"It worked out differently in my head." He took a drink.

"How's that?"

"Mean-Dog got scared of us and paid us, and then everyone else heard about Sophie and got scared of us, too."

"Even though she was chained up in a cowshed?"

"Well, she got out, didn't she?"

"Was that part of the plan?"

"Not as such."

"So, in the plan we just scared people with a dead fat woman in a shed."

"It sounds better when it's only a thought."

"Most things do." We toasted on that.

Mean-Dog Mulligan said, "Ooof."

"Oh dear," I said, the jug halfway to my mouth.

We both turned and there he was, Mean-Dog himself with a pick-axe in his chest and no blood left in him, struggling to sit up. Next to him Killer Muldoon was starting to twitch. Mean-Dog looked at us and his eyes were already glowing green.

"Was this part of the plan, then?" I whispered.

Pat said "Eeep!" which was all he could manage.

That's how the whole lantern thing started, you see. It was never the cow, 'cause the cow was long dead by then. It was Patrick who grabbed the lantern and threw it, screaming all the while, right at Mean-Dog Mulligan.

I grabbed Pat by the shoulder and dragged him out of the shed and we slammed the door and leaned on it while Patrick fumbled the lock and chain into place.

It was another plan we hadn't thought all the way through. The shed didn't have a cow anymore, but it had plenty of straw. It fair burst into flame. We staggered back from it and then stood in his yard, feeling the hot wind blow past us, watching as the breeze blew the fire across the alley. Oddly, Pat's house never burned down, and Catherine slept through the whole thing.

It was about 9 p.m. when it started and by midnight the fire had spread all the way across the south branch of the river. We watched the business district burn—and with it all of the bars that bought our whiskey.

Maybe God was tired of our shenanigans, or maybe he had a little pity left for poor fools, but sometime after midnight it started to rain. They said later that if it hadn't rained then all of Chicago would have burned. As it was, it was only half the town. The church burned down, though, and Father Callahan was roasted like a Christmas goose. Sure and the Lord had His mysterious ways.

Two other things burned up that night. Our still and Aunt Sophie. All we ever found was her skeleton and the chains wrapped around the burned stump of the oak. On the ground between her charred feet was a small lump of green rock. Neither one of us dared touch it. We just dug a hole and swatted it in with the shovel, covered it over and fled. As far as I know it's still up there to this day.

When I think of what would have happened if we'd followed through with Pat's plan... or if Mean-Dog and Muldoon had gotten out and bitten someone else. Who knows how fast it could have spread, or how far. It also tends to make my knees knock when I think of how many other pieces of that green comet must have fallen... and where those stones are. Just thinking about it's enough to make a man want to take a drink

I would like to say that Patrick and I changed our ways after that night, that we never rebuilt the still and never took nor sold another

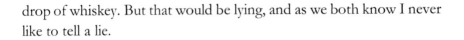

drop of whiskey. But that would be lying, and as we both know I never like to tell a lie.

HISTORICAL NOTE: There are several popular theories on how the Great Fire of Chicago got started. It is widely believed that it started in a cowshed behind the house of Patrick and Catherine O'Leary. Historian Richard Bales asserts that Daniel "Pegleg" Sullivan started it while trying to steal some milk. Other theories blame a fallen lantern or a discarded cigar. One major theory, first floated in 1882 and which has gained a lot of ground lately, is that Biela's Comet rained down fragments as it broke up over the Midwest.

About the only thing experts and historians can agree on is that the cow had nothing to do with it.

226

The Third Option

DEREK GUNN

"I fucking hate dead people," Deputy William Boyle whined as he reached for his hat. Outside the wind howled and threw sand against the windows of the small jail, the sound crackling like bacon sizzling on a pan. "I mean why can't we just put them back in the ground where they belong?"

Sheriff Amos Carter waited impatiently for his deputy and tried to ignore the pounding in his head. Boyle was a good man but inexperienced. He also asked way too many questions, but he had just become a father yesterday and they had celebrated far too much the previous night. Carter decided he would allow him a little leeway, but only as much as his throbbing head would tolerate, and his limit was fast approaching. "Now, Will," Carter sighed, "you know as well as I do that the Governor has ordered that these dead folk be left alone until they can decide whether they have a legal right to walk around."

"And what if they decide that they don't?" Boyle pressed him.

"Then," Carter sighed and slapped his thigh impatiently, "you can put them back in the ground. Now hurry up. We have to let him know about our town rules before he goes and breaks any of 'em."

"I'm coming," Boyle pouted, "but I still can't figure out what the good Lord was thinking 'bout when he sent 'em back to clutter up the place."

"It had nothing to do with the Lord's work as you well know." Carter pushed the younger man out the door where his startled cry was ripped from his mouth by the wind.

The day was young. The sun was still climbing in the sky. Sand swirled around the two men and forced them to pull their bandanas up over their noses and mouths. Carter cursed as his eyes were assaulted by the sand and he hunched up further as the wind snapped at him. It was June. Normally the sun would already be hot enough to fry an egg, but the sand was so thick after a dry month that the wind had whipped it up easily and it was blocking most of the heat. He squinted upward but could only see a vague outline of the sun through the storm. The weak glow cast the town in an eerie, diffused light.

The two men hurried to the saloon. Carter was thankful the storm cut off any further questions Boyle might have had. The subject of the dead walking around was confusing enough to him without having to come up with answers for an over-eager deputy as well.

Of course it would be easier to just kill them all, but one of the buggers had petitioned the Governor that the dead still had rights. He had argued that the fact that they no longer breathed did not necessarily change their legal status and the Governor's legal experts did not have any counter to that argument. Until the lawyers got their act together, they would have to put up with their share of visitors, although few of them came this far upstate.

It had all started two years ago as an act of final defiance by an Indian shaman before his tribe had been kicked off their land. Nobody knew for certain what had happened. The accepted version was that an Indian shaman had put a curse on the white man that "the dead would rise and ravage that which he held most dear." Carter assumed that the Shaman had meant for the dead to kill the living but something had gone wrong. The dead *did* crave that which the white man held most dear, there was no argument about that, it was just that the shaman had miscalculated on the white man's priorities. It wasn't life that the white man held most precious. Out here in the west, it was gold that men lusted after. Gold meant power. Of course some idiot had gone and killed the shaman in the meantime so the curse could not be reversed. So for now at least, they were stuck with the dead folk.

The two men reached the wooden boardwalk, which stretched from Tracy's Hardware to the hotel. The saloon was about half way along, past a barber shop, a few houses and the doctor's office. The path boasted a wooden canopy so they were shielded from the brunt of the storm as they continued walking. Unfortunately this also meant that it afforded Boyle the opportunity to launch into another question and, as if on cue, he did just that. "It's kind'a weird, don't you think?"

"What's that?" Carter rolled his eyes and reminded himself that Boyle was the only able bodied man in the town willing to work for the wages that the state paid.

"This gold thing."

The dead craved gold and needed it to survive. They needed it as surely as man needed food. "Is there anything in particular or is it everything in general that you find weird?"

"Well why do they drink it?"

Carter could understand the young man's confusion. He had been incredulous himself when he had heard it. He had since found out that hundreds of years ago kings and queens in Europe frequently took gold in the same fashion, believing that anything so expensive must be good for them. The problem now was that the living also coveted gold, and so trouble had begun almost as soon as the dead's cravings became common knowledge.

Carter sighed and stopped. Boyle didn't notice for a moment and continued on and had to hurry back. He smiled sheepishly. "Look. These things are dead. If we left them alone they'd eventually rot away and solve all our problems. Unfortunately that shaman worked some weird shit and gold slows their rotting. And before you ask I don't know how." Carter put his hand up to enforce his statement. "Anyway their teeth ain't as strong as they used to be so they have to take it in a drink or as a handful of finely shaved dust." Carter had had enough questions. "Bill," he placed a shoulder on the young man's shoulders. "I'll handle this. You go on over to Muriel in the hotel and let her know the Governor will be here later today. No doubt he'll want his usual suite."

"That's the fourth time this month," Boyle grinned lasciviously. "Those bedsprings must be bust by now."

"The Governor's sexual antics are no concern of yours," Carter admonished him and then grinned. "Mind you keep your mouth shut though. If his wife finds out he'll probably fire us just for spite."

The younger man grinned and headed off toward the hotel, giving Carter a moment to collect his thoughts before he entered the saloon. He pushed open the battered swinging doors to the saloon and winced as the hinges creaked and sent pain stabbing through his already delicate head. He stood for a moment and breathed a sigh of relief as he brushed dust and grit from his clothes. Outside, the church began summoning the faithful to worship and the incessant tolling of the bells reverberated painfully in his head.

Carter looked around the saloon, taking in his surroundings in a practised glance. He hadn't survived twenty years as a lawman by being stupid. He had long ago perfected the ability to read the occupants in a room by their stance or the looks on their faces when he entered a room, even when he was suffering from a hangover. Long slabs of wood lay on top of numerous barrels and dominated the room in front of him. The wooden planks acted as a bar until the new one arrived from St. Louis. The owner had promised the town a beautiful mahogany bar, with brass fittings, though Carter would miss this beer-stained monstrosity when it went; it had a certain charm. Large ornate oil lamps hung from the low ceiling. They burned merrily and cast deep shadows into the corners of the room. Tables lay scattered around the room in a chaotic jumble that seemed to have no plan other than to fit as many customers as possible into a relatively small space.

His eyes were drawn immediately to three Mexicans in the corner. The three men leaned in on the table conspiratorially with their elbows on the edges. Their quick, furtive glances toward Peterson behind the bar intimated some illicit activity, though their harsh accented voices and guttural laughter were far too loud to suggest anything he needed to be involved in. They were probably looking for somewhere to ride out the storm and had their own bottle hidden under the table rather than pay the exorbitant prices Peterson charged. Their clothes were simple and of poor quality. They did not appear to have weapons of any kind. He eyes continued to scan the room.

It was early yet so only two girls prowled the floor. Their gaudy colours and heavy makeup were more suited to the dim lighting of the evening. The morning's brightness, though somewhat subdued from the storm, illuminated their tired faces and lustreless hair more than they probably would have liked. They looked up with hope in their eyes as the doors creaked and announced his entry but they quickly lost interest when they saw him. The "moral majority" in the town constantly put him under pressure to run the girls out, but the law still tolerated their profession. Until that changed he could do nothing, though he did make sure that he was seen as neutral and that meant keeping his distance from both groups.

John Peterson stood behind the bar in his usual boiled white shirt and brocaded vest. He sported an overly-large moustache as if to compensate for the lack of hair on his head. His ruddy complexion hinted at an addiction to the liquor he sold. He rubbed furiously at a glass and moved his head toward the far corner of the bar. Carter nodded and glanced over toward the indicated table near the window where a lone man sat.

He spent another moment casually brushing dust from his clothes and used the time to look the stranger over. The man's boots and jeans were almost the same colour, with the natural fading of the materials and the dirt encrusted liberally over them both. He wore a dark blue shirt of good quality, though the material was worn in places and the collar was frayed. A black vest with three silver buttons, dulled from lack of attention, completed the man's wardrobe. He also wore a matching black hat that cast a shadow over his face but Carter could see that he was relatively clean shaven and that his hair was still quite short, the ends only curling slightly above the frayed collar.

Not dead that long then, he mused as he continued to study the figure. Hair had become the accepted method of judging the duration of a dead person's existence. Hair seemed to grow for quite a while after death, so many of them had long hair and uneven, scraggly beards. The dead seemed to have no interest in hygiene, so most of them smelled foul, somewhere between rotten meat and an open sewer. Their hair was usually matted and infested with all kinds of parasites.

Carter came to a stop at the table. The man moved his head slowly and regarded him with a cool appraisal of his own. The man had a strong jaw line but his desiccated skin was pulled too taut over the bone. This made the man's face angular rather than strong. His nose seemed too long and narrow with the flesh having receded in death, giving him a hawkish appearance that threw shadows over his already sunken eye sockets. His eyes bore the hallmark of the dead. Skin stretched tightly at the sides making them appear as if they were constantly squinting. The high cheekbones, where the bone protruded and stretched the skin around his mouth, gave the stranger an insane-looking grin. It was unnerving, looking at someone who grinned constantly, but it was the eyes that held him, as they always did. They were yellow with a small bead of black in the centre. There was no sense of life in those eyes as they regarded him, nothing but dark ovals of purest black.

The recent Civil and Indian wars had left thousands dead. The graveyards full to capacity. When the dead had begun to rise, there had been no shortage of corpses. Suddenly towns and cities filled with ambling corpses that, while they seemed to pose no immediate threat to the population, did make everyone uncomfortable. The first response had been to kill them. Thousands died, again, but the dead did not simply stand still and let it happen. Once they got over the shock of finding themselves walking around, the dead began to regain their wits and began to protect themselves. They were also bloody difficult to kill. They could survive almost any wound and only finally died when their brains were destroyed.

The figure nodded to him and Carter nodded back as he finished his appraisal. The man might be dirty and rotting but the two colts strapped to his sides were in beautiful condition. Even the holster shone with a recent oiling and the weapon's worn bone handles testified to long years of use. He also noted that both guns were tied low on the man's thighs. *A gunfighter,* Carter cursed his luck. He was not slow on the draw himself but he just knew as he looked into the stranger's eyes that he would be no match for this man. Dead or not, this man exuded competence. The dead tended to move more slowly than they had in life—something to do with the blood stagnating in their veins he had been told—but this corpse did not look slow. He had moved with an easy grace when he turned to face Carter and not the exaggerated slowness of many of his kind. Carter also noted that the man had cut his fingernails short to accommodate a fast draw and he felt his heart beat faster.

People had begun to grow worried when the dead began to defend themselves. It was assumed that, strange as it was, the phenomenon was still an isolated incident and once they killed off the walking corpses, things would return to normal. It was only when they realized that even those who had recently died also rose again that things had gone to hell. The government had been forced to call for a cessation of hostilities on both sides until something could be done. The most popular solution seemed to be that a reservation, similar to that put in place for the Indians, would be provided and everyone seemed to calm down while plans were laid.

The subsequent discovery that the dead needed gold to survive threw everything into chaos. Hostilities broke out again. It had been at that point that one of the dead had written a legal paper citing that the dead still had rights and as such should have access to all the protection that the law could provide. The paper also called for the return of all the dead's assets. The banks disagreed. The banks had gotten used to keeping the money and assets that the dead left behind, when no beneficiaries were involved, and they did not want to have to give these assets back. Cases were brought against the banks by a growing number of dead people, but until the question of their rights was addressed there could be no decision on who owned the money. This of course meant that the dead had no means of purchasing the gold they required to survive.

That left the dead with few choices. If they wanted to continue to exist they only had two options; either they earned their money or they would have to steal it. Most of the living would not employ the dead, so many of them were forced into crime to survive. It was this fact that branded all of them as criminals. This had the result of the dead being shunned. Violence had a habit of breaking out regularly when they came to town. While Carter was not allowed to throw the dead out of his jurisdiction, just because they were dead, he did make sure to warn any who came through that he took a dim view of anyone causing trouble in his town.

He took a deep breath and addressed the man. "Morning," Carter managed finally, pleased that his voice didn't break. The corpse nodded back, his mouth still grinning insanely at him. As a law officer he was not allowed merely to kill the stranger on a whim. Until the lawyers ruled one way or the other, this corpse had as many rights as any of the town's citizens. His hands were tied.

Only the elite Texas Rangers could kill without recourse, and they hardly ever came this far north. The Governor had made the Rangers exempt in an attempt to mollify his richest supporters. He had dressed it up in fancy language extolling the Ranger's proud history and supporting their judgment when on missions. It just wasn't practical, he had stated in his address to the papers, to force these men to check in before they acted. It would be suicide for these trusted men to be second-guessed for every decision. The result was that the Rangers had become untouchable. Carter had heard stories of Rangers combing the state and quietly executing the dead. It seemed that the Governor was making sure that whatever might be decided by the government about the issue of the dead's rights, it would not have an impact on the Governor's own finances.

Stories were becoming more frequent of Ranger death-squads sweeping the state trying to accomplish their mission before the lawyers came to any decisions. Carter didn't really care one way or the other. The dead were dead. Who cared if they were put back in the ground? Carter knew more than most about the current situation because the Governor's mistress lived in his town. Each time he came to visit, Carter made sure that he got an update from the Governor's bodyguards.

Carter shifted on his feet nervously. Most of the dead he dealt with were easy prey. He could intimidate them easily, but this corpse seemed far too confident. He had never seen such confidence in the dead before, and it worried him. He cursed himself for letting Boyle go on to the hotel. He could have done with the younger man's support. Outside the bells finally stopped tolling and he sighed in relief as the pounding in his head began to subside. The sun flared briefly outside in momentary relief from the wind and its glare blazed through the glass and reflected off something on the man's chest.

Carter frowned as he blinked and then the glare suddenly stopped as the wind picked up and the sand once again drew its veil over the sun. He studied the man's chest and saw that there was a badge there of some sort. *Was he a lawman too?* That would certainly make things easier. A lawman, even a dead one, would understand his predicament. He looked harder at the badge; the edges were not pointed like his own and it was more rounded just like...

Oh shit! Realization flooded through him. He's a Texas Ranger. A *dead* Texas Ranger. No one had foreseen that. Did that mean he still had his immunity to the law? *Shit.* He had to warn the Governor.

Suddenly a terrible thought struck him. If this ranger killed the Governor, would the Governor still retain his powers of office after death? That could turn the whole state upside down. The dead already outnumbered the living in the state. If they were in charge, they might be able to pass laws that would make living in the state almost impossible. Up till now the dead had been limited to two options to obtain the gold they coveted—employment, which was unlikely, and crime, which gave the living an excuse to kill them. It struck Carter they had discovered a third option to their problem. If they controlled the law, they could control the gold. Up till now people had considered the dead to be stupid, merely an inconvenience rather than any real threat. If they were capable of such planning, it showed an intelligence that sent a cold feeling of fear flooding through his veins.

These thoughts flooded his throbbing head in a flash. The Ranger merely smiled insanely at him.

He had to do something. He dropped his hand to his own weapon, adrenaline speeding his reflexes. The Ranger moved in a blur and suddenly Carter was staring at the barrel of the Ranger's colt before he even slapped leather. He looked into the Ranger's dead eyes and thought for a moment that he saw a widening of the corpse's grin. Maybe that damn shaman had got it right after all! By making the dead dependant on gold he had forced them to strike at the cornerstones of the country itself—its wealth and power. For a second he wondered what it would be like being dead.

Then he heard the shot. Darkness swept over him.

The Loaned Ranger

John Peel

The filthy black storm clouds hovered over the mesa as they had all day, threatening Heaven's vengeance on the small group of riders far below. The six Texas Rangers were moving slowly toward a box canyon, following a fresh trail. When the thunder broke it wasn't from the skies but from the rocks alongside the canyon walls. Rifles and handguns barked and pounded. A metallic rain slashed through the six men.

A couple of the unprepared victims strove to draw and raise their own guns, but they were cut down with no chance of returning a shot. One by one the Rangers jerked in their saddles, their bodies dancing as bullets tore into them. Then they fell into pools of their own blood. Screaming, terrified horses bucked and whirled. In the withering fire, most of them fell too, bleeding and gasping beside their riders. In moments, it was over. The flashes of fire from the rocks ceased. Then flashes began far above in the skies.

Cavendish made his way out of hiding, his gun trailing smoke as he walked slowly down to the fallen men. His gang followed him, their arms at the ready. One of the Rangers moved, his fingers inching toward his fallen revolver. Cavendish took quick aim and blew the man's brains all over the dust. That seemed to trigger a wave of ferocity in his followers. Gunfire erupted for another thirty seconds, bullets plowing into the fallen corpses.

"Enough!" Cavendish finally called, holstering his hot pistol. "The sons of bitches are dead."

Thunder cracked above his head as if to underline his pronouncement. He glanced upward. Rain started to hammer down from the Texan sky. Cavendish grinned. "This downpour'll cover our tracks in a matter of hours, boys. By the time the Rangers find their fallen compadres, we'll be untraceable. Back to the horses and let's vamoose."

The rain poured about them, pooling and washing at the blood on the ground, as if to scour the earth clean. Lightning cracked across the sky above them.

"Almost Biblical in its wrath," one of the gang noted. "A presage of the apocalypse even."

"A presage of our splitting the loot from that bank," Cavendish growled. His men were a cowardly, superstitious lot, and he didn't want them getting any wrong ideas. Their lust for the stolen gold would keep them contented for now though.

Above them on the rim of the canyon a lone figure watched and waited. He observed with hooded eyes as the killers recovered their hidden horses, mounted and rode off through the downpour. None of them looked back toward their fallen victims. Once he was certain that he had not been observed, the watcher mounted his own pony, and rode carefully down the trail. Already, the dust was turning to mud. The way was slippery, but his pony was sure-footed and made it down the wall of the canyon without mishap.

The Indian shook his head. Damn these Anglos and their bloodlust! He had no idea what had caused this fight, but he had no choice but to intervene. Ignoring the rain, he vaulted from the bare back of his pony and approached the group of fallen men.

The bodies being washed clean in the rain looked grotesque. They had fallen with twisted limbs and frozen expressions of fear and shock on their faces. The horses too were warped where they lay. Blood-laced rivulets ran from the soaked corpses. The Indian, sighing, studied the dead. Most were so bullet-ridden they were useless. He needed one without injury to the brain, but the outlaws' blood-lust had led them to almost obliterate the features of their foes.

The last man lay slightly apart. He'd been holding back somewhat, maybe worried about the way they were riding. He was one of the few who'd managed to draw his weapon. His revolver was still clutched in his dead grip. He had been shot several times in the chest. One shot had creased his forehead just above the eyes leaving a bloody furrow. The Indian crouched to examine the head. Not too bad, all things considered, and the brain hadn't been penetrated. It wasn't a good subject, but it was his best bet. The other corpses were completely unusable.

He glanced around and saw there was a slight overhang off to one side, giving some shelter from the rain. There might be sufficient room for a small fire for warmth—and other matters. He whistled for his pony, then manhandled the body he'd chosen across its back. He set off for the overhang, his pony trotting obediently behind him.

It took him some time to make a fire, but finally it caught and grew, crackling and spluttering with wind-driven drops of rain. Once it was going, he took a small pot from the pack on the horse's back and his herb bag. He sifted through the herbs, pulling out the ones he needed. He went over the blending in his mind several times, to be sure he had it right. He had not had cause to use this potion often, so it was important that he recall it exactly. Once he was certain it was correct, he broke and mixed the herbs with rain water in the pot and set it on the fire to boil. Then he turned his attention to the fallen man.

He wasn't the perfect choice for this, but there was none better. His companions were all too damaged to use. This man was almost intact—at least in the necessary areas. His heart had been destroyed, but that wasn't essential, and other bullets had ripped through organs that had once been vital.

Now the only one that mattered was the brain, and that appeared intact.

The Indian began the incantation. The potion was important, but without the right frame of mind, the correct prayers to the Manitou, and the proper respect shown to the other dead, this would never work. The prayers were long and involved, but he managed them without faltering. His pony stood, the only observer, beside the fallen body.

Once the words were done, it was time for deeds. He reached for the pot, stirring the thick potion with a stick until he was certain it was of the right consistency. Then he took it from the fire using a rag, and set it down beside the cooling body. It had been almost an hour since the man had died, but it wasn't yet too long.

Using the potion, the Indian drew signs and shapes across the man's face. Then he tore open the man's shirt and worked around the bullet holes to finish the markings. He began the invocation again, then poured the last of the potion between the dead man's lips. His prayers reached their fevered pitch, and he threw his hands up to the Heavens beseeching the Manitou to hear his words, to return the spirit of the slain man—even if only temporarily.

The Indian glanced down at the fallen white man. Nothing. Perhaps it was too late, after all? No, it couldn't be. He *had* to make this spell work. He repeated his prayer, filling his words with all the desperation that he felt. Then he threw up his hands again, thanked the Manitou for his power and looked at his patient.

The fingers of the man's right hand—the one that hand been clutching his gun before the Indian had removed it—twitched slightly. Not much movement, but *any* movement meant that the ritual had worked. The Indian grinned slightly, then breathed a sincere prayer of thanks to the gods.

The hand twitched more and the eyelids opened. Cold blue, dead eyes focused on his face. The dead man's mouth moved, but only a croak came out.

"Talk later," the Indian advised. "Rest for now. The storm will soon be finished." He returned to his pouch, and made a fresh selection of herbs. The undead man would require strengthening, so the Indian started another pot brewing. The white man nodded slightly and appeared to fall asleep. His chest didn't rise and fall nor did his heart beat, but he was still alive—or, at least, nearly alive.

By the time the Indian's brew was ready, the white man had opened his eyes again and watched as his companion brought him a cup of the potion. The Indian supported his head and urged the Ranger to drink of the cup. It took the dead man a few minutes to get the hang of using his mouth to swallow, but then he drained the cup. The icy eyes fixed on the Indian.

"What happened?" he asked. His voice was as chilled as his eyes. A whisper of death ran through the voice.

"You died," the Indian explained. "Shot." He pointed to the holes in the white man's chest. "Pretty bad."

"Then why aren't I still dead?" the Ranger demanded.

"I brought you back," his companion explained. "Your spirit is on loan from gods. Maybe short time, maybe long. Who can say? Gods are not too predictable."

The white man struggled to sit up and accepted help gratefully. He stared at the Indian. "Let me get this straight," he said. "You used some heathen ritual to reanimate my corpse?"

"Pretty much, yeah," the Indian agreed. "Potions, too. Deep mystery, few know." He tapped his chest and grinned. "I know. The gods give you back. I asked nicely."

"Okay." The Ranger closed his eyes and gathered his strength before reopening them. "Why in God's holy name did you do that? Out of the kindness of your heart?"

"No, not kindness. Leaving you dead is kindness." The Indian gestured at him. "Your body is in rough shape. Heart gone, liver gone. Manhood…" He made a gesture. "But the brain is okay, and brain is important. Without brain, no life." He gestured into the still-falling rain. "Other white-eyes too damaged. Only you were workable."

"Fine." The Ranger gave a sigh that seemed to come from the depths of an ancient tomb. "But *why* in perdition did you bring even *me* back to life? Is this your idea of fun, maybe?"

"No, not fun—necessity," the Indian protested. "Think about it. Six dead Rangers, one live Indian. If White-eyes find me, who will they blame?"

"I take your point." The man sighed again. "But I'm hardly a credible witness that you're innocent of my murder, am I?"

"Not witness," his companion said. "Vengeance. You get the real killers."

The Ranger glared at him. "You think I can take on six murderous outlaws all by myself? I'll be shot to pieces the next time."

The Indian grinned. "You're already dead—damn hard to kill again."

"You mean I can't die?"

"No, you can die," The Indian said. "It's just hard. Silver can do it, through the brain. Incantations and prayers, too. But the killers do not know my magic, so you should be okay there."

The Ranger examined his hands, cold and white. Even the warmth from the fire couldn't help there. "I'm not entirely sure I *want* to stay alive," he said. "This body doesn't feel quite right, and I kind of miss some of the pieces you couldn't restore."

"Sorry. I did best I could." The Indian shrugged. "I need you to get killers. Then maybe you can die again, if Manitou says okay."

The Ranger fell back to the ground. "I am not entirely certain I have the best of this deal," he complained. "Now I must rest. I may be alive again, but dying seems to have tired me somewhat. Wake me when the rain stops."

It took more than an hour before the Indian judged that the storm had finally spent its fury. He shook the sleeping dead man awake. The Ranger rolled over and caught sight of his face in one of the pond-sized puddles. He reached up slowly to touch the furrow above his eyes.

"This looks bad," he commented. "I won't be an acceptable sight in polite society. I need some kind of mask to cover it up, or people will stare at me."

"If you wear a mask, won't people stare?" the Indian queried.

"Yeah, but at the mask—not at *me*." He went to where one of his fallen companions lay. "Lucky stiff," he muttered. Then, using his knife, he cut himself a crude mask that would cover the scar, and used a rawhide thong to tie it into place. Then he studied his reflection again. "Better," he decided. He glanced back at his fallen comrades. "I'll be back to bury you when I've avenged you," he promised them.

Only one of the Rangers' horses had survived the massacre. It had been skittish before, but had calmed down during the storm as it stood with the Indian's placid pony. The Ranger swung himself into the saddle. He watched curiously as the Indian did likewise.

"You aiming on accompanying me?" he asked mildly.

"I brought you back," his companion explained. "Now I am responsible for you."

"Okay," the Ranger decided. "But we'll have no more of your heathen magics, you hear? When I kill these men, I want them to stay dead. You understand?"

"Fine by me," the Indian agreed.

Together they rode off in the direction the Indian had seen Cavendish's gang take. Their horses splashed through puddles that were already starting to shrink. Tracking the gang wasn't hard; not expecting pursuit yet, they hadn't bothered hiding their tracks. They had probably also sat out the storm, so it was clear they weren't far ahead.

"You with me in this fight, or do I go it alone?" the dead man asked his companion at one point.

"It's your fight," the Indian answered.

"Yeah. I kind of thought you'd say that. Stay back when we find them then. Wouldn't want you getting plugged by no stray bullets."

"My thought also."

It was getting on toward night when they could hear the sound of riders ahead on the trail. The Ranger took a moment to check that both his pistols were loaded, then his rifle. With a grim smile he plunged on. The Indian followed, but at a slower pace.

Rounding a bend in the trail, the Ranger could see that the men he was after were only about a quarter of a mile ahead. Perfect. He urged his horse onward.

One of the riders turned in his saddle and called something to his companions that the wind snatched away. The others reined in and turned to look back. Immediately they drew their weapons.

Their pursuer didn't care; he had been dead already.

"Jesus H. Christ!" one of the men swore. "Ain't that one of the men we done killed already?"

"I guess he survived somehow," Cavendish snarled. Bringing up his pistol, he fired three shots in quick succession.

Two whistled harmlessly past the Ranger. Hitting a riding man from the saddle was never an easy feat, which was one reason he hadn't bothered trying any shots himself. The third slammed into his shoulder.

He felt no pain, just the puncture of the impact that rocked him back in the saddle. Then he bent forward to ride on.

"What the hell?" Cavendish growled. "I'm sure I winged the lawman…"

"Not enough," the Ranger growled. He was close enough now and reined in his steed. His hands whipped down to his weapons, but the gang already had theirs drawn. A barrage of shells slammed into him, knocking him from the saddle and into the mud.

"That should bury him this time," Cavendish decided.

The Ranger sat up.

Three of the gang swore, and fired again. They could all see the bullets batter their target. He fell back again.

"What does it take to kill him?" one gunman wondered.

"More than you've got," the Ranger replied. His guns came up as he rose to his feet. He commenced firing.

Men and steeds screamed. The thunder of the guns was deafening. By the time it was over, five of the gang lay bleeding and dying on the ground. Their horses, howling, bolted. Only Cavendish remained untouched. The Ranger looked up from the steaming corpses of the men he had killed.

"Your turn," he said.

Cavendish emptied his revolver into the man's chest, to no apparent effect. Then he threw it at the Ranger, who simply ducked. Cavendish followed his weapon, slamming into his target and knocking him into the mud. Gripping his powerful hands about the man's throat, he squeezed hard. "Go to hell," he growled.

The Ranger didn't seem to be at all bothered by the death-grip. Cavendish of course didn't know the Ranger had no need of air. The man reached up, pushing back on Cavendish's chin until the grip about his throat ceased, and he could speak again.

"After you," he answered. With a twist, he heaved Cavendish into the mud. He leaped upon the man, and his hands clenched the outlaw's throat. "This works much better on you." Relentlessly he squeezed. Cavendish struck out, punching and chopping. The Ranger felt the blows but without pain. His nerves were dead, and the punches had little effect on him. His grip, however, was different. Cavendish's face was turning purple as the man struggled for breaths that weren't ever going to come. "Die, you lucky bastard." He gave one final squeeze and felt Cavendish convulse as he died. He threw the broken body aside and moved to each of the fallen outlaws in turn. Carefully, even if they were dead, he shot each one through the head. Returning to Cavendish, he put two bullets through the man's face.

The Indian had ridden up as this was going on. He'd caught all of the loose horses, and trailed them behind his pony. "What are you doing?" he asked, amused.

"Removing temptation from your path," the masked man answered. He glanced up and saw the horses. "What are you doing?"

The Indian shrugged. "Horses are worth twenty bucks apiece. Figure to sell them. Owners do not need them any longer."

"Damned right they don't." He grinned. "There's a bounty on the gang, too, about five hundred, all told. Their loot should be in their saddlebags. When we return it, there'll be a reward. Should earn us both a tidy sum."

"Why do you need money?" the Indian asked. He hopped from his horse to help load the slain outlaws across their steeds and to tie them in place.

"Well, not for food or whores now, that's quite clear," the Ranger replied. "But I do want to get me some silver bullets."

His companion scowled. "What for?"

"You did say that the only sure way to kill me again was with silver through the brain. I'd kind of like the option, should I decide I've had enough of this second life of mine. I do seem to be unable to savor things the way I used."

The Indian shrugged. "That is a problem with being dead."

"So I noticed." His task done, the Ranger swung back into the saddle of his horse. "Now I've got to go back and bury my friends—the lucky dead." He swung his steed around. "You coming?"

"Sure." The Indian vaulted onto his pony. "I have a feeling we are stuck with each other now."

"Yeah." The Ranger spurred his horse to start it moving. "I was kind of afraid of that." He glanced down at his shirt, which had been shredded by all of the bullet hits. He could see the holes in his torso created by the bullets. "You think we could dig these slugs out sometime? I hate having so many holes in me."

The Indian shrugged. "Tough."

Awake in the Abyss

RICK MOORE

'**E**re, what the hell's he playing at? What's he doin' to that woman? Cut her from neck to navel, he has. I've never seen such a sight... Never in all my...

Hold on a mo... That's... That's not possible. That's me, that is. It's me. How can I be up 'ere in the air looking down on meself? How can...

Hey up! You down there. Gerroff me. D'ye hear?

Oh my Lord. He's only gone and killed me. That's what he's done. Gone and killed me, he has. I'm... I'm dead.

Look at the blood! Never would've thought there was that much blood inside a body. There'll have a hell of a time getting it off the cobblestones in the morning. Hell of a time... What the hell am I on about? I must be losing me marbles. There I am, dead as a doornail, and all I can think is what a job they'll have cleaning up. God, look at it though. I've never seen so much blood. Not even that one time when I had to have me little operation. Well, it wasn't my fault. If you ask me, I did the nipper a favor, I did. What sort of life could somebody like me offer him? Not much. I could barely put food in me own belly, let alone provide for two. If I had had him, he'd be without a mother now, wouldn't

247

he? Shipped off to the workhouse sharpish he would have been, you mark my words. Yes, he'd be all alone now, now that bugger down there's gone and done me in.

What's he doin' now?

Why the bare faced cheek of it. Cutting me bits off, he is. The filthy blighter. Helping himself to a keepsake. That's me done for I suppose. Finished. Dead at the hands of him what they call Jack the Ripper.

Just my luck. But what's a girl to do? It's not my fault. I had to make a living somehow. Had to put food in me belly. Had to have a couple of pennies to rub together when I went about town of an evening. Had to make sure I had a couple more coins to pay for me doss at the end of it. I'm a, a—what do they call it?—victim of circumstances. Yeah that's what I am, a victim of circumstances.

Now what's he up to?

He isn't.

He bloody is, you know. Please, Jack, not there. Anywhere but there. Not me face. Have a heart, Jack. Not me face.

Where's a copper when you need one? Where…

Well stone the crows. Here comes one now. Never had that sort of luck when I was alive, mores the pity. Hurry up Old Bill. You've had a good long blow on your whistle, now get after him. Hurry up. Come on. He's getting away.

Too late. Well don't stand there looking at me body, get going. Oh go on then, blow your whistle again if it makes you feel better. You're a bit late now though mate. Could have done with you about five minutes ago. Still, at least he didn't mess me face up. That's something I suppose.

'Ere, now what's going on? Everything's gone all dark. So dark… Never known dark like this before… Is this the end? Suppose it must be… What a lousy way for a life to end. For that matter, what a lousy life!

* * *

What the hell am I doing back here? I thought all this was over and done with and I'd get a chance for a decent bit of kip for a change. I liked it in the dark. It was warm, and I felt safe, and there were no thoughts and no people or anything, just silence inside and out, like it is when you wake up of a morning, and you're all cozied up so you decide to have just five more minutes, and it's like you're not awake and you're not asleep, but somewhere in between the two. Lovely it was.

Would you look at all this commotion. All for little old me. What a palaver. 'Ere, I know him. Seen his boat race in the papers, I have. Abberline, yeah that's his name. Famous he is. I suppose I'll be famous too now. Imagine that—everyone in the whole of London knowing my name.

No good looking down there inspector. That poor cow can't tell you anything now. You want to look up here, that's what you want to do. Cooeee, here I am, floating right above your head. I can tell you what he looks like. Cooeee.

What's that he's saying? Keep a tight lid on it? Keep it out of the papers? What does he mean they don't want to cause the same widespread panic they had when the murders were being reported? You can't keep something like that from the public. It's not right. Well that's scuppered my dreams of being famous.

Blimey. What a sight I look in daylight. What a mess. Still, at least he didn't touch me face. The inspector must like the look of it. He's been staring at it long enough to give himself a nosebleed. What's he keep looking at me face for? Almost looks like he's about to well up... He isn't, is he? He bloody is, you know.

Oy! You down there! Cut that out. Don't you dare gave me that sympathetic look Inspector Abberline. Don't you dare! I didn't need sympathy from the likes of you when I was alive, and I most certainly do not need it now I'm dead, thank you.

Flaming cheek. Who the hell do you think you are? Looking at me like you care how I must have suffered when I died. If you must know, I hardly felt a thing. Pissed as a newt, that's why. Three sheets to the wind. And he was ever so quick with the knife that ended me life, was our Jackie boy. That much I will say in his favor. I've known some men, terrible brutes they was, what hurt me more with their fists than that last one did killing me, and I've known one or two who hurt me far worse and all it took was a few little words. Even now I smart at the pain of their false promises. Even now I ache from the bruises of disappointment.

Show the old cow's mangled body a look of tenderness will you? Well you know what you can do with your sympathy and tenderness—shove it up your arse. You couldn't even begin to know the life I led. You, with your fancy name, and your Scotland Yard, and your hoity toity friends. Looking at me like you care. Where were your caring eyes when I was alive, eh? Where was the kindness when I looked for it? Nowhere. Not here, that's for sure, not in London's Abyss. Fingers bled to the bone and a belly with no food in it. That's the best life had to offer the likes of me. Maybe what Jack did to me was a blessing in disguise. At least now I'll never again have to fear I'll end up back at the Spike, breaking me poor old back for a bowl of watery gruel. At least now the suffering is finally over, or it would be, if I could just find me way back to that lovely, lovely dark. Oh, it was lovely there. If I could...

-*Don't you ever shut that trap of yours?*

'Ere, who said that? Who's there?

-*Give the rabbiting a rest I said.*

Who is that? Hello? Hello?

-*Listen 'ere you fat arsed tart. A job needs doing and you're not going back in the dark until it's done.*

Cheeky mare. Who you calling a fat arsed tart?

-*Do you want to get him what murdered you or don't you?*

Course I do.

-*Well all right. Then listen...*

* * *

Who'd have ever thought such a thing was possible, eh? I followed Dark Annie's instructions, did everything she told me, used the will power of the other five unquiet souls to give me the power I needed to make it work, focusing on the fact we were us all wronged by the same hand, me spirit voice calling out at the same time as theirs, all of us demanding justice, demanding our pound of flesh—over and over and over—and bugger me if it didn't go and work. I'm back in me body. I'm alive. But not alive. I haven't got a heartbeat, and there's this deep yearning like nothing I've ever known, this yearning to… Well, never mind that now, the point is, I really am back from the grave. Or at least I will be, once I can find a way to get out of the bloody thing.

* * *

Well I buggered up one of me knees kicking through the lid, but I made it out in the end. When all that earth poured in I thought I'd suffocate for sure. That is until I remembered I couldn't, not with me being already deceased. I just kept wriggling and pushing, wriggling and pushing. They'd only buried me the day before so the earth in me grave was still loose and soft. When me hands broke through the surface, other hands grabbed mine and hauled me out.

I brushed dirt off me burial dress and looked around. There was fog swirling around me legs, and a mass of it a few feet from where I stood. Then the fog across from me cleared and I saw them. They were all there—Polly Nichols, Dark Annie, Long Liz, Kate and Ginger. I'd read the descriptions of what he'd done to Kate and Ginger's faces in the papers, but that didn't begin to prepare me for seeing them in the flesh. I tried not to look at them and focused on the faces of the other three. Polly, whose given name was Mary Ann Nichols, had lacerations to the right side of her jaw, but other than that looked fairly normal—pale and sunken eyed, but that look wasn't so uncommon, what with half of London in a state of near starvation. The same went for "Dark" Annie Chapman. Elizabeth Stride, who went by the name "Long Liz" was by far one of the prettiest girls I ever saw. She had some cuts on the right side of her neck, but even now few would recognize her for a ghoul. Beneath their burial dresses, they were all five the same as me of course. It was a relief not to have to look at the wounds Jack had inflicted with his knife, wounds later stitched together with catgut by the police surgeon.

"'Ello girls," I said. "It's a real pleasure to make your acquaintance."

"Likewise," said Polly, her voice sounding like she'd swallowed a pint of mud climbing out of her grave.

Dark Annie just nodded.

"Hello," said Long Liz, and hearing her accent, I remembered she was originally from Sweden.

I gave a smile and a nod to Kate. He'd carved her up bad, the bastard. There were deep gashes across the bridge of her nose and all down both sides of her face.

"I have come back," said Catherine "Kate" Eddows, "to earn the reward offered for the apprehension of the Whitechapel murderer." Her eyes, which before this had been pits of darkness, turned as white as snow. "I think I know him."

I didn't understand why what she'd said should strike any of them as funny, but all the other girls laughed at this, so I joined in and laughed along with them. Truth told, seeing her eyes go white like that, sort of put the frighteners on me.

Now for the hard part, I thought, and forced myself to look beyond the mutilated face and find the eyes of Mary Jane Kelly, the one the papers said went by the name of Ginger. She didn't have a face at all really. I saw something move in that mess of carved up flesh and realized it was what had once been her mouth.

"All right sweetheart," Ginger said, her voice sweet and musical. Ginger had been younger than the rest of us. I remembered reading in the rags she was only four and twenty when she died.

* * *

We knew where to find him without even needing to think about it, like it just came into our heads, all at the same time.

I closed the cemetery gates behind me and turned to look at the others. "Fairclough Street?" I asked.

Dark Annie nodded.

"Fairclough Street," Polly said.

The six of us set off arm in arm, walking down the lane that led from the Park Gate cemetery back to the Abyss, back to our final date with the one they called Saucy Jack.

Nobody noticed us at first. They went about their business hurrying to and fro most of them heading from alehouse to alehouse, gallivanting about. Two men saw us coming toward them and stopped in their tracks. They could only stand there as we got nearer, legs trembling, paralyzed by fear.

"Well fancy seeing you two here," said Long Liz. "Look girls, it's Harry Harris and his mate Joe Larende."

"All right Joe," Polly said to the cigarette salesman, a streak of brown liquid coming out of her mouth. "Got any fags on yer?"

"Ghouls!" Harry Harris cried, looking from the ones he recognized to the faces of Kate and Ginger . "All of them—ghouls from the grave!"

Harry and Joe turned tail and scarpered, wailing for their mothers as they went.

People turned to look, rubbed their eyes, blinked. The pandemonium was instantaneous. They ran screaming, ran for the alleyways and buildings nearest them, ran with the warning shout of "ghouls." What a lark!

Arm in arm the six of us walked the suddenly deserted cobblestone streets toward our destination. While it was fun at first to see the effect our appearance had on people, the silence, broken only by the occasional man or woman whimpering in a shop doorway or beneath a cart, weighed heavy on me heart. I'd had a lifetime of being an outcast and not being welcome—and here that feeling was all over again. Even though it no longer beat, I got that old sensation in me chest, the sensation of being crushed under the weight of all the shit life throws at you, not because you can't bear it, but because you always have to bear it alone. Ginger, bless her, must have been feeling the same thing; and I dare say all our spirits were lifted a little when a sweet sound rose into the air around us, as she sang "Only a violet I plucked from my mother's grave."

* * *

It was me what got picked to lure him in, on account of me being the last to die, and looking less dead than the rest of them. I stood with me back to the wall, that same fog from the graveyard swirling around me legs. As he got closer I felt a flutter of nervousness, but then I remembered he was just a man, not a real monster like I'd so long been led to believe.

"'Allo handsome," I said as he approached. "What's a fine looking gent like yourself doing in this neck of the woods then, if I might be so bold as to inquire?"

I saw a look in his eyes, as though for a moment he thought he knew me, but then the recognition went out of them.

"Are you a good girl?" he asked.

"I'm any kind of girl you want me to be, darling," I said.

He smiled that horrible thin-lipped smile of his. "You would say anything but your prayers."

Two coins were pressed into me palm.

"Will you?" he asked.

I nodded, "Yes."

"How cold your hands are," he said.

"No need to fret," I said, pulling him close. "Me hands might be cold, but I'm nice and warm where it counts."

I led him down the alleyway. Turning me back to the wall, I faced him. I saw his hand go into the pocket of his overcoat, reaching for his knife. He moved closer.

"Jack," I said, "don't you recognize me? It's me, your little Nelly."

He frowned, his eyes studying my face.

I pulled open me blouse, the buttons popping off, revealing the surgeon's catgut stitch work.

"What about now?" I asked. "Remember me now, Jack?"

Jack backed away from me. "You lived?"

"She lives tonight, Jack," said Liz right at the moment he backed into her. He whirled around looking up into her face.

"We all live tonight, Jack," said Ginger, stepping from the shadows into the light.

Seeing her face, knowing she could not possibly look like that and be alive, Jack let loose a wailing sob of terror. He turned toward the mouth of the alleyway, intending to run.

Polly and Dark Annie stepped from the darkness, blocking his exit.

Jack's hand came out of his pocket holding the knife that had stolen all our lives. He swung upwards, a wide arc that tore open Polly's throat. Soil and earthworms poured from the opening. A trickle of muddy water spilled from her mouth. "You can't kill me twice, Jack."

The Ripper screamed, so terrified the knife fell from his hand and clattered as it hit the ground. He spun around, looking for another way out.

"There'll be no escape for you," Dark Annie said. "Not tonight, Jack."

His knees buckled, and the man who'd struck terror into the hearts of so many fell sobbing to the ground. I bent and picked up his knife. I plunged the tip of the blade into his shoulder.

Jack screamed.

We took turns with it, stabbing and slicing, making sure none of the blows were fatal, cutting his flesh to ribbons. Jack sobbed and whimpered, screamed and wailed, begged for mercy. After we gutted him open he went sort of quiet. He just lay there making gurgling sounds and softly laughing.

All that cutting helped us work up quite an appetite. As I swallowed the first bite I understood the yearning sensation I'd experienced in my coffin.

"We're dining in style tonight girls," Polly said, ripping a strip of flesh from Jack's cheek and shoving it into her mouth. "He's ever so succulent. Ain't he tender?"

"Oh he is," Long Liz agreed, stuffing her mouth with Jack's steaming kidneys. "Not a bit of gristle on him."

"Well dig in girls," Dark Annie said. "Eat your fill."

"Aren't you having any?" I asked.

"Oh don't you worry about me, my dear," said Dark Annie. "The parts I have in mind won't be to everybody's liking, but I'll make short work of them, you just wait and see if I don't. Now go on, get it while it's hot."

I smiled and nodded. Realizing something existed far better than the darkness, I bent low, and using me teeth, ripped free another chunk of his flesh.

The Travellin' Show

Douglas Hutcheson

"**S**tep right on up, ladies and gentlemen! I guarantee you will see the most awesome and the most weird, from sophomoric silliness to give each belly a guffaw, to the most vile and pernicious of spectacles not fit for women, children and others prone to weakness of the heart! But step on up if you fair folk dare, just take the strong arm of one of these robust specimens of manhood from your own industrious town and hope he is not weak in the knees! Only a quarter a couple, or fifty cents gets in the whole family to strike your eyes full of fantastic phantasmagoria live in total and terrific color!"

Sweat dribbled like holy water from the caller's brow as he surveyed the crowd already shoving one another, bustling over stray dogs milling in the muck, babies catching blind elbows in mewling mouths. Hot as hell, the caller thought, but worth every coin. He had been right to steer them to Traverston this day, even if it meant bracing up for the heat of Texas that was still raging into September.

Word had spread before the end of last month as to how the poor town had lost a sizable portion of its meager population when a coal mine collapsed and trapped many men and not a few boys in its black caverns. The other carnies had figured to give them until the end of October at least, but why wait so long, the caller wondered? Nothing set the need to seek out a little zest for life and amusing distractions like down-in-the-bone tragedies.

"You, sir, you look like a man of means and importance!" The caller pointed his staff, which appeared to be made out of a combination of femurs and some shrunken head at the top, wound about and held fast by what looked like a golden snake whose mouth stood fixed perpetually about to engulf the little terrified head. "Yes, you, sir, with the jaunty feather!"

A plump man in a velvet frock coat and a top hat adorned with a wild guinea feather pointed to himself. He looked slightly embarrassed by the accoutrement that he eased it off, regarding the hat while he spun it carefully in his hands, then eyeing the crowd as it stared at him. "Go on, take a bow, Mayor!" someone yelled. The mayor did as he was told, sweeping his hat as he bent in a flourish.

"So this is the MAYOR, eh? Do step up and take your place here, sir, take your proper place! Regale us with your temporal wisdom, sir, at once!" The caller stepped aside from the podium and clapped while waiting for the portly man who heaved himself up on the stage with no little help from various grime-covered hands in the crowd.

"Yes, well, thank you, Mr. Black, for that, um, kindly observation." The mayor fiddled even further with his hat before he finally decided to simply plop it down on the podium. He pulled a cotton handkerchief from his waistcoat pocket and mopped his brow hastily before beginning to speak. "Yes, indeed...."

"Louder! " someone hollered. The mayor was about to try again but then another person cried, "And taller!" Laughter coursed through the assembly as the mayor looked on blankly, his hat's feather whipping in front of the town's foremost political nostrils.

Mr. Black's hand shot out toward the mayor and removed the hat from the podium. He waved the mayor up to his tiptoes. "Pray, sir, proceed for the benefit of your citizens."

"Ahem. As I was saying, indeed, I am certain we all would wish to thank Mr. Black and his traveling sideshow for crossing so many obstacles to bring us entertainments both amusing and inspiring during this erstwhile sorrowful time following our recent, um, *unpleasantness*. What say you all to a big round of applause for Mr. Black and his performers? Most talented, I am sure!"

The mayor led off the clapping, at which the caller nodded slightly, his eyes almost twinkling. Quickly Mr. Black shoved the mayor aside again. "Yes, thank you, Mayor Snotgrass...."

"Snodgrass."

"Yes, SNOTgrass, for those exuberant blessings of appreciation for our humble motley. And now, if you will, dear citizens of Traverston, please *entrez vous*! And remember we must request only Union legal tender! We, unfortunately, can no longer accept Confederate scrip, God remember the Cause."

An urgent murmur pressed forth with the surge of flesh, silver jingling, gold and jewels shining from ladies' necklaces and men's pocket chains, much of which Toadfrog, Mr. Black's lugubrious hopping midget, would have from them too, plucked from within the shadows, before the night had met its nadir.

"Have care, now, my new friends," Mr. Black grinned. "All will have their chance tonight to be taken like never before to heretofore untold extremes of wild abandon!"

* * *

The crowd thrilled at first to the many antics of the carnies. Jasmine, the Arab beauty who preened and batted her painted eyes, sauntered into the ring first, performing the Dance of the Seven Veils. Victor, the German strongman, followed her, flexing his massive oily biceps and lifting any and everything—including women volunteered from the rickety pew seats, looking up their bustles and plotting the rest of his evening. Next the Spanish Desdemona appeared in a puff of purple smoke and, with a wrathful mien, set forth to test herself as if she might be a witch of olden days, pricking her cheeks with bodkins and skewering her bosom with swords, though she did not bleed.

Then Mr. Black rolled out into the ring Bertha the Fat Bearded Woman, who spun like a giant ball. Once he had her upright, Mr. Black set fire to her whiskers. She watched them sizzle and smoke until they reached her skin. The crowd, even stalwart cowpokes, clambered to the edges of seats, barely able to gaze ahead and still keep their beers steady.

At last Churchmouse the Clown bounded out beside her, tumbling and flipping while keeping a full bucket of water from spilling, finally dowsing the crispy-faced behemoth. He laughed and ran with the empty bucket, holding it aloft to the crowd as if begging for change. When a few more-well-to-do folks tossed him some coins, he smiled and cartwheeled, but Mr. Black chastised him and he stood still.

Mr. Black ordered the clown to hand over his profits, but Churchmouse clung steadfast to the bucket. "Now, now, fool—we know the ringmaster always gets his due!" Mr. Black grimaced, pointing his staff. Sparks erupted from the bucket. Churchmouse shook it and squealed; when he looked again and offered it for the crowd to inspect, there remained nothing inside. From the other side of the ring, Mr. Black held aloft the coins and grinned, while Churchmouse figged him off and made sick faces at all the knee-slapping assembly.

Finally Simon the Snakeman slithered, legless and armless, into the center ring. He flicked his tongue as Mr. Black rolled eggs, then shoved biddies and lastly a grown bantam rooster toward Simon's mouth for him to gulp down within his massive jaws. When Simon finished his swallowing, he lifted his rear end and extruded a baby rattle from between his buttocks that he shook with gustatory satisfaction.

"Ah, but wait, Vile Serpent, for your feasting is not yet done!" Mr. Black motioned for Simon to come closer and rise up on a crate. The Snakeman crept his way atop and waited, his tongue still working fast over his ample teeth. "We have one final act for you ladies and gentlemen—well, for those of you not departing like your more-delicate fellows. Those of you who wish to remain, please drop a tip to Mr. Toadfrog as he makes his way among you."

Toadfrog appeared in the shadows as if from nothing and hopped his way from person to person, motioning for each to deposit a pittance into his voluminous and swelling jowls. A few more folk stood in disgust and Victor kindly escorted them out of the tent.

When everyone settled down again, Mr. Black called for the lantern-light to dim, which it did right on cue. "Citizens of Traverston, neighbors, *friends*—I invite you to look upon a thing so fantastic, though you see it this night, I defy you to believe! Is it a thing of good? Or of pure evil? You must decide for yourselves how your faith is tested! Behold…. Wait! Wait! Wait! Has everyone been to the concessions stand yet? We have buttered popped corn, sweet sugar treats, red candied apples, crisp sarsaparilla cold from the ice box…."

Laughter again from the stands and cries of "Get on with it!"

"Very well. Don't say you weren't warned," Mr. Black grinned. "Here, now, the greatest abomination ever witnessed by man!" He flung open the door to the crate. The crowd inhaled a collective gasp and whispered at the darkness within. Then, ever so tentatively, out stepped a lamb, shining with brilliant white wool and dewy eyes in the glaring limelight.

The crowd seemed ready to explode, half with giggles and the other half with curses. The din rose to nearly deafening volume, and children began to hurl peanuts and corn at the lamb as it trembled and tried to step back. The Snakeman leaned down as if to nuzzle the creature, instead coming away with the lamb's throat slathered in gouts of blood.

Women fainted, children spilled their gorges, and men spat and huffed and turned crimson. The lamb went to its knees, gurgling as it tried with all it had left to bleat. It twitched and kicked at the frothing bloody mud around its hoofs, but in a minute its eyes glazed milky, its tongue lolled out and it struggled no more.

"Now, I know what you must all be thinking: What kind of monsters are these people who would come into our benighted little hamlet with promises of amusements and diversions, take our money and our time, only to leave us with this ghastly scene of horror the likes of which no civilized humans would tolerate? Hmmm? And it ain't even Easter! No holiday for lamb stew, eh?"

Some of the bigger fellows were already trying to make their way down to the ring, their belts knotted in their hands or their knives sliding glistening from sheathes.

"Wait, gentle Traverstonians, wait! We would not leave you with such a bleak spectacle, especially not in such trying times as these. I pray you! Behold a man of the cloth, come to deliver salvation to the lost!"

With that a candle flame appeared from the dark back wings of the tent. As it drew closer, a haggard face, cast down, emerged out of the shadows—a tall slender man, not in showy primary colors like the rest of the carnies, but arrayed in simple black and white, though the collar he wore showed grey. "I give you the Right Reverend Dr. Tool, our own fair parson, bearer of the Word, a balm to sinful souls, who pierces for us this night that veil most mysterious and awful!"

The discomfort of the crowd was palpable. The old minister gritted his teeth as if every eye that lit upon him burned like coals. Still, he looked not into the scattered wide faces, only knelt down to the beast. Delicately he edged his candle beside its head.

Mr. Black bent with him, put his hand on the reverend's shoulder, but the reverend glared at him. Mr. Black withdrew his grasp, but not his eyes, though he lifted the candle and stood. "A candle lit can be extinguished, like a life, in so many dreadful ways." Mr. Black drifted his hand over the flame, then through it, before easing his palm down on the fire and squashing it to the crackle of sizzling flesh and the gloom of oily smoke wrapping his fingers as if grasping back at him.

He held the candle aloft and waved it around. He passed it to a little girl to examine. "The candle can, of course, be lit again." As he said this a crimson flame erupted from the wick. The girl yelped and jumped, almost dropping it.

Mr. Black snatched it back. "Surely, another trick, some slight of hand only." He blew it out. It erupted again. He blew it out. "Or, of course, one could merely strike a Lucifer to do the work." He produced a match, popped it on his nail, and tendered fire to the candle once more. "Child's play." He handed the light back to the girl, who accepted it finally with some prodding from her mother.

"But who among us here today, though the life be snuffed out, can return it to its proper hearth of the body? Who can be the Prometheus of that most holy fire? Why, no one, sadly—no one except the great believer, the miracle worker, the good shepherd here, the Right Reverend Dr. Tool! See now, and believe!"

The reverend eased his fingers under the lamb's neck and cradled its head in his arms. He looked skyward like a statue of an angel in a cemetery. His lips quivered though none heard what he spoke. His face shone haloed in the growing light and his hands almost sparkled with sweat as if catching ablaze. This went on for several minutes, then the glow, whatever it had been, faded.

The reverend bent to kiss the lamb's neck, then tucked its head back upon the ground. He stood and took a step backward.

Everyone but the reverend and Mr. Black gasped as the lamb jerked back to life. "Quickly now, Toadfrog, get the shackles on it!" Mr. Black shouted.

Toadfrog landed beside the creature in an instant, latching a chain around its neck, and just as suddenly bounding away. The lamb rose faltering at first, then almost stretching as if it had merely been sleeping. Most of the crowd roared in awe and clapped in thundering waves. Some though stomped the boards and shouted invectives, while others fell to their knees hollering, "Holy! Holy! Holy!"

Then, searching about itself, the lamb spied the people. It bared its teeth and bleated a most terrible and low sound that did not seem to end for long seconds.

Mr. Black bowed ever so slightly to the assembly, then waved toward the exit. "Yes, thank you all for your patronage! Thank you, and good evening! That's enough! Yes, that's enough for now! Thank you, ladies and gentlemen, thank you all for coming!"

"It's a trick!" One of the big fellows had made it down to the ring at last. He was just about to leap inside when Victor stepped out from behind a curtain and dwarfed him.

"It's okay, Victor. I suppose one of this town's own dutiful citizens should verify that this is not some sleight-of-lamb trick, right? Please, then, if he must have satisfaction, escort the gentleman into the ring, would you, Victor?"

"You show him, Joe!" several folks taunted.

Victor took the man's arm and shoved him toward Mr. Black and the beast. "You want proof, then? Here, sir, is your proof!" Mr. Black grabbed the man's hand and thrust it upon the back of the lamb.

"No!" shouted the reverend, who moved to intersect their course. Victor easily blocked his way. "No, you mustn't!"

The lamb whipped its ragged neck around as if to bite Joe's hand. He managed to break Mr. Black's hold and jerk it away, staggering backward. "It's alive! I can see the hole in its neck but it's alive!"

The lamb tugged at its chain, spittle dribbling from its gums.

"Yes, alive! Resurrected, you might say," agreed Mr. Black. "Is your curiosity now satisfied, sir, or would you care for another grope?"

"No, sir. But how? How can it be?"

"Glorious isn't it? As we shall all be healed someday in bodies of perpetual bliss, isn't that right, Reverend?"

But the reverend was already stalking off.

"Resurrected! Not only healed of the grave, but filled with a new gusto for life!" shouted Mr. Black. The crowd was dispersing though. He had lost his audience for now, but he had held their attention long enough.

The lamb began to bleat again, but Mr. Black kicked it in its throat and slammed the door to its crate.

* * *

The next day, just before noon, a small group of concerned citizens gathered at the church. Directly a mighty commotion issued from the white slats of the building, and soon it spewed forth the mayor. He marched at first toward the edge of town, the host of upright citizens monitoring his backside from the church steps. He had nearly advanced into the fairgrounds when he happened upon the saloon and almost leapt inside.

Nearly half an hour later he emerged again like a groundhog fearing its own shadow. He paused to throw back one last tumbler of whiskey, then rested it upon an outside stool. Plopping his hat on his balding head, the mayor strode, then staggered, then strode up to the carriage with the hanging shingle that read: "Mr. Black, Spinner of Tales, Extraordinary." He knocked ever so gently.

"Come in! Come in, my dear mayor!" resounded the immediate reply from within. The door creaked open and the mayor heaved himself inside. Mr. Black reclined upon his cushioned seat like the proverbial spider in its web; he spun his staff like a drill bit between the fingers of his left hand while holding aloft a big maduro-wrapper cigar with his right. He creaked forward and breathed a stinging haze into the mayor's face. "What shall be your desire today, then, Mr. Snotgrass? Could I tempt you with a cigar? Bertha rolls them herself, you know."

"Snodgrass," the Mayor coughed. "And no, but thank you, sir." As the mayor leaned back against the other side of the carriage, his eyes widened over the various vials of strange liquids and bottles of herbs arrayed about the walls. He reached to touch one jar that seemed to hold something like the green phosphorescence of fireflies, but Mr. Black slapped away his hand as if it were a child's.

"Ouch!"

"Sorry, Mr. Mayor, but these ointments and unguents and such are precious to me—my medicines, you might say. I am, sir, a *sick* man."

"I see."

"To what do I owe this pleasure, sir?"

"Well," the mayor's gaze flitted about other nastier recesses of the carriage before deciding at last to settle for his host's face, "Mr. Black, I am afraid that many of the citizens were, um, too well-shocked at the amazements of your show. It was, of course, like nothing they had ever seen and, that is, like something, um…."

"Yes?"

"Well, to come directly to the point, to not beat about the brush but be men about it, sir, it was something perverse, sir! Something devilish even!"

"You wound me, Snotgrass!"

"I mean, I am not so easily strained! I am a man of the world myself. I have traveled as far as our own Alamo and seen the heights of man's glory and the depths of his debasement."

"Indeed?"

"But these fair folk of Traverston, sir, they are too kindhearted, too genteel. I am afraid they have charged me hither on their behalf to request your show to depart, or they will burn your tent and carriages to the ground by dusk and hang the corpses of the scorched lot of you."

"I see."

"There was nothing I could say."

"I am sure."

The two stared at one another a minute.

"I suppose I should just go then." The mayor rose to leave. "Appointment over at the saloon, you know—busy, busy."

Mr. Black's nails dug into his arm. A little shriek escaped the mayor's lips.

"I will need at least until midnight, if you must insist on our departure and that with any haste. We require time to disassemble the rings and to take down the tent, among other tacks. Certainly you can persuade your compassionate and not-at-all-bloodthirsty good citizens to allow us that much leeway, don't you think?"

"I… I believe I can do that much."

"Yes. Believe it, and let it be so, Mr. Snotgrass." Mr. Black relaxed his grip and the mayor bounded away more swiftly than he had ever run in his life, his hat falling away to the dust and blowing with the breeze like a dandy tumbleweed.

* * *

That night the fairgrounds seemed almost deserted. The carnies had packed up the tent and rings and had closed the front of the concession stand. Nothing showed in the darkness save the flickers of a few candles here and there in the windows of the carriages.

"What they waitin' for?" said Joe.

"I don't know," said Harry, "but if we gon' do this thang, we best git with it."

"Well, let's be about findin' that preacher then."

The little cabal wove its way among the carriages and crates, inspecting each door as they passed, until they found the one marked with a cross.

"This must be the place."

Joe stuck a spike to the lock on the door and, with one solid hammer smash, struck it off. The preacher looked up, not at all startled, and shook his head just before the blow dropped him into darkness.

* * *

"Wake up, holy man."

The Right Rev. Dr. Tool awoke with a throbbing head. He blinked at the torchlight as Joe yanked a burlap hood off him.

"What do you want?" asked the reverend, but as his eyes focused into the night beyond, he saw the gaping black maw of the coal mine. "You don't want to do this. All of you, listen to me, y'all don't want this!"

They hefted the reverend to his feet. "You know what happened here. I know you heard. Hell, ever'body in a hundred miles has heard tell by now. This shouldn't have happened."

The reverend shook his head. "Who can say?"

"I can, by God! Ain't no reason for all them good hard-workin' souls to not be on this old earth right now, not down in a pit! They was only doin' they jobs! Ain't it enough we apt to catch the black lung down in them hell holes?"

"You people don't know what hell is."

Joe produced a Bible and rapped the reverend across the face with it. The blow rang out into the night for a moment like thunder. No, that was thunder. It looked like a storm sweeping in. "Don't tell me what I know. I lost my son in there! I was down sick that day but my boy… my brave boy went to work on his lonesome that day and died down there for it! Lots of families lost sons, young and old alike! You tell me that's right!"

The reverend spat blood and wiped his mouth on his sleeve. He tugged at his grey collar and tried to suck in a clear draught of air. "I can't say that it was right, but I know this is wrong. I *know*…."

Joe came around with four railroad spikes in his other hand and held them before the reverend's face. "You got a choice to make, preacher. You can have this here Bible in this hand and do the Lord's work, or we can give you these spikes from the other hand. We got us a cross all stood up over there in the rocks, and we ain't afeared to do the Devil's work, if that's what it takes to brang our families back together like they belong to be. Now git the hell up and git busy."

The reverend scrabbled to his feet taking the Bible in his hands. "It's always the same with people. You always want what ain't really yours to have. You think I don't know hurt? You think I ain't lost all that was most precious to me? I had a family once too and they were taken from me! I'm here to tell you, you're better off letting them go! Let them rest in the bosom of the earth where they belong."

"It's the hard way then. Take hold of him, boys," Joe said. The men slung the reverend down against a boulder. The reverend dropped the Bible on the rock as they commenced to stripping the coat and shirt from his back with their bowie knives. They pulled his arms out wide.

Harry stepped forward. "Rev, it'll go easier on you to just do the right thang."

The reverend rested his head against the Bible and was silent until the whip bit into him.

* * *

After awhile—he couldn't remember how long—he was begging them to stop. He cried and hollered and promised many things that shocked them to come from the mouth of a holy man. At last they released their hold on him and he collapsed. Joe gave him whisky to sip and it spilled down his blood-flecked cheeks. He gagged and coughed.

"Reverend?" said Joe.

The reverend clawed himself up against the rock. He pulled the Bible to his naked chest and stumbled toward the opening of the mine.

Lightning flashed around him as he raised the book. He looked like a gnarled old tree about to catch fire as he glared one last time over his shoulder at the men. "Lord, forgive them…. Y'all want this, y'll all have to answer for it!"

He began a low murmur that rose in pitch and intensity. The wind burst forth and swirled the dirt around him like a shroud as he spoke. "Arise, you bones, and be made flesh! Taste the breath of life and arise! Arise! As promised in the Word, I claim resurrection of these dead in the name of their lord!"

The mine belched forth fire and smoke and ash. The reverend staggered back and away before he was knocked over.

The other men, shaking, clambered toward the hole. Silhouettes appeared as if dancing within the furnace of the flaming mine.

"There! Lord, be praised! There is my little William!" Joe shrieked.

Others fell to their knees as their kin stumbled stiffly forward. As the lightning flashed again, the men looked upon their flesh and blood but saw that they were moldering and putrefied, with great gashes in their heads and bones jutting from terrible angles through their cracked and seeping hides.

"Oh, dear Lord!" Joe yelped. Little William, eyes hollow, jaw baring his ragged teeth, was the first to embrace his living kin, shredding Joe's jugular with one bite, chewing the gristle of his ear with another. So the reunion feast began.

* * *

The reverend loped back into camp, his wounds stinging in the sandy gusts.

Mr. Black stood waiting for him. "It is done?"

"To hell with you, Black, and all your kind." The Right Reverend Dr. Tool came around with a railroad spike and planted it with all his remaining might squarely between the wide eyes of the caller.

Mr. Black jerked back, blinked, then collapsed to the ground, flopping for a moment like a decapitated chicken.

"You don't control me anymore," said the reverend, turning toward a carriage not his own. He unhobbled the horses and climbed upon its seat.

Mr. Black shot up suddenly, gripping the spike in his hands. He pulled at it, but to no avail. "You... can't save them... you know."

"I know. Nothing can save them. They're beyond that now, but they're my responsibility, as always." The reverend cracked the reins over the horses' backs and the carriage lurched off toward towns unknown.

Mr. Black ceased tugging at the impaling implement, but slumped grinning at the faces that showed back through the carriage window—a woman and a little girl, blank eyes that seemed to stare through him and off into forever, the twitch of hunger on their twisted mouths.

Edison's Dead Men

Ed Turner

Allow me please to begin this story with its moral: Thomas Edison is a being of pure and unimaginable evil. I loathe Thomas Alva Edison.

My name is William Joseph Hammer, electrical engineer and personal assistant to the being known as Edison. I am about to record the events of December the thirty-first, 1899. I am reciting into this modified phonograph, one of many horrific but damnably useful little devices with which Edison has constructed his empire. Doubtless any papers I write will be uncovered and destroyed by his team of spies; it is my sincere hope that they will not suspect this unassuming vase to be holding any of his terrifying secrets. I am aware of the grim irony of undermining the man with his own device; it pains me to know he is as useful as he is evil.

Let not my effete accent and cultured tongue mislead you—I am a gentleman and, being raised as such, I lack the vocabulary to elucidate properly the degree to which I would like to perform an act of grisly murder upon Mr. Edison's person. However, when the opportunity arose... no, I am getting ahead of the narrative. I do not know if this story will ever be heard, but I know I cannot contain it any longer. Whoever may hear me, this is the story of Edison's dead men.

It begins on the Eve of the New Year. Much of the world was in mid-carouse. Edison had closed his Menlo Park laboratory, a rare thing indeed and cause for much celebration among those souls in his employ. One of the few truths that has slipped through the expansive propaganda campaign surrounding Edison is that he works his employees to the bone. That he had given them a day off was out-of-character to a mind-boggling degree.

Of course, I had no such luxury. I, being Edison's so-called favorite, had been called upon to design a display for some upcoming fair or another, and was expected to have completed my plans in the time that a reasonable employer would have expected me to have writ my name upon the page. Thus, while I technically had the day off, I was nonetheless condemned to my study, blearily completing the assignment as opposed to, for example, eating. As usual, I was throwing more and more light bulbs at the problem. They were growing rather old hat in the cities, but shiny things still played well in Appalachia. I was putting one final bleary embellishment on the design when the telephone on the wall chirped.

I glared at the damnable machine—an infinite capacity to better the world whose only practical application appeared to be in allowing Edison more effortlessly to irk me. I contemplated ignoring the call, but realized that whatever annoyances the man had planned, passing on them now would just put them in my lap later, after they'd had time to grow larger and more complex. With undue resignation, I lifted the earpiece and leaned into the telephone. "Ahoy hoy," I said. Edison hated that particular greeting, due to some petty grudge with Mr. Bell, who invented it. Needless to say, I used it at every opportunity.

"Hammer!" bellowed my employer. "Come to the laboratory! I've use for you!"

"May I ask for what, specifically, you need me?" I asked, not expecting much by way of an answer.

"A scientific discovery of an untold scale! Progress, Hammer, progress!" With that, the connection was lost. Progress, for Thomas Edison, was the end by which even the meanest of means would be justified. Especially if such means might inconvenience me.

While not a large man, Mr. Edison, he is imposing, and powerful in the more political sense. He also is possessed of a look—not the public smile you have likely seen in newsprint or in one of his films, which is humble but beatific. Rather, he can achieve a manic glint and perfectly awful twist of the mouth, a terrifying look that seems to say, "You are but one misstep away from being killed and consumed."

Had you ever been on the receiving end of such a look, you will know why, minutes after the telephone call, I had abandoned the warmth and comfort of my home for the chill in front of Menlo Park, where I found Edison, wearing his vest but no overcoat, seemingly oblivious to the snow surrounding us.

"What seems to be the trouble, sir?" I asked, as graciously as possible. Edison smiled and beckoned me into the building. Dutifully I followed through the front door, down the hall to his office, over to a lighting sconce on the wall which Edison twisted, upon which an unassuming section of wall swung open, revealing a narrow staircase. Edison began to descend, but I felt it would behoove me to express verbally my increasing discomfort with the situation.

"What in blazes?" I exclaimed, after a moment's hesitation.

"Ah yes!" he exclaimed. "You've not seen my private laboratory, have you?"

"You keep a secret laboratory hidden beneath your actual laboratory?" I said. "That is the logic of a madman!"

Edison cocked his head to the side and let his eyes twinkle in an unnerving way. "What's that?"

"Nothing, sir," I answered, feeling I did not have much incentive to experience the man's wrath. The acuity of our employer's hearing was a subject of much debate at Menlo. While some were certain he was stone deaf and only able to communicate thanks to a remarkable facility for reading even the lips that were far to his periphery, I and many others, on the other hand, believed it to be just another facet to the man's false front. This position was bolstered by the fact that one was only ever asked to repeat oneself when one had said something best left silent.

"I was quite sure you said something, Hammer."

"I... what is that stench?" I blurted out. It was a diversion, but an apt one, for I was just then aware of the horrific smell wafting up the narrow stairway.

"Death," Edison said. He bounded down the steps by twos. I followed with considerably more trepidation.

The secret laboratory, I must say, was much like the one upstairs—crammed full of too many tables overflowing with papers and partially-completed experiments. I noticed, however, that many of the devices littering the desks had stocks and sights, there were a number of bubbling tubes and concoctions about one side of the smallish room, and most distressingly, at the rear of the room was a cage with three men locked in it, struggling against the bars.

One, judging by his clothing, was a doctor; the second was a Negro; but it was the third that was the most interesting (and here I must take an aside to point out that if one is singling out an individual as "the interesting one" out of a trio of caged men in a secret laboratory, he must be interesting indeed). The creature looked like nothing so much as a corpse, some months rotted away. His gray skin was falling off in places. Along his shins I could see the bone. His hair was coming off in clumps, and he was dressed in rags and tatters. So shocking was the apparition that I did not notice that the others were similarly, albeit far less extensively, decrepit, and they were sporting large and unpleasant-looking—though surprisingly bloodless—wounds, the doctor on his wrist and the Negro on the shoulder.

"You... you... what is this?" I sputtered. "Are you harboring some sort of advanced lepers?"

Edison shook his head, smiling in the direction of the rotted men. "These are not lepers," he said. "They are dead."

"They are upright," I countered. "They are upright and seem inclined to escape the cage you have them in."

"They are not, admittedly, the traditional sort of dead. They are a new, progressive sort of dead. And you, Hammer my boy, are to see what makes them tick." Edison clapped me upon the back and spun on his heel, striding away in a manner quite familiar. I had no intention of playing his cannot-hear-your-shouted-objections game on that day, however. I darted around the table in the middle of the floor so as to halt the man's progress.

"What?" I asked. It was thoroughly insufficient in expressing the depth of my confusion, but Edison did stop and sigh.

He grabbed a beaker full of brown liquid from a nearby bench and thrust it into my hands. "Drink, while I explain." Mr. Edison was not a man who often saw fit to explain himself, so I was not about to pass on the opportunity to experience it, even if it required me to drink a mysterious concoction that turned out, rather unsurprisingly, to be rank and tepid coffee.

As another aside, I shall point out that it would not have surprised me if every bubbling phial in the laboratory was some variation on the theme of coffee. Edison was not much of a chemist, you see, but he had grown enamored of the beverage some years ago when he discovered that, technically speaking, it made sleep optional. It was an imperfect system, and for a while led to irritability and above-average levels of mania on his part. Also, he once showed up to work having neglected to wear clothing of any sort. When Nikola pointed out this fact, Edison grew confused and began babbling about magnets. Since then, however, he seems to have adapted.

"Three weeks ago," Edison expounded, "a cargo ship was returning to New York from California. They had just passed the Southernmost tip of Argentina when a storm blew them off course. They arrived at an island somewhere thereabouts, uncharted and uninhabited but for the most grotesque of those men in the cage. The captain of this little schooner, being in my employ for reasons best left unspecified," (by which he almost certainly meant his under-publicized cocaine habit,) "realized that he would likely be rewarded handsomely for bringing so fascinating a being to my attention. He hurriedly created a slapdash brig amongst his cargo proper."

As he spoke, Edison was setting up a film projector. Here, he began a brief film strip, and the room was just dim enough that I could see what was happening; the wildly thrashing corpse was being unloaded from the ship by several large burly men. "At first, they assumed the being to be a savage or cannibal, whose violent behavior could be explained away by being untouched by civilization." Here there was an edit to the film, and the same men were unloading the wildly thrashing Negro. "However, when the cabin boy was bit in the course of apprehending the rotten man, he turned ill and died on the trip home. The entire crew testified to the fact that he was well and truly dead. Then he awoke as violent as the rotten man had been. The condition that causes the active death, it would seem, also causes madness."

Here there was another edit. The film showed the more rotten corpse, strapped to a table, thrashing wildly as a rather uncertain looking doctor examined it. I could not make out his face, but I had no doubt he was the same man who was now in a nearby cage, shambling mindlessly and reeking of death. "We yet know little," Edison said,. "but these somewhat-living men are truly dead; there is no circulation and no respiration. We know nothing of what causes the condition except that it is contagious."

I sipped my coffee, when a sudden realization caused me to spurt it out in a manner that might have been most comical were not the situation anything but. For you see, the coffee tasted exceedingly rank because of the scent filling the room, and it was then that I realized my nose was being assaulted by particulates of a contagious dead man's flesh. "I have no desire to be a dead madman!" I shouted, somewhat muffled as I was covering my mouth and nose.

"Only men bit have died, Hammer. It is a disease borne of the blood, it seems. That much we know. I want you to figure out the rest."

"Mr. Edison!" I cried. "I am an electrical engineer! This is not my forte! I daresay this is no man's forte! An immensely talented physician may find this his mezzo-piano!"

For one brief moment, Edison was not only caught wordless but a tad sheepish as well. I realized why, for on the screen before us, the dead man broke free of his bounds and attacked the physician attending him. There was only a moment of struggle, before the film ended, but it was… well, it was quite bloody.

"Good lord, sir. Why? Why have you not killed these monstrosities?"

"Two reasons. The first is practical." Edison extended his arm toward the cage and a shot suddenly rang out. The doctor was thrown to the back of the cage with a bullet hole on his coat. A moment later, he was back at the bars, struggling to escape and oblivious to the wound.

"Do you have a revolver hidden beneath your shirtsleeve?" I asked.

"That is not what we're about right now," Edison said gruffly. "We are on the cusp of a new century, Hammer."

I opened my watch. "One half-hour away," I said, then noted the error in my maths. "One half-hour and a year, rather."

"The cusp!" he continued, ignoring me, as usual when he felt the desire to pontificate. "But I intend to see the next one, Hammer, and the one after. I do not intend to leave the great march of progress in the hands of lesser leaders because of something so mundane as death. With judicious experimentation, it may be possible to separate the immortality from the madness." He smiled at me, a mad glint in his eye.

"Judicious experimentation on violent and cannibalistic corpses who evidently killed their last experimenter!" I pointed out.

"Ah, yes, I almost forgot," Edison said. He rummaged through the junk on a nearby desk, finally pulling out something that looked like a wooden revolver with a steel sphere on the end of the barrel. A wire connected the device to a large cuboid, which I recognized as the alkaline battery Edison had been publicly toying with recently. "The electricity gun," he said. "Bullets do not stop the dead men, but this stuns them something awful."

"It looks like a smaller version of Nikola's theoretical teleforce weapon," I said without thinking. Edison frowned and shot me.

It was not fatal, obviously, and it did not even cause me to void my bowels, but that was not owing to any attention to sanitation on my part, but rather because the arc of lightning emanating from the sphere and terminating on my chest was causing me to spasm far too quickly for any such motion to occur.

"And that's just setting two of ten!" exclaimed the madman. "I've not yet tried out the more powerful levels as the power used increases geometrically and I suspect they would be dangerous indeed."

"You SHOT me!"

Edison grinned. "Are you ready to get to work now?"

"I don't even know what to do!" Of the many insane things that had so far happened, it seems odd that that was the one I latched on to at the moment, but my mind was still somewhat rattled from the shock. It was not the worst I'd ever received—working closely with electricity as I do—but it was high up on the list.

Edison's face softened and he flashed the beatific-yet-humble smile of which the newspapers were so fond. "Hammer... William. I trust you... you are like the son I never had."

"You have four sons."

"Yes but Dash is sort of a prat and... four? Are you quite sure?"

I nodded. This, I must point out, was a moment that strengthened, rather than shattered, Edison's pleasant façade, though that may seem counterintuitive to those out of his employ. The overworked atmosphere at Menlo Park meant that everyone's personal life was lived in a sort of dreary somnambulism. It was not uncommon to forget about loved ones completely. I myself was surprised recently to realize that I had married Alice White. Somehow I managed to sleep through the proposal, ceremony, and consummation. The former two I had been assured were romantic. The latter I have not yet worked up the nerve to ask about.

"Regardless," Edison continued, "I trust you. I think you will be successful. When you are, I will gladly let you become immortal with me."

It shames me to think it, but my heart was warmed. For a moment I was under the spell of the monster before me. Then the implication of the carrot dangled before me became clear. "Wait. Are you saying you intend to decide who lives and who dies?"

Edison's face hardened. "There are some types one does not want to spend eternity with, Hammer." I was aghast. "Obviously this isn't for everyone! You think everyone will have access to the electricity gun? To the omniplex telegraph? To the extended-play phonograph? Any number of the inventions I've created that would grow uncontrollably powerful in the world at large! What is the point of progress if the world progresses in the wrong direction?"

That was it, the line that pushed me into rebellion. "No!" I said. "No! You are a sick, sick madman, and not only do I quit, I am marching straight to the constabulary. I don't know if anything here is, properly speaking, illegal, but I'll see to it that you are closely watched for the rest of your natural and unnatural life!"

It was not the wisest move of my life, though it was terrifically refreshing for the moment. However, Edison did not like to lose control over situations, and he was also armed. This time I felt a higher charge of the electricity gun. While my trousers again remained unstained, I was thrown several yards backward, crashing into a table that splintered.

"I cannot let that happen, Hammer," he said. "Fortunately, I could always use another specimen." He extended his arm toward the cage and his unseen revolver fired again, this time causing the padlock that kept the door shut to shatter. A thicker lock might have survived the blast, but Edison was remarkably spendthrift, you see.

This brings me to the strangest leg of the story, an assertion that bears repetition. I am relating a story about walking dead men in a secret laboratory, and the strangest bit is yet forthcoming.

I am not the strongest of men, I will admit, but when called into action due to necessity or rage, I am capable of feats of grand masculinity. Shaking off the effects of the gun and the desk far quicker than expected, I leapt to my feet and then to Edison, who was attempting to beat a hasty retreat up the stairs. In an adrenaline-fueled frenzy, I grabbed the man and threw him to the back of the room, toward the shambling horrors even now fighting each other to get through the door of the cage.

There was a sickening crack as the most rotted of the corpses misstepped and his shin splintered. Slowly it toppled forward, snarling, and landed inches away from Edison's sprawled form.

"No!" I cried. I was angry at the man, certainly, but throwing him to the corpses was a gut instinct to prevent his escape, and not a desire to turn my admittedly demonic employer into one of those beasts. In the throwing, I had caused Edison to drop his electricity gun, which I seized and fired in the general direction of the dead men. This was foolish on my part: instinctively I was treating the device as I would a proper revolver, assuming it would fire more-or-less true to the direction pointed. The arc of lightning, however, twisted chaotically as such things do and stopped well short of its intended target, pouring instead directly into Edison's arm. I released the trigger, but though he had received only a split second's worth of power, his limb was spasming in a most violent way, dragging the man behind it, and landing with a regrettably memorable crunch in the brainpan of the downed corpse.

I ran toward the chaos to aid Edison. The spirit of humanitarianism, even toward those whom I hate, was instilled in me a long time ago. I bounded forward while Edison scrambled to his feet, his arm limp and lifeless in a most abnormal way. It was in this brief moment I noticed that while the doctor and the Negro were still shambling, the corpse whose skull was now in pieces was still.

"Sir, the rotten one..." I said breathlessly. "Destroying the brain killed it!"

"It was already dead," he rejoined as he slapped his arm, trying to restore some life to it.

"Properly dead!" I yelled, having no time for nuance. "You shoot the doctor, I shall take the Negro!"

I was not sure how Edison was supposed to deal with his corpse, his injured arm being the one where the seemingly invisible revolver hid. I was too busy working on my own problem; I had electrocuted a number of animals in order to justify Edison's esoteric grudge against alternating current. I was attempting mentally to rectify the shocks I'd felt with the shocks I'd delivered and come up with an approximation of the amperes the upper levels of the device would deliver, and how long I would have to maintain the charge until the creature's inner meats would begin to boil away. I ended up dialing the charge to level seven and holding the sphere directly against the Negro's bare chest for about ten seconds. It created an unpleasant visual I am loath to describe in detail, but suffice it to say his already putrescent form turned quite nauseous before he fell to the ground, still.

I turned to see how my employer was faring, and my heart turned in an odd way. It first fell, for Edison had failed to dispatch the doctor, who was now gnawing on Edison's injured arm. Then my heart lifted because I hate that man. I am not proud to have felt that way, but given what has transpired, I think you cannot blame me. Still, being a gentleman, I addressed my employer with sympathy.

"My lord, sir," I said, grasping for the right words. "I... I'm not... I won't let you live in madness," I settled on, and aimed the electricity gun at him.

"Don't you dare, Hammer," he shouted, evidently unconcerned with the pain one would expect a chewed-on arm would deliver.

"Immortality is not worth becoming one of these beasts!"

"Yes but... damn!" he said. "I was hoping not to have to reveal this." And with that, he performed a complicated action on his shoulder with his free hand, and his right arm fell off, shirtsleeve and all, trailing a small length of cable behind it. The corpse, having been denied the leverage it was relying on, fell forward with Edison's disembodied arm in its grip and mouth. As he hit the ground, the arm slammed against the concrete floor and split. Escaping springs and gears tore the sleeve to tatters, and I could see a wooden shell filled with a complicated array of wires and levers and tubes and pulleys and other, unidentifiable components. "All right, Hammer, help me get him back in the cage."

"What... in the name of Hell... are you?"

"I am a man interested in progress, Hammer!" he shouted. Through the now-useless armhole of his vest, I could see tiny cogs turning, as his left arm raised in a defiant manner. I presume he was unconsciously being symmetrical.

"You are a machine!"

"I am the future!"

"How much of you is even human anymore?"

Edison grabbed the slightly-stunned doctor by the back of the coat and hurled him into the cage in a display of inhuman strength. "My head, of course. Most of my trunk. There are some important organs it's proving difficult to replicate. Hence, the interest in progressive death, to render them unnecessary." He strode over to the cage, wherein the dead man was attempting to right himself. Edison's one arm was strong enough to twist the bars of the door around its frame in such a way that it would not be opened any time soon. "I fear my supply of subjects has run low," he said to himself. "No worry, society abounds with vagabonds."

"You intend to kill people in a horrific way and torture their corpses so that you, and whomever you deem worthy, will live forever," I said.

"Well, I would like someone else to do the actual experimentation, as I am a busy man, but that is the core of the plan."

"You are sick."

"I am Progress."

If this recording survives, and you are listening to it, I suspect that the bile has risen in your throat the way it rose in mine. There's being a megalomaniacal madman, yes, but then there's—honestly, I don't know what that level of insanity could be called. I did not speak. I turned the dial of the electricity gun all the way to ten, aimed at the cage, and fired.

Edison gave me his private look, which I now recognized as harboring more than just a mania. There was a distinct undertone of disgusted superiority. Meanwhile, I held the trigger down, the doctor roasted, and the smell of death was replaced with the smell of frying flesh.

"Your revolver was built into your lost arm," I said. He nodded. I knew he would have stopped me if he could have. Sure that the doctor was well and truly gone, I aimed the electricity gun at the madman before me.

That's when it struck twelve o'clock. Usually, the church bells were silent at night, but as this was the dawning of a new century, they rang in celebration. Their reverberations sounded loud and clear even down there in the underground laboratory. That gave me pause.

It was the cusp of a new century, and it had been an amazing one—the telephone, moving pictures, the light bulb, the weapon in my hands and every other minor miracle that this man had conceived or improved. If you looked away from his obvious madness for a moment, you'd find someone who had made the world a better place. The newspapers presented him in the most incorrect of all possible lights as a person, but he was a genius. Perhaps it was a most inopportune moment of philosophy that the new year brought, but I passed on the opportunity to rid the world of one of its more heinous villains, a decision which has haunted me since.

Still, I know his secrets. I must be forever on my toes, but he must be forever wary of me. If he goes too far, I can reveal his true nature to the world. That's why I am making this recording. Should I die under mysterious circumstances, my will stipulates it be played. It's regrettable that I must go to such lengths to control a madman, but he's a genius too. I was right to let him live.

Whether I was right to dial the electricity gun back to four and shoot him in the face, the only bit of him I knew still to be human—well, that I'm not sure of, but I must admit it was the most satisfying experience I think I'd ever felt. It also allowed for my unmolested exit with all the items of interest I could carry.

As for the so-called progressive dead men—I've not yet heard any other tales of their kind. I hold out hope that the ones I saw were unique exemplars of a bizarre plague whose last remnants were cooked away by me. Perhaps the twentieth century will never see a living dead man, but goodness knows, the world is rarely that fortunate.

About the Authors

JENNY ASHFORD is a writer and graphic designer hailing from central Florida. Her stories have appeared in the *DeviantLit* webzine and anthologies such as *ChimeraWorld* #3 and #4, and *Macabre Underground Vol. 2*. Visit her at www.myspace.com/jennyashford.

REBECCA BROCK, mild-mannered librarian by day, has had stories included in *Love, Damned Love; Decadence of the Dead; Brainchild; Cold Flesh;* and *The Book of More Flesh.* She provided research for over a dozen DVD commentaries for Joe Bob Briggs, as well as Briggs's books *Profoundly Disturbing* and *Profoundly Erotic.* She writes book reviews for Bookgasm.com and contributes a regular column on writing to *Ology* magazine (www.ologymagazine.com). She's currently working on adding to her collection of rejection slips by writing more horror stories and novels, as well as the occasional script. Visit her futile attempt at a website at www.thehorrorhack.com.

JAMES ROY DALEY is cool—like, really cool, you know? He's cooler than that dude with that fuzzy thing, and the big stick. You know, the guy that looks like he's going to puke but doesn't? He's in that movie with the Mexican that looks like a black Fonzie. Anyways, if you get a chance, you should meet

Roy, give him a hug. You'd like him 'cause he's hot, and he has beer—cold Canadian beer. He's from Canada. He lives in an igloo. He plays in a band called the Amber Room, and likes Slayer. He's great.

LINDA DONAHUE, an Air Force brat, spent much of her childhood traveling. For 18 years, she taught computer science. Now, when she's not writing, she teaches tai chi and belly dance. She also performs with the dance troupe Rave-nar. More of Linda's stories can be found at Yard Dog Press, Fantasist Enterprises, From the Asylum Books, Elder Signs Press and soon from Carnifex Press. In non-fiction, Linda has an article in the 2007 Rabbits USA annual. She and her husband live in Texas and keep rabbits, cats, and sugar gliders for pets.

DAVID DUNWOODY hails from Utah, where he lives with his wife of seven years. His most recent zombie fiction appears in *The Undead* volumes 2 & 3 from Permuted Press, and *Read by Dawn 2* from Bloody Books. His serial novel *Empire*, which will appear in print from Permuted Press, can be read online at www.empirenovel.com.

LEILA EADIE wanders around a lot but is currently based in London, UK. She has probably seen the insides of more dead people than you and gets slippery story ideas from them and many other sources. She has sold her horror and dark fantasy stories to various print and online venues, and her website is www.scarystories.org.uk for those who would like to know more.

DEREK GUNN, *www.derekgunn.com,* is the author of *Vampire Apocalypse: A World Torn Asunder* (Black Death Books, 2006). Derek's debut novel has made a big impact with reviewers and the film/TV rights were snapped up by a Hollywood producer. It is currently being developed simultaneously as a movie and TV series. Derek's stories have also been featured in *The Undead* (Permuted Press, 2005) and *The Blackest Death Vol. II* (Black Death Books, 2006) and in *Vol. III* (due out 2007). Derek lives in Dublin, Ireland, with his wife and three children.

In 1980 JULEIGH HOWARD-HOBSON won the Australian ANZAC Day Award for poetry regarding dead soldiers washed up on the beaches of Gallipoli. Since then, not much has changed with her usual subject matter. Her work featuring death and/or war has appeared, or will appear soon, in *Dead Letters, War Journal, Bewildering Stories, Going Down Swinging, Aesthetica, Loving The Undead* (From The Asylum Books), *Dead Will Dance* (1018 Press), and *Black Sails* (1018 Press). A recently selected Million Writers Award "Notable Story Writer," she was also a 2006 Morton Marr Poetry Prize finalist with a sestina... about a cemetery. Oh yes.

"The Rev. Dr." DOUGLAS HUTCHESON is reeling under the weight of history. Despite his work having appeared in such varied places as *Luminary, Analecta, Stillpoint* and *Staccato*, his past and his personal writing demons are not fully exorcised. When not hollering and having fits, he hopes that one day the publication of the books he is working on—including a collection of Southern gothic, *Dead Relatives*, and Western horror, *Dust Devils*—might be a balm to his haunted soul. One of his selves occasionally confesses his torments at www.myspace.com/douglashutcheson.

SCOTT A. JOHNSON is the author of several horror novels, including 2005's *Deadlands* and 2004's *An American Haunting*. He also functions as the Paranormal Studies Editor for Dread Central (www.dreadcentral.com) and is a paranormal investigator. Currently, he teaches in the undergraduate English program at Waynesburg College and in the Masters in Writing Popular Fiction program at Seton Hill University, both in Pennsylvania. When not writing, teaching, or poking around in haunted locations, he plays golf (poorly), teaches Kajukenbo Karate, and spends time with his wife and two daughters. Visit his official website at http://www.americanhorrorwriter.com.

CAROLE LANHAM's work has been published in *Son and Foe, Midwest Living, Thunder Sandwich, Eclectica, Ragged Edge Publishing* and in numerous anthologies. She lives in St. Louis with her husband and two children, and is a member of Midwest Horror Writers and the Horror Writer's Association. Some of her favorite pastimes include tracking down a home for her reincarnation novel *Law of the Last Thought* and hiking around Death Valley.

JONATHAN MABERRY is the Bram Stoker Award-winning author of *Ghost Road Blues* and *Dead Man's Song*, as well as 17 nonfiction books, including *Vampire Universe* and *The Cryptopedia*. He's a board member of the Philadelphia

Writers Conference, a writing mentor for the Horror Writers Association and the Mystery Writers of America, a founding partner of The Writers Corner USA, a speaker for the National Writers Union, co-founder editor of *The Wild River Review*, and publisher of *Cryptopedia Magazine*, an online horror magazine. He lives in Warrington, Pennsylvania with his wife, Sara, and son, Sam. Please visit his website, www.jonathanmaberry.com.

JOE MCKINNEY is a homicide detective with the San Antonio Police Department. When he's not solving murders, he's writing horror and mystery stories. His new police procedural novel, *The Murder Squad*, is due out in 2008. Also due out soon are the horror novels *Darkness Visible* and *Quarantined*. His first novel, *Dead City*, is currently under option to become a major motion picture. Joe lives in the Hill Country north of San Antonio with his wife and two beautiful daughters.

RICK MOORE is originally from the Midlands village of Thurmaston, England. Richard moved to the U.S. in 2000 and now lives in Chandler, Arizona. His fiction has appeared in *Dark Animus*, *Chimeraworld 3*, *Embark to Madness* and *The Undead: Flesh Feast*. Online venues include *Camp Horror* and *Homepage of the Dead*. In 2004 Richard co-founded *Red Scream Magazine* where he was fiction editor for 2 years, before taking a back seat to focus on his writing.

CHRISTINE MORGAN was warned by an aunt at age ten that reading horror would warp her for the rest of her life. Happily, it turned out to be true. She works the overnight shift in a psychiatric facility, where she spends much of her free time writing on the company clock and trying to chew through the restraints of self-publishing. Her previous works include the *MageLore* and *ElfLore* fantasy trilogies, the *Trinity Bay* series of horror novels, and the *Silver Doorway* kids books. She loves to hear from like-brained folks and can be reached through her site at www.christine-morgan.com.

KIM PAFFENROTH is Associate Professor of Religious Studies at Iona College. He is the author of numerous books on the Bible and theology. His book *Gospel of the Living Dead: George Romero's Visions of Hell on Earth* (Baylor, 2006) won the 2006 Stoker Award in the non-fiction category. His first novel, *Dying to Live*, is also available from Permuted Press.

JOHN PEEL was born in Nottingham, England, but currently lives in New York with his wife and far too many dogs. He has written several teen horror novels (such as *Talons, Shattered* and *Poison*), created several series (*Shocker* and *2099*) and penned several media tie-ins (*Star Trek, Outer Limits* and *Doctor Who* among them). He is probably best known for his teen fantasy series *Diadem*. Visit him online at www.john-peel.com.

PATRICK RUTIGLIANO is a lifelong devotee of weird literature and an aspiring professional writer. This anthology marks the first successful sale of one of his stories. Patrick currently resides in Fort Wayne, Indiana with his fiancée. He usually divides his time away from the keyboard between reading the collected works of his favorite authors and watching classic horror movies.

PAULA STILES is a forty-year-old Templar historian and citizen of the world who, in addition to this twisted little tale, has sold stories to *Far Sector, Albedo One, Neometropolis, Not One of Us, Strange Horizons* and *Black Gate*. She also has co-written a novel, *Fraterfamilias*, found at Virtual Tales. Her website is at geocities.com/rpcv.geo/other.html.

ED TURNER is an aspiring writer (read: unemployed layabout with an overactive imagination) who's written a couple novels and a whole mess of shorts about robots and zombies and people arguing and such, but this here would be his first actually published story. Needless to say, he's excited, and may well still be doing a ridiculous little jig. He maintains an Internet presence at www.thestrangestbit.org if you're interested in that sort of thing.

RAOUL WAINSCOTING is a longtime fan of speculative fiction who recently turned his attention to writing as a hobby. The voices in his head are most pleased with this new outlet for expression. He is confident that, if fueled by enough donuts, he will be able to contain them. Raoul also enjoys chasing and failing to catch ducks. *History is Dead* is Raoul's first fiction sale. Interested readers are directed to raoulwainscoting.blogspot.com.

Jonah Caine, a lone survivor in a zombie-infested world, struggles to understand the apocalypse in which he lives. Unable to find a moral or sane reason for the horror that surrounds him, he is overwhelmed by violence and insignificance.

After wandering for months, Jonah's lonely existence dramatically changes when he discovers a group of survivors. Living in a museum-turned-compound, they are led jointly by Jack, an ever-practical and efficient military man, and Milton, a mysterious, quizzical prophet who holds a strange power over the dead. Both leaders share Jonah's anguish over the brutality of their world, as well as his hope for its beauty. Together with others, they build a community that reestablishes an island of order and humanity surrounded by relentless ghouls.

But this newfound peace is short-lived, as Jonah and his band of refugees clash with another group of survivors who remind them that the undead are not the only—nor the most grotesque—horrors they must face.

DYING TO LIVE
a novel of life among the undead
BY KIM PAFFENROTH

www.permutedpress.com

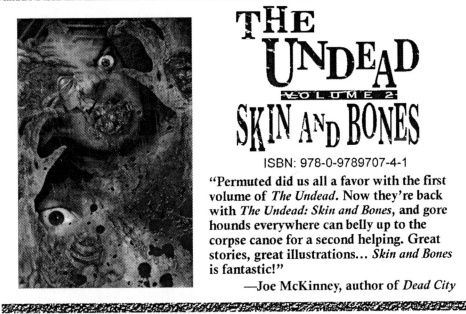

JOHN DIES AT THE END
by David Wong

It's a drug that promises an out-of-body experience with each hit. On the street they call it Soy Sauce, and users drift across time and dimensions. But some who come back are no longer human. Suddenly a silent otherworldly invasion is underway, and mankind needs a hero.

What it gets instead is John and David, a pair of college dropouts who can barely hold down jobs. Can these two stop the oncoming horror in time to save humanity?

No. No, they can't.

ISBN: 978-0-9789707-6-5

THE OBLIVION SOCIETY
by Marcus Alexander Hart

Life sucks for Vivian Gray.
She hates her dead-end job.
She has no friends.
Oh, and a nuclear war has just reduced the world to a smoldering radioactive wasteland.

Armed with nothing but pop-culture memories and a lukewarm will to live, Vivian joins a group of rapidly mutating survivors and takes to the interstate for a madcap cross-country road trip toward a distant sanctuary that may not, in the strictest sense of the word, exist.

ISBN 978-0-9765559-5-7

Printed in the United States
217471BV00004B/21/A

9 780978 970796